THE DUKE'S GAMBIT

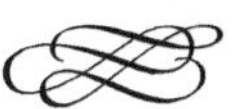

TRACY GRANT

The Duke's Gambit

ISBN-13:978-1986977081
ISBN-10: 1986977080

NYLA Publishing
121 W 27th St., Suite 1201, New York, NY 10001
http://www.nyliterary.com

DEDICATION

For Mélanie Cordelia, who is becoming a wonderful story teller

ACKNOWLEDGMENTS

As always, huge thanks to my wonderful agent, Nancy Yost, for her support and insights. Thanks to Natanya Wheeler for once again working her magic to create a beautiful cover that captures Mélanie Rannoch and has just the right hint of mystery and for shepherding the book expertly through the publication process, to Sarah Younger for superlative social media support and for helping the book along through production and publication, and to Amy Rosenbaum and the entire team at Nancy Yost Literary Agency for their fabulous work. Malcolm, Mélanie, and I are all very fortunate to have their support.

Thanks to Eve Lynch for the meticulous and thoughtful copy-editing, to Raphael Coffey for magical author photos, and to Kate Mullin for her insights into the story as it developed.

To all the wonderful booksellers who help readers find Malcolm and Mélanie Suzanne, and in particular to Book Passage in Corte Madera, for their always warm welcome to me and to my daughter, Mélanie. Thank you to the readers who share Mélanie's and Malcolm's adventures with me on my Web site, Facebook, Twitter, and Google+. To Suzi Shoemake, Betty Strohecker, and Kate Mullin, for managing a wonderful Google+ Discussion

Group for readers of the series, and to all the members of the group, for their enthusiasm and support, and making me see new things in the stories and characters.

I am very fortunate to have a wonderful group of writer friends near and far who make being a writer less solitary. Thanks to Veronica Wolff and Lauren Willig, who both understand the challenges of being a writer and a mom. To Penelope Williamson, for sharing adventures, analyzing plots from Shakespeare to *Scandal,* and being a wonderful honorary aunt to my daughter. To Jami Alden, Tasha Alexander, Bella Andre, Allison Brennan, Josie Brown, Isobel Carr, Catherine Coulter, Deborah Crombie, Carol Culver/Grace, Catherine Duthie, Alexandra Elliott, J.T. Ellison, Barbara Freethy, C.S. Harris, Candice Hern, Anne Mallory, Monica McCarty, Brenda Novak, Poppy Reifiin, Deanna Raybourn, and Jacqueline Yau.

Thank you to the readers who support Malcolm and Mélanie Suzanne and their friends and provide wonderful insights on my Web site and social media.

Thanks to Gregory Paris and jim saliba for creating and updating a fabulous Web site that chronicles Malcolm and Mélanie Suzanne's adventures. Thanks to my colleagues at the Merola Opera Program who help me keep my life in balance. Thanks to Peet's Coffee & Tea and Pottery Barn Kids at The Village, Corte Madera, for welcoming me and my daughter Mélanie and giving me some of my best writing time. And thanks to Mélanie herself, for inspiring my writing, being patient with Mummy's "work time", and offering her own insights at the keyboard. This is her contribution to this story - Malcolm is our new kitty, I love Zannie as well and Cordy. — Mél

DRAMATIS PERSONAE

*INDICATES REAL HISTORICAL FIGURES

At Dunmykel

Malcolm Rannoch, former Member of Parliament and British intelligence agent
Mélanie Suzanne Rannoch, his wife, former French intelligence agent
Colin Rannoch, their son
Jessica Rannoch, their daughter

Laura Fitzwalter, Marchioness of Tarrington, Colin and Jessica's former governess
Lady Emily Fitzwalter, her daughter
Raoul O'Roarke, Laura's lover, Mélanie's former spymaster, and Malcolm's father

Lady Cordelia Davenport
Colonel Harry Davenport, her husband, classical scholar and former British intelligence agent
Livia Davenport, their daughter
Drusilla Davenport, their daughter

Malcolm Traquair, Duke of Strathdon, Malcolm's grandfather
Gisèle Thirle, Malcolm's sister
Andrew Thirle, her husband
Ian Thirle, their son

Lady Frances Davenport, Malcolm and Gisèle's aunt, Strathdon's daughter
Archibald Davenport, her husband, Harry's uncle
Chloe Dacre-Hammond, Frances's daughter

Aline Blackwell, Frances's daughter
Geoffrey Blackwell, her husband
Claudia Blackwell, their daughter

*Prince Talleyrand, retired French statesman
*Dorothée de Talleyrand-Périgord, his nephew's wife

Tommy Belmont, Malcolm's former fellow attaché and agent
Stephen Drummond, innkeeper and smuggler
Dugal, his son,
Rory Drummond, Stephen's brother
Alec, footman
Marjorie, Gisèle's maid

In London

Valentine, the Rannochs' footman
Gilbert, Lady Frances's footman

Hubert Mallinson, Earl Carfax, British spymaster
Amelia, Countess Carfax, his wife
Lady Isobel Lydgate, the Carfaxes' daughter
Oliver Lydgate, her husband

David Mallinson, Viscount Worsley, the Carfaxes' son
Simon Tanner, playwright, David's lover

Jeremy Roth, Bow Street runner
*Sir Nathaniel Conant, chief magistrate of Bow Street
*Lord Castlereagh, British foreign secretary

Rosamud Hartley, proprietress of the Barque of Frailty
Miranda Spencer, employed at the Barque of Frailty
Daisy Singleton, employed the Barque of Frailty
Gerald Lumley, Miranda's friend
Faith Harker, Miranda's friend

Bertrand Laclos, French émigré
Rupert, Viscount Caruthers, his lover
Gabrielle, Viscountess Caruthers, Rupert's wife and Bertrand's cousin

Lord Beverston
Roger Smythe, his son
Dorinda Smythe, Roger's wife
Kit Montagu, Roger's friend

Charlotte Leblanc, former French agent
Pierre Ducot, former Scout in the Peninsular War
Victor Ducot, his son
Sam Lucan (Sancho), former French agent and arms dealer
Nan Simcox, his mistress
Bet Simcox, her sister
Robby Simcox, their brother

Alexander (Sandy) Trenor, Bet's lover
Matthew Trenor, his brother, aide to Castlereagh

Hugh Derenvil, MP
Lady Caroline Lewes, his fiancée

*Emily, Countess Cowper, patroness of Almack's
*Henry Brougham, MP
Aldous Morningtree, Viscount Gildersly
Lady Langton, the Rannochs' neighbor
Marianne, her daughter
Sir Lucius Brandon

Henriette Varon, former seamstress to Josephine Bonaparte
Manon Caret Harleton, actress and former French agent
Margaret O'Roarke, Raoul's estranged wife

Billy Hopkins, agent for Carfax
Thomas Ambrose, agent for hire
Julien St. Juste, agent for hire
Sylvie, Lady St. Ives

Though I am not naturally honest, I am so sometimes by chance
—Shakespeare, *The Winter's Tale,* Act IV, scene iv

CHAPTER 1

MALCOLM RANNOCH STARED at the footman who had just told him his sister had left her home on a snowy New Year's Day with the agent of his enemies. "Mrs. Thirle got in a carriage with Mr. Belmont and drove off?"

"Yes, sir." Alec's gaze was wooden yet somehow at the same time sharp with sympathy.

"Did she say anything?" Gisèle's husband Andrew had been standing by in white-faced silence, but now his sharp voice cut the still air of the hall. "Give you a message?"

"No, sir." Alec hesitated. "They appeared to be in a hurry."

"Did she seem distressed?" Malcolm asked. "Were they—could Mr. Belmont have had a weapon pressed to her side?"

Alec hesitated again, shifting his weight from one foot to the other. "No, sir." Apology shone in his eyes and rang in his voice, as though he wished he could have claimed Gisèle had been coerced. "They were conversing. They appeared to be in a hurry, but I saw Mrs. Thirle turn back to Mr. Belmont and—"

"What?" Andrew asked, voice taut with agony.

"She was laughing," Alec said, as though admitting to a glimpse of some terrible calamity. Which, in a way, he was.

"What's happened?" As though responding to a stage cue, Malcolm and Gisèle's aunt, Lady Frances Davenport, came down the stairs. She had Ian, Gisèle and Andrew's baby son, in her arms. Malcolm's wife Mélanie was just behind, holding their two-year-old daughter Jessica by the hand.

Andrew turned to the woman who had raised his wife. "Gelly's gone off in a carriage with Tommy Belmont."

In his thirty-one years, Malcolm had rarely seen his aunt's composure break to display shock or hurt. Now he saw both emotions flash across Frances's well-groomed features. "Did she—"

"She doesn't appear to have been coerced," Malcolm said.

On the step behind Lady Frances, Mélanie's gaze had also gone white. She picked up Jessica, as though to reassure herself, but her gaze went to Alec. "Did Marjorie go with Mrs. Thirle?"

"No, ma'am," Alec said.

Marjorie was Gisèle's maid. Mélanie, as usual, was thinking clearly in a crisis. "Thank you, Alec," Malcolm said. "Perhaps you could ask Marjorie to join us in the library."

"Of course, sir. Right away."

Inside the library, Malcolm poured sherry, despite the early hour, and pressed it into everyone's hands. Andrew stared into his glass as though he wasn't sure what to do with it. Frances took a quick swallow, then pressed a kiss to Ian's forehead. "I take it she didn't leave any sort of note?"

Andrew shook his head. "Only last night we were talking about taking Ian sledding today. Either something changed very quickly, or she's an actress on a level I never imagined—" He drew a sharp breath.

"It's possible," Mélanie said. "But Gisèle isn't a trained agent." Unlike Malcolm and Mélanie herself, and any number of their friends and family. Malcolm met his wife's gaze over their daughter's head. Jessica squirmed to be put down and walked over to investigate the chess set by the library windows.

"Andrew." Frances took another sip of sherry and fixed Gisèle's husband with a firm stare. "I'm sure I don't need to point out to you that Gisèle isn't her mother. Or her aunt."

Andrew gave a faint smile that didn't reach his eyes. "I'm sure Gisèle would quite like to be compared to you, ma'am. But she'd be the first to admit she's different."

"Well, then." Lady Frances's tone was brisk. Perhaps a shade too brisk. "Having grown up with this family and been married into it for almost two years, I'd think you'd understand how often our behavior is inexplicable."

"And I'd be a fool to claim any insights?" Andrew said. "You make a good point, Lady Frances. But—"

Ian gave a squawk and kicked his legs against Frances's stomach.

"He's hungry." Andrew took his son from Frances's arms. As though in confirmation, Ian grabbed at the neck of Andrew's shirt.

"I'll feed him." Mélanie held out her arms for the baby. "Jessica's old enough to share and I think I still have enough milk."

Andrew looked down at Ian as though the reminder that their son was still nursing made him realize just what Gisèle had walked away from. He put his son in Mélanie's arms. "I can't believe she—"

"We don't know what she's done." Frances put a hand on Andrew's arm. "Drink that sherry, you're going to need it.

Jessica looked up from the chess pieces as her mother took Ian, then went back to them without concern. Malcolm watched his wife settle Ian at her breast. Mélanie, one of the best agents he had ever met, who had spied on her own husband for years, had never spent the night away from either of their children. Which made Gisèle's actions even more inexplicable.

A rap sounded on the door and Marjorie slipped into the room. She was scarcely older than Gisèle. Her mother had been a housemaid at Dunmykel in Malcolm's childhood, and she had grown up playing with Gisèle. Her red hair was pulled into a neat knot, but strands escaped about her face, as though she'd been tugging on them, and her nose was pink beneath the freckles. "I didn't know, Mr. Thirle. Mr. Rannoch. Mrs. Rannoch. Lady Frances." Her gaze darted round the company. "I swear it."

"No one's suggesting you did," Malcolm said. "Sit down, Marjorie. When did you realize Mrs. Thirle was gone?"

"This morning when I took in her tea." Marjorie moved to a chair and twisted her hands in her print skirt. "That is, I saw she wasn't in her room. But I didn't think—"

"If she chose to get up early for some reason it wasn't your place to tell anyone," Malcolm said with a smile. "I quite understand."

Marjorie returned his smile, but her lips trembled "I never guessed—"

"Of course not," Mélanie said, rocking Ian in her arms. "Did she pack a bag?"

Marjorie drew a breath. "I didn't realize it at first. Not until after I learned she was gone. Then I looked in her trunks, and a small valise is gone with her nightdress and one gown and her dressing case. Nothing else."

Which made it less likely Tommy Belmont had pressed a pistol to Gisèle's side. Though it wasn't entirely beyond the realm of possibility for Tommy to have packed for her.

"I know you don't want to betray Mrs. Thirle's confidence," Mélanie said. "But had she seemed—distracted in any way lately? Worried? Concerned?"

"No—that is—She'd had a lot to do with the holidays, of course. And with all the guests." Marjorie drew a breath, as though realizing that referred to most of the people sitting before her. "She didn't say anything, but I think she'd been concerned about—"

"All the family issues," Malcolm said. Such as his grandfather's efforts to persuade him it was safe to come back to Britain despite the risks of Mélanie's past as a Bonapartist spy coming to light.

"Yes." Marjorie met his gaze directly. "But she was happy everyone was here. She was excited about Master Ian's first Christmas. When I helped her into her nightdress last night she told me 'Happy New Year.' I can't imagine..."

Andrew, who had been staring at his hands, looked up as Marjorie's voice trailed off. "Did she ever say anything about Mr. Belmont?" He drew a rough breath. "I'm sorry, I know I'm the last person you must want to speak to about that. If it helps if I leave the room—"

"No." Marjorie shook her head. "I know Mrs. Thirle was worried about Mr. Belmont's wounds, and relieved he was recovering, but I never heard her say anything to suggest she might—might leave with Mr. Belmont. She loves you very much, Mr. Thirle."

Andrew gave a twisted smile. "Thank you, Marjorie. I know how loyal you are to Mrs. Thirle."

Frances put a hand to her head, tucking a blonde curl firmly back into its pins. "There'll be callers arriving for New Year's Day in a few hours. And we have a house full of guests who will be down for breakfast soon. I'll try to put them off. If—"

She broke off as two of those guests stepped into the room. Raoul O'Roarke, who had once been Mélanie's spymaster and was also—Malcolm had learned a year ago—Malcolm's own biological father. And Cordelia Davenport, one of Malcolm and Mélanie's best friends, whose husband Harry was presently in London on a mission. Malcolm wasn't in the mood to waste time on explanations, but he welcomed their help, and their faces said they had already heard some of it.

"We asked Alec where Gelly was," Cordelia said, "and he said—"

"She left with Tommy Belmont," Andrew said. "We don't know why."

"Good God." Cordelia glanced at Mélanie holding Ian. "Did she—"

They quickly brought Cordelia and Raoul up to date, Malcolm and Mélanie doing most of the talking. Malcolm saw the concern in Raoul's gaze, though he said little. He knew more about secrets than any of them. He had also, like Frances, known Gisèle since she was a baby. And he knew about the Elsinore League, the shadowy organization Malcolm and Gisèle's mother had spent years trying to bring down, with Raoul's help, of which they had recently learned Tommy Belmont was a member.

Alec came back into the room. "Forgive me, sir. But the carriage has returned. Not with Mrs. Thirle," he added quickly, on a note of apology. "She and Mr. Belmont changed to a post chaise at the Griffin & Dragon in the village. They sent the carriage back. With a note for Mr. Thirle." He held a sealed paper out to Andrew.

Andrew was already on his feet. He took the paper at once, but stared at it for a long moment, as though breaking the seal could smash all his hopes to bits. Then he slit the seal with the opener Alec gave him, scanned the note quickly, and held it out to Malcolm without expression.

Andrew,

I'm quite safe, but there's something I have to take care of. I'll be back as soon as I can. Please don't come after me. Please, please do everything you can to keep Malcolm from coming after me. (I know that's almost impossible, but try).

I'll write when I can.

Kiss Ian for me.

I love you.

Gelly

"It sounds like Gelly," Malcolm said. "And it's her hand. It doesn't begin to explain." At a nod from Andrew, he handed it to Lady Frances.

"Why send a note now instead of leaving one when she left?" Cordelia asked.

"If she'd left a note, someone might have woken early and seen it," Malcolm said.

Alec gave a discreet cough. "According to the groom who returned the carriage, she left instructions for them to wait until the afternoon to return the carriage and deliver the note. But the staff at the Griffin & Dragon know her and decided not to wait."

"We should talk to the groom," Malcolm said.

Andrew nodded. "O'Roarke? Will you come with us? If this is to do with the Elsinore League you know more about them than anyone. And you've known Gelly since she was a baby."

Raoul had been frowning at a glass-fronted bookcase as though it might hold answers, but he gave a crisp nod. "Certainly, if you wish it."

He hesitated a fraction of a second, as though searching for some way to give Andrew reassurance, then instead simply followed Andrew and Malcolm to the door. Malcolm understood.

Because, given what they knew, there really wasn't any reassurance to give.

LADY FRANCES WATCHED the men leave the room, an uncharacteristic line between her brows. In the cool January light, her rouge, usually expertly blended, stood out against her ashen skin.

Frances cast a quick glance at Mélanie. "I'll talk to the others. You tend to Ian, my dear. Keep her company, Cordy."

She moved to the door, then turned back and touched her fingers to Jessica's hair. Jessica smiled up at her and went back to arranging the chess pieces. Frances's hand went to her own stomach for a moment. She was seven months pregnant with twins.

Mélanie swallowed, hard. When she woke this morning, before she learned of Gisèle's disappearance, she had already known they were confronting multiple crises—their friend Harry in London in search of information, their enemy Tommy Belmont seemingly recuperating upstairs from wounds from an unknown assailant, facing a return to exile themselves. But in the last two hours the world had shifted in ways she could not yet fully comprehend.

"Look, Auntie Cordy," Jessica said. "The king and queen are getting married."

Cordelia dropped down beside Jessica for a few moments, her cherry-striped skirts and lace-edged white petticoats billowing about her, then got to her feet and went to join Mélanie on the window seat. "Laura's with the other children," Cordy murmured to Mélanie. "She still doesn't know what's happened."

Laura Tarrington had been governess to the Rannoch children and now lived with them, along with her own daughter. The children would be secure with her, though when they learned Gisèle was gone they were bound to have a flurry of questions Mélanie could not begin to think how to answer.

Cordelia looked at Ian. "I didn't want to say this in front of Andrew. But Gisèle left a baby. Who's still nursing. It can be a challenge even to leave a baby at home for an evening. One's body constantly reminds one of how long one's been gone, even if one's head doesn't. She packed things to be gone overnight at the least—"

"I know." Mélanie looked down at Ian, who had fallen asleep in her arms. "Some women fall into a depression when their babies are small. Usually earlier than this, but I've known women it's happened to months after the baby was born."

"But Gisèle wasn't depressed. We both saw her. Laughing on Christmas morning. Kissing Andrew at midnight only last night. I know she's Malcolm's sister, but I can't believe she's a good enough actress to have deceived us all about that."

"They're a talented family," Mélanie said, "but no, I wouldn't think so."

Cordelia regarded her for a moment. "What is it? Don't tell me you thought she was depressed."

Mélanie drew the folds of Ian's yellow blanket about him. "Not depressed. Preoccupied. Restless, perhaps. When I first met Gisèle I don't think she saw herself running an estate in the Highlands."

Cordelia laughed despite the situation. "When I was eighteen I didn't see myself married to a classical scholar and former spy and quite ready to turn my back on London society and live in exile."

"Cordy. You aren't—"

"Not yet, not precisely, but I wouldn't mind it in the least if we did. And I'm quite sure at eighteen you didn't envision yourself married to a British politician and living in Britain, let alone going into exile in Italy with him. I doubt Laura saw herself as the mistress of a married revolutionary. I'm quite sure even a year ago Lady Frances didn't see herself married again and expecting twins. The point is life takes us unexpected places. Unexpected and often surprisingly happy places. I know it may sound odd coming from a woman who once ran off with another man, but I love my husband quite desperately enough to recognize the emotion in another woman."

Mélanie stroked Ian's hair. She saw Gisèle on her wedding day. "I do think she loves Andrew. But loving one's husband doesn't stop one from wanting other things in life. As I'm sure Mary Shelley would tell us."

Cordelia snorted. "Gisèle is much happier in her marriage than Mary Shelley."

"You've felt it, Cordy."

"Restlessness?" Cordelia wrinkled her nose. "I suppose so. Yes, all right, I have. Certainly when Harry and I were apart. Even now we're together. I love Harry. I never thought I'd love being a wife so much. I love being a mother. But it's not enough in and of itself."

"No. And nor is being a hostess or running a household. Even a household like Dunmykel."

"Yes, but I'd never leave Harry or my children—"

"Of course not. And we don't know that Gisèle intends to. At least not permanently."

Cordelia watched her for a moment. "You're very matter-of-fact about it."

Mélanie met her friend's gaze. "I'm not. I'm worried sick. But I'm trying damnably hard to think it through from Gisèle's perspective. Something has to account for what she did. And she doesn't appear to have been coerced."

Cordelia pleated a fold of her cherry-striped gown between her fingers. "They seemed so in love. Only a few days ago I was thinking—" She shook her head. "How fortunate Gisèle was to have found that sort of love the first time. Perhaps a part of me wanted to believe in the fairy tale."

"As I did. As I did with Bel and Oliver as well. But we, of all people, should know love is much more complicated than a fairy tale. "

CHAPTER 2

THE GROOM who had brought the carriage and Gisèle's note back from the Griffin & Dragon was Rory Drummond, the younger brother of Malcolm and Andrew's childhood friend Stephen Drummond, who had inherited the inn from his father a few years ago. The Drummond family had been at Dunmykel only last night, the first guests over the threshold at midnight.

"I'm sorry, Mr. Thirle, Mr. Rannoch," Rory said. Malcolm remembered Rory as a gangly teenager with spots. Now he was a young man past twenty, but he had the same bright, steady gaze. "We weren't sure what to do."

"You couldn't have done otherwise," Andrew said. "Thank you for letting us know."

"Do you have any idea where they were bound?" Malcolm asked.

Rory shifted his weight from one foot to the other. They were in the slate-floored kitchen where Alec had brought Rory to have a cup of ale and warm up from the cold. "I confess I was concerned enough I was listening for clues. I heard Mr. Belmont say something about Glasgow. But I had the sense he meant me to hear it, if you take my meaning."

"Quite," Malcolm said. "Well done." Rory was an astute young man if he could outthink Tommy Belmont.

Rory's brows drew together. His blue eyes were dark with concern. "I wish—"

Malcolm touched his arm. "You've done well, Rory. Thank you."

He, Andrew, and Raoul left the kitchen, but of one accord paused in the passage by the base of the service stairs. A window high in the wall let in the winter light and a lantern hung in the stairwell warmed the whitewashed walls.

"Where do you think they've gone?" Andrew asked.

"At a guess, London," Malcolm said. "Though it's difficult to speculate without knowing *why* they've gone."

"We should look at Belmont's room," Raoul said. "Though I doubt he's left anything there."

The room in which Tommy Belmont had spent the past fortnight convalescing still smelled vaguely of Tommy's citrus shaving soap and the favorite brandy that he'd relied on to get past the pain of a serious chest wound. The blue-flowered coverlet was pulled neatly over the embroidered sheets. A dressing gown Malcolm had lent him hung from one of the oak bed posts. The dressing case Malcolm remembered standing on the chest of drawers was gone. Inspection of the wardrobe and chest of drawers also showed those bare. Malcolm and Raoul looked beneath things and tapped the paneling to be thorough, but Tommy was too seasoned an agent to have overlooked anything. Malcolm held the writing paper on the escritoire up to the light of the windows. "If he wrote anything, he managed not to leave an impression in the sheets below."

Raoul set down the poker after a fruitless examination of the ashes in the grate. "If he had, I'd think it was meant to mislead us."

"Quite," Malcolm said.

"You worked with Belmont in the Peninsula." Andrew was frowning at the leaded glass panes of the window. He'd only met

Tommy Belmont once or twice before Tommy's recent unexpected arrival at Dunmykel.

"We were both attachés officially," Malcolm said. "And agents unofficially. At the Congress in Vienna, as well."

"But now you've learned he's working for this Elsinore League you're all investigating." Andrew turned his gaze to Malcolm.

"Tommy admitted as much to me in this very room." Malcolm grimaced, wondering just what he had let into the house and all their lives when they gave shelter to Tommy. He had inherited Dunmykel with the death of his putative father a year and a half ago, but Andrew and Gisèle managed the estate, and in many ways it was theirs. Malcolm had hoped it could be a haven for them away from the intrigues that engulfed the rest of the family.

"Do you think the League have something to do with why Gisèle left with Tommy?" Andrew asked.

"Did Gelly ever talk about them to you?" Malcolm kept his voice level, but he felt the tension that ran through Raoul. His mother had done her best to keep her children away from the League. Malcolm hadn't known of it himself until a year ago. His putative father, Alistair Rannoch, had begun the organization with a group of friends at Oxford over three decades ago, with the aim of manipulating the world to their advantage. The League remained mysterious, though in Italy they had acquired a list of the membership.

Andrew shook his head. "Only to say a few days ago that the more she learned about her mother, the more surprised she was."

"Do you think she could have been trying to discover more?" Raoul asked.

"I wouldn't have thought so." Andrew drew a breath. "Now I'm questioning everything I thought I knew about her."

For an instant, Malcolm was thrown back a year ago to the moment he'd discovered that his own wife was a French agent who had married him to gather information. And that the man he'd recently learned was his father had been her spymaster. He'd been sure he'd never trust anyone again.

"Gisèle has a good head on her shoulders," Raoul said. The faint roughness in his voice told Malcolm he was having some of the same memories. "And there's no reason to think Belmont intends harm to her."

"She trusts him," Andrew murmured.

"Andrew." Malcolm took a step towards his brother-in-law. "You read her note."

"She'd have written something like that no matter what," Andrew said. "I may not be a spy, but I can tell that much. She was doing her best to have us not follow them, though she probably knew there was little chance it would work." He met Malcolm's gaze. "I have to go to London. Or wherever else their trail takes me."

Malcolm, who had been determined from the moment three weeks ago when he stepped off the boat on the Dunmykel dock to get his family back to Italy as quickly as possible, inclined his head. "And I need to go with you."

"DAMN IT." Malcolm pushed the door to and took a turn about the bedchamber. "She wouldn't just disappear."

"Darling." Mélanie studied her husband's face, the tension in his jaw, in the set of his shoulders. They were alone in the room. Ian was asleep in the care of his nurse. Jessica was with Laura and Cordy and the other children while Cordy updated Laura on recent events.

"There has to be an explanation." Malcolm scowled at a Boucher oil of two young girls in a garden on the wall opposite. "She must have been coerced. If Carfax thought he could use her against us. Or the League—"

"Malcolm." Mélanie crossed to her husband's side and put her hands on his shoulders. "I'm as worried as you. But Tommy's with her." Whatever else one might say about Tommy Belmont, he could take care of himself and anyone with him.

"Precisely. So the League are probably behind it."

"That's one explanation."

"Mel, for God's sake—"

"It didn't sound as though she was coerced. And we have her note."

"Christ, Mel." Malcolm broke away from her hold. "You know as well as I do not to be taken in by appearances."

"Of course."

He stared at her. "But? What?"

"Only that we need to consider every possible explanation."

"I know. But she's my sister." He started pacing again. "You've only seen her a handful of times. I know her." He stopped short, staring at the Boucher oil again. "God, that's rich, I suppose, coming from the brother who abandoned her."

"Darling." Mélanie stepped up behind him and slid her arms round his shoulders. "No one would say you abandoned her."

Malcolm gave a short laugh. "Gelly did. More than once. But I thought we'd mended matters."

"And you had. I saw you together. I saw her with Andrew and Ian. I'd have sworn she was happy."

Malcolm turned in her arms. His gaze darted across her face. "But?" His voice was gentler as he said it, but inexorable.

Mélanie drew a breath. "I caught a restlessness sometimes. Nothing I could define. Nothing that made me think she intended anything. But in retrospect—"

"You're wondering if Gelly ran because you once thought about running?"

Mélanie held her husband's gaze with her own. "I never thought about leaving you, Malcolm."

"Never?"

"Only in the sense I knew I needed a plan if you ever learned the truth and tried to take the children away. But I know—"

"What?"

Mélanie drew a breath, seeing the flashes she'd sometimes caught in her young sister-in-law's gaze. Remembering moments from her own life as a London hostess. "What it's like to be happy in one's life and still be restless. To be happy, but feel society's constraint."

A muscle tensed beside his jaw, but he merely gave a crisp nod.

"Darling, I'm not—"

"I know. You'd never run out on your responsibilities. I suppose one could argue Gelly's a bit less responsible than you. At least she was. She was still throwing tantrums when you were an agent stealing papers from the ministry of police. I'd have said she changed. It could be argued that I wanted her to have changed. That I wasn't the best judge." He scraped a hand over his hair. "But Tommy was wounded and bent on the Elsinore League's business. Even granted he wouldn't cavil at much, it's hard to see him as bent on seduction."

"No," Mélanie agreed. "Unless it was part of his mission."

"To use Gelly against us?" Malcolm drew a hard breath. "That, I confess, has the ring of the League. And Tommy. But how—"

"They might want to get you to London."

"And I'm playing right into their hands? But I don't see how I can do otherwise but follow her." Malcolm's gray gaze settled on her own, at once determined and tender. "I need to leave with Andrew at once. For London or wherever her trail takes us."

Mélanie nodded.

Malcolm stared at her. Usually any suggestion that he take action without her met with quick resistance.

"Andrew will need your help and support. I don't want to leave the children, and you'll travel more quickly without us." Mélanie put her hands on her husband's chest. "Besides, you're in relatively little danger in London. I'm the problematic one."

His brows drew together. "If you get the least hint you're unsafe here—"

"I can pack up the children and go back to Italy. Don't worry, darling. I don't like to run, but I've never been afraid to do it when the situation calls for it."

"Ha."

"Seriously, darling. I may be reckless, but I've never been foolhardy. I wouldn't have survived in the game this long if I was. I'll pack a valise for you. If you need more, you can get it from Berkeley Square. Valentin will be there. Assuming the trail takes you to London."

Malcolm nodded. "We'll change horses at the first posting house and send the team back." He put his hands over her own and gathered them into a hard clasp. "This is serious. I know we've said that before. But this may be the most serious foe we've ever faced."

"We're equal to it."

CHAPTER 3

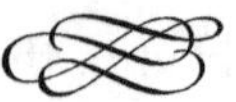

THE ROOM KNOWN as the old drawing room was unexpectedly quiet after the chaos in the house that morning. Most of the guests had retreated to their rooms. Cordelia had gathered the children in the library for charades. Laura Tarrington found herself alone with her lover for the first time since the news of Gisèle's disappearance. She walked up beside Raoul O'Roarke and slid her hand into his own. They had been lovers for almost a year and she was five months gone with their child, but long before that Malcolm and Gisèle's mother Arabella had been his lover for over twenty years. "I know you must be desperate to be doing something."

He had been frowning at the mullioned panes of the window, but he turned his head and gave her a faint smile. "I'd only complicate things if I went to London with Malcolm and Andrew. I'm not sure what they're facing, but they're likely to need to move in London society." His gaze went back to the window. His brows were drawn, his mouth set, his gray eyes haunted in a way they only got in unguarded moments. "I keep seeing Gisèle toddling across the lawn holding Malcolm's hand. Or at seven with a grubby face and one of Arabella's coronets on her head. I always thought Arabella must have been a bit like that as a girl. Before her life got unbearably complicated."

"I hadn't thought somehow—that you'd have watched her grow up."

"Not as much as Malcolm, but I saw a fair amount of her. I remember carrying her about on my shoulders the way I do with Emily and Jessica now."

"Darling." Laura turned to face him and tilted her head back to look up at him. "Do you know who Gisèle's father is?"

"No," he said, without hesitation. "Only that it wasn't Alistair."

Laura drew a breath. But some things she'd once have shied away from she could now say. "It couldn't—"

Raoul looked down at her with that reserved tenderness she'd come to know so well. "I've always been fond of Gisèle, but if she were my daughter, don't you think she'd mean to me what Malcolm does?"

"Of course. I just—"

"Wondered if I wasn't sure? It's true there's a great deal I don't know where Arabella's concerned, but we weren't lovers from my marriage in '95 until after the Uprising in '98, when Gisèle was several months old. There's no way I could be her father. Arabella could be frank about her love affairs—sometimes franker than I'd have wished—but she said nothing about her pregnancy save that it was unexpected."

"Do you think—could that have something to do with why Gisèle left? Searching for her father? Or because she learned who he was? We now know Tommy Belmont was working for the Elsinore League—"

"And Gisèle's father may have been a member? It's possible. Arabella did employ seduction in her attempts at gathering information."

As Mélanie had done. As Raoul had himself, Laura knew.

Raoul glanced at the Broadwood grand pianoforte. It had been Arabella's instrument, and this room, less formal than many of the rooms at Dunmykel, one of her favorites, according to what Laura had heard from the family. "Arabella was secretive about Gisèle's parentage. Unusually so."

"Especially with you."

His mouth lifted in a faint smile. "She didn't tell me everything. Far from it."

Laura put her hands on his chest. "Does Frances know who Gisèle's father is?"

"I don't know. I've never asked her. Though I think perhaps I have to now." He was silent for a moment. "Gisèle had a quick temper as a girl. She was always more mercurial than the boys. I know Frances worried about her growing up, but I never saw any sign that she'd inherited Arabella's illness."

"Even if she had, it wouldn't make her suddenly run off and leave her family."

"No," he said. "But something did."

RAOUL RAPPED at Frances's door and at her subdued summons stepped into the room to find her sitting on her dressing table bench, staring at a silver-framed miniature as though pleading for answers. Raoul had known Fanny since she was fourteen and he'd never seen such a lost look on her face.

She looked up and met his gaze. "Only last night she was talking to me about the babies and how wonderful it would be that they could play with Ian. I should have seen—"

"None of us saw," Raoul said, leaning against the door panels.

"But I'm—"

"Her mother to all intents and purposes. And she couldn't have a better one."

Frances shook her head. "Don't talk reassuring twaddle, my dear. We've known each other far too long."

"It's the truth. I don't think anyone else could have raised Gisèle as you did after Arabella died."

Fanny gave a twisted smile. "I love her as much as my other children. I may worry about her more. Difficult not to, when Arabella—"

She broke off, but there was really no need to put it into words. They were both all too familiar with Arabella's brilliant intensity and bouts of depression. "Gisèle could be moody," Raoul said. "But I never saw any sign that she suffered from Arabella's affliction."

"No," Frances said, "nor did I. I tried hard not to drive her mad watching for signs of it." She looked down at the miniature again. "The past two years I worried less about her than I have since Arabella died." She shook her head. "Malcolm twitted me on it once, being happy when they all got married and had babies. And God knows I don't think that's the only path to happiness. Even now I've risked it again myself." She spread her fingers over her rounded stomach. "But it is one sort of happiness. And I thought Gisèle was genuinely happy with Andrew."

"I think she was. Is." Raoul pushed away from the door and dropped down on the carpet in front of Frances. "Fanny, did Bella ever tell you who Gisèle's father was?"

Frances's eyes widened. "You've never asked before."

"No," he said, his gaze steady on her own. "I didn't think it was any of my business. But now—"

"You think that's why Gisèle ran off? Because she's trying to learn who her father is?"

"It's one possibility. Something made her run. With Belmont. I know Andrew's fears, but I doubt she's fallen in love with Tommy Belmont. She could think Belmont can make it easier for Malcolm and Mélanie to return to Britain, but she's sensible enough I think she'd be likely to confide in Malcolm if that were the case. But if she thought he might know who her father was—"

"You're suggesting her father might be an Elsinore League member?"

"Do you think he might be?"

Frances's fingers tightened on the silver filigree frame of the miniature. Raoul could see the image now, Gisèle at about sixteen, her mother's sharp cheekbones just starting to emerge from round-faced girlhood, her eyes as brilliant as Arabella's, her honey-blonde curls a darker version of her mother's. Whoever her father was, the resemblance wasn't obvious.

"She never told me," Frances said. "Bella never told me who Gisèle's father was. Mind you, I didn't tell her who the fathers of all my children were. At least, I don't think I did." Frances's penciled brows drew together. Of her five children, only the eldest had been fathered by her late husband. "But I confess, I was curious. After all, she told me right away with Malcolm, even though I was not yet fifteen, and she was very direct about Edgar being Alistair's. I'm a firm believer in everyone's right to secrets, but one night after we'd come home from the theatre and were drinking whisky together, I asked her straight out about Gisèle's father. Bella went still, in that way she would sometimes. Then she laughed, almost as though she was laughing at herself, and said it was much better for me not to know." Frances linked her hands together over the curve of her stomach. "Of course, at the time I didn't know about the Elsinore League. I didn't know a lot when it came to Arabella."

"Nor did I, if it comes to that." Raoul sat back on his heels. "Did Gelly ever ask you?"

"Once, when she was about fifteen. I told her honestly that I didn't know. She just nodded and said she supposed it didn't much matter. But there was a look in her eyes—" Frances shook her head.

Raoul laid his hand over Frances's own. "Did Alistair ever ask you?"

Frances went still. Arabella and Alistair Rannoch had been

estranged for most of their married life, but Alistair had been Frances's lover for over two decades. "Alistair rarely talked to me about Arabella. He had that much delicacy. But he did ask me once, when Bella was pregnant with Gisèle, in the most detached sort of voice, if I had any idea who the father might be. Of course, I told him no. And that if he really wanted to know, he should ask Bella."

Despite everything, Raoul found himself giving a wry smile. "And?"

"He said he didn't suppose it much mattered. Much as Gisèle later would. But I'm not sure either of them meant what they said. If—"

She broke off, as the door opened to admit her husband, Archibald Davenport. Archie hesitated on the threshold. "Sorry, I can—"

"Nonsense." Frances got to her feet and went to take her husband's hand. "I won't go so far as to say we none of us have secrets from each other, because at our age, with our lives, we know that's not true, but in this we're all united."

Archie lifted his wife's hand to his lips. "You've both known Gisèle far longer than I have."

Raoul pushed himself to his feet. Fanny and Archie were two of his closest friends, and he was a man with few he'd call friends. "Did Arabella ever say anything to you about Gisèle's father?"

Archie raised his brows. "Surely, if she didn't say anything to either of you—"

"Bella and I were franker with each other than many lovers, but still not entirely frank. And she was keeping the Elsinore League from Fanny."

Archie's brows drew together. "You think Gisèle's father may be a member of the League?"

"It's one possible explanation for why she's run off with Belmont."

Archie's frown deepened. He'd been a League member himself

for years, but early on he'd grown concerned by their ambitions and had begun passing information to Arabella and to Raoul, and then had moved on to passing information to Raoul about Ireland and France. "It's no secret to either of you that her investigation into the League sometimes took on intimate aspects. But she said nothing to me. And I can't remember anything from round the time Gisèle would have been conceived that would suggest who her father might be."

"Archie," Frances said. "This changes things."

Archie looked down into his wife's eyes. "You want to go back to London."

"I have to. It's all very well to worry about safety, but—"

"Of course." He pressed a kiss to her forehead. "We won't travel with Malcolm and Andrew and slow them down, but we can leave tomorrow."

Frances tilted her head back to look up at her husband. "Thank you."

"My darling, I could hardly do otherwise."

MALCOLM FOUND his father back in Tommy's room, tapping the paneling round the fireplace where they had already searched. Raoul turned to him with an abashed smile. "Trying to make one more search for clues."

"As I suspected you would be." Malcolm pushed the door to. "Andrew and I are leaving within the hour. For London or wherever their trail takes us."

Raoul nodded. "I assumed you would be, as soon as we heard Gisèle was missing."

Malcolm scanned his father's face in the cool light from the window. Raoul wasn't one to stay out of things, any more than Mel was.

Raoul gave a faint smile. "Of course, I want to go with you. I want to do anything I can to help. But I'd only create complications."

"Mel's agreed to stay. Which surprised me even more." Malcolm drew a rough breath. He knew what he had to do. And doing it was one of the hardest things he'd ever done. "I have no idea how long I'll be gone. And I'm leaving nearly everyone I love under this roof."

"It's far from ideal." Raoul spoke in the crisp tones of a commander acknowledging a risky battle plan. "But Mélanie should be safe here, especially while the winter weather holds. Difficult for anyone to come this far into Scotland. And, if necessary, we can be on our way to Italy quickly."

"I know you must need to get back to Spain." Malcolm recalled the taut urgency of his father's letters from Spain, where rebellion against the Bourbon monarchy was brewing and Raoul was in the process of setting up a network.

"My dear Malcolm. Mélanie and Laura are perfectly capable of getting the children to Italy on their own, as either would be the first to tell you, but you can't imagine I'd leave before this is resolved."

"You're running a network."

"I've made arrangements."

Malcolm met his father's gaze for a long moment. "Thank you."

Raoul nodded, face contained. As often, much between them remained unspoken.

"Malcolm." Raoul hesitated, fingers taut on the mantel. "I can't claim to know Gisèle as you do. But I saw a fair amount of her growing up. It strikes me that one reason for her seemingly inexplicable departure might be that she thinks Belmont can help her find her father."

Malcolm's gaze locked on his own father's. The thought had been there at the back of his mind, to the extent he'd had time to analyze at all, ever since he'd heard of Gisèle's departure. "I've thought of it," he said. "Especially since in Italy she realized I'd finally learned conclusively who *my* father is. That might have made her more curious to find her own."

"It's not me," Raoul said. "There's no way it could be."

"I didn't think it was," Malcolm said. "That is, I know you and Arabella were apart during your marriage to Margaret, and—" Presumptuous to say, *I know you're fond of Gisèle, but it's not like what's between us.*

Acknowledgment flickered through Raoul's gaze. "Arabella also never gave me any indication of Gisèle's father's identity. I just asked Fanny, and apparently the one time she asked, Bella told her she was much better off not knowing."

"You think it's someone in the Elsinore League?" Malcolm asked.

"I think it's a possibility. More to the point, Gisèle might think it's a possibility. And that Belmont could help her."

"And Tommy could be playing upon that because he and the League have other reasons for wanting Gisèle."

Raoul's mouth tightened. "It's possible. It's all still only a theory."

Malcolm looked into the gray eyes he now knew were the twin of his own. "I never thought I'd have to ask you this. But I'm going to need a list of Arabella's lovers who were members of the Elsinore League."

Raoul reached inside his coat and drew out a folded sheet of paper. "The names of all those I know of, and what I know about dates. There could well be others I don't know about."

"Thank you." Malcolm had never been so grateful for Raoul's matter-of-factness, and for the fact that he'd written the list down instead of Malcolm having to question him.

Raoul gave a crisp nod. "The dates aren't right for any of them to be Gisèle's father. But Arabella could have been involved with one before I realized, or resumed the affair later."

Malcolm tucked the list into his own coat. "The papers we found that Arabella had hidden, mentioning the Wanderer—

Gisèle would have been a baby when Arabella hid them. Could they have anything to do with her father?"

Raoul's brows drew together. Arabella had climbed in through Frances's window with these papers at a house party twenty years ago. Mélanie had found the papers just before Christmas, torn into pieces and hidden in Arabella's jewels. Once pieced together and decoded, the fragment of message proved to refer to something or someone called the Wanderer. The hand belonged to Julien St. Juste, an agent for hire who had once worked for Malcolm's spymaster, Lord Carfax, but had also served the French and many other masters. Carfax and the Elsinore League had both been searching for the papers, and a third group seemed to be after them as well. Cordelia's husband Harry had gone to London in search of more information.

"The timing's right," Raoul said, "but it's difficult to see how. Bella seems to have intercepted the papers. Likely from the League, though we can't be sure. Whoever or whatever the Wanderer is, it's unlikely it has to do with Gisèle's parentage."

"No, but the man she took the papers from could be Gelly's father."

Raoul's eyes narrowed as though he was sifting through the facts. "She took the papers from her lover, then climbed out the window and back in through Fanny's room so it would seem like the thief came from outside? It's possible. In fact, it sounds damnably like Bella."

"It's still only a theory, as you say." Something to ponder during sleepless nights at inns, as he and Andrew tracked Gisèle and Tommy Belmont. Malcolm moved to the door, but turned back, his hand on the doorknob. "Father? I couldn't leave as easily if you weren't here."

Raoul went still. Only then did Malcolm fully realize what he'd said. He gave a faint smile. "I've never said it, have I? I've thought of you that way for some time. But it's what I called Alistair. So I didn't—But damn it, I'm not going to let Alistair own a word you're much more entitled to."

"My dear Malcolm, that means—a great deal." Raoul drew a breath like that of a man stepping onto uncharted ground. "Now, find your sister and try not to worry about the rest of us."

CHAPTER 4

MÉLANIE CARRIED the valise she'd packed for Malcolm downstairs. She found Andrew in the study writing with a quick hand. "Malcolm's gone up to speak to the duke," he said. "I'm just writing out instructions for Tim." Tim Gordon was Andrew's assistant in running the estate. "He's been in charge before, when Gelly and I've been in London, and when we went to Italy last autumn." Andrew set down the pen. "You saw a fair amount when you and Malcolm visited in the past couple of years. Obviously, you can speak for Malcolm in his absence."

"I'll do my best," she said. Running a large estate was far outside her field of expertise. On the other hand, when she married Malcolm she hadn't known anything about managing a large household or being a diplomatic and political hostess, and she'd become quite adept at both.

Andrew nodded and sealed his letter for Tim. Mélanie set down the valise and moved to a shield-back chair beside the desk. Andrew's drawn face and the set of his shoulders betrayed the appalling strain he was under. But her investigator's instincts had been racing ahead from the moment they'd learned Gisèle was missing. This was her last chance to put those to use. And to ask questions Malcolm might not be prepared to ask.

"Andrew—" Mélanie hesitated.

Andrew set down the Dunmykel seal and studied her, his face gray in the morning light. "You're wondering if I'm not telling you something."

"Of course not. I know how you feel about Gisèle. It's plain you're desperate to find her."

"But you're wondering if I knew she was unhappy. If I have some reason to suspect she might have run off."

The torment of doubt in one's spouse. For all they had battled through, neither she nor Malcolm was a stranger to it. "I saw you and Gelly together. Unless I've completely lost my ability to read people, you love her, and she loves you. I also know love is a complicated thing. So is marriage."

Andrew glanced through the mullioned panes of the windows at a snow-flecked line of birch trees. "I still remember the moment I looked at her and realized she wasn't my friend's little sister anymore. That first evening I kissed her. She was wearing a white wool cloak and snowflakes dusted her hair." He drew a harsh breath. "I'm thirteen years older. I should have known."

"Not to let yourself fall in love?"

"It was too late for that. On my side, at least. But I took shocking advantage of her. She'd scarcely had a chance to explore her options."

"As I heard it, you insisted Gisèle go back to London and go about in society before you'd let her commit to anything. Gelly claimed you were so scrupulously honorable it drove her mad, but at the same time that she loved you for it."

Andrew gave a twisted smile. "None of which changes the fact that in the end I gave way to impulse and let her tie herself to me when she'd seen little of the world and was far too young to be sure of what she wanted."

"I imagine Gisèle would say growing up in this family she'd

seen a great deal of the world. And, as I recall, she was quite sure she wanted you."

"At the time." Andrew glanced out the window again, the look in his eyes both sweet and wistful. "And after. But it's damnably hard at nineteen to know what one wants for the rest of one's life."

"I was nineteen when I married Malcolm."

Andrew met her gaze across the oak and leather and chased silver of the desktop. He knew something of her past now, but not the full story. At least, she and Malcolm were convincing themselves he and Gisèle hadn't worked it all out. "You'd been through more than Gelly had," he said.

Mélanie studied him. "I think perhaps you're having one of Malcolm's overprotective moments. Perhaps having known Gisèle since she was a child, you find it hard to believe she's grown up."

Andrew gave a bleak smile that nevertheless told of past joys. "Believe me, I'm very aware she's grown up."

"In some ways. But perhaps in others you aren't giving her enough credit. *You* haven't changed since you married. Why should she?"

"I was older. I'd seen more of the world. And I suppose—" He returned the cap to the sealing wax with unwonted care. "A part of me could never quite believe she loved me."

"I know something about that."

Andrew's gaze shot to her face. "For God's sake, Mélanie. It's plain Malcolm adores you."

"Malcolm's not the type to adore. I do think he loves me. But that doesn't stop the thoughts about 'what if he sees the real me?'"

"My dear girl." For all his own crisis, Andrew's face was warm with concern. "You have nothing to worry about."

"Relationships can be so precariously balanced. For a long time I don't think I gave Malcolm enough credit. Perhaps that's what you're doing with Gisèle."

He watched her for a moment. "You're kind, Mélanie. And

remarkably reassuring. But I know what you've been thinking. You can't help but wonder. Malcolm doesn't like to think it about Gelly. I don't think Lady Frances and O'Roarke do either. But you saw the possibilities at once."

"Seeing the possibilities doesn't mean I believe them."

"But you don't think we should ignore them."

"I think we need more information. But whatever Gisèle's done, I'll never believe she doesn't love you."

"And yet I think you're well aware of just how complex love can be."

"And what it can endure."

Andrew drew a hard breath. "Surely there are things you want to ask me. Things Malcolm wouldn't ask."

Mélanie swallowed. But she had wanted to seize her chance. This was it. "Did you have any reason to think Gisèle was unhappy?"

"Unhappy? No. If I'd thought that, I'd have—" He shook his head. "I'm not sure what. Tried to fix it somehow. Asked her. But she's seemed—" He drew a breath as though fumbling for words the way he might hunt for a lost child's toy under the sofa. "Preoccupied. I'd catch her in unexpected moments, staring off into space. And then she'd turn to me with a bright smile as though she hadn't a care in the world."

Mélanie knew that look all too well. It was one she gave Malcolm loweringly often.

Andrew returned the pen he'd been using to its silver holder. "I thought she might be worrying about Malcolm and you. And not want to talk about it because perhaps Malcolm had confided in her but not in me. Which I'd understand. But it went on after you came here. And she seemed—restless somehow." He looked up quickly and met Mélanie's gaze before she could armor herself. "You saw it too."

"Perhaps. It could mean a lot of things. I'm restless at times myself."

Andrew aligned a stack of writing paper on the ink blotter. "Gelly loves Dunmykel, but I don't know that she'd ever have chosen life here on her own. It's yet another reason I worried about her marrying me too young. She grew up in London, in Lady Frances's household. She could have reigned over society like her aunt. Like her mother."

"Gisèle isn't Frances or Arabella. In any way."

Andrew settled a bronze paperweight on the writing paper. "She told me once that Dunmykel was a haven. The place she'd been happiest as a small child and was happiest now. But I'm not sure a haven is a place one wants to stay forever, all the time. Not if one has Gelly's appetite for life."

The villa on Lake Como shot into Mélanie's memory. White walls. Tile floors. Flowers spilling over the balustrade. A sense of being cut off from the world that was at once soothing and terrifying. "Wanting more from life doesn't mean wanting life away from you."

Andrew drew a breath. When he spoke, she had the sense he was at last voicing a fear he'd been terrified to utter. "Gelly always liked Belmont."

Innocuous words. Which turned a phantom hanging in the air into a tangible reality, hovering before them. "With this family," Mélanie said, "the obvious explanation very often isn't the correct one."

"Very often," Andrew agreed. "But not always."

MALCOLM FOUND HIS GRANDFATHER, the Duke of Strathdon, in the sitting room of the suite the duke occupied on his visits to Dunmykel, pacing the floor. In his one-and-thirty years, Malcolm could not recall a time he had seen his grandfather pace.

"Wanted to stay downstairs," the duke said, turning to the door as Malcolm came into the room. "Had some illusion that I could be doing more at the heart of the house. But thought it would be easier for us to talk here."

"Thinking like an agent, sir." Malcolm advanced into the room. "My compliments."

Strathdon waved a hand, brows drawn together. "You think they've gone to London?"

"That's my best guess, from the way they tried to obscure their trail. I could well be wrong. But I think I'll be able to read clues along the way. Tommy's good at covering his tracks, but I'm more than passably good at uncovering them."

Strathdon gave a crisp nod. "Why the devil—"

"I don't know, sir." Malcolm clasped his hands behind his back. His fingers were taut with strain. "At a guess, I'd say she thinks she can do something to help Mélanie and me return to Britain."

Strathdon's frown deepened. "She didn't know my plan. Not the whole of it. I wanted to keep her out of it."

"So did I. But that may only have piqued her interest." In fact, three weeks ago, on the night of Jessica's birthday, Gelly had expressed her frustration to Malcolm at all the family secrets she didn't know. A conversation that in retrospect haunted him. "It's folly to blame yourself, sir," Malcolm said. "More information may have made her more inclined to involve herself." He hesitated a moment, but his recent exchange with Raoul echoed in his head. "O'Roarke and Aunt Frances also think it's possible Gelly's searching for information about her father."

Strathdon went still.

"You knew Alistair wasn't her father," Malcolm said. It wasn't quite a question.

"Credit me with a bit of sense, lad. By the time Gisèle was conceived, I'd have been shocked if Arabella and Alistair got within ten feet of each other, let alone close enough to make a child."

"But you don't—"

"Good God, Malcolm. You can't imagine Arabella would have confided such a thing to me. Or that I'd have asked."

"That doesn't mean you didn't have suspicions. You did about my father."

Strathdon met Malcolm's gaze, his own blue eyes more open than usual. "True enough. But what was between your mother and O'Roarke was fairly obvious." He hesitated, glanced at the fire in the grate for a moment, coughed, looked back at Malcolm. "I don't think—"

"O'Roarke and Mama were apart when Gelly was conceived. He doesn't know who Gelly's father is. Nor does Aunt Frances. She says Mama told her not to ask."

Strathdon's gaze clouded, genuine concern overlaying the awkwardness of the subject. "You know I always let my daughters go their own way, for better or worse. One can argue I should have paid more attention—"

"Arabella was very good at keeping secrets, however hard you'd have tried. This may have nothing to do with why Gelly's disappeared." Malcolm hesitated, then touched his fingers to his grandfather's arm. "I know how difficult it can be to wait, but I beg you, try not to worry too much, Grandfather."

"Don't waste your energies on me, Malcolm," Strathdon said, in more of his usual tones. "I may have pretended to ill health to get you back from Italy, but I am perfectly fit and hardly likely to be overset by worry. However serious the situation. I may not be an agent, but life in this family has taught me to expect the unusual."

"That I know full well, sir." Malcolm held his grandfather's gaze. "Mélanie, O'Roarke, and Laura may have to take the children back to Italy before I return. Should they think it necessary to do so, please do everything you can to assist them."

"My dear boy, we may disagree on the possibility of your returning to Britain, but I would hardly attempt to stop your wife or your father or the charming Lady Tarrington from doing what they thought they must. Not that I have any illusions I could do so if I tried."

"No. Though I wouldn't care to put it to the test."

Strathdon's gaze flickered over Malcolm's face. "You'll be safe in London?"

"You were convinced enough I should be able to go back there."

"Talleyrand hasn't tried to bargain with Carfax yet."

"There's no evidence Mel's past is generally known. Even if it were, it doesn't implicate me unless they think I was working with her. And even in the worst case, it wouldn't be the first time I've got out of enemy territory."

The duke continued to frown. Malcolm touched his arm again. "Don't look so grave, sir. You've got your wish. I'll be on British soil a bit longer." He hesitated a moment after he said it, aware of the sudden rigidity of his fingers on the dark blue cassimere of his grandfather's coat sleeve.

Strathdon's brows snapped together in a very different way from his frown of concern a moment before. "You think Gisèle and I orchestrated this to get you and Mélanie to stay in Britain?"

"The thought could not but at least occur to me, sir."

"By God." Strathdon ran a hand over his smooth white hair. "I can't say for a certainty I wouldn't have tried it. But in truth, the thought never even occurred to me."

"I'm relieved to hear it."

"Do you believe me?"

"I think so, sir." Malcolm stepped back, prepared to turn to the door. "Which, coming from me, is a fair degree of certainty."

THERE WERE two other people Malcolm needed to speak with before he went downstairs to join Andrew. He left his grandfather's suite and crossed the central upstairs passage to the bedchamber allotted to Prince Talleyrand. Talleyrand opened the door himself. He was fully dressed, in a frock coat and diamond-buckled shoes, his wig powdered and securely in place on his head, though after a brief appearance at breakfast he had retreated upstairs. As befitted a guest in the wake of family tragedy. And yet, Talleyrand had been friends with the Duke of Strathdon long before Malcolm was born. He had come to Dunmykel in secret because and he and Strathdon had concocted a gambit they claimed would allow Malcolm and Mélanie to return to their life in Britain. A gambit far too dangerous to risk.

All of which suddenly seemed irrelevant in the wake of recent events.

"I assume you're off to look for Gisèle," Talleyrand said.

"With Andrew. And our search will most likely take us to London. Where a week ago, on Christmas night, I told you I wouldn't risk returning to, despite your kind offer. The irony isn't lost on me."

"The board has shifted."

Malcolm surveyed the prince. He had first met Talleyrand as a boy of five, when the prince sought refuge in England from the Reign of Terror. They had crossed diplomatic swords at the Congress of Vienna and in Paris after Waterloo, though Malcolm had also found Talleyrand an ally who went out of his way to protect Mélanie. "I don't know how long I'll be gone, but I suspect you'll have left for France by the time I return."

"Possibly." Talleyrand cast a glance at the connecting door to the room occupied by his nephew's wife, Dorothée. "I don't wish to leave so long as our presence can give support to your grandfather. I'm quite fond of your sister as well, you know. And I know Dorothée will be concerned about Mélanie."

"You've been a good friend to our family," Malcolm said with truth. He stepped forwards, where the light gave him a better view of Talleyrand's face. One needed all the help one could get to read the prince's expression. "Aunt Frances and Raoul wonder if Gelly may have run because she's trying to learn who her father is."

"And you think Arabella might have told me, when she didn't tell her sister or her longest-term lover?"

"She told you about Tatiana."

Talleyrand had helped conceal the birth of Tatiana, Malcolm's illegitimate half-sister, and had looked over her childhood in France and later made her his agent. "Actually, your grandfather told me about Tatiana," Talleyrand said. "Or, rather, told me Arabella was with child, at seventeen and unwed, and they needed my assistance. Which, of course, I was happy to give. There'd have been no such reason for Arabella to confide in me about Gisèle's parentage."

Malcolm held the prince's gaze with his own. "Which wouldn't stop you from having suspicions."

"True enough." Talleyrand's gaze was as shrewd and inscrutable as across the negotiating table, yet tinged with warmth. "I counted your mother a friend, Malcolm. I flatter myself that she shared things with me that she didn't with many others. And I with her. Perhaps more than I should have. But she wasn't in the habit of talking about her lovers. And yet—"

Malcolm knew that look in the prince's eyes. Weighing information, weighing how much to say. "What?" he asked. His voice came out sharper than he intended.

Talleyrand glanced down at the diamond buckle on his shoe, sparkling in the light from the fire blazing in the grate. "I was busy with France's concerns at the time your sister would have been conceived. But I did see Arabella once when she was pregnant with Gisèle. Arabella came to France in secret to see Tatiana, as she did frequently. She stopped to see me. She wanted to talk about Tatiana. And she had concerns about the uprising that was brewing in Ireland. She wanted my assurance that I'd help O'Roarke if he needed to flee the country. Which, some time later, he did indeed need to do."

"And you were indeed of assistance, as I hear it."

"Yes, I believe I was. Not for entirely altruistic reasons. I've always found O'Roarke useful. But I've always liked him as well. In any case, that was all in the future when Arabella was with child. We didn't speak much of her pregnancy, but I offered her my wishes for a safe delivery. She said—" Talleyrand stared into the fire, his expression oddly arrested. "She curved her hand round her stomach, much as I've seen Frances and Lady Tarrington do in the past days, much as I've seen many pregnant women do through the years. She said she wasn't unhappy to be having another child. But that she feared the pregnancy might be a mistake that would come back to haunt her."

Malcolm held Talleyrand's keen gaze. "Because of the father."

"Presumably."

"Arabella was apparently at pains to keep his identity secret. Unusual pains."

"And that makes you think there may be political ramifications?" Talleyrand asked.

"There's something that made her determined to keep it from Aunt Frances, in particular." Malcolm studied the prince. "You must have wondered?"

"Obviously. But, as I said, I knew few details of her personal life in those months."

Malcolm was aware of the list Raoul had given him tucked inside his coat. His mother's love affairs had been a part of so many investigations he could almost speak of them with equanimity. Almost. "It's no secret Arabella had lovers in her pursuit of the Elsinore League."

Talleyrand twitched a frilled shirt cuff smooth. "The thought, of course, occurred to me at the time. I confess I even made inquiries of one or two agents in London. Arabella was unusually circumspect in her personal life in the weeks round which your sister must have been conceived."

"Gelly never asked you about the League, did she?"

"No. But that doesn't mean she didn't have suspicions. Your sister is an astute young woman, Malcolm. It runs in the family."

"And I begin to think trying to protect her may have been one of my worst mistakes."

Talleyrand continued to watch Malcolm. "If I knew who Gisèle's father is, or knew anything that I thought would help you find your sister, I'd tell you, my boy."

That was quite an admission, coming from Talleyrand.

Malcolm almost believed it.

THE LAST PERSON Malcolm had to see was his cousin Aline, who was like a sister to Gisèle. He found her in an upstairs sitting room. Her husband had taken their daughter downstairs to play with the other children. Allie had never been overly demonstrative, but she crossed right to Malcolm and hugged him tight.

Malcolm's arms closed round his young cousin.

Allie pulled her head back and looked up at him. "I keep thinking I should have seen something. I was so busy with that wretched code on Boxing Day—"

"That code may prove vital." It had revealed that the information his mother had intercepted two decades ago, that both the Elsinore League and Malcolm's former spymaster, Lord Carfax, were suddenly bent on finding, concerned something or someone called the Wanderer. "None of us saw anything, Allie," Malcolm said. "Gelly hadn't said anything recently to make you think she was planning anything?"

"No. Well—" Aline frowned. "Yesterday morning, we were playing with the children, and she looked at Ian crawling after Claudia and said it was good he'd always have so many people to love him." She looked at Malcolm, in that fearless way she'd always been able to confront hard truths. "Do you think she was planning to leave then?"

"I don't know," Malcolm said honestly. "But I don't see how you could possibly have guessed it if she was. Allie—did Gelly ever seem curious about her father?"

Aline's eyes widened. "You think that's why she left?"

"It's one possible reason."

Aline rubbed her arms. "We talked about it off and on, growing up. But not as much as you'd think, considering neither of us knew the identity of our father. We hadn't discussed it in years. But only a week ago—no, a bit more, it was before Christmas—we were wrapping presents in the old drawing room. And she suddenly asked me if I ever wondered about my father. I said truthfully that I had much more important things to think about these days, and it really didn't matter. Gelly got an odd look in her eyes. She said she used to feel that way. But lately she'd been thinking it might matter more than she'd ever have dreamed possible."

MALCOLM FOUND Mélanie in the study with Andrew. Andrew was frowning, as though in contemplation, but at Malcolm's entrance he rose and moved to the door. "I'll see if the carriage is ready."

Andrew had always been tactful. This was probably his and Mel's last chance for a private goodbye.

Mélanie got to her feet as well, and gestured to a valise beside her chair. "All the essentials."

Malcolm nodded and crossed to her side, but instead of taking the valise, he put his hands on her shoulders. God knows he'd left often enough—too often—during the war, but on missions within Spain. The dangers may have been worse, but his return hadn't been so open-ended. And she hadn't been at nearly as much risk herself. "Promise me—"

"At the least hint of danger, I'll leave for Italy."

Malcolm looked down into his wife's face. He remembered

saying goodbye to her the first time he'd left after their marriage. The same brilliant sea green eyes and winged brows and ironic mouth. The walnut brown hair escaping in tendrils about her face. Yet he knew her so much better now. "Why do I not believe that?"

"Darling." She put her hands on his where they rested on her shoulders. "We have to trust each other to make the right choices."

He took her face between his hands. "The stakes have never been higher, sweetheart. And we've never been a continent apart."

"And if things go well, we won't be." Her throat tightened. "We always find our way back to each other. It's a bit redundant, but be careful yourself, darling."

He kissed her and pulled her into a tight embrace, committing the moment to memory.

Somehow, the longer they were together, the more he was aware how fragile everything between them was.

Mélanie clung to him for a moment, then pressed her lips to his cheek. "I love you, darling. Don't forget that until I'm here to tell you again."

CHAPTER 5

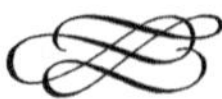

CORDELIA CAST a glance at the lamplight spilling over the delicate blue and gold of an Aubusson carpet and the pale blur of furniture under Holland covers. "What are we looking for?"

"Anything out of the ordinary," Mélanie said. "The Elsinore League built these rooms. Tommy works for the League. Gisèle left with Tommy."

"Nothing in these rooms could be called ordinary," Raoul murmured.

Mélanie lifted her lamp. The carpet was spread over a dirt floor, but the walls were painted. With a series of floor-to-ceiling murals, depicting characters from Shakespeare plays, though no production Mélanie had ever seen featured the scenes displayed here. Malcolm had searched the rooms, cut into the rock off the secret passage that led from Dunmykel's library to the beach, for clues to his mother's missing papers, and come back grim-faced, but this was the first time Mélanie had seen them.

Hamlet—he seemed to be Hamlet judging by the black clothing and clichéd wild-eyed stare—was ravishing a golden-haired, white-clad Ophelia against a stone wall in a bizarre perversion of the "get thee to a nunnery" scene. Gertrude disported with Claudius, Polonius, and a third man who was probably supposed to be old King Hamlet, though whether he was a ghost or in the flesh remained unclear. Romeo and Juliet were twined together in a position that appeared to defy the laws of physics. Desdemona and Othello were making the beast with two backs while Iago observed them from behind a tapestry. A black-veiled Olivia was enjoying the ministrations of an identical pair in blue doublets who must be Viola and Sebastian.

Mélanie stood still, breath caught at the sheer audacity of it, skin flushed with reluctant heat. Crude, blatant, yet undeniably arousing.

Laura broke the silence, her voice unusually dry. "Were you ever here?" she asked Raoul.

"No." His voice too was dry, his gaze even more dispassionate than usual as he scanned the walls. "Archie told Arabella and me about the rooms. Bella may have explored them. I never did. And I profoundly hope Strathdon has never seen them. I doubt his morals would be shocked, but I'm not sure he'd recover from the perversion of Shakespeare."

He lifted a corner of the Holland cover on the object in the center of the room. The lamplight gleamed off the polished wood of a table. The other Holland-covered objects proved to be a set of chairs upholstered in a tapestry that echoed the theme of the murals and a marble-topped Boulle sideboard with gilt comedy and tragedy masks on the doors. The interior was filled with crystal glasses etched with more erotic scenes and bottles of whisky, brandy, claret, and port.

"The brandy's been moved," Raoul said, studying the dust in the cabinet in the light of his lamp. "Within the past fortnight, I'd say."

"The League can't have met here in at least a year and half," Laura said. "Not since Alistair died."

"One wouldn't think so," Mélanie said. "Though they could

have pulled up by water and gone through the passage. But presumably not in the past three weeks while we were here."

"Tommy likes brandy," Cordelia said.

"So he does." Raoul moved towards one of the archways opening off the main room. Laura went with him. Mélanie and Cordelia moved to another. The archway gave on to a smaller room. It, too, was painted with murals. These depicted the four lovers from *A Midsummer Night's Dream* in every possible combination. Titania's court were engaged in an orgy in a mural on the ceiling. A carved four-poster bed took up most of the chamber, a fairytale creation of white and gold and gauzy hangings. Nude nymphs twined themselves round the table legs and the gilded bedposts. Something else gold glinted at each of the four corners of the bed. Finely wrought handcuffs and leg irons.

"A lot of the images aren't much different from what one sees for sale in stalls in the Boulevard St. Martin," Cordelia said. "But I have to say there are some it's never even *occurred* to me to try."

"There are some I don't think are physically possible," Mélanie said.

They turned back the sheets and mattress, tapped and twisted the gilded nymphs, unscrewed the finials, pushed back the Turkey rug to tap the floorboards. The other side rooms proved to be decorated with variations on *Measure for Measure, Troilus and Cressida*, and *The Merry Wives of Windsor*. More beds, a chaise-longue, a hamper of fancy dress—with a great many low-cut bodices and codpieces, all manner of swords and daggers, and a collection of birch rods.

They met Raoul and Laura in the *Merry Wives of Windsor* room. "Damn it," Mélanie said, as they shared their lack of success. "Now I'm going to have these images running through my head the next time we go to the theatre. I can only imagine how Malcolm feels." She started to drop down on the edge of the bed, thought better of it considering what had no doubt transpired there, and found herself staring at bit of gilding on the dark wood. Only this wood wasn't gilded, it was inlaid with silver filigree. She bent down and picked up a piece of gold braid, her fingers suddenly nerveless.

"What's that?" Cordelia asked.

"I think it came from the gown Gisèle was wearing two days before she disappeared," Mélanie said.

"IT DOESN'T PROVE ANYTHING," Cordelia said, hands curled round a glass of whisky. They had retreated upstairs to the library.

"No, but combined with the brandy being moved, it strongly suggests Gisèle was in the secret rooms with Tommy." Mélanie took a sip from her own glass.

"If he convinced her he had information about her father and that her father is an Elsinore League member, he could have taken her there to tell her about her father," Laura said.

"Quite," Raoul agreed. "Or to show her some evidence, though if so they took it with them or we missed it. And I refuse to believe Tommy Belmont could outwit all four of us."

"So do I," Mélanie said. "And you're right, Tommy and Gisèle obviously spoke together before they left New Year's Day morning. It doesn't change so very much that they spoke in the secret rooms. Save to put the League squarely in the middle of it." And to put Gisèle and Tommy in a setting designed for seduction.

"The bedsheets were clean," Laura said. "Unless they stripped the sheets and had one of the maids make the bed up fresh, nothing happened there recently."

Mélanie met her friend's gaze. That was perhaps the most reassuring thing she'd heard all night. Yet just the fact that Tommy had taken Gisèle into the rooms suggested they were on terms of intimacy that could not but be disturbing.

~

ANDREW PUSHED a piece of his scarcely touched beefsteak round his plate in the coffee room of the White Hart in York. "Almost certain they're headed for London now."

"Almost," Malcolm agreed. Rain lashed the inn windows and beat on the roof. "Though they laid some good false trails. Enough to convince me we're probably right about their destination."

Andrew pushed his plate aside and rested his elbows on the table. "When we get to London, I'll go down to Kent to talk to Judith. She may have heard from Gelly. And you'll have better sources for scouring London."

Malcolm nodded and took a sip of ale from his tankard. It wasn't a bad plan. His cousin Judith, Frances's second daughter, was also like a sister to Gisèle. "I don't have the connections I once did. But there are people I can call on." Including some former Bonapartists he'd helped Mélanie settle in London.

Andrew reached for his own tankard but turned it in his hands instead of drinking. "You must have better sources than Darcy."

"Darcy?" Malcolm asked. Usually he was quicker to catch clues.

"Darcy scours London for Lydia and Wickham. He manages to find them."

"Andrew." Malcolm's hand shot across the table to grip his brother-in-law's own. "I'm still not quite sure what this is. But it's no simple elopement."

"It's certainly not simple." Andrew tossed down a long draught from his tankard. "If Mélanie left you, you'd try to find her, there's no sense in even asking that. But what would you do if, when you found her, she didn't want to come home?"

Malcolm kept his fingers steady on his own tankard. The question was closer to what he had actually imagined than Andrew could possibly know. "I'd never want Mel to be anywhere other than where she wanted to be. Not that I think I could compel her in any case."

"Quite." Andrew stared into the depths of his tankard.

"But I flatter myself I know her enough to know her happiness is with me. And I flatter myself I know Gelly enough as well."

Andrew's gaze shot up to meet Malcolm's own. "You haven't seen much of her in ten years."

Malcolm accepted Andrew's gaze. "True enough."

Andrew scraped a hand over his hair. "I shouldn't—"

"No, that was above the belt. Nothing more than I myself point out frequently." Malcolm curled his hands round his tankard and leaned forwards across the table. "Look, Andrew." He searched for words and found himself wondering what his father would say in the same circumstances. "We can never really be sure of what another person might do. Even with those closest to us. I've had that lesson driven home more than once through the years." With the pain of a dagger thrust at times. "So you're right, I can't promise you Gisèle didn't leave the child she seems to adore and the man she seems to be head over ears in love with and elope with Tommy Belmont. But I can tell you that explanation goes against all my instincts. And for all my sins, I'm still a decent judge of my fellow humans. It also goes against everything I know of my sister. And for all I was gone for a decade, I do think I know her reasonably well."

Andrew's gaze locked on his across the table. "Have I told you you're a good fellow, Malcolm?"

"That has nothing to do with why I said it."

"No. And I do—appreciate it. Value your judgment. I just can't —help but worry."

Malcolm took a sip from his tankard. "My dear fellow. Who can?"

Andrew gave a quick smile that didn't quite reach his eyes. Malcolm looked round to order another round of ale. The coffee room, low-ceilinged and dark-paneled, as such rooms often were, was crowded with a combination of travelers and locals. Damp greatcoats and pelisses steamed on a settle by the stone fireplace. Waiters bustled in and out with trays and tankards. Malcolm had just caught a waiter's eye, when the door of the coffee room burst open. A man in a damp greatcoat, hair streaming rainwater, was flung onto the coffee room floor. A second man, who had done the flinging, strode in after him and slammed the door shut. "Keep your filthy hands off my wife."

A woman two tables over from Malcolm and Andrew screamed. Another woman in the corner put her arms round her two young children.

The man with the dripping hair pushed himself to his knees and lunged at the second man's ankles. They went crashing into a table. "Bloody hell," a stout man sitting at the table yelled as his ale tipped over.

The man with the dripping hair, now on his feet, drew back his fist to hit his attacker and instead hit the stout man's companion as he jumped up from the table. The companion gave a grunt of rage and punched back.

"Let's get out of here," Malcolm muttered to Andrew.

The route to the door went past the table engulfed in the brawl, which somehow now included three more men. Others in the coffee room pushed back their chairs and either moved out of the way or ran to join the fight. As Malcolm and Andrew neared the door, one of the brawlers skidded on the spilled ale and crashed into a waiter who had tried to back out of the fray. A covered dish, two tankards of ale, and three glasses of wine fell to the floorboards. The waiter shouted. Malcolm and Andrew dodged round the chaos. The man in the damp greatcoat, now grappling with the stout man, lurched against Malcolm. Malcolm felt a sharp slice across his ribs. He twisted away and pushed after Andrew to the door.

A tankard went flying over his head and dumped a stream of ale down his back. He and Andrew jumped over a fallen chair and stumbled through the door. They went down the slate-floored passage and up the pine stairs to their room without speaking. Inside, Andrew leaned against the closed door, breathing hard. "As if we don't have enough to contend with without stumbling into a random brawl."

Malcolm glanced down at his coat. There was a rent in the drab cloth and in the waistcoat and shirt beneath. When he drew his hand away, blood showed on his fingers. "I'm not sure it was random. Someone tried to stick a knife in me on our way to the door."

CHAPTER 6

MÉLANIE STARED down at the menu she was supposed to be reviewing. In Gisèle's absence, she was, for the first time, acting as mistress of Dunmykel. Running a large household wasn't anything new to her. But now words like *salmon beurre blanc, orange jelly,* and *damson tart* swam before her eyes. Only two days since Malcolm and Andrew had left, and her throat was knotted with frustration, her fingers tense with the need for action.

A splat on the window made her look up quickly. A snowball fight was in progress on the terrace and a snowball had landed on one of the mullioned panes, leaving a white trail down the glass. Outside, the window, her five-and-a-half-year-old son Colin gave her a shrug of apology. Mélanie smiled at him just as Livia Davenport hurled a snowball that caught him in the back of the neck. Colin snatched up a handful of snow and ran after Livia. He nearly collided with Laura's daughter Emily, who was throwing a snowball at Laura. Laura scooped snow up in her gloved hand and tossed it back at her daughter. Jessica threw a small handful of snow at Colin that fell short of its target. Dorothée bent to help her, as Cordelia was doing with her younger daughter Drusilla.

The door clicked open behind her. Raoul came into the room

and stood watching for a moment. "I feel like I'm getting a glimpse of the girl Laura was in India," he said, as Laura knelt in the snow, titian hair escaping the hood of her scarlet wool cloak, to snatch up two handfuls of snow.

Mélanie managed to smile, though she could still feel tension shooting across her shoulders. "Excellent distraction for the children. And there's nothing like distracting children to distract adults." Frances and Archie and Frances's youngest daughter Chloe had left the day after Malcolm and Andrew, along with Aline and her husband and daughter. Other than Mélanie, Raoul, Laura, Cordy, and the children, only Talleyrand, Dorothée, and Strathdon remained at Dunmykel. She set down her pen, leaving a streak of black ink on the menu. "How far do you think Malcolm and Andrew have got?"

"York, if they're lucky." Raoul moved to the escritoire where she was working.

"Days before they even get to London. Assuming that's where the trail leads them. Longer before we can expect to hear anything." She drew a breath and felt the frustration shoot down her recently injured shoulder.

"They may send word from the road." Raoul stepped behind her and rubbed the knotted muscles at the base of her neck. "It won't heal properly if you aren't careful."

Mélanie leaned her head back against his arm. For years they'd scarcely touched each other. They could now. So much had shifted while the world was falling apart and remaking itself about them. "If we hear from them, at least we'll know they're all right. Or were when they sent the message. But they're unlikely to have learned anything. Unlikely to send anything we can—"

"Act on?"

Mélanie looked up at him with an abashed smile. "Caught. But it's damnable not to feel we can do anything."

Raoul pressed a kiss to the top of her head. "It's the hardest part," he said. "Waiting."

"Which is why you avoid doing it?"

"Whenever I can. I've paced the floor more than once when you were off on missions."

Mélanie met his gaze. He gave a faint smile, though his gaze remained serious. "I sent you into unpardonable danger, *querida*. I could rightly be questioned for my actions. But I did worry."

She reached out to stroke their cat Berowne, who had curled up on a stack of paper beside the blotter. "You let me make my own decisions and run my own risks. I always appreciated that."

"You were completely fearless. It was bloody terrifying."

"So you decided I was better off married to Malcolm?"

"That wasn't the only reason." Raoul moved to the window. He waved to Emily, who was scooping up snow, then turned back to Mélanie, hands braced on the sill. "The bandits almost killed you. They came as close to killing you as I ever want to see with anyone I love. I realized then what was at stake. And that was before—"

"I was pregnant with our child?"

Raoul cast a quick look at her. "He wasn't—"

"He was then." Mélanie watched her son run to pick up Jessica, who had stumbled in the snow. The concern in Colin's gray eyes and the way his dark hair fell over his forehead were so very like Malcolm. "Don't get me wrong, I'm glad he's Malcolm's son. But I think you were worried about both of us."

"My God, I was."

Berowne batted at Mélanie's hand. She scratched him between the ears. "I always used to think you didn't think you had time for personal ties. Now I think you didn't think you'd survive."

"I didn't think so for much of the war. At least I knew there was a very reasonable chance I wouldn't."

"That was true for all of us."

"Yes, well, I was hoping to do my best to make sure it wasn't the case for you."

"So you decided I was better off sidelined."

"You were hardly sidelined."

"Poor word choice, perhaps." She studied him for a moment, outlined against the cool light from the window, this man who had shaped so much of her life. Whom she had once thought of as a Machiavellian spymaster, for all she'd loved him. "At the time I'd have boxed your ears. Now I'm rather grateful."

"*Querida*—It doesn't diminish what you did."

"Malcolm said much the same. And he should certainly know." She slid her fingers through Berowne's soft gray fur. Raoul was still leaning against the window, but she could read the restless energy in his posture. She remembered him in the old days, scarcely stopping to sleep, dictating orders while breaking a code, riding through the night from one part of his network to another. "I can guess what it must be costing you to be here when you have work waiting in Spain."

"My dear girl. Whatever the frustrations of waiting, I have no doubts about where I need to be at present. For one of the few times in my life."

"Because you're worried about us."

"Because so much is unsettled."

"And then you'll be back to Spain."

"Eventually."

"When you think we're safe." She stroked Berowne beneath the chin.

"I'll be back before the baby's born. If humanly possible."

Mélanie studied him for a long moment. Behind the tension, behind the conflict of competing loyalties, lay the stark terror of uncharted territory. "Being terrified is a quite normal part of expecting a baby. Though you and Laura have had a lot more practice now than Malcolm and I did the first time."

"I already know Laura is a wonderful mother. As for me—I'm trying."

"And, as you've often told me, that's all one can ask of oneself."

"I'm not sure about that in this case." He glanced out the

window over his shoulder. Emily had run to hug Laura, knocking her into the snow. Both were laughing, in a tangle of scarlet wool, white petticoats, and titian hair. "I fully recognize Laura and Emily and the baby deserve more. I don't want to let them down."

In all the years she'd seen him acknowledge risks and calculate odds, which frequently weren't in their favor, she'd rarely heard such doubt in his voice. She got to her feet and put a hand on his arm. "You've done everything you could for both your children. You'll do everything you can for Emily and the new baby. I'm just glad you'll be able to enjoy it more."

"*Querida*—" He hesitated as the past hung between them. "Thank you."

"No regrets," she said. She'd never said it before, not in so many words. It occurred to her that they had got to the point where she could. "We're both happy where we are. But—if you were worried about me when I was pregnant with Colin, doesn't the same apply to you now?"

"To me?"

"You have Emily. You're going to have a baby. If I needed to be careful, don't you?"

He watched her for a long moment, the lines of his body taut. "Are you asking me to—"

"Give up being a field agent? No, you wouldn't be you." She hesitated. "It's a challenge. Being true to one's children and partner and being true to oneself. I often think I'm failing on both fronts. But I don't think it's fair to ask one's children to live with one if one can't live with oneself. "

"A novel way of looking at it."

"Or perhaps of letting myself off the hook."

"I rather think I've always been far more guilty of that than you, *querida*."

"You haven't made yourself responsible for people. Or you haven't let them know that you felt responsible. Perhaps because it seemed safer for people not to be linked to you. Or because you were afraid of letting them down."

"Caught."

"I don't think Laura wants you to be anyone other than who you are. I don't think any of your children do, or will, as they grow up and understand. Including Malcolm." And yet, she could hear the fear and frustration in her husband's voice in Italy over the risks Raoul was running. *I don't know how to keep him safe.* "You've never played dice with other people's lives as much as you wanted the world to think," she said. "You need to accept that you can no longer play dice with your own as you once did."

His mouth twisted, but he kept his gaze steady on her own. "Easier said than done perhaps."

"Oh, my dear," Mélanie said, "none of this is easy. For that matter, being a parent isn't easy. You must have realized that by now."

"It had dawned on me. I think the moment I first learned I was going to be a father. If—"

He broke off at a rap on the door.

Alec stepped into the room. "Mr. Drummond has called with young Dugal, madam. Shall I show them in here?"

"Yes, please do. And send in some wine, and some cakes for Dugal."

Alec inclined his head. "Stay," Mélanie said to Raoul. Raoul nodded, brows drawn together. Stephen Drummond ran the Griffin & Dragon, one of the last places Gisèle had been seen.

Stephen was a tall man with a shock of dark blond hair and an easy assurance in his bearing. He'd been formal when he first met Mélanie, but had relaxed towards her as he and Malcolm rekindled their friendship. Dugal, his eight-year-old eldest son, had been on the floor playing with the other children on New Year's Eve, but today he was solemn-faced, sticking close to his father.

"We're sorry to disturb you," Stephen said, after they had exchanged greetings. "I know it's a difficult time."

"In truth, we're very pleased to see you and to have guests to break up the quiet," Mélanie said. "But I don't think this is a social call."

"I didn't know." Dugal's voice burst out. "Truly."

"Of course not." Mélanie smiled at the little boy. "Why don't you sit down and tell us about it."

Alec came in with wine, tea, cakes, and lemonade as they were settling themselves round the fire. Mélanie supplied Dugal with a cup of lemonade and a large slice of seed cake, but though he took a grateful sip of lemonade, he barely picked at the cake. "It was Hogmanay," he said, hands wrapped tight round the cup. The Drummond family had been the first over their threshold at midnight, a mark of good luck on a Highland New Year. "I didn't think anything of it at the time. He just asked me to post a message."

"Who did?" Raoul asked, in the sort of level, friendly voice he used with the children.

"The Englishman. Mr. Belmont."

Mélanie cast a quick look at Raoul. "Mr. Belmont asked you to deliver a message to someone?"

"To post it. And I did, the next day. It was only later that day that I heard Mrs. Thirle was missing, and even then no one told me she'd left with Mr. Belmont."

Mélanie met Stephen's gaze. Of course, she realized. The Drummonds had been trying to protect Gisèle's reputation and avoid gossip. So if Dugal hadn't happened to see her with Tommy, they wouldn't have mentioned it to him.

"It was only today when I heard Rory and Daddy talking and they mentioned Mr. Belmont. That was when I realized it might be important."

"Excellent deduction," Raoul said. "Dugal, do you happen to remember anything about the letter? The address? Or the name?"

"Oh, yes." Dugal's face brightened. "I don't think Mr. Belmont realized I can read. But I remembered because the name was so interesting. The address was Leicester Street. And the name was Charlotte Leblanc."

Mélanie sucked in her breath. She could feel Raoul's stillness beside her. She'd been prepared to be surprised. But not to learn that Tommy Belmont, former British agent and Elsinore League member, had been in communication with a former French spy.

CHAPTER 7

"TOMMY BELMONT WAS WRITING to someone you used to work with?" Cordelia asked. She and Laura had joined Mélanie and Raoul after the Drummonds left.

"She wasn't one of my agents," Raoul said. "But she was a colleague. I helped her settle in London after Waterloo."

"Could she have been a double?" Laura asked.

"It's possible. God knows my judgment has proved questionable lately. But I wouldn't have thought so."

"I knew her." Mélanie took a turn on the hearth rug. She'd found it difficult to sit still since the Drummonds had left. "Not as well as Raoul did, but I worked with her on one or two missions." She could hear Charlotte Leblanc's dry voice and see her raised brows. "She was a pragmatist. But loyal."

"Perhaps Harry and Malcolm are wrong and Tommy was working for the French," Cordelia said. She shook her head. "Funny how calmly I can say that. I remember when spies seemed like something out of a novel."

"Perhaps," Raoul said. "Or Charlotte could have formed an alliance with the Elsinore League after the war. I would have thought—but again, I've misjudged people in the past."

"Either way, this changes things," Mélanie said. "Malcolm and Andrew need the information. It could lead them to Gisèle."

"I could go to London," Cordy said. "There's no reason for me to be in danger."

"For that matter, I could go with you," Laura said. "I don't like to separate us—"

"Nor do I," Mélanie said. "But I think Raoul and I also need to be there. It's not just getting Malcolm and Andrew the information, it's getting Charlotte to talk. We know her." She cast a glance at Raoul.

He nodded. "I can't say she'll talk to me—or that I'd trust her if she did—but she'll say more than she would to a stranger. We were friends." He cast a glance at Laura. "A bit more than friends on occasion, though it never went much beyond."

"My dear." Laura reached for his hand. "The details of your past may be a surprise but the fact that you have one isn't."

"Thank goodness, for a change, it's not *my* ex-lovers we're encountering," Cordelia said.

"Cordy and I could stay here with the children," Laura said, "while the two of you go to London."

Mélanie folded her arms over her chest. Her fingers bit through the gathered garnet gros de Naples of her sleeves. "No. I don't want to leave the children, but it's more than that. I don't want them to be in a situation where they could become—"

"Hostages to fortune," Laura finished for her.

Mélanie dropped down on the sofa between Laura and Cordy. "It's not that I don't trust the two of you with them. I trust you both with my life—with my children's lives, which is a far greater trust. But the more we're all separated, the more risk there is someone will use some of us against the others."

Raoul was frowning, still leaning against the back of the sofa and holding Laura's hand. "It's a fair point."

"So, we all go." Mélanie glanced at Raoul over her shoulder. "Don't you dare suggest you go without us."

She could sense him weighing all the options. The three of them and the children, alone in the Highlands. "Surely you aren't suggesting the three of you couldn't protect yourselves?"

"It's not our safety I was worried about."

He smiled. "A point."

"Besides, you may need my help with Charlotte."

"Also a point."

"And London's a port. We can leave from there as easily as from here. And we'll all be together. We're too separated as it is."

"YOU'RE SURE IT'S SAFE?" Dorothée asked as she watched Mélanie pack a valise.

"I'm not sure anything's safe. Including staying here. But if we go, we're safer together."

"And you're relieved beyond measure not to be sidelined anymore."

"Well, yes." Mélanie looked up, a nightdress in her hands, and met her friend's gaze. "No sense in denying that. And, as I said, we can leave London as easily as we can leave here."

Doro's brows drew together. "You aren't just going back to London. You're talking to someone from your past. That makes the risks greater."

"Talking secretly." Mélanie twitched the pink ribbon at the neck of the nightdress smooth.

"Still." Dorothée held her gaze across the valise. "I don't know about being a spy. But I do know about having a complicated past. And confronting it can have all sorts of challenges."

Mélanie reached for her dressing case. She could scarcely deny the truth of Doro's words. "I hate to run, but I agree with Malcolm that we didn't have a choice six months ago. To stay would have been foolhardy and put our friends at risk as well as ourselves. It's different now. We don't have much choice *but* to go back to London."

"You're going to leave Ian here?"

"I think it's safer for him. We may need to leave straight for Italy. He'll be here when his parents come back. And he has Elspbeth." They had found the wife of one of the Dunmykel tenants to be Ian's wet nurse. She had moved into the house temporarily with her own baby, and Ian was feeding well and crawling everywhere.

Dorothée nodded. "He was giggling quite delightfully this afternoon when I played peek-a-boo with him. But I think I still catch him looking round as though wondering where his parents are."

"I do too." Mélanie's fingers bit into the linen as she put the nightdress in the dressing case.

"I've been away from my own children a great deal," Dorothée said. "Sometimes it's hard when I come back, but we're always able to get back to where we left off. Or close to it."

"Yes. Given time they should be all right." Assuming Gisèle came back. Assuming they all got through this safely.

"I remember how you used to worry in Vienna when Malcolm was off on a mission," Dorothée said. "Now I know you were running those same risks yourself."

"So I know what I'm doing." Mélanie picked up a folded chemise.

Dorothée held her gaze, her own concerned. "That doesn't make it safe."

~

"So, once again the board shifts." Talleyrand put a glass of calvados into Raoul's hand. "I assume in London you'll be able to look for news of the Wanderer."

"Depending on what else we encounter." Raoul's fingers tightened round the glass. He was still sifting the implications of the news about Charlotte, how much he could share with Mélanie, Laura, and Cordelia, how much he had to keep to himself. "So far as you know, did Charlotte Leblanc know anything about the Wanderer?"

"So far as I know?" Talleyrand tossed down a swallow of calvados. "No. But then I didn't know Arabella knew anything either. And Charlotte being involved is likelier than Arabella." He cast a glance at Raoul. "A clever woman, Charlotte Leblanc. She'd make for a dangerous enemy, I always thought."

Raoul took a drink of calvados. It had a strong bite tonight. "So she would."

"You were fond of her."

"So I was. So I am."

"Which could be a complication."

"My dear Talleyrand. I assure you I haven't gone entirely soft."

"No." Talleyrand turned his glass in his hand. "It's a question of degrees."

Raoul took another sip of calvados. "Wondering if you can trust me?"

"I've always wondered how much I could trust you, O'Roarke. I'd be rather insulted if you didn't say the same about me."

"Fair enough. But in this we have few allies."

"As you say. But you might decide that you had other uses for the Wanderer."

"So might you." Raoul held Talleyrand's gaze. "In fact, you can't tell me you haven't considered it."

"I try to consider every eventuality, O'Roarke. As do you. In the right circumstances, the Wanderer could help further your cause."

Raoul swirled the calvados in his glass. Once a whirlpool was set in motion, one couldn't tell what it would pull under. Or dredge up. "That's not a way I choose to fight."

"You used to not be so squeamish."

"No? Perhaps not. I've violated my sense of what's right and wrong more times than I can count, but I like to think I've always had practical limits, if not moral ones. I don't like to think of what the Wanderer might unleash."

Talleyrand lowered himself into an armchair. "Nor do I. I've given up the illusion that I can control events, but some are too unpredictable to risk. In any case, I think we're both agreed that the Wanderer in the League's hands is unacceptable."

"Quite." Raoul moved to a chair opposite the prince. "What are your own plans?"

"I can't quite say. They rather depend on how the board continues to shift. But for the present I think I'm better off in Britain. Should I leave, you can reach me through the usual channels." Talleyrand turned his glass in his hand. "We're going to need each other, O'Roarke. As you said, we have few allies in this. Including those closest to us."

Raoul took a drink of calvados. "I told Laura about my past history with Charlotte. She didn't seem disturbed, which was what I'd have expected. So there, at least, I'm not keeping anything back."

"There, at least."

Raoul downed the last of the calvados. "It won't be the first time I've lied to people I'm close to. And I'm not fool enough to think it will be the last. What that means for my relationship with my family is my lookout."

STRATHDON'S GAZE moved from Mélanie to Raoul to Laura to Cordelia. "I'd be lying if I didn't say this concerns me."

"It concerns all of us," Mélanie said. "But we have few options."

"You don't think the children would be better off here?"

She drew a breath, trying to sort out safety and her own instincts. "If we're separated, there's that much more chance they can be used against us. If we have to leave for the Continent suddenly, better we all do it together." Her hands locked together in her lap. "And if I'm arrested, they won't arrest the children."

Strathdon settled back in his chair. "I always knew you were a formidable woman. But even after I learned the truth of your past, I don't think I realized quite how formidable."

"We have limited moves open to us, sir. We have to do the best with those we can make."

"That sounds eminently logical, my dear. But it doesn't decrease the danger."

"Malcolm and I are used to living with danger. We're used to protecting the children from it." Mélanie's fingers tightened. "I know it's not the sort of marriage you'd have wanted for your grandson—"

"On the contrary." Strathdon took a sip of whisky. "Or if not, it's a failure of my imagination. Because it's far better than any marriage I could have imagined for him."

CHAPTER 8

THE BERKELEY SQUARE library smelled as it always had. Ink and leather and the dusty aroma of books. The candlelight bounced off the glass-fronted bookcases and gleamed off the Carrara marble of the library table, which brought an unexpected shock of memory of Italy.

Malcolm lifted his candle to the book spines. He needed distraction. The house echoed with memories. And yet, the sound of his children's feet clattering up and down the stairs and of his wife's laughter were all too absent. He studied the book titles. Not Shakespeare. He could scarcely glance at a page without seeing a quote he and his wife had tossed back and forth. Not Ludlow. Mel had given him his first edition, and even if he read a newer copy, it made him think of her. He reached for *Pride and Prejudice,* then thought of Andrew's comment at the White Hart.

He and Andrew had completed their journey without further attacks after the brawl at the White Hart. Except for a faint sting along his ribs, the incident might never have happened. Save that Malcolm remained convinced it hadn't been coincidence. He and Andrew had had countless discussions about the possible reasons on the remainder of their journey, but whether the Elsinore

League, or whoever had attacked Tommy, or someone else entirely had been behind it was impossible to determine. Given the danger, he probably ought to be all the more relieved Mélanie was in Scotland. Instead, he missed her damnably. Not just her presence and warmth, but her insights into the dangers they faced.

Andrew had not even come into London. He and Malcolm had parted ways at an inn outside the city. Andrew had headed south to see Frances's daughter Judith. Malcolm had arrived in Berkeley Square well after dark. Tomorrow he would see Harry Davenport and also enlist the aid of their friends Rupert and Bertrand. Bertrand, who secretly helped Bonapartists find refuge in London and had once done the same for Royalists, had excellent sources in the city. Malcolm's brother Edgar was in France, and Malcolm had yet to write to tell him of Gisèle's disappearance. He'd been hoping they discovered her first. And perhaps he was being craven. He and Edgar had had a strained relationship since their mother's death, for reasons he did not fully understand himself.

He looked further down the shelves. *The Odyssey?* That seemed appropriate. Except that he was already home, though without his family and without any expectation of staying.

Malcolm shifted the library steps to reach for the book, then went still. A sound echoed through the house. The front door bell, he realized. He'd sent Valentin to bed. He was accustomed to not having servants see to all the details of the household after Italy, but he hadn't been expecting a caller in the middle of the night. He moved into the hall, carrying his candle. The spy's wariness settled over him like a familiar cloak—no one should know he was in London yet. At the same time, a shred of hope tugged at his chest. Could Gelly have found her way home?

He pulled open the heavy front door. Familiar blue eyes blazed into his own.

"Harry." Malcolm went forwards to embrace his friend, then hesitated as he saw the man standing beside Harry on the front steps. Not that he wasn't glad to see him as well. But— "It's good to see you, Jeremy." Malcolm gave Harry a quick hug and then bestowed one on Bow Street runner Jeremy Roth. He could feel the tension running through both men.

"We wouldn't have come so late," Harry said, "but we thought this shouldn't wait. It's nothing to do with Gisèle," he added quickly, no doubt seeing the fear shoot through Malcolm's gaze.

Malcolm stepped away from the door. "Come in out of the cold. I can't promise a fire, but I do have plentiful whisky."

He flung open the library doors, returned his candle to the library table, where a brace of candles already burned, and went to pour whisky. Harry shrugged out of his greatcoat, but Roth made no move to do so.

"I know," Roth said. "You don't want to tell me why you left Britain or why you're back."

Malcolm turned from the decanters, a glass in each hand. "Jeremy—"

"And I agree I'm better off not knowing. God knows, I miss you, and I'd like you to come back, but that's not why I'm here."

Malcolm put a glass in Roth's hand and gave another to Harry.

"I went to see Carfax when I got to London," Harry said, "as we had agreed."

Malcolm nodded. The plan had been for Harry to try to draw Carfax out over Carfax's proposal that they work together against the Elsinore League.

"I arrived at Carfax House to find Roth there," Harry said.

Malcolm cast a quick glance between the two men. "Carfax summoned you?" he asked Roth.

"No, Carfax was discovered in the Barque of Frailty."

Malcolm frowned. "The Barque of Frailty is—"

"A brothel," Harry finished. "The one sort of intrigue I wouldn't think to find Carfax involved in." But for all the irony, his face was intense.

"No." One of the few things Malcolm didn't doubt about his

former spymaster was Carfax's love for his wife. "But no one would summon Bow Street because Carfax was in a brothel, whatever the law."

"No," Roth said. "They summoned Bow Street because Carfax was in a room with the dead body of a young woman."

Malcolm stared at his friend. "Good God. What did Carfax say?"

"Very little," Roth said. "He's been arrested for murder."

If anything, that was even more surprising than Carfax being found with the dead woman. Malcolm scraped a hand over his hair. "What's the woman's name?"

"Miranda Spencer. Mid-twenties, I'd say. According to the staff at the Barque of Frailty, she'd been employed there for almost three years."

"It's horrible," Malcolm said. "But it's also the sort of thing Carfax could talk his way out of in ten minutes, however he was found, whatever he was doing there. Whether or not he killed her. As it is, I'm surprised there wasn't pressure on you not to make the arrest."

"Quite the opposite," Roth said. "To own the truth, I hesitated. Not because it was Carfax, but because the circumstances didn't quite add up. Carfax says he went into Miss Spencer's room and found her dead. He'd gone upstairs with her over and hour before. He says he left the room and went to a sitting room down the passage, but he doesn't give any account of why or what he was doing in the interval or of why he went back to Miss Spencer's room. The person who discovers a body is always of interest and often does indeed prove to be the killer, but I'd have expected a man like Carfax to have a better story. Miss Spencer was found in the bed, but there was a bruise on the back of her head. It looks to me as though she hit her head on the edge of the marble night table. I suspect the killer pushed her and perhaps she lost consciousness. From the pooling of her blood, I think she was smothered on the floor and then moved to the bed. It looks to me like a crime of impulse, not too neatly done. Which isn't what I'd expect from Carfax."

"No," Malcolm said. "Carfax was a field agent once. If he was going to kill with his own hands, he knows how to do it. And I can't see him losing his temper and pushing someone in an argument."

Roth nodded. "I pointed all that out to the chief magistrate. But I was informed in no uncertain terms that I was to make the arrest forthwith."

Malcolm stared at his friend. "The chief magistrate told you that himself?"

"Yes, but I was under the impression that Sir Nathaniel was acting under instructions from the home secretary."

Harry crossed to the drinks trolley, poured a third whisky, and put it in Malcolm's hand before Malcolm quite realized what he was doing. Malcolm's fingers closed round the glass. He took a long swallow. "So Sidmouth wants Carfax arrested. Or he in turn is being pressured by someone who does. I can't believe the murder of a woman who worked in a brothel would rouse the government's ire. Or that she'd have friends powerful enough to pressure the home secretary."

Harry took a drink from his own glass. "My first thought was that someone set up Carfax. Most likely the Elsinore League, given that we know they're targeting him. Given their use of blackmail, I could believe they could pressure Sidmouth. A few months ago I'd have said Sidmouth could be a League member himself, but now that we have the list, we know he isn't. Assuming the list is complete. Which it may not be."

"The League are the most likely explanation," Malcolm said. "Though it's also possible the government have decided Carfax is a liability on their own, and want to get rid of him. But either way, what I don't understand is Carfax's keeping quiet. He has to know he's being set up. He's the last man to put up with that."

"So he thinks he has something to gain from not talking."

Harry twisted his glass in his hand. "Trying to throw his enemy off guard? I'd think his enemies would find his behavior as puzzling as we do. But the only other option I can think of is that he's protecting someone."

Malcolm nodded. "But other than David, who's on the Continent, the only people I can imagine Carfax going to prison to protect are Lady Carfax, Bel, Mary, Georgiana, and Lucinda. And it's difficult to imagine any of them being implicated in such a murder."

"Could he be being blackmailed?" Roth asked. "By someone who knows his secrets?"

"They'd have to be pretty serious secrets to make it worth staying in prison for murder and risking hanging," Harry said. "But then, we know Carfax's secrets are on the serious side. Still, he'd have to feel the implications were worse than prison and possible execution."

"We don't know he doesn't have a plan he thinks will get him out before it comes to that." Malcolm stared at the candlelight bouncing off his glass. "Carfax would risk a lot for what he sees as the good of the country. If he thought Britain's interests could be harmed by whatever information he was concealing, I can imagine him keeping quiet." He drew a breath, turning over possibilities. "Has anyone written to David?"

"I haven't," Harry said.

Roth shook his head. "But the family may have."

Harry met Malcolm's gaze. "You think—"

"That Carfax would let himself be arrested to get David back to London? Possibly. Carfax will go to fairly extreme lengths when it comes to David." Carfax had told his son David the truth about Mélanie in an effort to cause a rift between David and his lover Simon Tanner and persuade David to marry. He hadn't succeeded, but the revelations had driven Malcolm and Mélanie into exile, and now David and Simon had gone abroad as well.

Harry studied Malcolm in the library shadows. "There's no

need for you to get involved. No one could claim you owe Carfax anything."

"I'd be the first to agree with you there. But I do think there's need for me to be involved. For one thing, it may involve the Elsinore League. And for another—I'd cheerfully leave Carfax to his fate if I thought he was guilty, but I'm damned if I'm going to stand by and leave a likely innocent man in prison. Even Carfax."

Harry gave a sudden grin, his first of the sort since he'd arrived at Berkeley Square. "I couldn't agree with you more. In fact, I'd have investigated myself even if you hadn't."

THERE WAS something about the gray light of prison that seemed to strip people to the bone. Malcolm had noticed it when Laura was in Newgate, and he noticed it now looking across the cell at the man who had once welcomed a lonely young boy into his home. Who had set one of Malcolm and David's best friends to spy on them as undergraduates. Who had offered Malcolm employment when Malcolm was rootless and mired in despair. Who had employed Malcolm for a decade during which Malcolm had violated nearly every principle he possessed. Who had used the truth of Malcolm's wife's past to drive a wedge between his own son and the love of his son's life, and between David and Malcolm. Who, even now, could destroy nearly everyone Malcolm held dear.

Carfax's face was haggard, his cheeks sunken, but the gaze he turned on Malcolm was sharp as ever. He might have been summoning Malcolm into his study, all the cards in his hand, not facing him in prison. "You've always been able to surprise me. I thought you'd come back to London eventually, but I didn't think this is what would do it."

"It isn't. I was here in any case."

Carfax's gaze flashed in acknowledgment. "For what it's worth,

I can do rather less to protect you now than I could in my previous situation."

"I may be slow, sir, but I'd never rely on you for protection." Malcolm drew out a chair—carved oak with the look of Hepplewhite, Carfax was well taken care of even in prison—and sat opposite Carfax. "I don't know if Oliver told you that I turned down the offer you sent him to Dunmykel with just before Christmas."

"Rather moot at this point, but yes." Carfax pushed his spectacles up on his nose. "Then why are you here?"

"Because I don't think you did it."

Carfax regarded him. For a moment, Malcolm would have sworn he'd shocked his spymaster. Then Carfax removed his spectacles and folded them, with the same ease he'd displayed when he was in command of a scene. "You're a keen judge of people, Malcolm. But your tendency to want to see the best in them is your besetting sin. Don't make that mistake with me."

"After six months ago, can you imagine I would?"

"I wouldn't have thought so. But old habits die hard. You have to know this wouldn't be the first time I've killed. Or at least ordered someone killed."

"Quite. But it's a bit different to do it oneself."

Carfax adjusted the spectacles on the table, as he'd once arranged objects on his ink blotter. "I was a field agent once. And I've never been squeamish."

Malcolm regarded Carfax in the winter light slanting through the high, barred window. The bones of his face were even sharper and more hawk-like than usual, the planes and angles harder. His eyes gleamed with understanding, but even without the spectacles, they appeared veiled. Somehow, whatever the illumination in the room, Carfax was a master at hiding in the shadows. "I don't doubt you'd be capable of it. To own the truth, when I first heard the story, I thought you were probably guilty. But the details don't add up. If you were going to kill with your own hands, you wouldn't begin by losing your temper and pushing your victim. And then, your being in the brothel at all makes no sense."

Carfax raised a brow. "My dear Malcolm. Surely there's a very obvious explanation for that."

"With nine men out of ten. Not with you."

Carfax gave a short laugh. "I don't know whether to be shocked at your naïveté or relieved you still have any sort of faith in me. For all your ideals, you've always been refreshingly free of illusions where I'm concerned. And surely if you had any doubts, the last six months have convinced you that I'm capable of any sort of betrayal."

"Of most. Of many I'd have once thought might be beyond you. But not all, I think."

"I'd rather have thought learning the truth about your wife would have helped you realize the people closest to one can commit betrayals that seem unthinkable."

Malcolm kept his fingers steady on the table. Even behind bars, Carfax knew how to draw blood. Which meant Carfax wanted to change the subject. Which was interesting in and of itself. "Actually, my wife taught me that, perhaps especially when someone's stock in trade is deception, certain loyalties become very important. I never had illusions you wouldn't betray me, even long before last June. I no longer have illusions you wouldn't betray David. But I'm quite sure you wouldn't betray Lady Carfax."

Carfax turned his folded spectacles in his hands. "That's a rather large assumption about a man you admit is morally bankrupt."

"Don't forget I've been in and out of your house since I was a boy." Carfax was always using their association that went back to Malcolm's childhood to his advantage. Malcolm could do the same. "I used to envy David his family. I knew it had its challenges. In some ways, even then, I was glad not to have the burdens David did. But I always envied the security that came from having two parents who loved each other."

Carfax gave a faint smile that might have been acknowledgment or irony. "Surely after all your time on the Continent, you realize love is no guarantee of fidelity."

"I wouldn't have had to leave Britain to know that. But even you've admitted I'm a reasonably shrewd judge of character."

"Without doubt. I've found it very useful on occasion. But as I said, your besetting sin is wanting to see the best in people. And your other besetting sin is your love of mysteries."

"I'm rather good at solving them."

"So you are. But sometimes you see mysteries that aren't there."

"You're avoiding the facts, sir. A sure sign that they don't support your thesis."

Carfax settled back in his chair for all the world as if it were the wingback chair in his study, instead of straight-backed oak. "My dear Malcolm. I'm expert at taking care of myself. Why wouldn't I seek your help if I were innocent?"

"My thoughts precisely. It's very like Laura's behavior last March."

Carfax snorted. "I doubt O'Roarke would care for the comparison. I assure you, whatever the outcome, I am not going to run off to Italy with a revolutionary."

"No, I know you have other priorities. And I would think you'd want to get back to them."

"My dear Malcolm. You can trust me to take care of myself."

"My dear sir. You aren't doing a very good job of it just now." Malcolm studied Carfax for a moment in the gray light. "You obviously had a reason other than the obvious for being in the brothel. To collect information? It's the obvious assumption."

"The second obvious assumption."

"I assume you came back into the room to find Miranda Spencer dead."

"I did, as it happens. But I see no particular reason why you should believe me more than anyone else does."

Malcolm shifted his position, trying to get a better view of Carfax's expression through the swirl of dust motes. "I've been wracking my brain to think what endgame would be served by your being in prison. But I can't come up with any. Which could be a failure of imagination on my part. The other explanation is that you're protecting someone."

Carfax lifted a brow.

"Yes, I know," Malcolm said. "I doubt David, or Lady Carfax, or Bel, or Lucinda, or Mary, or Georgiana killed Miranda Spencer. But their safety could be threatened."

"You think someone is blackmailing me into accepting a murder charge? If I could be so easily controlled, surely someone would have tried it years ago."

"Unless they had new information." Malcolm settled back in his own chair. "It did occur to me that you might think your being in prison would get David to return to London."

For a moment, the armor in Carfax's gaze cracked, and Malcolm had a glimpse of something raw as a wound to the bone. "Considering the terms my son and I parted on, that hardly seems likely."

"Don't play games, sir. You know David's loyalty. If nothing else, he'll be concerned about his mother and sisters."

"He didn't show a great deal of concern when he left Britain without saying goodbye to his mother."

"Sir." Malcolm held Carfax's gaze with his own. "You know your son."

Carfax hooked his spectacles over his ears. "I thought I did."

Malcolm paused, but much as he hesitated to share anything to do with David and Simon, Carfax needed to know. In this, perhaps they were allies. Or at least their interests briefly aligned. "Did you know the League were trying to get incriminating information about David and Simon?"

Carfax went still as granite.

"You didn't know."

"Can you imagine I'd have stood by?"

"I'm not exactly sure what you could have done."

"They tried to get the information from you?"

"I think they knew they wouldn't have a prayer of success. They tried to blackmail Percy and Mary Shelley into getting Simon to commit something to writing. I don't know whom else they may have approached."

Carfax's hands closed white-knuckled on the edge of the table.

Odd how the fear in Carfax's gaze brought a sympathy Malcolm would have sworn he'd never again feel for his spymaster. "The Shelleys are both too good friends to have agreed," Malcolm said. "And Simon and David are too careful, I think, to commit anything to writing that could be used against them if it fell into the wrong hands. They've always been scrupulously careful, even when writing to Mel and me."

"But we don't know whom else the League may approach." Carfax looked up. "It's always been a risk of this—of their relationship."

"The relationships of anyone connected to spies are always subject to being used."

"If David understood—"

"David understands enough to protect the people he loves. David's at risk because he's your son. And because the League see you as an enemy."

"Are you suggesting I shouldn't be?"

"I think the risk posed by the League is one of the few things we agree on."

Carfax's mouth tightened. "If David isn't careful—"

"I'm quite sure he will be careful. He knows what he has to lose. Ironically, you helped him learn that. He's been very careful and hardheaded in protecting his family. More so than I gave him credit for six months ago."

Carfax stared down at his clenched fingers. "I wanted to protect him. You should understand that."

"You wanted him to do what you wanted."

Carfax unfolded his spectacles and hooked them back over his ears. "Because it was better for him."

"Are you protecting him now?"

"You mean, did the League blackmail me over David to get me to accept a murder charge? I'm not so easily manipulated."

"I wouldn't have thought so. But if they had hard evidence—"

"You just pointed out that David and Tanner wouldn't be fool enough to give it to them." Carfax adjusted his spectacles. "Have you seen David?"

It was said in the same level tone as his other comments, yet Malcolm had the oddest sense it wasn't calculated. "No."

"But you've heard from him."

"I'm the first to acknowledge a parent's feelings, but given your own actions regarding your son, do you seriously expect me to share any information concerning him?"

Carfax removed his spectacles again, pulled a handkerchief from his pocket, and began to polish them. "I miscalculated. Though there were limited moves open to me."

"You didn't give David and his feelings for Simon enough credit."

"I rather think I gave David too much credit in thinking he'd do what was right for the family. But you're right that I may also have misjudged the strength of his attachment."

Malcolm continued watching his spymaster. "I'm impressed you can recognize that."

"I'm not entirely blind to the power of love. I've felt it myself."

Said in that same mild voice, it was, in its way, a shattering admission for Carfax. "Which is precisely why I'm convinced your wife is the one person you wouldn't betray." Malcolm pushed himself to his feet. "You could think playing along is a way to get information on the Elsinore League. Is that it?" He leaned over Carfax, hands braced on the table.

"I'm obviously not much use against the League in here."

"Which makes the question of why you aren't trying harder to get out all the more interesting."

Carfax spread his hands on the scarred oak of the table as though it were the gilded ink blotter on his desk. "I'm quite good at taking care of myself, Malcolm. If we agree on nothing else, we should agree on that."

It was true. So why, looking at this man who had threatened so much of his life, did Malcolm find his throat gripped by dread?

CHAPTER 9

ARCHIE CLUNKED down his coffee cup and looked from Harry to Malcolm. "The Barque of Frailty?"

"We know it's a brothel," Harry said. "But not much more."

"And you assumed I might possess more knowledge?" Archie smiled, though he was still pale from the news about Carfax. "Your lack of illusions is always refreshing, Harry."

Harry sat back in his chair. "You can't deny you've had a more active career in certain areas than either Malcolm or I, sir. And that your pursuit of the Elsinore League has taken you some interesting places."

"True enough." Archie reached for his coffee. He and Frances and Chloe had arrived in London the night before as well. They had left a day after Malcolm and Andrew and had traveled more slowly, but had also taken a more direct route. Malcolm had already been to see Carfax at Newgate, but the hour was early for the fashionable world. Frances wouldn't be up for another hour, at least. "I've never had much taste for brothels, though," Archie said. "Seems as close as I can imagine to sacrilege to turn something that should be mutually enjoyable into commerce. I've never patronized the Barque of Frailty. But I do have a—past acquaintance—with Rosamund Hartley."

"The woman who runs it?" Malcolm sat forwards in his chair, his own coffee forgot at his elbow.

Archie nodded. "Though she didn't then. She was one of the loveliest opera dancers at Covent Garden."

"She was your mistress," Harry said.

"For a time. A quite agreeable time, I confess. I left her with some handsome pieces of jewelry and a large parting gift. Some of which I suspect went into setting up the Barque of Frailty." Archie frowned into his coffee. "I confess, I never thought too much about what I was financing."

"A woman who wants to make her own way in the world without family and fortune has limited options," Malcolm said.

Archie met his gaze. "I can't but admire Rosamund's enterprise. But what's perhaps more interesting, in light of present circumstances, is that she left me for Lord Beverston."

Malcolm's fingers closed on the edge of his chair. Beverston was one of the founding members of the Elsinore League. He had recruited into it both his son, John Smythe, who had died in their adventure in Italy, and his godson, Tommy Belmont. Who had run off with Gisèle. "Are you saying the League are behind the Barque of Frailty?"

Archie's brows drew together. "I've never heard a suggestion of that. Rosamund was always ambitious to be independent. But I wouldn't be surprised if Beverston's money also went into it, either directly, or because he too bestowed expensive gifts on Rosamund. And I know several League members who patronize the establishment. Rosamund met Beverston at one of the League's parties when she was still my mistress. I wouldn't precisely say he took her from me—the affair was already beginning to run its course by then—but she did leave me for him. And I believe he still visits the Barque of Frailty."

"Have you ever heard any mention of Carfax's being connected to it?" Harry asked.

Archie's frown deepened. "No. Nor of Carfax's visiting a brothel or having a mistress. Despite the circles I moved in. I'm quite sure you're right that he was at the Barque of Frailty in search of information. Very likely about the League. But as to why the devil he isn't talking now—" Archie shook his head. "Carfax is nothing if not challenging."

Malcolm's fingers tightened on the walnut of his chair. "Did you ever hear mention of Tommy Belmont in connection with the Barque of Frailty?"

Archie met Malcolm's gaze, his own warming with compassion. "No. I'm sorry. But as I said, I've had little to do with it in recent years."

"When did you last see Mrs. Hartley?" Harry asked.

"Not for some time. Though she's still to be found at Elsinore League parties, my own attendance has been dwindling. But if I write a letter of introduction, I think that will get you through the door." Archie pushed himself to his feet and went to his writing desk, but he paused as he went to dip his pen in the inkwell. "Odd to remember those days. They seemed amusing enough, at the time. But my life with your aunt is so much more agreeable."

Malcolm hesitated in front of the Barque of Frailty. Portland stone, lace curtains at the windows, a shiny brass knocker, window boxes neatly pruned for winter. Nothing on the surface like the Gilded Lily in Seven Dials, with its cracked windows and gin-soaked floorboards, which he and Mélanie had visited last June. But fundamentally the same inside, in many ways.

Harry touched his arm. "It's no different from Le Paon d'Or."

Where Malcolm had got quite at home in the weeks in Brussels before Waterloo, calling to get information from Rachel

Garnier, one of his best agents. He had paid a fair number of visits to brothels in his life, but only as an agent or an investigator. Intimacy was difficult enough for him. He'd never been able to bring himself to pay for a substitute. He'd always swallowed a distaste for intimacy as commerce, and the circumstances that left women with no other recourse, but he'd been fairly matter-of-fact, working with women like Rachel and taking advantage of their ability to gather information. Until—"I didn't know about Mel's past then," he said. Thank God he could say that to Harry now. "It shouldn't make a difference, but it—"

"Drives home the point," Harry said. "Yes, I can see how it would." Harry studied the building in front of them. "A fellow soldier once used a word about Cordy that would imply she worked in a brothel. When we were separated. I punched him in the jaw."

"You're a good man, Davenport."

"Whom Cordy slept with was her own business. I saw no reason to call her names for doing something half the men in the beau monde do."

After another moment's hesitation, they climbed the steps and rang the bell.

A footman opened the door. Powered wig, blue satin livery, silver-buckled shoes. He might have worked at any house in Mayfair. Though, in point of fact, this *was* a house in Mayfair. He surveyed them with raised brows. This was the sort of establishment that only admitted regulars.

Malcolm gave him his card and Archie's note. "We're here to see Mrs. Hartley."

The footman studied the card for a moment. He clearly knew how to read. And he was well enough versed in the Debrett's to recognize the Rannoch name. His gaze moved over the card with instant recognition. He inclined his head and took their hats and gloves. "If you will come this way."

He conducted them down a marble-tiled entrance hall

complete with pier table and silver basket for calling cards (who, Malcolm wondered, actually left a card there?) to a sitting room hung with rose-colored silk in the sort of shade that cast a flattering glow in any lighting.

"If you will wait here, gentlemen, I'll inquire if Mrs. Hartley is at home."

"One can't but imagine the scene that might ensue if someone stumbled into the wrong house thinking they were calling on an acquaintance," Harry said.

"Simon could build a play on that. An intriguing take on *She Stoops to Conquer*." Malcolm glanced round the sitting room. The furniture was Hepplewhite or a good imitation, covered in a watered silk that complemented the walls. The paintings on the walls were by Boucher and Fragonard. Tasteful and elegant, but a bit more suggestive than what most hostesses would have in a receiving room.

After a few minutes, the door opened to admit a tall woman with hair the color of a pale sherry, twisted into an elegant knot that showed her handsome pearl earrings. Her face was strong boned yet delicate, her eyes a clear blue. She wore a gown of corded lavender silk (was the color a nod to the death in what might be called her family? Malcolm wondered). The neck was high, edged with a small lace ruff, the sleeves long and tight, but the cut betrayed that she still had the lean, elegant body of a dancer.

"Mrs. Hartley." Malcolm bowed, as did Harry. "Thank you for agreeing to see us."

"I could scarcely not respond to a letter from Archie." She gave a smile that somehow warmed her face without quite touching her eyes. Her gaze moved over Harry. "There's no need to introduce yourselves. You're very like your uncle in the days when I first knew him. He was always exceedingly proud of you."

"You're kind, ma'am. I trust my uncle had more interesting

things to discuss with a beautiful woman than my schoolboy exploits."

"On the contrary. He was eager to share them, and I found them most entertaining. I understand he's about to become a father himself now."

"To his surprise and, I think, delight."

"Odd where life can take one. Though hearing him talk about you, I always thought it a shame he didn't have other children." She gestured to the chairs. "Do sit. As agreeable as it is to meet Archie's nephew, I know this isn't a social call. I assume you're here about Miranda."

"Our condolences," Malcolm said.

Mrs. Hartley met his gaze as she sank into a chair and settled her skirts. Her own showed neither surprise nor irony. "Thank you. I was fond of her, as I am of all the girls I employ."

"How long had she worked here?" Malcolm asked.

"A year. No, more than two. It was late in '16. Daisy Singleton told me she had a friend in need of employment. I have to be careful about whom I take in, but Daisy's been with me a long time, and I trust her judgment."

"Do you know where Miss Spencer came from?" Malcolm asked.

Mrs. Hartley's hand stilled for a moment on the ruched folds of her gown. "She said she was a widow whose husband had fallen at Vitoria, that she'd worked as a governess but had lost her employment when her charges' father took an interest in her. That she'd scraped together a living as a seamstress for a time but could no longer do so."

"But you didn't believe her?" Malcolm asked.

Mrs. Hartley studied a sapphire ring on her left hand. "It's a common enough story. Perhaps too common. Some girls go into this life because it's preferable to the life they're born to. But Miranda Spencer was clearly born to something better. For girls like that, there's always a story. Sometimes it's the obvious one. But more often I've found there are more layers."

"Did you have any clues as to what Miss Spencer's true story might be?" Harry asked.

Mrs. Hartley twisted her ring round her finger. "She was clearly educated. She could read, and she wrote the sort of copperplate hand that's learned from a governess. Quite unlike my own cramped fist. She also spoke French fluently."

"Do you think there's any chance she was French?" Malcolm asked, keeping his voice conversational.

Mrs. Hartley's finely arced brows drew together. "Mr. Rannoch, are you asking me if Miranda could have been a French spy?"

"Do you think she was?" Malcolm returned.

"I wouldn't have thought it. But I know your reputation. I know the reputation of Lord Carfax, who stands accused of her murder. I can guess what might lie behind your question. Better to confront it head on than to have you thinking my establishment is cover for a French spy ring." She folded her hands in her lap, her gaze steady on Malcolm's own. "It isn't, by the way, though I suppose I'd say that even if it were."

"Yes, very likely. Though I'm not sure you'd be so quick to admit to the possibility. Unless you were very cool headed indeed." Which, in point of fact, Rosamund Hartley showed every sign of being.

"This business takes a cool head. But I'm not sure I'd have the temperament for the spy business. In any case, as to Miranda herself—she came to me over a year after Waterloo."

"Which was far from the end of the spy game." Malcolm settled back in his chair. "Leaving aside your own role, did you have any reason to believe Miss Spencer was French, and/or a spy?"

Mrs. Hartley frowned again seemingly in genuine consideration. "She had no trace of an accent. But her French was also without noticeable accent—at least to my ear, and I've spent a fair amount of time round French dancers and French émigrés. If I had to hazard a guess, I'd say she probably had a French governess or had spent time in France. As to her being a spy—as I said, it never occurred to me. But she was rather secretive. She wasn't the only one of the girls to be so. In this business, one often needs to find something of one's own to hang on to."

"Did she have friends outside of Miss Singleton? Or family?"

"She had a brother who visited her several times. At least, she said he was her brother. I confess, I wondered, though if he was her lover there was no need for such secrecy. What the girls do on their off days is their own business, and several of them have young men. It's not unheard of for them to leave to get married." She smoothed the ruffle on her sleeve. "I suspect that shocks you."

"On the contrary." Malcolm kept his gaze steady, while in his head he heard his debate with his wife about whether or not he'd have married her if he'd known she'd worked in a brothel. "I grew up in the beau monde, after all."

Mrs. Hartley gave a faint, appreciative smile. "In any case, if this young man was Miranda's lover rather than her brother, I saw no sign of romance between them. But I can't say there was much family resemblance. He has brown hair, while she was very blonde. And he's stocky, where she was fine boned."

"Do you know his name?" Harry asked.

"Gerald Lumley. According to Miranda. She said he had a farm in Devon. But as to why he couldn't help her in her straitened circumstances—that was never clear."

"Had she seen Lord Carfax before?" Malcolm asked. He said it abruptly, hoping to catch Mrs. Hartley off guard. But she didn't so much as blink.

"No. At least not here. Not unless he climbed in a window."

"Had Lord Carfax ever been here before?" Harry asked.

"No. I was shocked to see him in my drawing room."

"I don't imagine it's easy to gain entrée to your house," Malcolm said.

"It isn't." Mrs. Hartley folded her hands in her lap. "One has to have an introduction from someone already known to me. Needless to say, you wouldn't have got past my footman without Archie's card."

"I don't doubt it," Harry said.

"Who brought Carfax in?" Malcolm asked.

"Lord Waitely. He's been a frequent guest here for years. I couldn't refuse him. Not that I'd have refused Lord Carfax if he'd simply walked in my door. I know enough about him to have a healthy respect for his powers."

"Did you speak to him?" Malcolm asked.

"I speak to all the gentleman in my drawing room. He was polite. Thanked me for admitting him." She cast a brief glance at Harry. "He mentioned that he understood I was an old friend of Archie Davenport's. I didn't realize they were much acquainted."

"I don't believe they are," Harry said. "But Carfax has certainly met Archie at the Rannochs', and I'm sure elsewhere." And Carfax might know Archie had been a French agent.

"I didn't want to linger or appear overly interested," Mrs. Hartley said. "But I confess I wondered if Carfax had come in search of information."

"Did he ask to meet Miss—Mrs. Spencer?" Malcolm asked.

"He didn't ask me, but later in the evening I looked across the room and saw him speaking with her. It looked innocuous enough. Hardly the stuff of seduction. But then, I've found some men are more interested in someone to talk to, who'll listen to their problems, than in the more obvious reasons for visiting a brothel. Not that it stops them from indulging in other activities. Thinking back—" She shook her head. "If I could tell you how many times I've gone over my glimpse of them talking, of the moment I saw them leave the room together. Asked myself what clues I might have missed, what clues might have got me to intervene—" She put her hand to her mouth, gaze sharp with grief and self-reproach.

"You saw them leave the room together," Malcolm said. "Did anyone see them go into Mrs. Spencer's room?"

"I don't know. But obviously she was found there, with Carfax beside her."

"Which makes the question of whether they were in the room together until the murder particularly interesting."

Mrs. Hartley's gaze locked on his own. "You don't think Carfax killed her."

"I think the facts as we know them don't quite add up. I'm quite prepared to find Carfax guilty if the additional facts we uncover point that way."

"You used to work for him," Mrs. Hartley said.

"We all have things in our past we're ashamed of."

Her brows lifted and she inclined her head in acknowledgment.

Malcolm settled back in his chair. "I understand you're also well acquainted with Lord Beverston."

This time, he'd swear he caught her off guard, though she concealed her faint start of surprise with admirable aplomb. "What does Beverston have to do with this?"

"I'm not sure. But as a member of the Elsinore League, he can't but be of interest."

Her gaze locked on his own.

"You must know we're aware of the League," Malcolm said. "My— Alistair Rannoch was one of the founders, after all. Along with Beverston."

Her hands locked together in her lap. "Archie confides a great deal in you."

"We're passably good at uncovering information on our own," Harry said. "It seems several members of the League are frequent guests in your establishment."

Mrs. Hartley drew a breath, as though armoring herself. "If you know anything at all about the Elsinore League, you must realize their members are to be found at many establishments such as mine."

"But not all such establishments are run by people who number members of the League as former protectors."

"I assure you, the Barque of Frailty is under my control, not some sort of operation of the League's. Though, I suppose, as with being a front for French spies, I'd say that in any case. But I somehow can't bear to have you think something I built myself is the province of others."

"I have no doubt the Barque of Frailty is entirely yours," Malcolm said. Which didn't account for what else Rosamund Hartley might be involved in.

She held his gaze in a moment of acknowledgment. "I can understand your interest in the Elsinore League. But surely it's a side issue to what happened to Miranda."

"Not when one considers that Carfax is a sworn enemy of the League."

Mrs. Hartley's eyes widened in surprise. Or a good counterfeit of surprise. "You think Carfax was here in search of information about the League."

"I think it's highly probable." Malcolm paused for a moment as that information settled in Mrs. Hartley's eyes. "Did Mrs. Spencer have League members who were regular clients?"

Mrs. Hartley's fingers stirred against the folds of her gown. Keeping the secrets of her clientele would be as ingrained in her as keeping sources secret was ingrained for a spy. So when she spoke, Malcolm sensed it was a sign of how very much she wanted to learn the truth of what had happened to Miranda. Unless she was playing a very complicated game indeed. "Lord Beverston took an interest in Miranda," she said. "She wasn't the only girl in my employ he patronized, but he definitely sought her out more than once. He's always had a taste for delicate blondes." She hesitated a moment, then added, "You might not credit it, but I had something of that look when Beverston first knew me."

"If Beverston had a scrap of sense, ma'am," Harry said, "he wouldn't have looked away from what was before him."

"You're very kind, Colonel Davenport."

"I'm nothing of the sort, Mrs. Hartley, as you must know if my uncle was remotely accurate in what he told you about me."

"Did she ever attend any Elsinore League parties?" Malcolm asked.

Mrs. Hartley drew a breath.

"We know about their parties," Malcolm said. "Being a Hell Fire Club may be cover for the League, but it's not entirely without truth."

"Archie says you're to be found at their parties still," Harry added.

"Upon occasion. Though I haven't seen your uncle at one since Mr. Rannoch's aunt entered his life. I don't supply girls to the parties, if that's what you're asking. And I never saw Miranda at one. But it's true she was out a number of evenings in Lord Beverston's company. I can't swear to where they went."

"Was she close to other League members?" Malcolm asked.

"My dear Mr. Rannoch, even I don't know every League member. Miranda had spent time with Riversby and Dunstable, but she wasn't as close to either of them as to Lord Beverston."

"Were any of them here the night she was killed?" Malcolm asked.

Mrs. Hartley's gaze locked on his own. But then she seemed to give it honest consideration. "Beverston and Riversby were." Mrs. Hartley twisted her ring round her finger again. "Beverston was most distressed when Miranda's body was discovered. The house was in chaos, as you can imagine. I can't be sure of where everyone was. I was trying to keep Miranda's room clear until Bow Street arrived, but Beverston pushed his way in and dropped down beside her. There were tears on his face."

Which said a lot about Lord Beverston's relationship to

Miranda Spencer. But did not, in Malcolm's estimation, in any way prove he hadn't killed her.

"I'd like a list of everyone who was in the house that night," Malcolm said.

He half thought she would deny she kept such a list, but Rosamund Hartley nodded.

"And we'd like to speak to Miss Singleton."

Again he thought she might protest, but Mrs. Hartley got to her feet. "I thought you would," she said. "I warn you, she's taken it very hard, but I think she'll be willing to talk to you." She moved to the door, but turned back, gripping the handle. "Mr. Rannoch. Colonel Davenport." Her gaze moved between them.

"Yes?" Malcolm asked.

"Find out who did this to Miranda. And try to make sure some sort of justice is done."

CHAPTER 10

DAISY SINGLETON HAD a heart-shaped face that would have been bewitchingly pretty were it not blotched with tears, her nose red and eyes puffy. She wore a simple muslin dress, with a blue sash that had been hastily tied, and her dark hair was pinned up in a haphazard knot. Mrs. Hartley had taken Malcolm and Harry to a small sitting room hung with blue-striped paper and filled with white-painted furniture, very different from the other rooms they had seen in the house. She brought Miss Singleton in and introduced her, but then did not stay. Another sign, perhaps, that she was more interested in learning the truth about Miranda's death than in controlling the investigation.

"This is where we receive our family and friends on our off days," Miss Singleton said, as though noting their reaction to the room. She put her fist to her mouth abruptly. "Miranda—"

"Miranda used to receive Gerald Lumley here?" Malcolm asked. "Mrs. Hartley told us about him."

Daisy nodded. "She was lucky, having someone to visit her. We don't all."

Malcolm started to put out a hand, but given her profession, he was even more reluctant to touch her than he would have been most people he was interrogating. She had little enough ability to keep herself to herself. "Tell us about Miranda," he said.

Daisy Singleton dropped into a straight-backed chair with a chintz cushion. Malcolm and Harry sat opposite her. "I met Miranda at one of the coffee stalls in Covent Garden," Daisy said. "I'd been to a masquerade. Miranda had a basket of flowers she was selling. I was tired and tripped over the basket and sent the flowers sprawling all over the pavement as well as spilling Miranda's coffee. I helped her pick up the flowers and bought her another coffee, and we sat and drank our coffee in the shade of the Piazza. Miranda had the sort of accent I try to affect, but her skirt was patched and her cuffs had been turned more than once. She told me her husband had been killed at Vitoria."

"Did you believe her?" Malcolm asked.

Daisy frowned. "I did at first. She was very convincing as she told it. But I couldn't make out why a girl with her background wouldn't have someone she could turn to. I thought there must be more to it. But not my place to ask questions. I saw her again the next week. Out late again," she added. "Mannerling's this time. We shared our coffee again. We took to meeting regularly. Miranda's clothes looked more threadbare, and she was obviously losing weight. And not in the way a girl wants to. Finally she confided in me that she was thinking about trying the streets. That was when I offered to introduce her to Mrs. Hartley. I'm not sure I would have otherwise. I mean, I don't mind this life, but I'm not sure I'd pull anyone else into it."

"How did she react?" Malcolm asked.

"She looked relieved, truth to tell."

Mélanie had said much the same about her own recruitment into a brothel. Food and a roof seemed like the promise of heaven, she'd said.

"Miranda always seemed nervous," Daisy said. "She'd glance round sometimes when we were sitting in Covent Garden. Almost as though she was afraid someone was following her."

"Did you ever ask her about it?" Harry said.

"I did once. A man crossed in front of us towards one of the coffee stalls, and Miranda went white as bleached linen. For a moment I thought she'd stopped breathing. Then he turned and she got a look at his face and let out a breath. When I asked her what was wrong, she said she'd thought he was a friend of her late husband, and she didn't want anyone from her old life to know what she'd come to. But I got the feeling it was more than that. Or at least, more than that she was ashamed of where she was now."

"What did the man look like?" Harry asked.

"Not too tall. Not stout, but not too thin, if that makes sense. Dark hair, I think. He was wearing a hat. Dressed like a gentleman. Quite a fine gentleman. One gets used to recognizing a good tailor in my line of work. He walked in a sort of brisk way—I think that might be what caught Miranda's attention, made her think it was the man she knew." Daisy frowned over the memory for a moment. "I think part of the reason Miranda may have been relieved at working at the Barque of Frailty wasn't just to have food and a roof over her head, though she needed both, but to be away from this man. Mrs. Hartley's careful about whom she'll take on," she added. "But she trusts me, and I told her I knew Miranda. Told her I'd known Miranda a bit longer than I had, actually. And she liked Miranda. Mrs. Hartley runs an elegant house, but even here Miranda was something out of the common way."

"How did Mrs. Spencer adapt to life in the house?" Harry asked. It was a blunt question, though put as tactfully as possible. Malcolm doubted he'd have managed it so well himself.

Miss Singleton regarded him frankly. "It's always a bit of an adjustment. Though it's been so long for me, it's hard to remember, truth to tell. She was better than some at meeting gentlemen in the drawing room. You could tell she'd been trained to it. Talking and pouring coffee and brandy and the like. She knew just how to do her hair and the right amount of rouge and scent to use. As to what happened after she went upstairs with a man and closed the door—she didn't talk about it much. Less than some of the girls. But she wasn't new to it, if that's what you're wondering. She'd been with a man before, and I'd guess more than one. She knew how to take precautions before I explained it to her."

"Did she ever see the man she was afraid of, that you know?" Malcolm asked. "Or think she saw him?"

Daisy shook her head. "Miranda didn't seem nervous in the Barque of Frailty, though when we were out together I'd see her glance about sometimes. Especially at first. And she was cautious about leaving the house with gentlemen."

"I understand she went out with Lord Beverston fairly often," Malcolm said.

"Yes." Miss Singleton fingered the end of her sash. "I remember the first time they met in the drawing room. His gaze went right to her. Almost as if—" She drew a breath.

"Yes?" Malcolm asked in a quiet voice.

"Almost as if he knew her," Miss Singleton said. "That probably sounds mad—"

"Not necessarily, if Miss Spencer had the sort of background you've surmised," Harry said. "Did Miss Spencer give any sign of knowing him?"

"Not precisely," Miss Singleton said. "But going out, away from the house, with him didn't seem to worry her the way going out with other men did. We all go out with gentlemen sometimes. To Vauxhall or a masquerade or a private party. Sometimes for a week at someone's hunting box. Most of the girls like it—a bit of a change. But Miranda didn't, as I said. Except with Beverston."

"Do you know where Miss Spencer went with Beverston?" Harry asked.

Miss Singleton shook her head. "She always dressed carefully, but then, any of us would, going out for the evening. She seemed —excited, almost. As though she was anticipating a treat instead of it being a chore. But she never talked about those evenings. She didn't share details much, as I said, but come to think of it, she would sometimes stop by my room when she'd come back from going out with another gentleman, mention the champagne they'd had, or the music that had been played, or how fine the carriage was. She never said anything about her evenings with Beverston. She never even stopped to chat."

"Did you ever get the sense she'd known any of the other men she met here, before she came to the Barque of Frailty?" Malcolm asked.

"No. Though I can't swear to it that she didn't." Miss Singleton frowned. Her face was still red and blotched with tears, but it now had the concentration of one turning her grief to a focus on learning what had happened to her friend.

"Tell us about Gerald Lumley," Malcolm said. "Mrs. Hartley said he was Mrs. Spencer's brother."

"Yes, that's what Miranda said."

"But you didn't believe her?"

"Mr. Lumley dressed nicely and arrived in a hackney and brought Miranda chocolates and hair ribbons and sometimes a bottle of wine. If he could do all that, and he cared for her as he seemed to, why couldn't she have gone to him instead of going to work at the Barque of Frailty?"

"A good point," Harry said. "But perhaps her family had cast her off and Mr. Lumley was dependent on them."

"Perhaps." Miss Singleton frowned. "They didn't look much alike. But they were comfortable together, like two people who've known each other a long time. I never got the sense he was a lover she was passing off as a brother, the way some of the girls do."

"Did you spend time with them together?" Malcolm asked.

"Not much, beyond an exchange of pleasantries sometimes when he arrived or left. Miranda usually kept their meetings quiet. But the last time he was here—a week ago Thursday." She drew a breath, as though shocked at how much had changed in that time. "I came downstairs to fetch my shawl and I saw Miranda saying goodbye to him. She stood on her tiptoes to kiss his cheek. Not at all what one would do with a lover. But it wasn't that that stuck in my memory. I heard her say, 'It's all right. I'm sorry it happened, but I won't say more. I promise.'"

Malcolm exchanged a quick look with Harry. "Do you know what she was referring to?"

Miss Singleton took her head. "I thought it must be some family business. That is, until—Do you think it had something to do with why she was killed?"

"You don't think Lord Carfax killed her?" Malcolm asked.

"You wouldn't be here asking questions if you thought he had," Miss Singleton pointed out.

"That doesn't mean you have to agree with us," Malcolm said.

Miss Singleton frowned. "It was odd that night. What I can remember of it. It was such a shock. Mostly I remember Miranda. The way she looked lying on the bed. But I caught a glimpse of Lord Carfax. He just stood there looking at her with this utter horror on his face. Like he was seeing into hell, though he wasn't a man who had believed he could. It wasn't the face of a killer. At least, not what I'd imagine the face of a killer would be."

"You're very astute, Miss Singleton," Malcolm said.

"I've had a lot of time to think about what happened to Miranda. And I want to learn the truth."

"Did you see her go into her room with Lord Carfax that night?" Malcolm asked.

Miss Singleton shook her head. "I was in the drawing room talking to Lord Beresford. I didn't even see her leave with Carfax. If only—" Tears welled up in her eyes.

Malcolm reached out and put a hand over her own. "One always questions what one could have done differently after a tragedy. But it's impossible to know, and folly to blame yourself. I'm sure Mrs. Spencer wouldn't want you to."

Miss Singleton met his gaze, her own wide and at once somehow the gaze of a very young girl and a woman who has seen too much of the world for her years. She inclined her head. "Thank you."

Malcolm settled back in his chair but kept his gaze on her own. "Do you remember anything else from that night?"

Miss Singleton tucked a loose strand of hair behind her ear. "Matthew Trenor was here. I don't remember him in the drawing room earlier in the evening, but he was there when we were all milling about upstairs, after the screams." She hugged her arms across her chest.

Malcolm frowned. Matthew Trenor was an aide to Lord Castlereagh, the foreign secretary. "Did Miss Spencer know him?"

"She'd been with him a few times. After one time, she had marks on her wrists. I told her she should complain to Mrs. Hartley—she'll bar a man from the house if he's too difficult—but Miranda just said she could take care of herself."

"Did he look upset the night she was killed?" Malcolm asked.

"He looked—" Miss Singleton frowned. "Numb. But then he started to cry. I never liked him much, but I actually felt sorry for him. I gave him a blanket. He was shivering."

"Is there a back way to get upstairs?" Harry asked.

"Yes. There are the servants' stairs, but there's also a small staircase that runs from just down the passage from this room up to the first floor. The girls use it sometimes to smuggle up young men who aren't clients."

"And the first floor passage," Malcolm said. "I assume it's empty much of the time?"

Miss Singleton nodded. "Though one couldn't count on it. The girls and the gentlemen are coming in and out of the rooms. But especially later at night it's quieter." Her fingers bit into her arms. "It was late when Miranda was killed."

"One more question," Malcolm said. "Do you know how to find Gerald Lumley?"

"No. That is, I don't have anything like an address. But he's sure to come wanting news of her. Unless he's heard she'd been killed already, but he may not have, living in the country."

Malcolm nodded. "You've been very helpful."

Her gaze fastened on his face again. "Do you think it will help you learn what happened to Miranda?"

"I hope it will."

Miss Singleton plucked at the white fabric of her skirt. ""There's one other thing. Miranda had a pendant she always wore. She had it on the night she died when we went down to the drawing room. I distinctly remember it. But it was gone when I saw her body."

MALCOLM PAUSED in the Barque of Frailty's portico and drew a breath. "Compared to similar houses, it's hardly the worst. But still—To see those women with no other recourse to stay off the streets—"

"Quite." Harry drew on his gloves.

"Rachel worked in a house like that. As the Barque of Frailty seems to be, Le Paon d'Or wasn't bad for a house of that sort. The women were comfortable and had some ability to say no. Still—It didn't occur to me to get her out, even to offer to get her out, until after Waterloo when she wanted to marry Rivaux."

"You needed her. You wouldn't have been much use in intelligence if you rescued every one of your agents and informants."

"And I was focused on being an agent."

"You were a good one. You got Rachel out eventually. We got Sue Kettering out last summer. The women at the Barque of Frailty have much more control over their lives than she did."

"That doesn't—"

"I know." Harry drew on his second glove. "Though at least they can say no to any particular man. One could argue whether it's much better to choose a husband simply to keep a roof over one's head and have no ability to avoid his bed."

Malcolm studied his friend's profile. He knew, happy as Harry and Cordy were, that Harry still worried that he'd proposed to Cordelia at a time when she was desperate for escape. "A lot of husbands wouldn't take advantage of that."

"No. But legally it depends on the husband, as Cordy or Mélanie would point out. Mrs. Hartley has more control over her life than a wife. One could even argue Miss Singleton does."

"In the end, Miranda Spencer didn't have any control at all."

"No." Harry turned to Malcolm. "On the face of it, it sounds as though she was a girl who ran off with a lover and was cast off by her family. In its own way as common a story as her tale of being a war widow. Too common, perhaps, as Mrs. Hartley said, though sometimes the likeliest explanation *is* the correct one."

"The jade pendant is interesting," Malcolm said. "If the killer took it, it could indicate he—or she—is connected to Mrs. Spencer's past."

Harry nodded. "It could also have broken when she fell or when the killer smothered her. Perhaps even got tangled up in his —or her—clothes."

"And then the killer stuffed it in a pocket to get it out of the way? Possible. It's also barely possible that someone else at the Barque of Frailty took the pendant after she was killed but before Miss Singleton saw her." Malcolm hesitated. "I took Tatiana's locket after she was killed." He would never forget those moments kneeling beside his murdered half-sister. Though he'd been dazed with grief, his instinct had been to protect the secrets of her birth.

"That would mean someone else at the Barque of Frailty that night knew who she really was," Harry said.

"So it would. Whoever she was, she seems to have been someone known to Beverston. Which could make her anything from the daughter of a tenant to the daughter—or wife—of a colleague. A fellow League member, perhaps."

"Which could explain Carfax's interest. Though it makes it less likely she was spying for him."

"Unless she was someone known to Carfax from the past. He had Sylvie St. Ives spying for him from when she was a teenager."

They started down the steps. "If Miranda Spencer was spying for Carfax on the League, any of them would have a motive to kill her," Harry said.

"So they would." Malcolm started down Jermyn Street, a decorous bustle of crested carriages, ladies in plumed bonnets, silk-hatted gentlemen, maids and manservants with parcels. "What did you make of Mrs. Hartley?" he asked as Harry fell into step beside him.

"I can see what attracted Archie. And I'm not talking about her appearance, though she's a beautiful woman. But she's plainly brilliant. And formidable. And she seems to have cared for Miranda Spencer. Which counts in her favor."

"Quite. She helped us more than I expected."

"Yes. And yet—" Harry frowned at a perfumer's sign across the street. "Archie did give her the money to set up the brothel."

"Yes, he admitted as much. And?"

"Archie was a French spy."

Malcolm stopped walking and looked at his friend. "Harry, are you suggesting your uncle set up a French spy ring in a brothel?"

Harry continued to frown at the gilt-painted sign. "I'm not saying I think it likely. But I do think it's a possibility to consider."

"All right." Malcolm continued to watch his friend. "Keeping feelings out of it—which I admit it's hard for me to do where Archie's concerned—Archie told us about his connection to the Barque of Frailty."

"Which he already knew we were investigating. I hope he credits us with enough investigative skills to have realized we'd trace it back to him eventually."

"Harry—"

"Damn it, Malcolm, tell me you don't wonder things about O'Roarke sometimes."

Malcolm hunched his shoulders and turned his own gaze into the distance. "Sometimes. Mostly I tell myself I have to trust him or life would be unbearable."

~

VALENTIN'S GAZE held a flash of warning when he opened the door to Malcolm in Berkeley Square. Malcolm was alone, as Harry had gone home to pack for their visit to Lord Beverston the next day. "Lady Isobel Lydgate called, sir. She's waiting in the library."

Carfax's daughter. The wife of his friend Oliver, whom he now knew had been an agent for Carfax himself. Malcolm nodded, gave Valentin his hat, and went into the library.

Isobel was standing before the fireplace but spun round at the opening of the door. "Malcolm." She was pale, her face tight and drawn inwards. Present circumstances could account for that, but Malcolm suspected it went back further. She came forwards but didn't hold her hands out as she once would have done unthinkingly. "I came to London to see Father and heard you were back. You've heard?"

Malcolm nodded.

"Can you help him?" The words seemed to tumble from her lips before she could properly frame them, probably before she had intended to speak them.

Malcolm took her arm and drew her to a chair, but she jerked away. "Don't. I don't need to be coddled." She drew a harsh breath, as though pulling herself together by sheer willpower. "I know Father had something to do with why you and Suzanne left Britain. I've asked Oliver but he says he doesn't know, and I think he's telling the truth. I asked David and he said we had to trust that you knew what was right for your family. I'm quite sure David knows the truth. I even asked Father, and he told me he hadn't the least idea. I'm quite sure he was lying. Now David's left as well, and I'm quite sure there's a connection." She put out a hand. "No, I'm not asking you to explain. What I'm saying is I understand you probably don't feel very charitable towards Father right now. Nor do I, after I learned he had Oliver spying on all of you. But—Malcolm, I can't believe he did this."

"Nor can I," Malcolm said. "That is, I have grave doubts. Not because I think Carfax isn't capable of murder. Because the facts don't add up."

Isobel drew another rough breath. "I know he's done unforgivable things. I know he's abominably hard on David. But, you must remember him when we were growing up. He was always busy, but he made more time than many fathers."

Countless other moments shot through Malcolm's mind. Carfax signing papers that would effectively end someone's life. Carfax telling Malcolm it was Malcolm's duty to uncover information, and—thankfully for Britain—Carfax's to decide what to do with it. Carfax trading papers with Julien St. Juste in Hyde Park. Carfax admitting Malcolm and Mélanie and their children were collateral damage in his efforts to manipulate his son. "I remember a lot of things."

"He loved you. Like one of his children."

"He was good to me. I think we both always knew I wasn't one of his children. Seeing what he put David through, I was always grateful for that."

"I think you were the son he'd have liked to have."

"I'd have driven him far madder than David."

Isobel spun away. The dark blue of her pelisse pulled taut across her shoulders. "He's never been an easy man for any of us. But I never thought he'd come between so many of us in so many ways."

"Bel." Malcolm took a step towards her and put a hand on her shoulders, heedless of the risk of her flinching. "Whatever's between your father and me, I'm still your friend."

She flinched but didn't pull away. "I've been so angry at Oliver, but at Father too. But I couldn't turn away from Father and Mama with everything they've been through. And now it's Father who needs me."

Malcolm turned her to him and hugged her for a moment. "That doesn't stop you from needing your friends. Or your friends from helping you."

Isobel went still for a moment, like a creature carved from ice. Then she clung to him, the way she would have when she was the girl he'd first met. "I'm glad you're back, Malcolm," she murmured, her face buried in his cravat.

He tucked a strand of hair behind her ear. "I'm only back temporarily, Bel. But I'll do my best to learn who killed Miranda Spencer."

Isobel lifted her head and gave a slow nod.

Malcolm released her and drew her over to the sofa. This time she sat beside him. "Did you ever hear Carfax mention Mrs. Spencer?"

"Malcolm, you can't think Father would have mentioned a trollop to his daughter?"

Malcolm's fingers curved inwards. He'd like to think he'd always have flinched at Bel's wording. But there was no denying her words cut more now that he knew the truth of Mélanie's past. "Probably not. But one of the things I always appreciated about Carfax was his plain speaking. Another was that he didn't try to wrap his daughters in cotton wool. Particularly you."

"He never mentioned her."

"Was he investigating anything lately?"

Isobel frowned. Her face was still drawn, but her gaze was more thoughtful than when she'd first stepped into the room. "He's always held things close, and since Louisa's death he seemed to do so even more. But lately—He got a message at Carfax Court over Christmas. He always gets messages when we're in the country. But this one—I was in the study with him when the footman brought it in. He slit it open immediately. The look in his eyes—" She paused for a moment, as though searching for the right word. "He looked afraid." Disbelief sounded in her voice even as she said it. "I think that may be the first time I've ever seen Father afraid."

"What did he say?"

"Merely that he was afraid he'd have to answer this at once and could I ask my mother to push back dinner half an hour. The next day he left for London. I didn't see him again before we got the news he was in Newgate."

"Where's Oliver?" Malcolm asked.

"Outside in the carriage."

"What?"

"He came to London with me. But he wasn't sure you'd want to see him."

"Oh, for God's sake." Malcolm strode into the hall, pulled open the front door, and waved to Oliver. His Oxford friend, whom Carfax had paid to spy on him, descended from the carriage and climbed the steps of the house, wariness in his posture.

Malcolm didn't embrace him as he once would have done, but he did touch his arm. "I thought we'd at least established when you came to Dunmykel that we're still on speaking terms."

Oliver met his gaze without flinching. "For which I'm inestimably grateful. But I didn't want your feeling about me to color your willingness to help Carfax."

"My dear Oliver. Whatever is between us pales beside what's between Carfax and me."

Malcolm led the way back into the library, where Isobel was waiting. Uncertainty flickered across her face, but she moved to Oliver's side, which was interesting in and of itself.

"What can we do?" Oliver asked.

"See if you can persuade Carfax to talk," Malcolm said. "Though I doubt anyone can. But after you see him, I think you both can both do the most at Carfax Court, making sure Lady Carfax and Lucinda get through this as well as possible."

Isobel nodded. "We're not at Carfax Court. We've removed to Spendlove Manor. It's closer to London. I brought Mama to see him once just after he was arrested. I'm not sure what they said to each other. But I think he asked her not to come back. I can't be sure what Mama's thinking or feeling. But then our family never show their feelings much. Lucinda's the most upset."

"Lucy can show she's upset," Oliver said. "Which is probably a very good thing."

"I know Father wants us to stay in the country," Isobel said. "I know Mama and Lucinda need us. But I feel so much better knowing you're investigating, Malcolm."

"I'll do my best to uncover the truth."

"Which will help Father because he's innocent."

"I can't be sure what it will do."

Isobel nodded, her gaze tight on his face. "I can't ask for more."

CHAPTER 11

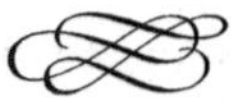

COLIN SCRAMBLED up the steps of the Berkeley Square house, Livia and Emily close behind him. Mélanie swallowed a pang as Raoul handed her from the carriage. Six months gone and the house was still home.

Home, where Malcolm was. For all the dangers and uncertainties, in a few minutes she would see him.

"Home," Jessica said from Mélanie's arms.

"Quite right, *querida*," Mélanie murmured as Raoul handed Laura and Cordy from the carriage and picked up Berowne's basket.

Valentin opened the door. Colin and Emily hugged him. Livia, who knew him almost as well, shortly followed suit. Valentin hugged them back and met Mélanie's gaze over their heads. "Mrs. Rannoch. We weren't expecting you. Mr. Rannoch's gone up to Surrey with Colonel Davenport for the night."

"Surrey?" Mélanie climbed the steps and stepped under the fanlight.

"Yes, madam, to visit Lord Beverston."

Tommy's godfather. Mélanie exchanged a quick look with Raoul, Laura, and Cordy as they all reached the hall.

Valentin glanced at the children. "I have some cakes in the kitchen. I can bring them into the library."

Jessica and Drusilla wriggled to be put down and ran after the older children. Valentin met Mélanie's gaze before the adults followed the children. "There've been some unexpected developments, madam. I'm sure Mr. Rannoch would have left you a letter if he'd known you were coming. Lord Carfax has been arrested for murder."

~

LORD BEVERSTON WAS A SHORT MAN, though he carried himself with a brisk purpose that made him seem much taller until one was actually face to face. As he and Malcolm were when Malcolm and Harry were shown into the study of his country house in Surrey.

"Rannoch. Davenport." Beverston crossed the Turkey rug to greet them. "I didn't know either of you was back in Britain, let alone in Ipswich."

"Most people don't. It's a quick visit. My condolences, sir. I can't imagine anything worse than losing a child." Whatever Malcolm thought of John Smythe, the condolences were owed. And Malcolm wanted to see how Beverston took them.

"Thank you." Beverston drew a breath. He had himself well in command, but the flash in his eyes said he wasn't entirely without parental feeling. "I understand you saw John in Italy."

"Both Davenport and I did," Malcolm said. "He was involved in some very complicated things, but what happened to him was certainly a tragedy."

"It's been hard to comprehend, as I'm sure you'll understand. I've been concerned about Diana. Though of course we're pleased about the news of the baby."

"As I think Diana is." That, Malcolm thought, was the truth. Diana Smythe's marriage to John had been a hell she could not but be relieved to have escaped, but though she'd seemed shocked to realize she was pregnant weeks after his death, she also seemed to be happy about the baby as something quite apart from John.

"But I don't expect you called just to offer condolences," Beverston said.

"Quite." Malcolm took a step forwards. "Given the offer your godson made to me in Scotland, we can dispense with the pleasantries, sir. Or, rather, with the fiction that the Elsinore League do not exist."

Beverston's gaze locked on Malcolm's own. "I always thought you were dangerous, Rannoch. In one of my last conversations with Alistair he warned me not to underestimate you."

"You surprise me. I never thought Alistair had much use for me. Or, rather, that he paid enough attention to have any thoughts about me at all."

"You should know by now that Alistair kept a great deal to himself." Beverston jerked his head towards three claret leather chairs before the fireplace. "I trust you've given proper consideration to our offer?" he said when they were seated.

"To protect us against Carfax?" Malcolm said. "He's hardly much of a threat now."

"That depends upon how much reliance you place upon his remaining in prison."

"Are you suggesting he didn't kill Mrs. Spencer?" Harry asked.

Beverston spread his fingers on the carved arm of his chair. "The more pertinent question is, do you think he did? And given that you're both apparently investigating her death, I would imagine the answer is that you don't."

"You know we're investigating her murder?"

"My dear Rannoch. I have excellent sources of information, even in the country. I also presume your investigation means that you're prepared to deal with the consequences of Carfax out of prison."

"Which should answer your question about your very obliging offer," Malcolm said.

Beverston held his gaze across the cold, hard marble of the table between their chairs. "You're a dangerous man, as I said, Rannoch. And in many ways your flexibility of thinking is impressive. But you're not seeing the full picture here. Carfax will always be a threat. To you. Certainly to your wife. And from what I understand of your parliamentary speeches, he's opposed to just about everything you believe in."

"Whereas the League are a hidden bastion of reform?"

Beverston settled back in his chair and crossed his legs. "I won't deny that most of our members are opposed to much of what you believe in. But fundamentally our actions aren't driven by setting policy."

"No, they're driven by enriching yourselves."

"And how, precisely, does that makes us different from nine-tenths of the men in the beau monde or Parliament?"

"They don't kill to do it," Harry said. "Or amass blackmail."

"I understand you were close to Miranda Spencer." Malcolm made the switch abruptly, hoping against hope to catch Beverston off guard.

A shadow that might have been grief flitted across Beverston's face. "Tragic what happened to her. But surely of all my activities, my friendship with a girl who was employed at the Barque of Frailty doesn't shock you."

"No, but it does when that girl was murdered and the League's greatest enemy stands accused of her murder."

Beverston's fingers curled on the chair arm. "I'm not sure I'd call Carfax the League's greatest enemy. But he's certainly high on the list."

"You were at the Barque of Frailty the night Mrs. Spencer was killed," Malcolm said.

"So I was. I'm there many nights. That may be hard for two men so known to be devoted to their wives to understand, but I doubt it surprises you if you have any understanding at all of most marriages in the beau mode. I saw Miranda leave the room with Carfax, as I'm sure you know from the investigating you have already done. To my eternal regret." Beverston shook his head. "If only I'd intervened. I almost did so."

"Because you'd have been afraid of what Mrs. Spencer might tell him?" Malcolm asked.

"For God's sake, Rannoch, do I seem like the sort of man who confides dangerous secrets to a young whore across the pillow? My sense aside, believe me, I had more important things to talk to Miranda about. Using 'talk to' in the loosest possible sense of the term."

"You took Mrs. Spencer out with you a number of times."

"So I did. The Barque of Frailty is convivial enough, but sometimes one wants a change of surroundings. I think Miranda enjoyed it too."

"According to those who witnessed your first meeting with Mrs. Spencer"—Malcolm didn't want to draw undue attention to Daisy Singleton—"you gave the impression that you recognized her from somewhere else."

"Did I? Usually I pride myself on not giving anything away. But there's no particular reason to be secretive about it. And I own it was a shock. Miranda was the daughter of the curate who had the living at one of my smaller properties. Woodbury in Bedfordshire. I'd seen her off and on as a child and young woman. She disappeared two years ago. The story was that she'd gone to stay with an aunt in Shropshire, but it was fairly common knowledge she'd run off with a half-pay officer. Given that, I really shouldn't have been surprised to find her at the Barque of Frailty. But it was still a shock to come face to face with her."

"You didn't think of—" Harry hesitated. Rare for him.

"Rescuing her?" Beverston raised a brow. "My dear Davenport. Miranda had already put herself outside the bounds of society. I suppose I could have tried to invent a history for her and find her a place as governess or companion, but the truth of her past would always be a risk. And she seemed content enough where she was. I'll own at first I simply spoke with her to learn of her past. But Miranda was—out of the common way. Had she still been the gently bred girl I'd known, I'd never have let my interests run in that direction, but given where life had taken her, our association seemed quite natural."

It was plausible. The third plausible story Malcolm had heard to account for Miranda Spencer's past. And he wasn't sure he believed it any more than the other two. "Mrs. Spencer had a jade pendant she wore a great deal," he said. "She was wearing it the night she was killed, but it wasn't found on the body."

Beverston frowned with a surprise that might have been genuine. "I know the pendant. She wore it a great deal. I assumed it must have been a gift from her family or her first lover. But if you're suggesting the killer took it because it meant something to him, I can't imagine any of her family or her former lover in the Barque of Frailty. One generally needs more exalted connections to get past Rosamund's doors."

"Mrs. Spencer didn't indicate to you that she'd recently seen anyone from her old life?"

"Certainly not. She didn't seem to wish to speak of it at all."

Malcolm watched Beverston for a moment. "When did you last see Tommy Belmont?"

"When I sent him to Scotland to make our offer to you. I assume you've seen him much more recently."

"Then you don't know he's back in London?" Malcolm hesitated, but at this point, shielding Gisèle's reputation seemed less important than finding her. "In company with my sister?"

Beverston raised his brows again, though whether at the facts themselves or at Malcolm sharing them, Malcolm couldn't be sure. "My word."

"That wasn't part of the plan when you sent Tommy to Scotland?"

"I don't deny the intricacies of our planning, Rannoch. Or that Tommy is very useful to us. But surely you realize a man like Tommy could have reasons for going off to London with a pretty young woman that have nothing to do with the League."

"He could. The League could also want to control my sister."

"Possibly, I'll grant you. But Alistair was quite fond of Gisèle."

"Alistair's dead."

"But still engenders a great deal of loyalty within the League."

"Damn it, sir." Malcolm lunged out of his chair and grabbed Beverston by the flawless lapels of his coat. "What do you know about my sister?"

"Rannoch, for God's sake." Beverston's voice was hoarse. "Do you think—"

"Yes." Malcolm tightened his grip.

"I don't know. Strangle me if you will, but that's the truth."

Malcolm threw Beverston back in his chair. "Convenient."

Beverston straightened his neckcloth. "I'm proud of Tommy, I confess. I've often lamented that he wasn't my son, instead of—but that is neither here nor there. I brought him into the League. I trusted him with things I would never have trusted John with. But I've never had any illusions I could control him. It's part of what I admire in him."

"Do you deny he undertakes jobs for you?"

"Not in the least. But he also undertakes missions for others in the League. The last time I saw Tommy was in early December, when I sent him to Scotland to make our offer to you. I received a curt response that he'd been unsuccessful. I haven't seen him or heard from him since. I certainly said nothing to him about running off with your sister."

Beverston's voice had the ring of truth. Though Malcolm no longer was as confident of his ability to judge such things as he once had been. "But you tasked him to look for the Wanderer," Malcolm said.

For a moment Beverston's face went still. Malcolm had the

dubious satisfaction of knowing he had shaken the other man. "That sounds fanciful for something I'd involve myself in."

"That rather depends on who—or what—the Wanderer is."

Beverston held Malcolm's gaze. "You have no reason to take advice from me, Rannoch. Or to believe I wish you well. But upon my honor, this is truly meant. Stay away from the Wanderer. You don't know what you're involving yourself in, and it will only lead to disaster for you and your family."

CHAPTER 12

"I WISH I could tell you more." Archie cast a glance round the Berkeley Square dining table, where Valentin had done an admirable job of assembling a cold supper out of a hamper from Fortnum's, supplemented by a salmon salad assembled from left-overs from Frances's kitchen. "But I only learned about Carfax myself yesterday morning, when Malcolm and Harry called on me."

"And to think I thought we were prepared for the unexpected." Frances took a sip of coffee. "I was tempted to call on Amelia, but I hear she's in the country. I did pay a round of calls on my friends yesterday—those who are back in London—and there are rumors flying, but precious few facts I could discern." She cast a glance through the open door across the hall to the library where her nine-year-old daughter Chloe had taken the younger children to play, but the shrieks of excitement suggested that even the sharp-eared younger generation weren't attending to their parents' conversation.

"I thought about talking to Rosamund myself—" Archie said.

"And I told you I hadn't the least objection," Frances interjected.

"But I decided to wait and see what Malcolm and Harry learned. They sent us a note yesterday afternoon saying they were going up to see Beverston." Archie picked up a walnut and cracked it. "So, whatever they learned from Rosamund must have sent them after him."

Frances's brows drew together. "I'm still surprised they didn't come to see us before they left."

"They'd have been in a hurry." Archie handed his wife half the walnut. "And they may not have been entirely sure what to tell me. Given my past connection to Rosamund, and my other activities."

Cordelia stared at her husband's uncle across the table. "But that's all in the past."

"Rosamund is." Archie crumbled a bit of walnut shell between his fingers. "As to the rest—these things are never fully in the past, as both Malcolm and Harry know. And they've both learned to question everything."

"If they hadn't already, some of us have taught them that." Mélanie frowned into her coffee.

"Are you saying the murdered girl—Miranda Spencer—was a French spy?" Cordelia asked. "Or Rosamund Hartley is?"

"Neither, to my knowledge," Archie said. "Which doesn't mean neither of them is or was. Or that Malcolm and Harry aren't wondering."

Raoul reached for an orange and began to peel it. "For what it's worth, Beverston never was an agent. At least, not that we know of."

"That's the only connection to Gisèle." Frances picked up her coffee again, as though she wanted to keep her hands busy, which was unlike her. "That Beverston is Tommy's godfather and recruited him into the League. But I can't think how—" She shook her head and set the cup down untasted.

"Jeremy must know what's going on." Mélanie stared at her untouched slice of fig cake on the silver-and-burgundy-edged plates Cordy had helped her choose at a china warehouse, in what seemed like another lifetime.

Raoul handed round segments of the orange. "We don't know how much he knows and what Malcolm's told him. Calling on him would only advertise your presence in London to Bow Street and the home office."

"There's no evidence they're looking for me," Mélanie said.

"No, but we don't know who knows what. And ironically Carfax being out of power leaves you with less protection."

They had been having a variant of the same conversation ever since their arrival a few hours before. The immediate impulse to seek more information after Valentin's startling revelation about Carfax had been checked by the realization that here in London, where they were all used to having a host of sources at their fingertips, there were few people to whom they could safely apply.

"Meaning, once again we have to wait," she said.

"For the moment," Raoul said. "I need to talk to Charlotte.

"You think she's hiding Gisèle and Tommy?" Frances asked.

"It's difficult to know," Raoul said, in a tone that warned Frances not to get her hopes up. "But we know Tommy wrote to her as they were leaving, so at the very least she's heard from him more recently than we have."

"Do you think she'll confide in you?" Frances asked.

"Charlotte's not precisely the confiding type. And, given that she's in touch with Tommy, I question if I knew her at all. But I think I can learn something." He glanced at Mélanie.

"You want to go alone," Mélanie said.

"I think I should, the first time. You can follow up if I meet with resistance. We may want the option of approaching her as though we aren't allies."

Mélanie nodded. It was sensible. Which didn't make the continued waiting any easier.

"I assume you aren't going to advertise your own presence in London," Laura said to Raoul.

"Charlotte is hardly the sort to consort with Bow Street."

"That you know of. You just admitted you don't know her as well as you thought."

"A palpable hit, sweetheart." Raoul leaned over to kiss her. "I'll take all the usual precautions."

"Given the life you lead, that's hardly reassuring."

THREE YEARS AGO, Raoul had helped Charlotte Leblanc establish herself in rooms in Leicester Street. But having made some discreet inquiries, he instead made his way to a coffeehouse in

Piccadilly, run by a Parisian émigré. Not, so far as he knew, anyone acquainted with the world of espionage. As with a Parisian café, there were more ladies present than would be found in a typical London coffeehouse. Matrons, some with children in tow despite the evening hour, shopgirls, governesses, ladies' maids. Possibly a few ladies who'd be considered less than respectable, but they were discreet. French accents assaulted his ears. He hadn't been in Paris in over six months. Since Waterloo even the thought of the city brought associations that were like a knife twisting beneath his ribs. Yet in some ways it would always be home. One of his homes. Just as the Berkeley Square house was, he had realized this afternoon from his shock of familiarity when he stepped over the threshold.

He saw her at the back of the café, a cup of coffee steaming at her elbow, the twilled sapphire blue fabric of her pelisse pulled taut against her shoulders as she wrote in a notebook, her dark blonde hair coiled against the nape of her neck. Her back was to him, but he knew her at once.

He made his way between the tables, without the haste that

could draw unnecessary attention, and stopped before her table. "*Bonjour*, Charlotte."

She looked up, her blue gaze hardening as it settled on him. "I'd say I was surprised to see you. Save that your appearances are always a surprise."

Raoul pulled out a chair and dropped down opposite her. "Then I haven't entirely lost my touch."

"Perish the thought." She closed her notebook. "Travel accounts. They sell remarkably well. Of course, I haven't visited any of the places I write about in three years and more, but I manage. Though sometimes the changing borders—not to mention names of countries—nearly trip me up."

"You've done well."

"I manage. Perhaps better than some." Her gaze flickered over his face. Her own was little changed. The shrewd eyes, the generous mouth, the sharp cheekbones and nose. "I didn't know you were in Britain."

"Few do."

She raised her brows. "These days I'd have thought secret missions would take you out of Britain, not into it. I understand you've been busy in Spain once again."

"It offers some unique opportunities."

She gave a faint smile. "You'll never give up on the cause, will you?"

"Not as long as I'm capable of thought and action."

Charlotte took a sip of coffee, without taking her gaze from him. "Though I understand you've also been spending time in Italy."

Raoul settled back in his chair. "You hear a great deal."

"I may have left the game, but old habits die hard. And information is always useful. You're living with the Rannochs."

"I've stayed with them in Italy."

"And you're wondering how much I know. When a former agent like Malcolm Rannoch abruptly leaves the country, there's bound to be talk among agents and former agents, whomever they worked for. The few people I've talked with who know the truth about Mélanie are even more intrigued. And, obviously, surprised by your presence in the household."

Raoul had never told Charlotte that Malcolm was his son—it was something he'd explicitly admitted to very few people, not even to Malcolm himself until recently—but he was fairly sure she'd guessed. "My ties to the Rannoch family go back a long way."

Charlotte gave a dry laugh. "Yes, I'm certainly aware of that. They're far older than your ties to Mélanie Rannoch, if not more complicated."

"You saw Mélanie when we brought you to London. She's very much in love with her husband."

"As I said. Complicated."

A dozen personal confidences welled up in his throat. He'd never cared much what anyone thought of him, but he was inclined to overreact to what people thought of Mélanie or Malcolm. "When have any of our lives not been complicated?"

"All too true." She closed her notebook. "I assume they ran because of Mélanie's past. And so I assume Malcolm Rannoch knows the truth."

"You can't expect me to answer on either count."

She tilted her head to one side. "That was the maddest mission I ever saw you orchestrate. I'm still not sure whether to be appalled, or stunned at your daring."

A dozen questions he'd never be able to answer shot through his head. "It was certainly one of the more dangerous and problematic things I've ever done."

"It made sense if your goals were as focused and hardheaded as you let on. But I'm not sure they are. It seems to have worked out all right, though, at least as far as the marriage. And I presume you're still on speaking terms with both of them.

"I'm on far better terms with both of them than I ever had any right to expect."

Charlotte raised a brow. "Since you're free of Mélanie, I could suggest we continue this conversation at my rooms. For old time's sake?" Her smile as she said it was open and familiar.

Raoul found himself smiling in return, as he had more than once in the past. "No offense."

"None taken."

"I'm not what might be called free."

"There's another woman in the household, I hear. Lady Tarrington?"

Raoul held her gaze. She might know already. In any case, it would help set the terms of their conversation as friendly. "Laura Tarrington and I are expecting a child."

Charlotte smiled again. "My felicitations. Though I imagine it's another complication."

"It's a number of things. But more than anything else, a cause for joy."

"That's a way I've never heard you talk before."

"A number of things have changed."

Charlotte tucked her pencil into the notebook. "If Mélanie is at risk of exposure, so are you. And yet you're back in London, when your work is in Spain, and the rest of your life is in Italy. Did the Spanish cause send you here?"

"No, this mission is of the more personal sort."

"You intrigue me. You didn't used to do much of anything for personal reasons. At least, not that you admitted to."

"It seems we can both surprise each other. I had no notion you knew Tommy Belmont."

Charlotte's gaze went as still as the water of Lake Como when the wind suddenly died. "You aren't going to believe me if I say 'Who?' are you?"

"Surely we know each other too well for a tiresome round of denials."

She tucked a strand of hair into its pins. "Are you asking if I was a double?"

"Were you?"

"I'd hardly admit it."

"What's the harm, after all this time? I'm not in a position to cause you mischief, and you'd have been on the winning side."

Charlotte smoothed the lace frill on her cuff. "So, if I tell you I wasn't, you'll believe me?"

"Let's say I'll be more inclined to believe you than I might be under other circumstances."

She was silent for a moment. "I never believed in it the way you do. I disliked the monarchy, but I could hardly have been called a committed Republican. But I also don't believe in going back on my word. That sounds rather stuffy coming from me, but there it is."

"Tommy."

"Tommy." A faint smile curved her mouth. "We crossed paths once in the Peninsula, though neither of us knew the other's true name. But when we happened across each other in London, we both remembered. And could tell the other did. As I said to you, with the war over there's little sense in pretending. Oh, perhaps I should have—I'm more at risk than he, certainly. But there seemed little sense in a denial he wouldn't believe. And sometimes one wants to talk to someone from the past, even if they did fight on the opposite side. Or have you never felt that?"

Raoul settled back in his chair and signaled to a waiter to bring him coffee. "I confess to knowing the feeling."

"Well, then. Sharing the past led to sharing more." She held his gaze for a moment across the scarred wood of the table. "Shocked? Surely not. You never were the jealous sort. At least, not when it came to me. And it's very like you and me, after all. Seeking escape and a few moments of solace. Not expecting strings or commitments. Quite unlike you and Mélanie."

"I never made a commitment to Mélanie."

"You never let her know you made a commitment to her. I rather think you didn't want to entrap her."

"My dear Charlotte. We were talking about you and Tommy. I'd hardly be surprised at two people seeking solace or escape or any other sort of joy they may find together. But it doesn't explain the letter he sent you when he left Scotland."

"He's been away. We're not what you'd call anything like an exclusive arrangement, but we do remain in communication."

The waiter deposited a cup of coffee before Raoul. Raoul blew on it and took a sip before responding. "I could almost believe that. Save that he sent the letter the night before he ran off with Gisèle Thirle."

"Who? I wish I could say I was surprised to hear Tommy had run off with someone, but I confess that's not my immediate reaction."

"Arabella Rannoch's daughter."

Charlotte's gaze locked on his own. "Oh, my dear. I'm sorry. I know what she meant to you."

"Insightful of you, as I'm not in the least sure myself what Arabella meant to me."

"Whatever passed between us tended to be when she drove you to distraction. Not that I'm complaining. I wouldn't give up the past for the world."

Charlotte's smile as she said it was intended to evoke memories. And distract him. He reached for his coffee. "Then you'll understand my concern for Gisèle. I've known her since she was a baby."

"And she's Malcolm Rannoch's sister."

"As you say."

Charlotte turned her coffee cup in its saucer. "Tommy worked with Malcolm Rannoch. You must know that. I've heard him complain more than once about Rannoch's tiresome scruples, but I think he has a certain admiration for him. Perhaps even affection. I wish I could say I believe that would have kept him from seducing Rannoch's sister, but knowing Tommy, I fear not."

"Charlotte." Raoul shot his hand across the table to grip her wrist. "You aren't fool enough to try to convince me its coincidence that Tommy wrote to you the night before he and Gisèle ran off."

Charlotte made no attempt to remove her hand from his grip but watched him steadily. "He wrote to me on New Year's Eve, if that's the letter you're thinking of. There's nothing exclusive about our relationship, as I said, but it's not without affection on either side. Something I'd also think you'd understand, based on our past. He wrote to wish me a happy new year."

"And the next morning he and Gisèle left Scotland for London."

"Well, he'd hardly have told me that."

Raoul released her wrist and sat back in his chair. "Damn it, Charlotte. You used to be better at coming up with a story. You can't expect me to believe that."

"What you believe or don't believe is entirely up to you. But you should realize that coincidences do occur."

"So they do. I'm also more than passably good at recognizing lies. And I'm quite sure you're lying now."

"You think I'd have helped Tommy run off with another woman?" Charlotte picked up her coffee and took a sip with deliberate control. "We may not have had an exclusive relationship, but I'd hardly have done so. For any number of reasons."

"No. But then I don't think Belmont and Gisèle ran off for romantic reasons at all."

Charlotte raised her brows.

Raoul hesitated. If she knew, he wasn't revealing anything. And if she didn't, she should be warned. "What do you know about the Elsinore League?"

Charlotte's gaze went still again. "If you think this is to do with the League, you can't be surprised I won't talk."

So. She was more than Tommy's dupe. Disappointment, the sort he'd thought he wasn't capable of feeling, coiled within him. "She's scarcely more than a child, Charlotte. She has a husband she loves very much and a young baby. She doesn't deserve to be dragged into any of this."

"I'm not sure what's more surprising. That you're appealing to sentiment or that you expect it to work on me."

She'd always had a hard edge. It was part of what had appealed to him, as both a lover and an agent. "You've never been cruel."

"And I'm not being so now."

"If you're afraid of the League—"

"My dear Raoul. You should know me well enough to know I'm not afraid of anything."

Raoul snatched up his coffee and tossed down a swallow, holding Charlotte with his gaze. "I won't attempt to play on your sympathies by reminding you that I helped you find refuge here. But I have a number of connections in London still. Surely I don't have to point out that I could make things quite uncomfortable for you."

"And surely I don't have to point out to you that you have secrets of your own to protect. You aren't even living in London at present."

He curled his hands round his cup. "I've always been prepared to take my chances."

"Are you prepared to take them with Mélanie?"

He should have seen it coming. To a degree he had, but he'd overestimated the extent of Charlotte's feelings of comradeship. Perhaps overestimated what had been between them. "Given your suppositions about the Rannochs' departure for Italy, you should realize Mélanie's secrets are not so secret anymore."

Charlotte put her notebook and pencil in the tapestry bag beside her chair. "We both know there are degrees of secrets. And that even after a secret is out to some, it can still do incalculable damage." She regarded him for a moment, her gaze hard as a polished knife blade. "I'll own to being full aware of what you could do to me. But you must be equally aware of what I can do to you. I trust we both see the folly of destroying each other." She picked up her bag and got to her feet. "This is dangerous, Raoul. You must know that. I doubt you'll take my advice, but as a friend, I'd counsel you to take your family, however you define them, and return to the Continent."

Raoul got to his feet. Common courtesy, and a way to keep them on the same footing. "Are we friends?"

"I rather think that has to do with how one defines friendship, my dear. I have no illusions that this is the last time I'll see you. But I presume you know I'll be on my guard."

She swept from the coffeehouse. Raoul watched her go. Nothing to be gained from following her, and this had always been an opening gambit, after all. He picked up his coffee cup and tossed down the last swallow, his gaze on Charlotte as she made her way to the door. Out of the corner of his eye he caught a gleam in the shadows of the coffeehouse. Pale hair. And something unmistakable about the angle of the head.

Damnation. He was going to have to start lying to his family sooner than he had anticipated.

CHAPTER 13

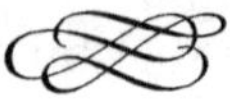

"Do you think she knows where Gisèle is?" Mélanie asked.

"At the very least, I'd wager she has a way to reach Tommy," Raoul said.

Frances's fingers curled inwards. "Damnation. I'd like to shake it out of her."

"Tempting," Raoul agreed. "But I don't think it would get us very far."

They were gathered in the Berkeley Square drawing room, while the children played at the other end. Frances and Archie hadn't wanted to leave until Raoul came back with a report. Frances, Mélanie had noted, had been unable to sit still much of the time.

"You trusted her," Laura said.

"I trust very few people," Raoul said. "Present company excepted. But I liked her."

"Do you think she and Tommy really are lovers?" Cordelia asked.

"I'm not sure anything she told me is the truth," Raoul said. "Though, like any good agent, Charlotte knows the value of basing a cover story in fact. I suspect she's telling the truth that she wasn't a double, and she and Tommy met in London after the war. They may have become lovers. And Tommy drew her into his work for the Elsinore League. Either because she wanted the funds, or because she missed the game, or perhaps both. Or possibly because of their personal relationship, though I've never known Charlotte to make professional decisions for personal reasons."

"So we're no closer to finding Gisèle," Frances said.

"Not entirely. We have a connection to Tommy and, therefore, Gisèle. I never had great hopes Charlotte would simply confide in me if she was involved."

"Shall I approach her?" Mélanie asked. "Pretend you and I aren't on the same side entirely?"

"Not yet, I think," Raoul said. "First, I'm going to do some reconnaissance. Ask questions about her neighborhood. I called on Pierre Ducot on my way home. I have him watching her lodgings, and trailing her if she goes out. She'll be on her guard, but Pierre's good enough she may not get wind of it."

Mélanie nodded. Pierre had been an able scout in the Peninsula. Since he'd settled in London, he'd once or twice undertaken errands for her and Malcolm.

"More waiting," Cordelia said.

"At least until Malcolm and Harry get back," Raoul said. "We'll know more then. About a number of things."

"And meanwhile, you get to have all the fun," Laura said.

"My apologies." He reached for her hand and laced his fingers through her own. "But before we're done, I'm quite sure there's going to be plenty of work to keep all of us busy."

"I LOST MY TEMPER." Malcolm scowled at the path ahead as he and Harry rode back towards London.

"With great provocation." Harry steered his horse Claudius

round a mud puddle. "And you didn't reveal anything to him. Except the extent of your determination. You may even have alarmed him."

"I doubt it. Beverston is much too secure in his position to fear anything I might do." Malcolm forced his hands not to clench on the reins, then reached forwards to pat Perdita's neck. It was good to be on her back again.

"Whatever he knows about Miranda Spencer's death, he's grieved by it," Harry said. "Which doesn't necessarily mean he didn't kill her."

"Quite. In fact, if he'd confided in her across the pillow and then thought she was talking to Carfax, he has an excellent motive."

"Quite. The more so as he appears to have had some genuine affection for her. To the extent Beverston is capable of feeling affection for anyone."

"If—"

Malcolm broke off as a report sounded from the trees. He fell forwards on instinct against Perdita's neck and felt a bullet whistle by. He heard a thud and looked up to see Harry sprawled on the ground.

"Harry." Malcolm flung himself down beside his friend in an echo of Waterloo, even as he was aware of the sound of retreating hooves from the trees.

"I'm all right." Harry pushed himself up on his good elbow. "Lost my balance."

"I think the bullet took off a lock of your hair." And it had left a scrape on Harry's temple.

"It's all right, Cordelia doesn't love me for my looks." Harry pushed himself to his knees. "Are they—"

"They're long gone, whoever they were."

"No permanent damage done."

"No," Malcolm said. "But it could have been."

CHAPTER 14

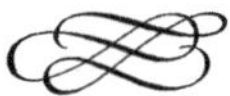

"SO MUCH WORRY AND URGENCY," Cordelia said. "And now London looks remarkably placid."

Raoul had left before breakfast to make further inquiries about Charlotte. The women had succumbed to the pleas of the children, who had been cooped up in a carriage for days, and taken the younger set to the Berkeley Square garden. Hardly a return to London society, yet it felt at once alien and oddly normal, Mélanie found, to be sitting on the wrought metal benches, beneath the leafless winter tracery of the plane trees, the children's laughter cutting the air, familiar brick and stucco houses all round.

Few people were abroad on a January morning. They'd glimpsed a nursemaid walking two young charges, but the group had continued out of the square without stopping in the garden.

"Odd to be so on edge here," Laura said. "When I was Colin and Jessica's governess, it seemed the center of my world." She smiled at the game of hide-and-seek that was in progress. Emily was persuading Jessica to stay hidden behind a gnarled tree trunk. Colin was behind another tree with Drusilla, who grasped the game a bit better than Jessica. Livia had her hands over her eyes and was counting.

"We have to snatch a few moments respite while we can," Mélanie said. "Or at least the children can." In truth, she found it damnably hard to sit still. She remembered Frances pacing the night before. She stroked Berowne, who was curled up in her lap, willing her body to relax.

"How did this happen?" Cordelia said. "The men are all off having adventures and we're sitting in a garden watching the children play. Not that I don't quite like watching the children play in the general run of things, but when we're in the midst of a crisis—"

"Maddening," Mélanie agreed. "But I'm trying to be sensible."

"I still wonder if I should be making a round of calls, as Lady Frances is," Cordelia said. "But I'd be bound to get questions about you and Malcolm and Italy. Besides—" She chewed on her gray-gloved finger. "I want to be here the moment Harry and Malcolm return."

Carriage wheels and horse hooves cut the air. Mélanie tensed instinctively, but the yellow and blue barouche that rolled into view bore the crest of Lord and Lady Langton, their neighbors across the square. On a chill winter day, the top was raised, so she didn't entirely relax until the carriage came to a stop and the footman let down the steps and handed down a fair-haired lady in a purple bombazine pelisse and a high-crowned bonnet lined with lavender silk who was unmistakably Lady Langton. She and Malcolm had not been on close terms with the Langtons, who were Tories, but they had been invited to the Langtons' larger parties and had invited them to their house in return. The family had six daughters, the elder two of whom followed their mother from the carriage. The younger two had occasionally played with Colin and Emily. Mélanie lifted a hand in greeting. Best to act as though all were normal.

Lady Langton didn't seem to see her. Marianne, the second daughter, waved. That caught her mother's attention. Lady Langton put a hand on her daughter's arm. Her gaze moved from

Mélanie to Laura to Cordy. Then she turned pointedly away and shepherded her daughters into the house.

"Well," Cordelia said. "Quite like old times. When Harry and I first separated, I received the cut direct so often it quite lost its sting."

It was actually the first time it had happened to Mélanie. Ironic, considering that if even a fraction of her true history were known, most doors in Mayfair would be barred to her. "I always thought Lady Langton was small minded," she murmured.

"She's worried about her daughters," Laura said in a quiet voice. "Felicia's going into her second season, and Marianne will be out this year. She has six daughters to see settled, and the title and most of the property go to Lord Langton's nephew."

"You're more charitable than I am, Laura." Cordy said.

"And you know more about the Langtons than I do," Mélanie said.

Laura shrugged. "The governess used to bring the younger girls to the garden when I was here with Colin and Jessica. She liked to settle in for a gossip. And it's nothing I wasn't expecting. I'm sorry for the two of you, though."

"It couldn't bother me less," Cordy assured her.

"Or me," Mélanie said. "In many ways it makes it easier. The less we talk to people, the less chance of exposure."

Colin ran over to the three women. "Why didn't Estella and Corinthia's mummy wave back at you?" he asked.

"I daresay she was just preoccupied and didn't see us," Mélanie said.

Colin's dark brows drew together against his pale skin. "Marianne saw you."

"Marianne has the eyes of a seventeen-year-old. I've long thought Lady Langton needs spectacles."

Colin continued to frown. Livia ran up and seized his hand. "People don't see things all the time when they're thinking about other things. Especially grown-ups. Let's get back to the game."

Livia, Mélanie was quite sure, remembered her mother receiving the cut direct and had a very shrewd idea of what it meant. Colin's brows were still drawn, but he let Livia pull him off.

"Your daughter's a diplomat," Mélanie said to Cordelia.

"I've always known she was observant, but I don't think I realized quite how much she was aware of at three."

"Her father's a scholar, after all," Laura said.

Cordelia turned to smile at her friend. "Yes," she said, "so he is."

Which was true. Cordelia might not be sure who Livia's biological father was, but Livia took after Harry in a number of ways.

Movement caught Mélanie's eye before she heard the sound of footsteps over the stir of the wind in the branches. A small figure seemed to be making for the Rannoch house, but when he caught sight of the group in the garden, he veered over to them. It was Victor Ducot, Pierre's son. Mélanie's pulse quickened. He'd brought messages from his father before.

Victor waved to the children—he'd tossed a ball with them in the past, but was bent on more serious business now. He opened the gate and trotted over to Mélanie. "Madame Rannoch. Papa sent me with a message for Monsieur O'Roarke. But he said he might be out and, if so, I should talk to you."

"Yes, he is out," Mélanie said. "But I'll make sure he hears whatever it is."

Victor nodded. He was thin and wiry like his father, with dark hair and pale skin. "Madame Leblanc hasn't gone anywhere unusual. But she sent a message about an hour ago. Papa had someone track the messenger. He went to St. Giles. Near the Red Lion. Papa thought it might be helpful for you to know right away."

Mélanie stared into Victor's intent blue gaze. "Thank you, Victor. That's very helpful, indeed." She turned to Cordy and

Laura. "I'm going to have to go out for a bit. If Raoul returns or Malcolm comes back, give them Victor's message."

MÉLANIE MADE her way through a maze of streets, yards, and courts. The close-set brick buildings, smoke-mottled and unleavened by greenery or ornamental white moldings, seemed to swallow one up. Once or twice a hand snatched at her mulberry velvet pelisse, but thanks to the cold and damp, few people were abroad. A light rain was falling and the tug of the wind promised more.

She paused in a narrow court, beside a public house with a faded sign proclaiming the Dolphin. The grimy glass of the windows was so thick that the scene inside wavered, like a charcoal drawing smudged with water. A scattering of customers was visible, but instead of studying them, she ducked through a gap between the public house and the next building over and opened a side door covered with peeling varnish.

A narrow passage with patches of damp on the peeling wallpaper stretched before her. The only illumination was the fitful light from the open door, which showed the outline of a staircase. The murmur of voices and clunk of tankards came through the wall from the common room next door. She climbed the splintery windowless staircase and eased open a door onto a small room that smelled of mildew, gin, and tobacco. A man seated over a game of solitaire spun round and pointed a pistol at her.

"What the hell are you doing here?"

"I'm here to see Mr. Lucan," Mélanie said.

The man gave a coarse laugh. "He's not here."

"You're just guarding the door on general principles?"

The guard got to his feet and walked towards her, pistol extended. He had a round, determined face, and while he was not overly tall, his shoulders were broad and he carried himself with the air of a man accustomed to using his fives. He'd not been the one on duty the last time she'd come here.

"Stand still," he said. "Arms out. No funny business."

Mélanie complied. It would be faster this way. She stretched out her arms, silver and silk reticule dangling from one gloved wrist. The guard stared at her as though she were a rare tropical bird, equally likely to break or bite him.

"It's all right," Mélanie said. "I'm not vicious when handled with care."

He gave a grunt that might have been annoyance or apology, took her reticule, and snapped it open. A scent bottle tumbled to the floor and rolled into a corner.

"Oh, dear," Mélanie said. "I'm afraid I have a shocking tendency to try to carry too many things at once."

The guard backed towards the corner, pistol still pointed at her, retrieved the scent bottle, took her silver nail scissors from the reticule and tested his finger on them, then returned the lot to the reticule, closed the clasp, and returned the reticule to her. He regarded her a moment longer, then patted his hands gingerly over her pelisse.

"Very politely done," Mélanie said. "Now will you be so good as to tell Mr. Lucan that Juana Murez is here to see him."

"Who the devil—"

"Tell him."

The guard disappeared into the inner room. Thirty seconds later he returned, scratching his head, and nodded towards the room beyond. "He says you're to go in."

The inner room was larger and the smell of mildew less pronounced. Perhaps the latter was due to the smoke from the tarnished brass lamp on the gateleg table in the center of the room. A man with thick side-whiskers and a lady with a cascade of curly dark hair were bent over papers on the table. The man pushed back his chair and got to his feet, gaze on Mélanie.

"*Hola*, Sancho." Mélanie stared at the man she vividly remembered drinking Rioja with in a Spanish tavern. Moments before a knife fight had them both under the table.

"Mélanie." Sancho stared at her with equal surprise. She'd been to see him a few times in London, but not in months. And their last encounter had been round the supposed Phoenix plot.

"Who is she?" The curly-haired woman came round the side of the desk and stared at Mélanie.

"Mélanie Lescaut. Also known as the Marquesa Ferante, Juana Murez, and a number of other names. Oh, and Suzanne Rannoch, which is what she calls herself now that she's living in Britain as an English aristo's wife."

"I'm calling myself Mélanie again. Malcolm isn't an aristocrat—at least, he doesn't have a title—and we're not living in Britain any more."

"You used to work with her?" the woman demanded.

"Don't come all jealous, Nan. Not that it's not appealing. She wasn't mine, she was O'Roarke's."

"I wasn't anyone's," Mélanie said. "Though it's true I used to be Raoul's lover. But these days I'm loyal to my husband. In all senses of the word."

"That must be challenging." Sancho regarded her, arms folded across his chest. "All things considered."

The curly-haired woman stepped on his foot. "Nan Simcox," Sancho said. "Sorry. Mélanie Rannoch, or whatever she's calling herself now. One of the best damn agents it's been my pleasure to work with."

"Thank you, Sancho. It's good to meet you, Miss Simcox."

Nan was eying her with less surprise and more curiosity. "You've had an interesting life. Or are having one."

"You could say that."

"Leaving aside the question of why you came to see me," Sancho said. "Not that I'm not pleased."

"I came in search of my sister-in-law. Why the devil she'd be hiding here—"

"Your who?" Sancho's look of surprise was very creditably done and might once have deceived her. Before she knew him.

"Spare me the denials, Sancho. Charlotte Leblanc sent you a message earlier today."

"Charlotte's an old friend."

"Charlotte is in touch with Tommy Belmont."

"Who?"

"Don't play games, Sancho. I know you sold weapons to both sides in the Peninsula. It's not a wonder you crossed paths with Tommy. I suppose I shouldn't be surprised he turned to you now. But I don't think you know who he really is."

Sancho's gaze hardened. "You know me, Mélanie. I've never been squeamish about who I do business with. You used to be a deal less squeamish yourself."

"We're talking about my husband's sister." Mélanie crossed to stand a handsbreadth away from him. "For God's sake, Sancho, she's only twenty."

"When you were twenty—"

"And she doesn't belong in this game."

Sancho looked down into her eyes. "I'm sorry, Mélanie. But you can't expect me to talk—"

Mélanie pulled a knife from her bodice and pressed it against his throat.

"Damnation. Mick was supposed to search you."

"He did. You need to train your men better. Raoul would rip you to pieces for employing such shoddy guards."

Nan gave a gasp that might have been either shock or appreciation.

Mélanie pressed the knife deeper into Sancho's flesh. "Where's Tommy Belmont?"

"You're not a cold-blooded killer, Mélanie. Unless marriage has changed you."

"Damn it, Sancho—"

"Don't, Mr. Lucan. There's no sense in more lies."

A side door had opened while they were intent on their confrontation. Mélanie recognized the voice, but it was a moment before her brain made sense of it. She turned and found herself staring into her sister-in-law's green eyes.

Gisèle wore a plain chestnut-colored gown. Her hair was simply pinned back, her color good. But her eyes had a hardness Mélanie had never glimpsed before. "I'm sorry, Mélanie," she said. "I shouldn't have put Mr. Lucan in the position of having to lie to you. But I was afraid—"

As she spoke, the door burst open. Four men ran into the room. Mélanie felt a rush of movement. Then a blow knocked her into the wall.

CHAPTER 15

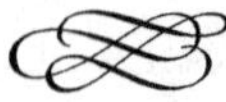

THE WORLD SPUN like a boat in a gale, then stretched into dreamlike slowness. Mélanie recovered her balance and slashed her opponent with her knife. He screamed. Then she felt the press of a pistol barrel against her temple. She caught a glimpse of the unconscious form of the guard through the open door. A yank on her arms forced her gaze back to the center of the room. One of the men who had burst into the room had hold of Gisèle, a knife pressed to her throat. A third man, apparently unarmed, was holding Nan.

The fourth, pistol in hand, walked up to Sancho. This man wore a snuff-colored coat, out of style, but of a cut that bespoke a good London tailor. The product of one of the secondhand clothes dealers in Petticoat Lane or Rosemary Lane, most likely. Where Mélanie had sent her companion Blanca to acquire costumes a few times. A cut above the rough homespun and corduroy of the other three men.

The man in the snuff-colored coat stared at Sancho for a long moment, then struck him a blow across the face. "Mr. Eckert wants to see you."

Sancho returned the man's stare. "Then he can bloody well come here himself."

"He knows you peached on him to Bridges."

"What?"

"No sense denying it. Got a tip this morning."

"From who?"

"Doesn't matter." The man flicked a glance at his companion who was holding Mélanie. "Come with us quiet, Lucan, unless you want your mort's brains all over the floor."

Sancho's gaze went to Nan, and then to Mélanie, with the pistol to her temple. "She's not—"

"Sam," Mélanie yelled, in North London accents, "do what he says or I'm dead for certain."

Sancho stared at her. Nan was sensibly holding her tongue. So was Gisèle. Mélanie locked her gaze on Sancho's. Two possible exits: the windows that overlooked the court and a door behind the table. Four of them, four of the others. Two guns. One knife visible, possibly more concealed. She curved her thumb and forefinger in. A count of three. Sancho inclined his head a fraction of an inch.

Three second later Mélanie sank back, twisted her head, and bit her captor's shoulder. The pistol went flying. At the same moment, Sancho sprang at the man in the snuff-colored coat and knocked him to the ground. The second pistol whistled through the air and lodged in the floorboards.

Mélanie kneed her captor in the groin and lunged for the fallen pistol. Nan yanked against her own captor's hold. Gisèle twisted away from the knife. Sancho tore off his coat and flung it over Snuff-Coat. Mélanie seized the lamp from the table and hurled it into the center of the room.

The chimney shattered. The smell of coal oil filled the air. The room was plunged into shadows, lit only by the fitful light from the windows. A second pistol shot cut the air, but it must have gone wide because Sancho and Snuff-Coat were both still on their feet. Nan tore away from her captor and jerked open a door, nodding at Mélanie. Across the room Sancho seized Gisèle's hand and pulled her to the windows. They hurled themselves at the glass, broke the ancient wood casements, and sprang into the street below.

Nan pulled the door to behind her and Mélanie. They were in pitch darkness, though judging by the close air the space was small, probably a closet or passageway. Nan tugged open another door and stepped into a small room, lit only by the light from a single window. It was furnished with a cot, a table, and three chairs. The window was framed differently from those in the Dolphin and the ceiling was lower. Mélanie realized they were in the next house over.

"Escape route," Nan said. "Always have one." She wedged one of the chairs beneath the door handle.

A crash sounded from outside. They ran to the windows to see Sancho racing across the street, holding Gisèle by the hand.

"Eckert's people are all over this part of town," Nan said. "We'll have to go carefully. Sam will know where to find me. Up, I think."

For the first time, Mélanie noticed a ladder leaning against the wall in the far corner of the room. Nan led the way up the ladder and pushed open a trapdoor. A cloud of dispersed dust greeted them. An attic, with a low, sloping ceiling and dormer windows black with mildew. Nan twisted her hair into a knot and tucked her skirt into her sash. "Can you go across the roofs in those clothes?"

"It's not the first time I've gone over the roofs," Mélanie said, with a vivid memory of a certain night in Vienna. She reached inside her gown, pulled loose the ribbon that gathered her chemise at the neck, and used it to kirtle up her gown and pelisse. Nan pushed open one of the windows and pulled herself up onto the slate roof. Mélanie followed.

A blast of rain-laced wind nearly knocked them into the street.

They half crawled, half slid over the rain-slick slates, dropped four feet to the next roof over, and then pulled themselves up five feet onto the one beyond that. The court appeared to be empty now, but it was difficult to see as they were clinging close to the roof slates. Mélanie pulled off her gloves, which gave her better purchase, but the cracked slates scratched her palms.

Then, instead of following the line of the roofs, Nan moved to two wooden planks that created a makeshift bridge across an alley. "They're safe," she mouthed, above the whistle of the wind. "Leastways, they were the last time I came this way."

Mélanie eyed the four-story drop into the alley and reminded herself that she had survived worse. She got a sliver in her palm and a gash in her silk stockings, but the planks held. They followed another line of roofs, turned a corner, and crossed another gap on more planks. At last, Nan stretched out flat and reached over the edge of the roof.

"Hold my ankles," she told Mélanie over her shoulder. She leaned halfway off the roof. Wood scraped against stone. "Good. The sash wasn't locked."

She crawled down through an attic window. Mélanie followed, more relieved than she cared to admit to have a roof over her head and a solid, dry floor beneath her feet.

They were in a small bedchamber, empty, though it had an inhabitant, judging by the frayed lace dressing gown tossed over the calico coverlet and the broken-toothed comb and chipped ewer and basin on the three-legged stool beside the bed. Mélanie also noted a bottle of vinegar and a washleather bag that she suspected contained sponges.

"Thank goodness," Nan muttered. "Sal's out on the street, despite the weather. She'd ask a damn sight too many questions if she was here. Help me shift the chest of drawers, will you?"

Behind the chest of drawers was another door, so low they had to bend double to go through it. It gave onto another dark passage, also cut between two houses. Nan opened a door at the far end onto a room that smelled of rice powder and cheap violet scent and was filled with moans and giggles and the rustle of bedclothes.

A blonde girl and a dark-haired young man were engaged in congress in the bed. The girl, who was on top at the moment, sat up, straw-colored hair spilling over her naked breasts.

"Bloody hell, Nannie, can't you at least knock?"

"Sorry, Bet, we're a bit pressed for time."

"Is Sam with you? Sam, you rotter, what have got my sister into now? You—Who the devil are you?" Bet asked, seeing it was not Sam but Mélanie who stood behind her sister.

Nan drew a breath. "That's part of the—"

She broke off, because the dark-haired young man, who had pushed himself up against the headboard, was staring at Mélanie with round, bewildered eyes.

Mélanie decided that this was one of those times when the truth was simpler than lies. "Mr. Trenor," she said. "It's some time since we've met. Lady Cowper's rout, I believe."

The Hon. Alexander Trenor, whom Mélanie had last seen in Emily Cowper's drawing room the previous June, turned paler than the linen of the sheet he was clutching to his chest. "Mrs.—Rannoch?" he said, as though even now he could not quite believe it.

"The same," Mélanie said, "though distinctly the worse for wear." She turned to Bet. "My name is Mélanie Suzanne Rannoch. Pray accept our apologies for bursting in so unceremoniously."

"Lord, it's not your fault. Nan does it all time." Bet grabbed a faded blue silk dressing gown from the foot of the bed and shrugged it on. "Here now, are you hurt?"

"Scratches," Nan said. "The roofs haven't got any smoother."

"You're both soaked." Bet picked up a shirt and breeches from the floor and tossed them to Mr. Trenor. "Put those on, Sandy—yes, the ladies will turn their backs—then go in the next room and start brewing some tea, there's a love."

Mr. Trenor gaped at her for a moment, but when the women turned their backs he scrambled into the clothes and beat a hasty retreat into the next room.

"Nicest customer I have." Bet twitched the rumpled bedclothes smooth, brushed two unused French letters from the night table into a drawer, and crossed to a wardrobe of rough deal planks in the corner of the room. "Do you really know him, Mrs. Rannoch?"

"His elder brother is a colleague of my husband's."

Bet turned from the wardrobe with raised brows. Then she stared at Mélanie. "I know who you are. I've seen your face in print shop windows. What's a society beauty doing in St. Giles with my sister? No, don't try to answer that yet, it's bound to take hours." She held out two gowns. "Put these on. Then you can have some tea and explain things."

"Thanks, Betty." Nan fingered the green poplin her sister had given her. "One more thing. Sam's on his way here, along with Mrs. Rannoch's husband's sister."

Bet rolled her eyes. "I might have known it. Do they have constables on their trail? Or someone worse?"

"Not if they've managed to give them the slip."

Bet banged the wardrobe doors shut. "That story had better be very good. Where's Sarah?"

"Safe. Mary Cornwell has her for the day."

"Sarah?" Mélanie asked.

"My little girl," Nan said. "I know better than to get her into trouble, truly, Bet. Not that I could have seen this trouble coming."

"Trouble's part and parcel of your life," Bet said. "Here, let me do the strings. Your fingers must be frozen."

She asked no further questions as she helped them out of their wet gowns and into the dry garments. "Best take off your boots too," she added, rummaging in the chest of drawers. Mélanie removed her boots, tugged off her ruined silk stockings, and pulled on the black cotton stockings Bet gave her. She smoothed her hands over the skirt of her borrowed cherry-striped sarcenet gown, a couple of inches too short for her. It seemed to be in its third incarnation, with a blond lace flounce added to the skirt, the neckline cut down, and cerise ribbon trimming the sleeves to cover where the fabric had been turned. Bet or whoever had remade the gown was a skilled seamstress.

Bet had discarded her dressing gown and was scrambling into a gown herself. Nan did up her sister's strings but stared at Mélanie over Bet's shoulder. "Why did you pretend you were Sam's mort instead of saying it was really me they should have held the pistol on?"

Mélanie tucked a wet lock of hair back into its pins. "Because I knew I could get away from the pistol."

Nan gave a slow nod. "For what it's worth, you have my thanks."

"And you have mine for the escape route. And your sister's hospitality."

Bet moved to the door. "If you helped Nan, you have my thanks too, for all she's often more trouble than she's worth."

She opened the door onto a small room with peeling flowered wallpaper, where Mr. Trenor had got a coal fire going in the smoke-blackened grate and was brewing a pot of tea over the spirit lamp. Bet set their wet boots before the fire and draped their gowns over the faded fire screen. Mr. Trenor, still not quite able to meet Mélanie's gaze, was pouring tea from a chipped cream lustre pot when a door banged open in the bedroom. A moment later, Sam appeared in the doorway. Mélanie released a breath she hadn't known she'd been holding, then looked behind him with a start of alarm. "Where's Gisèle?"

Sam pushed the door to. He had a cut on his cheek, a split lip, and the beginnings of a black eye. "I lost her. That is, I think she gave me the slip. Let go my hand and darted into the crowd." He met Mélanie's gaze. "I know it probably sounds like a story—"

"No." Mélanie returned his gaze. "I wish to God I thought it was, but it fits all too well with Gisèle's behavior. And what I saw of her before Eckert's men broke in."

His gaze swept the company. "Glad to see everyone's still alive. Kind of you to have us all, Bet."

"Didn't have much choice about it, did I?"

Nan stared at Mélanie. "What the devil is your husband's sister running from—"

She broke off as the door once again burst open. Mélanie spun round, poised for attack, and found herself staring at her husband.

Malcolm had a red mark on his jaw that was going to turn into a bruise, his hair was dripping rain onto his forehead, the shoulder seam of his coat was torn, his once biscuit-colored pantaloons were gray with rainwater and filth. His gaze took in the scratch on her cheek, the scrapes on her hands, the set of her arms that betrayed no broken bones. "You're hard to find, sweetheart."

"Malcolm, what on earth—"

"Laura and Cordy told me where to look. But then I had a bit of a dance catching you. I ran into some men working for someone named Eckert who seemed to take me for an enemy."

"Sorry about that," Sancho said.

"Sam Lucan," Mélanie said. "Nan Simcox and her sister, Bet. And you know Alexander Trenor, darling."

"Of course." Malcolm nodded at Mr. Trenor, who was standing by in breeches and untucked shirt, teapot in hand. Malcolm's gaze was easy, though Mélanie caught the quickest narrowing of his eyes. "Bit of luck running into you like this, Trenor."

Mr. Trenor inclined his head. His pale face was now tinged slightly green, but he met Malcolm's gaze. "Er—quite, sir. Tea?"

"Tea?" Sam said. "Good God, woman, surely you've got some brandy hidden about here somewhere?"

Bet regarded him, arms folded across her chest. "You haven't brought the constables down on me, have you?"

"The constables? No."

"Or anyone else?"

"Shouldn't think so. We managed to give them the slip. And then your sister gave me the slip, Rannoch."

Malcolm's mouth tightened, but he didn't appear over surprised.

Bet went to a dresser in the corner, a water-stained but once handsome piece, and took a bottle from inside. "Good stuff from France, fresh off a smuggler's boat. You can thank Sandy for it. He brought it me on his last visit."

The oddly assorted company sat down on an odd assortment of furnishings—a frayed damask settee with stuffing poking through the arms, two straight-backed chairs with cracked slats, a settle draped with a flowered silk shawl. Mr. Trenor finished pouring out the tea into a mismatched set of cups, chipped but clean and carefully dusted with his pocket-handkerchief. Bet passed round the brandy bottle. She cast a glance at Malcolm, the only one still standing. "Oh, bloody hell, you are a gentleman." She dropped down on the settle beside Mr. Trenor.

Malcolm sat beside Mélanie and squeezed her hand.

Bet looked from Nan to Sam. "Well?"

Sam took a long swallow of brandy-laced tea. "Had a bit of a run-in with Eckert's men."

"Eckert's?" Bet shivered. "Why?"

"Thinks I peached on him."

"Jesus bloody Christ. Did you?"

"Do I look the suicidal type? Bloody well would have been the end of me, if it wasn't for—" Sam looked at Mélanie. "I wonder if you're enough of a madman for your wife, Rannoch."

"One can only hope," Malcolm said.

"You saved Sam and Nan?" Bet looked at Mélanie. "Not that on the whole I'm not glad they're still alive, but why? And what were you doing in St. Giles in the first place?"

Mélanie took a sip of tea, to which she'd added a modest splash of brandy. "Looking for Sancho—Sam."

"Why?"

"I thought he might have useful information."

Mr. Trenor had returned the teapot to the spirit lamp. Now he got to his feet and tugged at Bet's hand. "Let's go to the Pig & Whistle and bring back some food."

"Why?"

"Because this'll be private business. They won't talk if we're about."

"But—Oh, very well. I don't know why Nannie always gets all the luck."

"We'll find some of those pies you like," Mr. Trenor promised, grabbing a blue velvet cloak from a hook on the wall and wrapping it round her shoulders.

"Before we speak further," Malcolm said, when the door had closed, "there's something we have to sort out. You appear to have exchanged a lot of information in the past hour."

Nan looked up at him. She had unpinned her hair and was leaning forwards to let it dry before the fire. "You mean because I know your wife worked with Sam?"

"I don't think," Malcolm said, in a gentle, inexorable voice, "that you know anything at all."

"I don't peach on my friends, Mr. Rannoch. Or do you think a St. Giles mort takes her word less seriously than a gentleman?"

"On the contrary. But I've learned anyone's word can at times give way to circumstance and exigency."

Nan tossed back her hair. "I doubt anyone who'd matter would believe me if I *did* try to peach. But anyways, you could ruin Sam, and even if I didn't care what became of Sam, Sam could ruin me, so I'd say we've all got jolly self-interested reasons to hold our tongues."

Malcolm nodded. "Now why don't you tell me what you were doing with my sister?"

"Tommy Belmont brought her here," Mélanie said.

Sam took a swig of tea and brandy. "We didn't know she was

your sister. That is, we didn't know you at all. Didn't know she was Mélanie's husband's sister. Belmont turned up with her, said she needed a place to stay where her family wouldn't find her. Introduced her as Mrs. Fraser."

"Our great-grandmother's name." Malcolm's fingers whitened round his cup, but his gaze remained steady. "Did he say why? Or did she?"

"I wouldn't be much of a success in my business if I asked questions, Rannoch. And Belmont isn't the sort to volunteer answers. Nor is your sister, from what we saw of her."

"Seemed like such a fragile thing at first," Nan said. "But then I saw her fight." She sat back, pushing her hair over her shoulder. "She has children, doesn't she?"

"What makes you think that?" Mélanie asked.

"She was good with Sarah—my little girl. I thought she looked a bit wistful at times."

Mélanie swallowed and saw Malcolm's mouth tighten.

"What did Charlotte send you word about today?" Mélanie asked.

"She didn't," Sam said. "That is, she sent a message, but it was for your husband's sister."

Probably a warning that they might be on to them. It had been a risk for Charlotte to send it, but she must have thought her messenger could outwit Raoul's watchers. "Do you still—"

Nan shook her head. "I saw her burn it after she read it."

"And Mr. Belmont?" Malcolm asked. "Where is he?"

"I don't know." Sam met Malcolm's gaze squarely. "That's the truth. He hasn't been staying here. Brought Mrs. Fra—your sister, and then took himself off. He's been back to see her twice, but the last time was two days ago."

"Did he leave you a way to contact him?" Malcolm asked.

Sam took a swallow of brandy. "Ah—"

"Through Charlotte," Mélanie guessed.

"That's the right of it. Rannoch's sister may have had a more direct way to reach him, but neither of them shared it with us."

"I could see Mr. Belmont drawing a woman away from her family," Nan said. "If anyone was going to."

Malcolm drew a hard breath.

"We don't know that's what's between them," Sam said.

"Seriously, Sam?" Nan swung round towards him. "When did you start ignoring the obvious?"

"We're dealing with people with whom the obvious answer isn't always the right one." Sam turned his mug in his hands, frowning.

"I won't pretend it isn't an uncomfortable subject," Malcolm said. "But we haven't got time for niceties. Do you think my sister was with Belmont because they were lovers?"

Sam drew a breath and met Malcolm's gaze for a moment. "I can't swear to what is or isn't between them. But I'm quite sure she wasn't with him just for—er—romantic reasons."

"It's true," Nan said. "They'd talk all secret-like sometimes. Not the way lovers talk secret."

"But you don't know what they were talking about?" Malcolm asked.

"I try to stay out of Belmont's business," Sam said. "He has a way of being involved in trouble. Though I suppose I can't blame today's disturbance on him."

"I'm not so sure," Malcolm said. "*Did* you peach on Mr. Eckert?"

"What the devil business is it of yours?"

"Your denials seemed singularly vehement. And if you really didn't peach on him, it looks to me as though someone set you up for the little scene that was enacted just now."

Sam struck his palm against his knee. "And you think that has to do with whatever Belmont and your sister are involved in?"

"I think it's possible. But then, you know more about your dealings with them than I do. Not to mention whatever else you may be involved in."

Sam turned his mug in his hands. "I must say, when Mélanie walked in it never occurred to me it was to do with Belmont and his friend. I thought you were on the trail of St.—"

"Bloody hell, does she know him too?" Nan asked in the silence after Sam bit back his words.

"Never mind." Sam sought refuge in his mug again.

But Mélanie had already jumped ahead, and she suspected Malcolm had too. "Sam, are you saying you've seen Julien St. Juste?"

Sam clunked his mug down on the floor. "Didn't say anything of the sort."

"If Julien was behind Eckert's men—" Mélanie said.

"That bastard." Sam punched his fist into the chair arm. "I should have bloody well shown him the door the minute he showed up."

"When?" Mélanie said. "When did he?"

Sam stared at her.

"Oh, for God's sake, Sam," Nan said.

He wiped his hand across his face. His lip was still bleeding. "A month since."

"What did he want?"

"Help in hiring a crew."

"What sort of crew?"

"He wanted someone who knew the ropes of a break-in and how to track and fight and could read and write. And who'd know where to hire on others, if needed."

Nan was staring at Sam with smoldering eyes. "You slimy bastard. What have you got Robby into?"

"Robby can take care of himself," Sam said.

"Robby?" Mélanie asked.

"My brother."

"You're an enterprising family," Malcolm said.

"We know how to look out for ourselves. But," Nan added,

swinging her gaze back to Sam, "that doesn't mean we can walk out of any danger unscathed."

Sam grabbed the brandy bottle from the floor and splashed more brandy into his tea. "He was eager enough for the rhino, wasn't he?"

"Of course he was. He's eighteen and he thinks he's as immortal as one of those Greek gods there're all the statues of in the British Museum. What good's that going to do him if he gets in over his head?"

"Nannie, I told you—"

"I know what you told me." She turned away from him, arms folded across her lace-vandyked bodice.

"What did St. Juste want Robby for?" Mélanie said.

"He didn't say," Sam muttered.

"When did you last see St. Juste?" Malcolm asked.

Sam took a swig from his mug, as though too tired to prevaricate further. "When he came to me a month ago. We haven't spoken since."

"And Robby?"

Nan chewed her nail. "He was here Monday last. Flashing his blunt and talking about his secret work."

"Did he tell you what it was?"

"No. I was tired of him putting on airs, truth to tell." She rubbed her forehead, eyes stricken.

Malcolm leaned forwards. "What's St. Juste planning?"

"I tell you, I don't know." Sam stared into his mug. "But it wasn't an isolated job. He was setting up an operation in London." He frowned for a moment. "You think someone connected to St. Juste set Eckert's men on me? To shut me up? Who?"

"Julien himself, potentially, if he thought he'd revealed too much to you," Mélanie said. She saw Julien St. Juste at their last meeting, in Malcolm's study in the villa in Italy. These days Julien just might be an ally, but she had no illusions about what he was capable of, and she knew Sam didn't either. "Someone trying to stop Julien, though it's difficult to see how they'd think attacking you would do that. Or whomever Julien is working for, if they were trying to tidy away loose ends."

"I didn't say—"

"But you had to have known he was working for someone," Mélanie said. She looked at Nan. "Why are you so worried about your brother?"

Nan started to speak, then bit her lip and looked at her lover.

"Why were you so afraid to tell us the truth, Sam?" Mélanie said.

"Mélanie—"

"Whoever sent Eckert's men at you, I helped you escape them."

Sam stared at her for a long moment. She remembered much the same look in his eyes once in Spain, when he'd been trying to decide how to tell her that the barn they were hiding in was surrounded by British soldiers. At last he set his mug down and turned to Malcolm. "Rannoch, could you leave the room for a minute?"

"Certainly, if you wish it."

"For God's sake, Sam," Mélanie said. "Haven't we established that Malcolm is to be trusted?"

"It's not that." Sam drew a long breath, gaze fixed on the cracked floorboards. "It's—"

"If you tell me alone, I'll just turn round and tell Malcolm."

"But that's a decision you can take for yourself." Malcolm started to get up.

Mélanie gripped her husband's arm. "Better for us both to hear it at once. Who's St. Juste working for, Sam?"

"Christ. Have it your own way." Sam snatched up his mug, took a long swig, and stared at her over the chipped enamel rim. "St. Juste is working for the man we all used to work for. The man you used to sleep with. Raoul O'Roarke."

CHAPTER 16

MÉLANIE STARED AT SAM. Beside her, she felt Malcolm go still as ice. "Did St. Juste tell you he was working for Raoul?" she asked.

"Course not. Since when does that bastard tell anyone anything?" Sam took a swig of tea and brandy. "I said I hadn't spoken with St. Juste since he came to see me a month since. Which is true. But I caught a glimpse of him in the Chat Gris last night. Sitting at a table towards the back. With O'Roarke."

"Did you speak with them?" Mélanie said.

"What kind of a fool do you take me for? If there was any profit in it, they'd come to me. Otherwise, I give them a wide berth, same as I did in Spain."

"So you don't know for a certainty that they're working together."

"What the devil in this life is a certainty? St. Juste is working for someone. He used to work for O'Roarke—"

"Among others," Mélanie said.

"—and now here they both are in London, conferring together. I didn't think O'Roarke was supposed to be in London."

"He's been in Italy. With us." Mélanie smoothed her hands over her cherry-striped skirt. "He arrived in London with me yesterday. When Julien first came to see you, Raoul was in Scotland with us."

Sam frowned. "I seem to have missed some developments. But it wouldn't be the first time O'Roarke engaged someone's services from afar."

Nan was looking back and forth between her lover and Mélanie, a gathering frown on her face. "Who the devil is O'Roarke?"

"Cove I—we—used to work for in Spain," Sam said.

"And you were his mistress?" Nan asked Mélanie.

"A long time ago."

"And now he lives with you and your husband?"

"He's also my father," Malcolm said.

Nan let out a snort of disbelief. "And you were worried I'd peach about your past. No bleeding fear of that. No one would believe me if I did." She took the teapot from the spirit lamp and refilled her cup. "What would this O'Roarke be wanting with St. Juste now? Last I checked, the war was over."

"Not for everyone." Malcolm scrubbed his hands over his face. "O'Roarke's half-Irish and half-Spanish, and a revolutionary on general principles. A William Godwin/Tom Paine sort of Radical. He sided with the French in Spain because he thought Bonaparte's regime offered the quickest route to reform. Now he's allied with the Spanish Liberals—many of whom fought against the French but oppose the restored Spanish monarchy."

"A monarchy which hasn't exactly proven itself friendly to the rights of anyone," Mélanie said.

"Quite," Malcolm said. "O'Roarke would like support from the British for a Liberal rebellion in Spain."

Nan added milk to her tea, then splashed in some brandy. "I don't see why he'd need St. Juste for that."

"No," Malcolm agreed.

Nan took a sip of tea. "So you think O'Roarke set Eckert's men on us?"

"Doesn't make a lot of sense," Sam said. "Not that O'Roarke's not cold-blooded enough to do so, in the right circumstances, but he should know I don't blab. Besides, he always tended to look after his own. He tried to make sure his agents were safe out of it after the war. Helped me get settled in London. It could have been St. Juste himself who wanted us out of the way, as Mélanie said. Or someone else. Even someone connected to Belmont."

"Could Belmont be involved in the same plot?" Nan asked.

"I doubt it," Malcolm said. "He's linked to O'Roarke's enemies."

"Wouldn't be the first time enemies have become allies," Nan said. "If—"

She broke off as a rap fell on the door. Trenor poked his head in and asked if they were done talking for the moment. As the questions about Raoul were exhausted, and she wasn't sure she wanted to reveal more to Sam and Nan, Mélanie nodded. Bet and Trenor entered the room with a parcel of warm pies and a pitcher of ale. Bet produced plates, in a variety of transfer-ware patterns, and served the pies while Trenor poured the ale into an assortment of cups and glassware.

"You'll have to lie low." Bet looked from her sister to Sancho. "You're no match for Mr. Eckert, Sam, and don't go thinking you are."

Sam grimaced and nodded. "We'll go carefully for a bit."

"We can't leave London, though," Nan said. "Robby might need us."

"Oh, poison." Bet clunked down her glass of ale. "Is this to do with that job you got Robby? Is he in danger?"

"We're not sure," Sam said round a mouthful of pie.

Trenor cast a quick glance from Sam to Malcolm, then looked at Bet. "If your brother's mixed up in something dangerous and those are the people who came after Sam and Nan, then you could be in danger as well. This settles it. You're coming with me."

Bet shook her head. "Stop talking like you're on stage at the Tavistock, Sandy. How'm I supposed to make a living?"

"You won't need to. It's high time we changed things anyway."

Bet turned to Mélanie. "Is Robby in danger?"

"We can't be sure," Mélanie said. "Do you have any idea where your brother might be?"

"Not in his old lodgings. He'd had to skip out just before Sam found him the job and when he was here last week, he told me he'd be hard to find as long as the job went on."

Malcolm pulled his card case from inside his coat. "Can you let us know if you hear from him? Trenor knows how to find me."

"I can read." Bet took the card he was holding out and frowned at it.

"It's all right, Betty," Nan said. "We can trust them. As much as we can trust anyone."

Bet tucked the card into her bodice. "If Robby's in trouble, it'll take more than Nannie and me to talk sense into him. I'll let you know if I hear from him."

"Thank you," Malcolm said. He handed another card to Nan, then turned to Sam. "If you hear from Belmont—"

Sam inclined his head. "I'll let you know. And do my best to keep him and your sister here if they show their faces again."

"That's good of you," Malcolm said.

"And you're not entirely sure you can take my word, given that I've been working with Belmont and taking his money. But Belmont's a client. Mélanie's saved my life more than once, including perhaps today. I may be flexible in my loyalties, but I don't forget a thing like that."

Malcolm nodded.

"One more thing," Sam said. "O"Roarke has his own loyalties as well, but if he's working with St. Juste, God knows what he's up to. Go carefully."

"Thank you," Malcolm said. "I always do."

~

MALCOLM LEANED BACK against the greasy squabs of the hackney he had flagged down. "Just when I think I know him, he surprises me."

"I don't think he'll ever stop." Mélanie kept her voice level, but she could hear the worn places beneath the polished veneer.

"I assume he didn't say anything to you about St. Juste?"

"No." Mélanie smoothed the folds of the scarlet cloak Bet had lent her. The yellowed ivory of her borrowed gloves pulled over her taut fingers. "Raoul went to see a woman named Charlotte Leblanc yesterday." She cast a quick glance at Malcolm. "That's why we're in London. Tommy wrote to her—"

"Yes, Laura and Cordy told me."

"Raoul said he found her in the Chat Gris last night. He could have simply happened across Julien there. Though that strains coincidence. Julien could have sought him out." She shivered, because the Elsinore League had wanted Julien to kill Raoul, and though Julien had refused, one never knew what could change. "Or Raoul could have got wind that Julien was in London and gone looking for him. He'd have wanted intelligence about the papers in Julien's hand about the Wanderer that your mother hid twenty years ago. But whatever the reason, he didn't say anything to any of us about seeing Julien."

She saw Raoul coming home last night, dropping down on the drawing room carpet with the children. Updating her, Laura, Cordy, Frances, and Archie. This morning teasing the children, kissing Laura before he went out. There'd been no hint of anything to do with Julien in his words, no hint he was keeping secrets in his manner. But then, with Raoul one could rarely detect secrets.

"He might not have done," Malcolm said. "If he was trying to figure out what St. Juste was doing and wanted to keep you out of it. At least until he knew more."

"Perhaps. Though he's shared other information about Julien."

"That would rather depend on what St. Juste is involved in. What Raoul thinks he's involved in."

"Or Raoul really could be working with him." She forced herself to say it.

"It's possible." Malcolm's voice was even. "He doesn't tell us everything about his work in Spain. I wouldn't expect him to. He could have found reason to work with St. Juste. Even to employ him."

"Yes, but Julien's in the middle of the fight against the League. Which we all share." She hugged her arms over her chest, fighting off a chill.

"True enough. But we'd be fools to think we can always share everything." He looked at her for a moment across the shadows of the carriage. "I told you in Italy that I choose to believe O'Roarke won't betray us. Because the alternative is unthinkable. That still holds true."

She swallowed. Hard. Sometimes the unthinkable had to be put into words. "I used to think I didn't know his limits. In the past year—"

"I know. He's a friend. He's my father. We're a family. I'd swear I know him. I've told him things I'd probably say to no one else but you." Malcolm drew a breath as though biting back further words.

Mélanie studied her husband in the shadows of the hackney. Sharp-boned face, intense eyes, shoulders curved, dark brown hair disordered where he'd pulled off his beaver hat. At once hardened agent and vulnerable schoolboy. "But you can't really fully trust anyone, can you? Thanks to me."

Malcolm met her gaze, his own at once open and uncompromising. "I'm an agent. I should have always known I couldn't fully trust anyone. But I refuse to live my life that way. I refuse to always suspect the people I care about. That doesn't mean I automatically believe everything they say, either. You and I both acknowledge we might have reason to keep things from each other."

"We wouldn't—"

"I'm not sure I'd hire St. Juste without telling you. But I might hire someone. Potentially someone we're both connected with."

"Raoul is—"

"I'm not fool enough to think that because O'Roarke's my father, because he raised me without admitting it and we've actually remembered how to interact as father and son, because he's Emily's father, maybe even Colin's father, Jessica's grandfather—that any of that means he's stopped being a spymaster. Mostly, I've been worried about the danger that puts him in, but it also could put him against us. Or, at least, against me."

"Malcolm, I wouldn't—"

"I'm not going to put you between the two of us, sweetheart."

"You can't think—"

"I think it would depend on the circumstances, and you'd decide accordingly. Depending on what Raoul's objective was and what mine was. You aren't really sure what you'd have done if the Phoenix plot had been real, are you? Or what O'Roarke would have done?"

Mélanie could hear Raoul's voice, as they had stood by the Serpentine watching the children, unsure if the plot to free Napoleon Bonaparte was real or a trap to catch former agents. *I want what's best for France. And I want you as far away from it as possible.*

"That was more than six months ago. I don't think he would risk getting involved with something like the Phoenix plot now. At that point, he hadn't quite acknowledged what Emily was to him. Now he's her father and he's about to have another child."

"And, like most parents, I think he wants the best world possible for his children. As you and I do. And fundamentally we all agree about that world. But we're not always going to agree about how to get there."

"But after our time in Italy—"

"We've been running for the past six months. We still are. That's made us allies."

"It's more than that." Scenes from their time at the villa ran through her mind. Sharing newspapers and coffee on the terrace. Sipping wine and watching the sunset. Jessica on Raoul's shoulders. Colin and Emily on his lap. Capping each other's Shakespeare quotes. Strategizing over the Elsinore League papers.

Malcolm's gaze remained steady and, at the same time, oddly warm. "True. We aren't the people we were when we left Britain. God knows, I'm not. But that doesn't take away the fact that we could end up on opposite sides."

She drew a rough breath.

"I wouldn't want either of you to do anything but follow the dictates of your conscience."

"That's the sort of thing that sounds splendid and rational, Malcolm. And it's hellishly difficult to put into practice."

"Fair enough. But we may have to learn how to do so." Malcolm frowned. "Did Trenor say anything of note before I got there?"

"Only if one were a dramatist like Simon, trying to capture the scene. He was trying desperately to hold on to his manners while being caught in a very compromising situation."

"He certainly seemed genuinely confused. And rather endearingly attached to the younger Miss Simcox. But his elder brother happens to have been one of Miranda Spencer's clients. And to have been in her room just after her body was discovered."

RAOUL LOOKED between Mélanie and Malcolm. "You're sure Gisèle ran on her own? I have a fondness for Sam, but I wouldn't say it extends to trust."

"Nor does it on my side," Mélanie said. "But Gisèle's running on her own fits with what I saw earlier when I spoke with her. She seemed—" Mélanie hesitated.

Malcolm watched his wife and was aware of Raoul doing the same.

"Like a different person," Mélanie finished.

Malcolm swallowed, picturing his sister as he had last seen her. He'd accepted long since that he'd never really known his elder sister Tatiana. But Gelly—"As I suppose we all can in the right circumstances," he said.

They were in the Berkeley Square library. Malcolm and Mélanie had returned to the house to find that Raoul had just got back from his inquiries into Charlotte Leblanc. Cordy had taken her daughters to the Davenport house now that Harry was back, and Laura, Colin, Jessica, and Emily had gone with them. Malcolm, Mélanie, and Raoul had the house to themselves, save for Valentin, who had produced coffee and then retired to the kitchen.

Raoul picked up his coffee and blew on the steam. "Gisèle has a lot of Arabella in her."

"Sam and his friend Nan thought it was more than that she and Tommy were lovers," Mélanie said. She hesitated. "Though they didn't rule that out."

"Nor would I," Malcolm said.

His wife shot him a look of surprise.

"I think she loves Andrew," Malcolm said. "But I'd be a fool to think that rules out—all sorts of things."

"Sam didn't know more about what Belmont and Gisèle were doing?" Raoul asked.

"He said not," Mélanie said. "And it had the ring of truth. He also mentioned seeing someone else recently." She splashed more milk into her coffee. "This is quite like old times, in some ways. I always used to take it for granted that you were keeping secrets. This time, I confess, it surprised me."

Raoul raised a brow. "You're a step ahead of me."

"Sancho—Sam—was contacted by Julien a month since."

Raoul let out a whistle. Entirely believable. "And?"

"Sam saw you in conference with Julien last night in the Chat Gris," Mélanie said. "Sam thinks Julien's working for you. That you're setting up a network."

Raoul's gray eyes gleamed with amusement. "*Querida,* even I don't have time to plot with everyone I hold a conversation with."

Mélanie picked up a spoon and stirred her coffee with methodical strokes. "Julien isn't everyone."

"No. Which is why, when I caught sight of him in the Chat Gris—quite by accident—"

"A very coincidental accident," Malcolm said.

"Not so very," Raoul said. "Considering St. Juste and I were both in London, it's not surprising we both happened to be in a coffeehouse frequented by French agents. It's where I found Charlotte."

"And?" Malcolm said.

Raoul returned his cup to its saucer. The silver-edged rim didn't so much as waver in the lamplight. "As I said, I caught sight of St. Juste, just as Charlotte was leaving. Given recent events, I was curious about what he was doing there. I also wanted to see if I could get him to talk about the Wanderer, and how Arabella got those papers."

"It didn't occur to you that he might be trying to kill you?" Mélanie asked.

"First you accuse me of plotting with him, then you're worried he's going to assassinate me."

"Both are reasonable possibilities."

Raoul sat back in his chair, one of the high-backed Queen Anne ones that flanked the fireplace. "He told you he wasn't going to agree to the Elsinore League's proposition."

Mélanie set down her coffee cup, rattling the china. "Since when have you taken Julien at his word?"

"I don't. But I tend to agree with you that, at the moment, he tilts more towards ally than enemy. Though given that he's recently had dealings with the League—not to mention that they tried to recruit him to kill me, not to mention that he's connected to Carfax, and that both Carfax and the League are after papers he wrote that Arabella stole two decades ago—I wanted to learn as much as possible. So I stood him a bottle of Bordeaux and spent an hour or so trying to discover what he was doing in London while he tried to discover the same about me. Along with more than one question about you, which I answered as evasively as possible. He flat out laughed when I asked him about the Wanderer and said that if I had any illusions he'd talk about that, Italy really had addled my brain. I told him Gisèle had disappeared. He showed very believable surprise, which may or may not have been feigned. In the end, the bottle was empty, we were both more fuzzy-headed than was good for us, and neither of us had discovered anything."

"And then?" Mélanie said.

"He left the coffeehouse. I waited until he was gone and made my back to Berkeley Square by a roundabout route. Unless I'm slipping, I wasn't followed, by Julien or anyone else."

Mélanie leaned forwards and fixed Raoul with a hard stare. Malcolm knew that look. It was almost impossible to hide from. "You didn't say anything about this to us when you got back last night."

"I was going to." Raoul gave a faint smile. "I fully accept that it's better to share information."

"That's a bit of a change," she said.

"Surely it would be stating the obvious to say we've all changed. Yet old habits die hard. I knew St. Juste's presence would worry you. I didn't have anything concrete to report. I didn't—"

"Want me going in search of him?"

O'Roarke gave a faint smile. "You can't deny your position in London is more precarious than it was. And while I'm inclined to think that on the whole Julien's feelings make him less of a danger where you're concerned, rather than more, there's no denying it's a complicated situation."

"So you were being overprotective, like Malcolm."

Raoul gave a self-deprecating shrug. "Call it what you will. It wasn't very sensible to think I could keep anything from either of you."

Malcolm studied his father. Raoul's words were entirely plausible. So was his demeanor. And yet, Malcolm was quite sure that his father, the man he had come to trust and confide in in the past year, had just lied to him.

CHAPTER 17

MÉLANIE SAT BACK in her chair and reached for her coffee cup, willing her fingers not to tremble. Raoul had lied to them. She didn't risk a glance at Malcolm, but she was sure he had felt it as well. She could only guess what it meant to him. It stabbed her like a knife cut, though at one time she'd have said she was quite prepared for her former spymaster to lie.

"I take it you got no more news from your surveillance of Charlotte Leblanc?" Malcolm said.

Raoul shook his head. "Not so far, beyond the report Victor brought Mélanie."

"Could St. Juste have been in the Chat Gris to see her?" Malcolm asked. His voice was cool and neutral, giving no hint of the storm that must be roiling inside him.

"I've been wondering just that ever since last night." Raoul picked up his coffee cup and turned it in his hands. "I don't know that they ever worked together, but they certainly could know each other from the Peninsula."

"In which case, does Julien have something to do with Gisèle's disappearance?" Mélanie asked, pleased to find she had command of her voice.

"As I said, his surprise when I told him about Gisèle was very believable," Raoul said. "Which I'd expect of Julien, in any case. We know the League have been attempting to obtain Julien's services. It seems more and more likely the League are behind Gisèle's disappearance in some way. Belmont works for them. Charlotte's working with Belmont. She as good as admitted she's working with the League too. Even though Julien turned the League down, it's not impossible that he's working with them now. Or Charlotte could have sought him out on behalf of the League."

"Beverston knows something about Gisèle, I'd swear it," Malcolm said. "I didn't do a very good job confronting him about it."

"You weren't going to get him to talk," Raoul said. "At least you got a reaction out of him. And then there's the question of the men who attacked you and Harry. Is that to do with Gisèle, or the Wanderer, or your investigation into Carfax's arrest?"

Malcolm's mouth tightened. He was staring at his hands. "You're both kind not to ask why the devil I'm spending time on Carfax's arrest at all. Though in truth I probably wouldn't have taken the time to go up to see Beverston were he not Tommy's godfather and an Elsinore League member."

"Darling." Mélanie reached for his hand. "No one would expect you to simply stand by while Carfax was in prison."

"No?" He looked up and met her gaze. "I was sorely tempted to do just that when I first heard. But I don't think he did it."

"Nor do I," Raoul said.

Malcolm's gaze shot to his father.

"Carfax is quite capable of murder," Raoul said. "But if so, he'd give himself an escape route. I want to know what he's concealing. And what he was after in the brothel. I can't claim to know Carfax anything like as well as you do. But I've observed him with Lady Carfax. Not that he couldn't surprise us, but I suspect he was seeking information."

"He wouldn't be the first spymaster to look for it in a brothel."

Mélanie met Raoul's gaze, remembering the first moment she'd been alone with him in that narrow room in the brothel in Léon, her confusion and dawning interest when she realized what it was he really wanted from her. She hadn't trusted him then. She'd learned to do so. "You wanted me to spy on someone who was a client."

"So I did," Raoul said. "And from the start your abilities surprised me."

"And I later recruited Rachel Garnier to do much the same," Malcolm said. "Miranda Spencer's client list reveals some interesting things. It includes several Elsinore League members. Not necessarily surprising—it was a popular brothel with those in prominent positions, and God knows League members frequenting a brothel isn't surprising. Any of them could account for Carfax's interest in Miss Spencer, though Beverston apparently saw more of her than any of the others."

"Carfax might have sought her out for information on the League," Raoul said. "Or she could have been working as an agent for him for some time gathering information on any number of people."

"Either of which might give a number of people motives to have killed her," Malcolm said. "She also numbered Matthew Trenor among her clients. Whose younger brother Mélanie happened to stumble across in her escape today. It's difficult to see how that could have been set up, and Alexander Trenor comes across as a very unlikely conspirator, but it's still surprising. Also, Daisy Singleton remembers Matthew Trenor being blank-faced after Miranda Spencer was killed. And said that Miranda had marks on her wrists once after she'd been with him."

"Their father's Lord Marchmain, isn't he?" Raoul said.

Malcolm nodded. "A powerful family. But I doubt Marchmain has the influence to have Carfax arrested to protect his son. Not unless Carfax was in on it."

They were analyzing the case, as they had so often in the past.

Proposing theories, building on one another's ideas. Mélanie remembered a moment in Italy, standing with Malcolm and Raoul on the edge of Lake Como, analyzing evidence and marveling at the alliance between them.

Save that Raoul's lies about Julien meant they weren't allies at all anymore.

~

"YOU'RE sure she ran off on her own?" Cordelia asked. "She might have been afraid of this Sam Lucan if Tommy left her with him."

It was a variant of the same question more than one of them had asked in the course of the evening. They had gone to Frances and Archie's for dinner and were gathered round tea and coffee in the drawing room while the children played round the fire with Christmas gifts.

"I could see it in her eyes," Mélanie said. "Before Eckert's men broke in. She came into the room to stop me from hurting Sam. She didn't want to see me, but she wouldn't let him be hurt. And she looked at me with—apology. Like a woman who knows the consequences but is very committed to her course of action."

Frances added milk to her coffee, fingers white round the eggshell porcelain of the jug. "At least we know she's unhurt. And her own mistress."

Malcolm shot a look at his aunt.

"Andrew's not here," Frances said. "I can be franker about the realities. It never made sense to me that Gelly had been forced away."

Mélanie tightened her grip on her own cup. Her fingers felt not quite steady, for any number of reasons. "Whatever's between Gisèle and Tommy, he wasn't staying with her at Sam's."

"But she'll have gone to find him now," Malcolm said.

"Which makes Charlotte our best avenue to find them," Raoul

said. "They'll be careful because we're on to them, but he'll almost certainly communicate with her again."

Which was probably true. Mélanie took a sip of coffee. God, it was hard to investigate without knowing if they could trust Raoul.

"Sanderson claims not to have heard anything about Gisèle." Archie had paid a visit to their source within the Elsinore League. "But he said there's something afoot. The League are after information and very excited about getting it."

"The Wanderer?" Harry said.

"I asked Sanderson," Archie said. "He heard the name once. He's not sure what it means. Save that it seems to mean access to power. But he did say that when Lord Wyncliffe died recently, he admitted on his deathbed to Lord Beverston that he'd retrieved information about the Wanderer twenty years ago and then lost it. That seems to be what set them searching at Dunmykel."

"Wyncliffe was one of Arabella's lovers. He was on the list you gave me." Malcolm cast a quick glance at Raoul, as though for the moment he'd forgot his questions about his father.

Raoul nodded. "In '98."

"And he was at the house party at Dunmykel when Arabella climbed into my room with the papers," Frances said. "So if Wyncliffe had them, perhaps Arabella took them from him, rather than directly from St. Juste."

"Tommy Belmont may well know we found information about the Wanderer in Lady Arabella's jewels," Laura said. "Perhaps the League think Gisèle possesses more information."

"That's certainly likely," Malcolm agreed. "But as to what Gelly thinks she's doing—"

"Investigating on her own," Frances said.

Malcolm met his aunt's gaze again.

"She's Arabella's daughter," Frances said. "And mine. If she got it into her head she could learn something that you couldn't—"

Malcolm nodded. "I forget sometimes that playing with fire is almost a family pastime."

"The Wanderer could be what the League want from Julien St. Juste," Cordelia said.

"Quite," Raoul agreed. "But not necessarily what Julien's doing in London. Unless he's decided to work with them."

Mélanie took another sip of coffee, pleased her fingers were steady. "Julien runs risks but not simply on a whim. The League want him. He's in London, where the League are based. Either he's made an alliance with them or he has other vital business."

"You said it was clear in Hyde Park six months ago that things weren't done between him and Carfax," Harry said.

Malcolm met Harry's gaze. "You think St. Juste has something to do with Carfax's arrest? Or Miranda Spencer's murder?"

"There's obviously an old and strong connection between Carfax and St. Juste. Carfax is in prison and acting strangely. St. Juste is in London."

"It's suggestive," Raoul agreed, in the voice of one sifting the evidence (as opposed to the voice of one possessed of evidence he wasn't sharing). "Though none of it explains what he wants with Robby Simcox."

"Unless—" Cordelia broke off.

Mélanie looked at her friend.

"He couldn't have employed Robby Simcox to kill Miranda Spencer, could he?"

Mélanie drew a breath. Funny. She'd have said she had few—no—illusions about Julien. But the thought of him being behind a young woman's murder still brought her up short.

"I would think it would have been difficult for Simcox to get into the Barque of Frailty," Malcolm said. "Mrs. Hartley is very careful."

"And Robby Simcox doesn't sound as though he has the finesse for that sort of job," Mélanie said. "But if Mrs. Spencer had information about Julien, it could explain Carfax's interest in her."

"And Beverston's," Malcolm said.

"Dear God," Frances said. "It's almost as though it's all connected. Carfax. Gisèle. This St. Juste."

"It may well be," Malcolm said. "Though I can't see how the pieces fit together at present."

"We know Carfax wants the papers about the Wanderer too," Mélanie said. "Perhaps he thought Miranda Spencer could tell him what the League know about them."

"And he's not talking because he doesn't want to reveal anything about the Wanderer?" Harry asked. "Given the secrecy and urgency surrounding the Wanderer, that has a certain logic."

Frances tucked a curl behind her ear. "Arabella certainly behaved as though the papers were valuable. And dangerous."

"So did Julien," Mélanie said. Eight years ago she and Julien had worked together on a mission helping the Empress Josephine's daughter Hortense conceal the birth of her illegitimate child. On their journey with Hortense, they'd been attacked by men trying to get the secret of the Wanderer from Julien. "And there's not much Julien considers dangerous."

"Yet another reason we can't neglect looking into the murder," Harry said.

"There's one other thing Sanderson told me," Archie said. He'd been frowning. Now he set down his coffee cup. "Apparently Beverston has a new mistress. Lady St. Ives."

Harry let out a whistle. Sylvie St. Ives had been an agent for Carfax until she and others, including Julien St. Juste, broke away from him six months ago. She also had a long association with Julien that none of them fully understood, save that Julien had told her the truth about Mélanie. and she had told Carfax.

"One wonders which of them is spying on the other," Mélanie said. "Is Beverston trying to get information about Julien from Sylvie St. Ives, or is she trying to get information about the League? Or both?"

"Or has she gone to work for the League now that she's broken away from Carfax?" Malcolm said.

"And how much did St. Juste tell her about the Wanderer?" Cordelia added.

"And if she's working for the League, how much has she told them?" Malcolm's voice was grim.

Mélanie reached for her husband's hand. "Several of the League already know about me, darling. Including Lord Beverston. I don't know that Sylvie could do that much more damage there."

"Lady St. Ives certainly has her reasons for wanting to destroy Carfax," Harry said.

"Are you suggesting she killed Miranda Spencer?" Cordelia asked her husband. "And framed Carfax?"

"Not necessarily—though it wouldn't be the first time she killed. But if the League are involved, she certainly might have helped push suspicion onto Carfax."

Malcolm grimaced. "We need to talk to Mrs. Spencer's brother. Or supposed brother." He drew a breath and glanced about the company. "And I think I should talk to Castlereagh about the government's attitude towards Carfax's arrest."

"Of course," Mélanie said.

Malcolm reached for her hand. "There's no 'of course' about it, sweetheart. I'd as lief Castlereagh had no idea we were in London."

"Darling." Mélanie tightened her fingers round her husband's own. "He almost certainly knows already."

"Yes, I know." Malcolm met her gaze, a rueful twist to his lips. "Deluding myself."

"Actually," Raoul said, "it would be good to have a sense of what Castlereagh knows. And there's nothing to suggest he knows about Mélanie."

"No," Malcolm admitted. "And I actually doubt Carfax would have shared such a valuable piece of intelligence. Still—"

"If he does know about me, darling," Mélanie said, "the more we know about what he knows, the better."

"I can't argue with that," Malcolm said. But he continued to frown.

MÉLANIE SET the shawl and reticule she'd taken to Frances's down on her dressing table. The polished walnut looked strangely bare with so many of her things still in Italy. She began to peel off her gloves, the events of the day echoing through her brain. Except for a flurry of dressing for dinner, with the children running in and out, this was the first time she and Malcolm had been alone together since their conversation with Raoul about Julien St. Juste.

Malcolm put Jessica, sound asleep on his shoulder, down in her cradle, then went to the chest of drawers and poured two glasses of whisky. Contrary to his usual habit, he took a long drink himself before he crossed the room and put a glass in her hand.

Mélanie met her husband's gaze as she took the whisky from him. His eyes had the steadiness of glass that could shatter at the slightest pressure. She took a sip of the whisky. It burned her throat. "Raoul was lying to us."

"I think so, yes."

Her fingers tightened round the crystal etched with the Rannoch crest. "He'd know we're likely to see through him. So if he thinks it's worth lying—"

"He has very strong reasons for keeping the truth from us." Malcolm took another drink of whisky. "Which could be to protect us."

"Including to protect us from whatever he's involved in." For a moment she was back in the Peninsula, a young agent, aware that, though her spymaster and lover trusted her far more than he trusted most people, there were innumerable things he kept from her.

"Possibly," Malcolm acknowledged. His hand was steady but his fingers were white round his own glass.

"We could confront him. Tell him we know he's lying. But he probably still wouldn't admit anything. And—"

"He'd be more on his guard. Quite."

"So we're left with trying to outthink him."

"Well, there are two of us and one of him." Malcolm swallowed the last of his whisky. "And he trained us well."

"So, we see what we can learn. While working with him to find Gisèle." She kept her gaze on Malcolm, the words not quite a question.

"You mean do I trust that he's trying to find Gelly?" Malcolm set his glass down. "As much as I trust anything. As we discussed at Frances's, everything seems to be intertwined."

"He's seemed as desperate to find her as the rest of us these past weeks," Mélanie said. "And he told Victor to come to me with news."

She swallowed the last of her own whisky. Their lives had always been impossibly complicated, but she suddenly, desperately wanted to go back to this morning, which seemed so much simpler it was almost like a fairy tale.

Malcolm brushed the backs of his fingers against her cheek. "It could be worse, sweetheart. We're together."

She met his gaze and went still, taking him in. In Spain they'd been apart for longer. But their marriage had been very different then, new and uncertain. And though he'd meant far more to her than she'd have admitted, he hadn't meant nearly what he now did. Nor had she to him, she was quite sure. And for all they'd been in the midst of a war, the risk of being separated by a continent hadn't overhung them. She found herself scanning his face, absurdly relieved to find a glint in his eyes and the familiar lift of his mouth.

She slid her arms round him, not taking her eyes from his face. His own arms closed round her with unexpected force. She lifted her head and his mouth came down on her own, raw with longing and relief, as though he were learning her anew.

"Reunions," she said, when he finally lifted his head. "The only good thing about a separation."

"I suppose we have to take what we can get." He stroked a thumb against her cheek. "I kept telling myself you couldn't come to London. That it wasn't safe. That I should hope to God you were sensible enough to remain in Scotland or go back to Italy."

"Malcolm, this is no time to turn Hotspur—"

"And all the time I was hoping against hope to see you every day." His other hand came up to cup her face.

She leaned her cheek against his hand. "You have no idea how I've missed you."

"Not possibly more than I've missed you. I'm very fond of Andrew, but I far prefer sharing a room with you."

She slid her arms round him and leaned into him for a moment, drinking in their closeness. He rested his chin on her hair companionably, but then she felt his sudden stillness. She lifted her head to look up at him. "What is it?"

"It's just—I never thought we'd be back in this room."

"I know." She kept her gaze on his face, but she was keenly aware of the soft blue-gray walls, the theatrical prints, the green and burgundy of the coverlet. The moss green of Malcolm's favorite chair.

"I've been sleeping in the dressing room," he murmured. "Where I swore I'd never sleep. But I couldn't face our bed without you. Not after being gone for so long."

"I understand. I slept in the nursery last night." She looked into his eyes and saw a hope she knew he wouldn't dare let himself put into words. She touched his face. "We're here now, Malcolm. Let's enjoy that."

"We haven't got time to enjoy it, sweetheart."

"We have tonight. We're not going to learn anything new before morning." She took his hand and drew him to their bed. "Might as well reclaim our bed. For as long as we have it."

CHAPTER 18

LAURA CLOSED the door of the night nursery. Strange to see the children back in their familiar beds, canework instead of the iron in Italy. And only Emily and Colin. Livia had been sharing the nursery with them for months. So much the same, yet different. She looked at Raoul. He'd gone into the nursery with her to tuck Emily and Colin in, and seemed as focused on them as ever, but now he was staring at a tapestry chair back as he laid his coat over it.

"At least we know more than we did at the start of the day," she said. "And we know that Gisèle is unhurt, and not a victim."

Raoul looked up and met her gaze. "No, there is that. Although—"

"The League can control people? As I should know better than anyone?" She went round the other side of the chair and knelt on it, facing him. "But I was without friends, and Trenchard was using Emily to control me. Gisèle's son is safe, and she has family and friends she must know she can turn to. And whatever she may have done, I can't imagine she feels the weight of guilt I did."

Raoul reached across the chair back to grip her hands. "She could be afraid for Malcolm, though I suspect you're right. That she's acting on her own. Which leaves the question of why. Though as you say, we're in a better position to answer that than we were last night." He turned her hands over in his and kissed her palms. "Have you thought about going to see your family?"

"I did." She smiled into his eyes, keeping her voice determinedly normal. "That is, I went to see James and Hetty today. I left Emily in Hill Street with Cordy." After they'd been cut by Lady Langton, she'd realized it was imperative she speak with her late husband's brother and his wife before they heard of her presence in London—and her pregnancy—from other sources.

Raoul's gaze darted over her face "I'm a brute not to have asked you sooner."

"We've had rather a lot to talk about, and scarcely a moment on our own." Laura tightened her fingers round his own. "I own I was rather dreading it."

"My darling—"

"You couldn't possibly have made things better by being there."

"No, I know. Quite the reverse, in fact. Which doesn't make me feel any less of a worm."

"It wasn't nearly as bad as my imaginings. James said you were a good man."

Raoul's gaze remained steady on her face. "Somehow I doubt that's all he said about me."

"He's concerned. I'd hardly call James a creature of society, but I think it's hard for him to imagine someone who could be at its heart choosing to live outside it."

"I imagine he's also concerned for Emily."

"Yes." Laura wasn't quite prepared to tell her lover just how strongly James had expressed those concerns. Though at least he hadn't gone so far as her deepest fear and said anything about attempting to gain custody of Emily himself. "I don't think he can fathom that I'd prefer my daughter not grow up a duke's granddaughter. But he acknowledges the security Emily's found with us and the Rannochs. And he said that after what his brother put me through, I deserved every happiness I could find."

"He's right there."

"Leaving aside the question of what I put Jack through." James didn't know his own and Jack's father had fathered Emily—and for both James's and Emily's sakes, Laura profoundly hoped he never did.

She didn't add that, in addition to James's concerns about her own and Emily's social ostracism, he'd expressed worries about the lack of stability in a relationship with a man who was gone for weeks, months even, at a time, risking danger and arrest. "Though I don't agree with O'Roarke's politics," he'd said, "I admire his commitment. But the man's already had to flee Britain once. He's in no position to be a husband and father, and the fact that he already has a wife is the least of it." Laura had countered that the same argument might have been made about her own father when he was an active soldier. James had gone silent at that, but the troubled look hadn't left his eyes.

"I said we'd be going back to Italy before too long," Laura continued. "I offered to stay away while we're in London to spare them embarrassment. James told me not to be foolish."

"One could make a fair argument that I'm not a good man, but James certainly is."

Laura tightened her grip on his hands. "He is. And so are you, there's no sense in trying to deny it. As I was leaving, Hetty ran after me. She said James was bound to feel he had to behave as the head of the family, but that she could quite understand being happier raising one's children in quiet. That she and James were happier than she'd ever dared hope to be, but that in many ways she missed the old days when they could retreat to the country without a staff of twenty and didn't have to dine out seven nights a week. She said she'd never have chosen to be a duchess, but she happened to have fallen in love with a man who became a duke.

So she could understand choosing a life that might not seem comfortable, because one had fallen in love with a different man."

"My dear—"

"I haven't made my life round you, sweetheart. I've told you that more times than I can count. We're making our life together. But I am grateful to Hetty for understanding. She said not to worry about James. That he could be stubborn, but with time he sees sense. Which is another way of saying Hetty helps him see sense." Laura leaned in to Raoul across the chair back. "I'll see my father and Sarah tomorrow. But I know from their letter that they're happy for us. Of all the things we have to worry about, this is the least of them. We'll be back in Italy before long, and society's opinion will seem singularly unimportant. But I'm glad James and Hetty know, and that I was able to tell them in person."

Raoul's gray gaze darkened. She knew what he was thinking. In the eyes of the world he had rendered her, the widow of a marquis, a fallen woman, outside the bounds of society. No matter that he had spent his entire adult life fighting against society's strictures, no matter that he claimed to care little for what people thought of him, it still bothered him. They were none of them entirely free of the code they had been raised on. And little as he might care for anyone's opinion of him, he cared very much what they thought of her and their children. And she loved him for that.

"I want to see your parents while we're here," Raoul said. "But probably best you see them alone first, for a number of reasons."

"Are you going to see Charlotte Leblanc again tomorrow?" She realized as she said it that it might sound as though she was suspicious, but she didn't think he would take it that way. They were beyond that sort of jealousy.

"Better at this point for Mélanie to talk to her, I think. I want to see if I can recruit some more people to keep watch."

Laura tilted her head up to look at him. "You're setting up a network."

"I suppose I am, in a manner of speaking. The first network I've had in London. A bit ironic."

"But a number of your former agents are here." She scanned his face. "Are you going to look for St. Juste?"

"I think it would be a waste of energy. Julien will appear if he wants to be found. But it's possible some of my contacts have wind of what he's doing."

Laura slid her hands from his clasp and put them on his chest. "It's just that I can't forget the Elsinore League wanted to hire him to kill you."

"And he refused." Raoul leaned over the chair back and kissed her. "I may not be able to claim to be a match for St. Juste, sweetheart, but I think I can say I have more experience than he does."

Laura pressed her head against his shoulder, hiding her face. "I fully believe you're a match for him, my dear. But it doesn't stop me from worrying."

Much later, lying in the bed that had been hers as a governess, that they were now openly sharing for the first time, his arm round her, her head in the hollow of his shoulder, she stared up at the frame of the canopy. For once, he had fallen asleep before she did. From the first night they'd spent together, the night before she'd found Emily, she'd always felt secure in his arms. It was the place she didn't have to worry or pretend. Tonight his touch was no less tender. His arm no less sure round her. Yet she was quite certain he hadn't told her the full truth when she asked about his network and Julien St. Juste. Not that there weren't other times he'd kept things from her, but he was usually open about it. This time he'd been concealing something.

She couldn't ask him about it. He'd never promised to tell her everything about his work, after all. And, she realized, she couldn't talk to Mélanie or Malcolm or Cordy or Harry. Not without jeopardizing Raoul's relationships with them. Which meant that she was alone. For the first time since she had found

Emily and Raoul and accepted that the Rannochs were her friends and family rather than her employers.

Once being alone had been a familiar sensation. Now it felt damnably uncomfortable.

A FAINT SPLASH and whir woke her. Mélanie rolled onto her side and watched her husband by the looking glass on the chest of drawers, whipping the shaving soap into a lather with the brush.

He caught her eye in the mirror and then turned to look at her over his shoulder. "I didn't mean to wake you."

"You didn't." She studied him, the lower half of his face white with shaving soap. "It's just a while since I've woken to the sound of you shaving."

It was such a hallmark of a British gentleman. When she first met him in the Cantabrian Mountains, he'd shaved every morning, even though they were camping in the snow. But in Italy he'd rarely bothered until later in the day, and occasionally he'd omitted shaving altogether. Just as he'd often gone days together without putting on a cravat. Or a coat on hot days.

He turned back to the glass and reached for the razor. "Yes, well. We're not in Italy anymore." He drew the razor along his jaw. "It's a while since I've unlaced your corset."

Mélanie studied the pile of their clothes on the foot of the bed. Well, strewn over the bed and floor, actually. Her corset was dangling half off the bed with a rose-embroidered garter caught on one of the hooks. "It took a bit of getting used to," she said. "It's a good thing I have so many front-lacing ones as I've been managing without either Blanca or you. Mind you, I thought about leaving it off." Odd, when six months ago she'd been so keenly aware of missing Britain, to be missing Italy. "But though we may not precisely be going about in society, given the people we're seeing, it feels—"

"Yes." He peered into the glass and drew the razor over a part of his chin he'd missed.

"We need entrée. We don't want to be denied admission anywhere."

"I'm sorry."

"Sorry?"

He looked at her over his shoulder again, the razor clutched in one hand. "To have dragged you back into"—he waved his free hand in a gesture that encompassed the house, Berkeley Square, London society—"all this."

"Darling. I don't deny I'm missing Italy far more than I'd have expected six months ago. But—" She sat up and drew her knees up under the sheet. "It's good to be home."

His gaze locked on her own for a long moment that echoed back to those moments in the Tavistock Theatre a year ago when he'd first learned the truth of her past. "We can't stay, sweetheart. For any number of reasons."

"I know. It doesn't stop me from enjoying being here." She hugged her arms round her updrawn knees and rested her chin on them. "Laura and Cordy and I received the cut direct in the square garden yesterday. From Lady Langton."

Malcolm's brows snapped together.

"Darling, we knew it would happen. Laura knew it would happen."

"Did the children—"

"Colin asked some questions." Mélanie stroked Berowne who was curled up at the foot of the bed. "And I think Livia understood. Because she'd seen it happen to Cordy. As Laura pointed out, Lady Langton has six daughters to marry off. She has to worry about appearances."

Malcolm turned back to the glass and dipped the razor in water. "I'm sorry beyond words—"

"Darling. Spare your energies for the things we do really need protecting from. Not that I admit to needing protecting."

Malcolm set down the razor. "It will be good to get back to Italy as soon as we can."

In some ways. And yet—She looked at the windows. The cool crystalline winter light would always say Berkeley Square to her. The sheet was soft beneath her fingers. Somehow, even the lavender smelled different here from in Italy. She gave Berowne a last scratch beneath the chin, pushed back the sheet, and reached for her dressing gown. "I don't think we're going anywhere right away. Not until—"

"We find Gelly."

"And Carfax is out of prison."

Malcolm was patting his face dry. He looked up at her, the snowy towel clutched in both hands. "I don't have to—"

"Darling, at the very least you need to learn the truth. Even I don't want to leave him in prison if he's innocent. I wouldn't wish that on anyone." She shrugged on the dressing gown. "Besides, we don't know how it might connect to the League—"

"We were dealing with the League from Italy." Malcolm tossed down the towel and moved towards her.

"But now we're here where it's so much easier." Mélanie met him in the middle of the room, wiped away a bit of shaving lather he'd missed near the corner of his mouth with her thumb. She drew his head down and reached up to kiss him. "We're back for the moment, and reasonably safe. We should take advantage of it."

He returned the kiss with great willingness, but when he lifted his head, he smiled down into her eyes, his own at once tender and hard. "I know that look. It usually means we're about to go into danger."

"It usually means we're about to discover information."

"Which can amount to the same thing."

She put her hands on his chest. "We need to find Gisèle. We need to learn who killed Miranda Spencer. We need to find out what the hell Raoul is up to. I think we have more than enough to keep us busy."

CHAPTER 19

"IT'S good to see you back in London, Malcolm."

There was no reason, Malcolm told himself, to look for irony behind the foreign secretary's tone. Castlereagh and Carfax were colleagues and allies, but wary allies. Malcolm doubted Carfax would have trusted so valuable a secret as the truth of Mélanie's past to the foreign secretary. Not unless he needed something very valuable indeed. And if Castlereagh did know, Malcolm very much doubted he'd have kept quiet. He was a brilliant man, but his thinking was narrow. Which made the risk, if he ever did learn the truth, all the greater.

"We came back because of my grandfather's health," Malcolm said, letting himself into the chair Castlereagh waved him to. "He's much improved, fortunately. He sent my brother-in-law and me to London on business." Malcolm settled back in his chair. "I arrived to the news about Carfax."

"A shock, that." Castlereagh frowned at his ink blotter. "Difficult to imagine a man one's worked with—"

"You believe it, then?"

Castlereagh rubbed at a smudge on the blotter. "It isn't up to me to judge that."

"And you weren't sure about me."

Castlereagh met and held Malcolm's gaze. When Malcolm had been arrested for Tatiana Kirsanova's murder in Vienna, the foreign secretary had remained scrupulously neutral. Malcolm could understand that diplomacy had required him to do so, in the midst of the Congress, with Malcolm arrested by their Austrian hosts. He had more difficulty accepting that he was also quite sure Castlereagh had had personal doubts about his attaché's innocence. Though, with the perspective of four years and a wealth of personal experience of betrayal, he was closer to understanding.

"I try not to let personal feelings cloud my judgment, Malcolm."

"Fair enough. So what's your rational assessment when it comes to Carfax?"

Castlereagh reached for the cup of tea beside his inkpot. "Carfax was found with the young woman's body."

"Which hardly proves anything. My dear sir, Carfax is about as likely to frequent a brothel for the usual reasons as you are."

Color touched Castlereagh's sharp cheekbones. He was notorious for his fidelity to his wife. "Carfax, on the other hand, would be more likely to have unusual reasons to frequent one."

"And to kill there?"

"For God's sake, Malcolm, you worked for the man. And for years he was in military intelligence. He was an agent in the field."

"None of which explains why he isn't offering an explanation. Or why the government aren't covering up the situation as a matter of course."

Castlereagh's shoulders snapped straight. "Rannoch, you forget yourself—"

"On the contrary, sir. Since I've stopped being your attaché, I've begun to remember who I am. Not entirely yet, perhaps, but I'm getting there."

"Malcolm—"

"A man privy to the most dangerous secrets in Britain is caught with a dead young woman in a brothel in suspicious circumstances. He refuses to explain himself. Even Bow Street have doubts."

"Obviously not enough—"

"Someone pressured Sir Nathaniel to have Carfax arrested."

Castlereagh's face went still. "You're involved in something very dangerous, Malcolm."

"Hardly for the first time. In the past, you were frequently the one who asked me to involve myself in danger."

"In the past, you worked for me."

"And you thought you could control what I discovered?"

"I never thought I could control you, Malcolm."

Malcolm sat back in his chair. "Did you know Matthew Trenor was one of Miranda Bentley's clients? And there the night she was killed?"

Castlereagh's brows drew together. "Yes, I learned that in the report from Bow Street. A number of men were there the night she was killed. And I fear Trenor was not the only one of my aides to frequent the Barque of Frailty. But none of them was in the room with her dead body."

"If Carfax had killed her, don't you think he'd have taken care not to be found in the room?"

Castlereagh pushed his chair back and strode to the windows looking out on Downing Street. "You've been out of Britain for six months. You've been out of the diplomatic corps for almost two years. The war's over. Things have changed. In ways you have no knowledge of."

"You mean the security of the country necessitates getting rid of Carfax?"

"Don't be ridiculous, Malcolm. I was sorry when you left the service. But you made a very cogent case for why you disagreed with official policy. You have a family to think of. Stay out of this. For their sake. And your own."

"And leave an innocent man in prison?"

Castlereagh shot a look at Malcolm over his shoulder. "Can you say with certainty he's innocent?"

"Can you say with certainty he's guilty?"

Castlereagh turned his gaze back to the window. "We have to let justice take its course."

"You'll forgive me if I don't believe that it will do so." Malcolm pushed himself to his feet. "Is this to do with the Wanderer?"

Castlereagh went still. Then he swung round and stared at Malcolm, his gaze gone cold with something Malcolm had rarely seen in the foreign secretary's eyes—fear. "What do you know about the Wanderer?"

"Frustratingly little. What do you know?"

Castlereagh tugged hard at a shirt cuff beneath his coat sleeve. "If concern for your family won't get you to stop, then have a care for the good of your country. For God's sake, leave this alone."

"THIS IS INTERESTING, I CONFESS." Charlotte Leblanc settled into a tapestry settee in a snug sitting room in her rooms in Leicester Street. Her maid had admitted Mélanie without hesitation. "Does Raoul think you can succeed where he failed?"

"I'm not sure Raoul thinks he failed," Mélanie said. She was seated in a straight-backed chair at right angles to Charlotte. The room was small but snug with a fire and furnished with the same casual elegance with which Charlotte dressed.

Charlotte lifted a silver coffeepot and poured Mélanie a cup. "Raoul's always been ruthlessly honest. He can't have deceived himself that he got the information he wanted."

"I'm sure he hasn't." Mélanie accepted the cup Charlotte was holding out to her. "And also sure that he hasn't given up."

"I have no doubt of that." Charlotte poured a cup for herself. "And so he sent an ally."

Mélanie took a sip of coffee. It had that indefinable Parisian taste. "And I'm not sure I'd say Raoul and I are allies."

Charlotte lifted a brow. "Interesting. Also a good tactic. Send an ally in pretending not to be an ally. I've done it myself."

"So have I. And Raoul and I discussed my talking to you. But things have changed."

"Obviously. You're married to an English aristocrat."

"Malcolm's Scottish and he doesn't have a title. But I meant things have changed in the past two days."

Charlotte's gaze remained steady, but Mélanie caught a spark of interest. "I confess you intrigue me. Go on."

Mélanie picked up her spoon and stirred her coffee. She was combining her genuine questions about Raoul with a strategy for drawing Charlotte out. Truth mixed with deception. A tactic she had learned from Raoul. "You know Raoul. Have you ever fully trusted him?"

"No." Charlotte took a sip of her own coffee. "But you have quite a different relationship with him."

"Had."

"Whatever's between you, you're obviously still close. And he's apparently close to your husband."

"Yesterday he lied to both of us. That changes things."

"It can hardly be the first time he's lied to you."

"No. But this is different. Were you meeting Julien St. Juste in the Chat Gris?"

"Julien was in the Chat Gris?" Charlotte sounded surprised. It was probably a genuine reaction. Probably.

"Raoul spoke with him after you left. But he didn't tell us until we had a report elsewhere that they were seen together. When we asked him about it, he said he happened across Julien. But Malcolm and I are both sure he wasn't telling us the truth. At least, not all of it."

"You think Raoul is working with Julien?"

"That's partly why I came to see you."

"You think Raoul would have confided in me?"

"I know the League have been trying to hire Julien."

"If so, that would seem to preclude his working with Raoul. And also my confiding in you."

Mélanie took another sip of coffee. "I think in this case, we might be able to offer each other beneficial information." Which wasn't entirely a lie. "Assuming Julien isn't working for the League, what do you think he and Raoul might be planning?"

Charlotte's eyes narrowed. "How well do you know your sister-in-law?"

Mélanie kept her coffee cup steady in suddenly nerveless fingers. "What does Gisèle have to do with this?"

"I don't know her, of course," Charlotte said. "I only have Raoul's story to go by. But do you think there's any chance she could be playing Tommy?"

Gisèle's gaze in the moments before Eckert's men burst in shot through Mélanie's memory. Hard and yet pleading. She had certainly seemed more in command of the situation than Mélanie had expected. But to what end it was difficult to say.

Charlotte turned her coffee cup on its saucer. "I doubt Tommy would admit he could be played. But from everything I've heard about Arabella Rannoch, her daughter must be a formidable woman. As must your husband's sister from what I've heard of him. And I don't think Raoul would be above recruiting Arabella's daughter."

Mélanie took refuge behind her coffee cup, not sure whether to be more horrified because she could imagine the truth of what Charlotte was suggesting, or because if it was true, and Charlotte suspected and was working with Tommy, Gisèle was at appalling risk. "It's an intriguing thought," she said. "But I think you're making the mistake of seeing Gisèle through the lens of our own lives. She's scarcely left off being a girl."

"The same could be said of you when I first met you."

Mélanie remembered that meeting. Charlotte had fascinated

her, a woman who had made a life for herself as a spy, much as the celebrated actress Manon Caret had. Though Charlotte, even more than Manon, had been an independent agent. "To say that Gisèle's life has been more sheltered than mine would be a gross understatement. Her family have been at pains to keep her out of the spy business."

"Which may have made her all the more curious."

Mélanie strongly suspected that was the case. "But not a trained agent. Raoul's always been careful about whom he employs. And it doesn't explain his meeting with Julien."

"No," Charlotte agreed, "it doesn't. If Raoul's working with Julien, he must be planning something quite significant." Her brows drew together. "He's worked against Britain for a long time, after all."

"In Spain. In Ireland. Not directly."

"No, but those other avenues are now closed to him." Charlotte leaned forwards to pick up the coffeepot. "We're all finding things to do with ourselves since the war. Interesting to contemplate what Raoul might have found. A little more coffee?"

CHAPTER 20

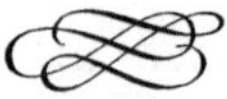

"CHARLOTTE THINKS I recruited Gisèle to spy on the League?" Raoul said, his gaze appraising. "I have to credit her for a clever scenario."

Mélanie had told him Charlotte's theory about Gisèle, though not her suggestions about what he might be plotting with Julien. She needed to hear his response. And to warn him and the others. They were gathered in the Berkeley Square library—Malcolm, just back from his interview with Castlereagh, Laura, and Harry and Cordy, who had just arrived.

"Yes," Malcolm said, watching his father. "It is clever."

"And you wonder if I'd actually have done it?" Raoul, who was standing by the fireplace, picked up the poker and pushed a log back into the grate. "Leaving aside my affection for Gisèle, my loyalty to Arabella and Frances, my loyalty to you—I wouldn't be a very good spymaster if I turned an untrained agent loose on an undercover mission against the Elsinore League."

Malcolm nodded. Like her, Mélanie was quite sure he recognized the logic of what Raoul was saying. While, at the same time, not being completely certain.

"But Gisèle could be trying to spy on Tommy and the League

on her own," Harry said. He gave no sign of noticing the undercurrents, but when did Harry not notice undercurrents?

"Charlotte seems to have wondered," Mélanie said. "I think that was genuine. And she implied that Tommy wouldn't listen to her concerns. Without outright admitting she knew anything about Gisèle's connection to Tommy at all."

"Which puts Gelly at risk from the League." Malcolm pushed himself to his feet and strode to the library windows. "Whether she's really working against them or not." He stared at the leafless branches of the plane trees in the square garden. He must remember playing there with Gisèle when they were children.

"It's a risk." Raoul's gaze fastened on Malcolm, at once uncompromising and startlingly tender. "But Belmont apparently doesn't believe whatever suspicions Charlotte may have, and the League are more likely to listen to him."

"And Gelly seemed very much in command when I saw her yesterday," Mélanie said.

"We know she's not a prisoner," Laura said.

"No," Malcolm agreed. "But if she was reckless enough to do this, she may be reckless enough not to leave when she should."

Cordelia frowned. "Do you really think—"

She broke off as the door swung open. They all looked round as Gisèle's husband strode into the room.

ANDREW'S GAZE fastened on Mélanie's face, like that of a drowning man who feels a rope slipping from his grasp. "Gelly ran away from you?"

"From Sam Lucan. But I think it was clear she didn't want us to find her." Mélanie made her voice as gentle as possible. But there was no point in keeping it from Andrew. In his place, she'd want to know. "I don't think we can begin to understand what's driving her."

"She seems much more focused and driven than I credited," Malcolm said.

"That's plain." Andrew wiped a hand across his brow. "Especially after what Judith told me."

"Judith heard from her?" Malcolm said.

Andrew met his gaze, a soldier giving a report even though the battle seems lost. "Gelly went to see Judith. Just after she got to London by my calculations. She told Judith she'd come to town on business for you. That Ian and I were in London. Judith was surprised, but didn't see any reason to be concerned or to try to detain Gelly or follow her."

"No, she wouldn't." Malcolm leaned forwards. "Tommy wasn't with her?"

Andrew shook his head. "That would have taken explaining. All Gelly said was that she needed a necklace Lady Frances had given Judith that used to belong to Lady Arabella. Diamonds and amethysts in white gold."

"I remember Judith wearing it," Cordelia said. "It's a beautiful piece."

Malcolm nodded. "Aunt Frances gave it to Judith just before her wedding."

"Judith said she was surprised, but she assumed Gisèle had her reasons." Andrew said. "She gave the necklace to Gelly. Gelly stayed to swallow a cup of tea and hug the baby and then left, promising to explain later." Andrew gripped his hands together. "She's obviously trying to find the rest of the papers Lady Arabella hid in her jewels. I think it's fairly plain now she's trying to help Belmont."

"Nothing is plain in this family." Malcolm stretched out a hand. "Andrew—"

Andrew jerked back. "Don't, Malcolm. I won't pretend it doesn't hurt like the devil, but I'm not the first man to lose his wife. I'll survive. We know she isn't being coerced. You know Gelly. She could have sought refuge with Judith. At the very least, she could have sent a message through Judith that would let you know she was in trouble. She certainly could have run with Mélanie instead of away from her. She wants to be with Belmont. She wants to assist him." He ran a hand over his hair. "I'd gladly give her a divorce if that's what she wants, but she seems to be bound up in the Elsinore League intrigues. And I'd hate to see her tie herself to a man such as you've described Belmont."

"I'm all for facing possibilities, Andrew," Malcolm said. "But they're still just that, possibilities. It's also possible Gelly's working against Belmont and the League."

"Charlotte thinks so," Raoul said, "and she has a keen understanding."

Hope shot through Andrew's gaze, only to be ruthlessly suppressed. "Why in God's name wouldn't she tell us?"

"Probably because she knew we'd try to stop her," Malcolm said.

"From going undercover with a secret group who are known to kill? By God, yes," Andrew said. "I'd try to stop you from doing so as well, though I'm not sure I'd succeed."

"Point proved, I think," Harry said.

"Malcolm's an agent," Andrew said. "Gelly isn't."

Mélanie spread her fingers in her lap, those few moments at Sam's etched in her memory. "I saw Gelly jump through a window without hesitation yesterday, Andrew," she said.

Andrew's gaze swung to her. "What are you suggesting? That Gelly's been spying for years? From Scotland? That someone—what—recruited her and trained her?"

"Charlotte apparently thinks I did," Raoul said in a steady voice. "But I didn't. I wouldn't."

Andrew stared at Raoul. "What if Belmont did?"

"But then she'd be working for the League," Cordelia said.

Andrew scraped a hand over his hair. "We don't know that she isn't. All you have are this Charlotte Leblanc's suspicions. Or she could have changed her mind and decided to work against them."

"That sounds more possible," Malcolm said.

Andrew's fingers tightened on his scalp. "Just a few weeks, and I don't feel I know her anymore. If—"

He broke off as the door opened again, this time to admit Valentin. "I'm sorry to interrupt," Valentin said, "but this just came for Mr. Rannoch. It seems important."

Malcolm took the letter Valentin was holding out and slit it open. "It's from Mrs. Hartley," he said. "Miranda Spencer's supposed brother has surfaced at the Barque of Frailty."

GERALD LUMLEY SCRUBBED his hands over his face. "I can still scarcely believe she's gone. I didn't even see—not that I'd have wanted to see her like that, but—"

"It can help, in an odd way," Harry said. "Seeing a person after they're dead. One can't avoid the reality. I know it was like that for my wife when her sister was killed."

They were once again in the white-painted sitting room at the Barque of Frailty. After some debate in Berkeley Square, Malcolm and Harry had gone to see Lumley alone, as they had already established a degree of trust with Mrs. Hartley. Mrs. Hartley had greeted them with relief and left them alone in the sitting room with the shocked Gerald Lumley.

Lumley met Harry's gaze. "I'd known her since we were children. That is—"

"We were already quite sure you weren't Mrs. Spencer's brother," Malcolm said.

Lumley flushed. "I wasn't. We were friends." He stared at Harry and Malcolm, his dark hair falling over his face "Oh, God. They don't know, do they? Her family?"

"I don't think anyone knew their names to inform them," Malcolm said. He held Lumley's gaze with his own. "What name was Mrs. Spencer born with?"

Lumley drew a breath, then went still, eyes wide with uncertainty.

"I know," Malcolm said. "You've been protecting her, and that's very commendable in you. But she doesn't need protecting now. She needs justice. And we need to know the facts of her life if we're to learn who killed her."

"You think she was killed because of who she was before she came here?" Lumley asked in shock.

"I think it's a possibility. And we have to explore every conceivable possibility."

Lumley drew another hard breath and nodded. "My father was —is—the vicar near her father's estate. In Surrey. Her father's name is Dormer. She was born Miranda Dormer."

"Her father is Sir George Dormer, isn't he?" Malcolm said. Sir George was an avid hunter, not often to be found in town. Not overly political. Not a member of the Elsinore League. At least, his name wasn't on the list. His elder daughter had almost married Malcolm's friend Kit Montagu. And his estate was not far from Beverston's. So Beverston may have been telling the truth about having known Miranda Spencer—Dormer—as a girl. Though not about her father being a vicar.

"Yes, Sir George is her father," Lumley confirmed. "Miranda is —was"—he shuddered—"his younger daughter. Always a bit of a rebel. Nothing too wild, but Sir George is the sort who likes ladies to be ladies, if you know what I mean."

Malcolm exchanged a look with Harry, thinking of their wives. "Quite," Harry said.

"Lady Dormer too. Also, she's not the sort to disagree with her husband. Miranda was over a decade my junior, but she played with my sisters, and I thought of her as almost another sister. I studied law and set up a practice in the village so I was about a good deal. Three and a half years ago I spent some time in Cornwall on a case. I returned to find Miranda gone. Her parents wouldn't talk about her. My parents wouldn't either. But my younger sister said the story was

Miranda had run off to London with a man. Sir George went after her, then came back and said they weren't to speak of her again."

For a moment Malcolm saw his sister's face. Different circumstances, but—"How did you find her?" he asked.

"I didn't. Not right away. I couldn't think where to begin looking. I had to go back to my practice and—I suppose I was a coward."

"You had little to go on," Malcolm said. "And no authority to ask questions where Miss Dormer was concerned."

"I've often wondered if only I'd found her sooner—" Lumley's face twisted with the pain of unanswered questions. "As it was, it was over a year and then only because I was in London and saw her walking in Green Park. She looked away at first, went on walking, but when I ran after her, she turned round. She seemed glad to see me."

"I'm sure she was pleased to see someone from her old life," Harry said.

"Yes, I think so, only she said we couldn't talk in public. She told me to meet her at a coffeehouse, to let her go in first and she'd be at a table in the back. I half thought she wouldn't be there, but she was. She was working at Mrs. Hartley's by then. Admitted it straight out. Said she was fortunate in many ways."

"Did she talk to you about her life before she came to Mrs. Hartley's?" Malcolm asked.

"Very little." Lumley shifted in his chair. "She made me promise not to tell anyone where she was."

"You mean her family?" Harry asked.

"I think she was worried about them discovering her, yes," Lumley said. "But I also think she believed they had disowned her no matter what. She was chiefly worried about the man she had run off with. I gather he had been—not kind."

His tone gave the words added weight. "She was afraid of him?" Malcolm asked.

Lumley nodded. "He was a cad, of course, to have done what he did and not married her. But it went beyond that. She never quite said so, but I believe he was violent. I can't imagine her being so afraid of him otherwise."

Images of Diana Smythe's distant gaze and the ironic turn of her mouth shot into Malcolm's memory. Married to her abuser, she hadn't even had a way to run. He wondered for a moment which was worse. "I begin to see why she found the Barque of Frailty a haven," he said.

"Yes," Lumley sat forwards in his chair. "She never came right out and said so, but I had the sense her being there had been arranged."

"Arranged?" Harry asked. "Daisy Singleton said they had a chance encounter in Covent Garden."

"Yes, Daisy said that to me as well," Lumley said. "And I think Daisy believed it was chance. But I had the sense someone else had set up their meeting. That perhaps Mrs. Hartley knew about Miranda in advance."

Malcolm and Harry exchanged a quick look. This might explain why Mrs. Hartley had taken in a girl she didn't know, without a known history, but it added a whole new layer of questions.

"Miss Dormer knew Mrs. Hartley before she came here?" Harry asked.

"I'm not sure. She's not—that is, I can't imagine she'd have met her before she left her family. But I don't know about her life in the year after she ran off."

Malcolm sat forwards in his chair. "Her former lover whom she feared. Do you think he might have found her here?"

Lumley's eyes widened. "You think he got in somehow and killed her?"

"She feared him and she ended up dead," Malcolm said. "It's an obvious possibility. Though if Mrs. Hartley knew of Miss

Dormer's past, I imagine she'd have been on her guard against this man."

Lumley frowned. "Miranda was panicked about seeing him when I first found her. In all the years I've known her, I don't think I'd ever seen such fear in her eyes. But lately she actually seemed a bit less worried. She even suggested we go out for a walk once or twice when I visited, and to a coffeehouse just a fortnight ago—" He drew a harsh breath, the reality of that being one of the last times he'd seen her sinking in.

"Miss Dormer had a jade pendant she wore a great deal," Malcolm said.

"Yes, it had been a gift from her parents on her seventeenth birthday. Do you know what's become of it?"

"No. Apparently it disappeared the night she died."

Lumely frowned. "And that makes you think her former lover might have killed her?"

"It suggests whoever killed her may be someone who knew her real identity. Had she said anything to suggest to you she'd seen anyone from her old life?"

"No, nothing at all. Truly. As I said she'd seemed less concerned about encountering her former lover in recent months."

"Miss Singleton accidentally overheard Miss Dormer say something to you about being 'sorry it happened' and that she 'wouldn't say more,'" Harry said.

"Oh that," Lumley glanced away. "Miranda ran into someone I was at Oxford with. At the—here. She recognized the name and was afraid she'd betrayed to him that it was familiar. She didn't want to create any awkwardness for me. I wasn't worried—my only concern was that it be awkward for her or somehow betray where she living, but she didn't seem concerned."

It was a plausible story and Lumley told it well, but something about the way he chose his words made Malcolm suspect it wasn't the truth. At least not all of it. "Did Miss Dormer ever talk about Lord Beverston?" Malcolm asked.

Lumley shook his head. "No. She rarely mentioned anyone by name. Not the—people she knew here. Some of the other girls, that is, but not—"

"I understand," Malcolm said. "Did she ever talk about where she went when she was away from the Barque of Frailty?"

Lumley shook his head. "As I said, until recently, she tried to avoid going out as much as possible. Except to visit—" He drew in his breath again.

"She knew someone else in London?" Malcolm asked. "Someone from her past? Or a man she loved?"

"No. It's not what you think—" Lumley's mouth tightened as though against the press of confidences.

"Anyone she knew may have information relating to her death," Harry said. "Even if that person doesn't realize the information could be important."

Lumley looked at Harry, looked at Malcolm, glanced away. "Miranda didn't tell me until over a year after I found her. And then she swore me to secrecy. She has a son. He's almost three."

CHAPTER 21

MANON CARET HARLETON looked up from the tiny bundle in her arms. "I heard rumors you were back, but I put them down to idle talk. I scarcely let myself believe you could really be here."

"I'm sorry." Mélanie met Manon's gaze across the satinwood table. Laura, Cordy, and the children had come to Manon's with her, but they had gone into the nursery with Manon's daughters to admire Christmas presents so Mélanie and Manon could talk. "I'd have sent word, but we're trying to keep a very low profile."

"I quite understand. I've told myself that if—when—I saw you again it would probably be much like this."

Mélanie moved from her chair to the settee where Manon sat and bent over the bundle in Manon's arms. A small face peeped out of a pale green blanket that Mélanie had sent from Italy. His father's thick brown hair and his mother's long lashes, closed against sleep-flushed cheeks. "He's beautiful," Mélanie said.

"I confess I'm inclined to think so, though I own to a distinct bias." Manon rocked her baby. "Crispin is besotted."

"You look distinctly besotted yourself."

A faint smile played about Manon's ironic mouth. "Perhaps. There's something about those early months after one gives birth that can turn the most sensible woman into a doting imbecile. I remember it being the same with the girls."

"You still dote on the girls. You just don't admit it." Mélanie held out her arms. "May I?"

Manon smiled and put the baby into Mélanie's arms.

"It seems like yesterday that Jessica was this size," Mélanie said, settling baby Roderick against her. "And suddenly she's such a little person."

Manon cupped her hand round her baby's head. "You're not back for good, are you?"

"We can't get back to Italy soon enough to keep Malcolm happy."

"Are you here because of Lord Carfax? I wouldn't have thought the news would travel quite this quickly."

"No. Though now we're here we've been drawn into it. Malcolm's sister's run off."

"His sister in Scotland?" Manon asked in surprise. "Doesn't she have—"

"A nine-month-old." Mélanie looked down at Roderick.

"New motherhood doesn't make every woman besotted," Manon said.

"No. Though I'd swear she loves her child. And though she left with a man, it's more than a simple love affair."

"'More than?'"

"It may not be a love affair at all. I can't be sure. But she's been drawn into a tangle that would challenge a seasoned agent." Mélanie studied Manon in the soft light of the lamp. They were in an elegant room in Manon's new husband's house, but they were still the women they'd been when they spoke by the light of a spirit lamp in Manon's dressing room. "Have you heard anything about Julien lately?"

"Good God, he's not the man Malcolm's sister ran off with?"

"No. It's not quite that bad." Though Tommy could only be called slightly less dangerous than Julien.

"But Julien's mixed up in this?"

"He seems to be. I'm not quite sure how. Raoul just saw him at the Chat Gris and tried to draw him out but couldn't get far." Somehow Mélanie couldn't bring herself to share her suspicions about Raoul. If Manon knew anything, she was confident her friend would tell her. Unless Manon was working with Raoul. In which case, confiding in her would do no good save to set Raoul more on his guard in whatever he was doing.

Manon's gaze showed no particular surprise. "The wonder would be if even Raoul could draw Julien out. The last I heard of Julien was when you told me he was here last summer. I've been on my guard ever since, and quite relieved not to see him."

"We saw him in Italy in September. Or rather, I did. He seemed to be an ally then. As much as one can ever tell with Julien. But the Elsinore League were trying to hire him to kill Raoul."

"Good God. Why? I mean, not that Raoul isn't formidable, but—"

"Why now? Precisely what Raoul says. He claims the League really want to engage Julien's services for other reasons and refuses to take the threat seriously."

Manon snorted. "That sounds very like him. I hope Laura's knocked some sense into him. He's going to be a father."

"And he is taking it seriously." Mélanie thought back to their conversation just before they decided to leave Scotland. "But he's still—Raoul."

"And always will be." Manon reached out to stroke Roderick's hair. "Which, in this changing world, is both comforting and rather terrifying."

"Quite."

Manon smiled down at the baby for a moment as he stirred in his sleep, then looked back at Mélanie. "It's odd. Here I am married to the father of my third child, and if not precisely accepted by society, accepted more places than I ever thought to be. And Laura—If anyone can face down society, I imagine she can. But she was born into it. Or at least on the edges of it. That must make it harder to be an outcast."

"Laura's remarkably matter-of-fact. It's Raoul who worries."

"That's both very surprising and not surprising at all. In the strangest way, he's always been overprotective."

"That's remarkably perceptive. I'm not sure I ever had perspective where Raoul's concerned." And she still wasn't. Mélanie tucked the blanket folds more closely about Roderick. "Have you heard of the Wanderer?"

Manon frowned in seemingly genuine puzzlement. "No. And I thought I was familiar with most code names, even if I didn't know whom they referred to."

"This isn't a regular code name. In fact, it may be a what, not a who."

"And it's to do with why Malcolm's sister's disappeared?"

"It seems to be."

Manon shook her head with regret. "I wish I could help."

"There's a man who broke into Dunmykel a fortnight before Christmas in search of papers relating to the Wanderer. He seems to have hired some of the locals to help him, so he was a stranger to Dunmykel. They describe him as tall, thin, 'middle years'—the men describing him are young, so that could mean thirties to sixties—and one thought he had a French accent, though the others claimed he was English. Keeping in mind these were people who mostly hadn't been out of the Highlands, so even an Edinburgh or Glasgow accent might sound foreign. Does that remind you of anyone? It's not a very detailed description, though the height seems to rule out Julien."

"I wouldn't put it past Julien to change his height by some sort of alchemy. But of all the disguises I've seen him in, I've never seen him tall."

"Nor have I. Anything that makes one taller makes action challenging. And Julien would have had to make himself a lot taller to appear tall to these young men—they're a tall lot themselves."

Manon frowned. "It's true it's not a detailed description. I probably wouldn't connect it if I hadn't just seen him. But as it is —it could be Thomas Ambrose."

"He's an agent? I don't think I've ever heard of him."

"No, you didn't work in Paris much, so it's not surprising you didn't cross paths with him. He was an agent for hire, much like Julien, though not at Julien's level. Few are. But quite capable. I crossed paths with him once on a mission involving some Royalist papers I was trying to intercept—did intercept. Our encounter was—interesting. Enough for him to linger in my memory. So when I saw a man who resembled him crossing the street near Covent Garden, I was quite sure it was he. I actually let out a gasp. Which, of course, confused Crispin. And given the nature of my past connection with Thomas, I didn't quite like to offer up a great many details to him. Not to mention that the girls were with us as well, and though they certainly know I have a past, there's no need to flaunt it in front of them."

"When was this?" Mélanie asked.

"The day after Boxing Day. We were taking Roderick to the Tavistock to show him off."

"So there'd have been time for Ambrose to get here from Dunmykel."

"Yes, I would think so. I did wonder at his presence in London, but who am I to worry at another agent seeking refuge here? Of course, it occurred to me that he could be here on business, but I told myself I was much better off not knowing." Her gaze flickered over Mélanie's face. "I'm sorry."

"You couldn't have known. I try to stay out of things myself these days."

"Ha."

"I said 'try,' not 'succeed.' How old is Thomas Ambrose?"

"We never shared birthdays, but I'd say about a decade older than I am. So, mid-forties now."

"Do you have any idea whom he might be working for?"

Manon shook her head. "He always laughed at the idea of any sort of ideology or loyalty. And that was during the war, when sides were a bit clearer than they are now. All I can say is that it must be someone who can pay well. Which means someone with a great deal of power."

A YOUNG WOMAN with smooth fair hair, delicate features, and calm green eyes answered the door of the rooms in Fenchurch Street to which Lumley conducted Malcolm and Harry. Her eyes widened in alarm.

"It's all right, Faith," Lumley said. "Mr. Rannoch and Colonel Davenport are trying to learn the truth about what happened to Miranda."

The young woman drew a sharp breath, but the gaze she turned to Malcolm and Harry was appraising.

"Miss Harker." Malcolm inclined his head. "I understand you've been raising Miss Dormer's child ably." Lumley had told them that Faith Harker, Miranda Dormer's maid, had accompanied Miranda when she ran away from home, and had looked after Miranda's baby since he was born.

Miss Harker drew a breath, as though sifting risk with her desire to seek justice for her friend. "I'd gladly speak with you, but it's not the best time—"

A child's cry cut the air of the narrow hall behind her. Not fear or anger but pure glee. "Do it again!"

"Of course, Danny," a man's voice said. "But you need to hold still. You'll knock it over."

Malcolm, who had recognized the man's voice at once, pushed past Miss Harker and flung open the door behind which the voices had come. A small boy with curly blond hair knelt on the hearthrug watching a man spin a blue and yellow top. The man's back was to Malcolm, but he looked round at the opening of the door and confirmed what Malcolm had been almost sure of when he heard the voice.

"Is this your son?" Malcolm asked Lord Beverston.

"My son?" Beverston pushed himself to his feet. "What do you take me for?"

Malcolm drew a breath, then realized the little boy was staring at him. Curious, not afraid. Not yet. Malcolm smiled at the child. "Good day, Danny. My name is Malcolm."

Danny gave the grin of a child used to finding adults friendly and the world a safe place. Beverston stood frozen for a moment, then took a half step towards the boy. Danny smiled and hooked an arm round one of Beverston's highly polished boots. "Grandpapa."

CHAPTER 22

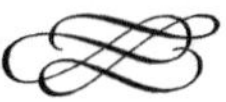

MALCOLM AND BEVERSTON stared at each other, neither willing to put more into words in front of Danny. The door opened to admit Faith Harker, Gerald Lumley, and Harry.

"Lord Beverston?" Lumley said with an amazement that suggested he had told the truth when he claimed not to know the identity of Miranda's lover.

"Lumley, isn't it?" Beverston said, his voice unwontedly rough. "Perhaps you and Faith could take Danny into the other room? I need to speak to Mr. Rannoch and Colonel Davenport."

Faith Harker met Beverston's gaze for a moment, with the look of a woman who recognized his authority but was also used to trusting him. She nodded and scooped up the little boy. "Come on, Danny. Uncle Gerald and I will show you more tricks with the top."

Lumley picked up the top and held open the door for Faith and Danny. Danny waved goodbye over Faith's shoulder.

Beverston watched the door close behind his grandson, Faith, and Lumley. His face was a study in conflict, from a man accustomed to being decisive.

"I should have realized," Malcolm said. "John abused his wife. She likely wasn't the first or only woman he treated in that way."

"I didn't know." Beverston's voice was low and still rough. "I had no notion until Miranda disappeared. Even when her father told me he couldn't find her trail. I don't think even Dormer knew the name of the man she'd run off with. John"—his mouth tightened—"gave no hint of anything. I heard he was keeping a woman in London, but that was hardly surprising." He hesitated a moment, gaze on the hearthrug where he'd been playing with his grandson. "It was a year later when my valet repeated a chance comment he'd overheard from one of the Dormer servants, and I pieced it together. I tracked Miranda down in London." He didn't elaborate on how, but then Beverston, as a senior Elsinore League member, would have considerable resources at his disposal. "I found her living in a garret with Faith and the baby. Scraping by with what she could earn by her needle. And on the streets." His mouth tightened. "She was terrified to see me. She thought I'd lead John to her."

"Did you know how John treated Diana?" Malcolm asked. His hands curled into fists at his side as he said it.

Beverston met his gaze. "No. That's the truth. I knew the marriage wasn't ideal, but what marriage is? And one doesn't like to think of one's son—" He took a turn about the room, moving with something like his usual brisk purposefulness. "I had to find somewhere for Miranda to be safe from John. The options were limited. That was when I went to Rosamund."

"You could have set her up in rooms of her own or in the country where she could have raised her child and not had to earn her keep in a brothel." Harry's voice was level but held an undercurrent of ice.

"And when John tracked her and Danny down?" Beverston asked. "She'd have had no protection beyond her maid. Rosamund keeps a tighter watch on the Barque of Frailty than many generals

I've known on their command posts. No one gets in whom she doesn't vet."

"Including a number of members of the Elsinore League," Malcolm said.

"But John certainly wouldn't." The contempt in Beverston's voice told volumes, and tallied with John Smythe's account of his father's attitude towards him. "Rosamund wouldn't have let him within a hundred feet of the place."

"Miss Dormer went out," Harry said. "I assume Mrs. Hartley didn't send a bodyguard with her."

"Mostly she went out with me," Beverston said. "Those outings were cover for her to visit Danny. Needless to say, Miranda and I did not have an amorous relationship."

"I don't see why that necessarily follows," Malcolm said. "You're clearly a man willing to cross a number of lines."

Beverston's gaze clashed with Malcolm's own. "I draw the line somewhere. Unlike O'Roarke."

"A palpable hit." Malcolm kept his voice even. Though the sting was less strong than it once would have been. "But you've rather proved my point about the lines people will cross."

"Perhaps." Beverston folded his arms across his chest. "Regardless, Miranda was never my mistress."

"No." Malcolm held Beverston's gaze with his own. "She was your agent, wasn't she?"

"My what? My dear Rannoch, I've never been a spy."

"That rather depends how one defines spying. You had Miss Dormer collecting information for you for the Elsinore League, didn't you?"

Beverston raised a brow, but his face remained impassive. "At the Barque of Frailty? A number of the clients were members of the League, as you yourself said."

"And the League don't always act in concert, as you've admitted more than once. You could well have your reasons for keeping an eye on your confederates. Then, of course, there are the other men who patronized the Barque of Frailty."

"In fact, that would be quite a good use of it." Harry regarded Beverston, arms folded across his chest. "Your fellow League members could bring men into the Barque of Frailty about whom you wanted to acquire information. Or on whom you wanted to gain a hold."

Beverston returned Harry's gaze. "The most careful men will reveal things across the pillow they wouldn't dream of saying anywhere else. Tell me both of you haven't made use of that in your work as agents."

Malcolm swallowed. He had with Rachel Garnier. Harry, he was sure, had in other circumstances. Though neither of them had ever put a woman into a brothel to work for them. Still, the tang of self-disgust he'd tasted when they first visited the Barque of Frailty bit him in the throat again. "Why was Carfax in the Barque of Frailty?"

Beverston's brows snapped together. "I would very much like to know that myself."

"You didn't lure him there for the reasons Davenport just enumerated?"

"My dear Rannoch. Surely you realize one doesn't lure Carfax anywhere?"

"Not in the general way of things," Malcolm agreed. "But then, in the general way of things, Carfax isn't arrested for murder either."

Beverston's mouth tightened. "If you're implying Miranda's murder was a ploy to entrap Carfax—"

"For the present, I'm doing you the credit of thinking you'd at least draw the line there." Which wasn't entirely true. Malcolm wasn't at all sure he had Beverston's limits. "Did you know Carfax was talking to Miranda?"

"Can you imagine I wouldn't have taken action if I had?"

"That would depend on whether or not you'd tasked her to uncover information from him."

Beverston gave a grunt of acknowledgment. "I knew Carfax had asked Waitley to bring him to the Barque of Frailty. We didn't have a lot of notice—Carfax saw to that. But Waitley sent word to Rosamund and Rosamund sent word to me. She pointed out it would be difficult to keep Carfax out, which I agreed with. And, truth to tell, I wanted to see what he was after. I told Miranda if he approached her not to try to avoid him. To listen to what he had to say and not reveal anything. I told her I had the greatest faith in her. Which was true." A muscle twitched beside his jaw. "To own the truth, I was relieved when I saw him go over to her. I wanted to know what the devil he was doing at the Barque of Frailty, and Miranda was my best chance."

"And then?" Harry's voice was level, but taut as a bowstring.

"I went to the Barque of Frailty that night, as you know, but stayed as far away from Miranda as I could and pretended to interests elsewhere. I wanted Miranda to learn what Carfax was up to, and I had no reason to think Miranda was in danger." Beverston drew a sharp breath. "I'll never get over the sight of her."

Malcolm watched Beverston closely. That fit with Daisy Singleton's account of his reaction. And, as he and Harry had discussed, didn't necessarily mean he hadn't killed her. "Did you take her jade pendant to keep her identity a secret?"

"Did I—No. I confess, I didn't even think about the pendant until you asked me about it the first time."

"You don't have an idea what Carfax asked her?" Malcolm said.

"I didn't see her after she left the room with him until—until I saw her body. Obviously I didn't ask Carfax." Beverston's hands were curled into fists at his sides. "She was the mother of my grandson."

"And your agent," Harry said.

The gaze Beverston turned to Harry was surprisingly open.

"Surely it's not news to you that one may care for an agent, Davenport. By God, if Carfax killed her—"

"Hardly logical if he came there for information," Malcolm said.

"That," Beverston said, "is the only reason I'm cooperating with your investigation."

"I thought that was because we tracked you down and learned who Miss Dormer was and gave you no choice," Harry said.

Beverston's gaze hardened. "Believe me, Davenport, if I didn't want to talk to you, I wouldn't."

"If Carfax didn't kill her, who do you think did?" Malcolm asked.

Beverston's brows drew together in genuine inquiry, but also in wariness. "I thought it was your job to uncover that. From what I hear, you're both quite good at it."

"By questioning those close to the victim. Until now, our chief suspect was Miss Dormer's seducer, but I think being in a grave is a fairly unshakable alibi."

Beverston grimaced. "I own she felt a degree of relief with John gone."

"Did any of her family know where she was?" Harry asked.

"Not that I know of. She said they'd washed their hands of her and she had no desire to expose herself to their scorn. And I've had no hint in my dealings with Sir George that he has any idea where she is."

"Surely—" Harry bit back the words.

"You're supposed to be a cynic, Davenport."

"If being shocked that a man doesn't wonder at the fate of his daughter makes me less than a cynic, then guilty as charged."

Beverston regarded Harry for a moment. "In his eyes, she'd ceased being his daughter. And no, I can't imagine doing the same with one of my daughters. I imagine you're shocked to find us agreeing about anything."

"On the contrary," Malcolm said. "I've learned I can see eye to eye with my greatest enemies over certain things. And quite fail to do so with my dearest friends over others."

Beverston met his gaze in a moment of measured acknowledgment. "If her family had learned where she was, I'd be shocked if they'd come to see her. Let alone had anything to do with her death. The only person from her past she was in touch with, besides Faith, was Gerald Lumley. I was a bit nervous when Miranda told me she'd seen him, but it seemed to comfort her to know someone from her old life. I don't think he'd have harmed her."

"Nor do I," Malcolm said. Though one could never rule anything out. "Whom else did you have Miss Dormer spying on?"

Beverston's mouth tightened. "She wasn't—"

"For God's sake, Beverston." Malcolm took a step forwards. "You said it yourself. She was the mother of your grandchild. I'm not happy to be standing here talking to you either, but for the moment we're allies in wanting to learn who killed Miranda. At least, I think we are."

Beverston let out a rough sigh. "Hugh Derenvil."

Malcolm frowned. Somehow he'd been expecting a cabinet minister or a crony of the prince regent. Hugh Derenvil was a generation younger, but an up-and-coming young Tory. He'd been a year ahead of Malcolm at Harrow, a serious young man and a good scholar. Not one for the usual public school hijinks. Not one, judging by rumors, to visit the girls in the village with whom a number of students experimented. He'd then gone into the army. Malcolm had seen him a few times in the Peninsula and Brussels. And more recently in the House of Commons. He pictured Derenvil sitting on the Tory benches, face focused and intent, eyes on whoever was speaking, actually listening, which was rarer than one would think among MPs. Not the sort of man one would think to find in a brothel. Though by now, Malcolm thought, perhaps he should realize there was no particular type.

Derenvil was a protégé of Lord Castlereagh. Rumor had it Derenvil might be in line for a minor cabinet post. And—

"He's sponsoring a fishing rights bill," Malcolm said. He might be away from Parliament, but he followed the news closely in the English papers. "Which I assume you take more of an interest in than I would have thought."

"No comment," Beverston said. "Save that I have extensive property in Derbyshire."

"Which would be impacted by the bill."

"Derenvil's also about to marry Caroline Lewes," Harry said. "It's the social event of the winter season."

Malcolm looked at Harry. So did Beverston.

"My wife still follows such things," Harry said. "And occasionally I listen."

Caroline Lewes was the eldest daughter of Lord Thorsby, whose grandfather had made a sizable fortune in shipping and been elevated to the peerage. His daughter was a considerable heiress and Thorsby was a force in the Tory party himself, well positioned to assist Derenvil's career. "And his involvement with Miss Dormer put you in a position to disrupt the marriage," Malcolm said to Beverston.

Beverston lifted a brow. "I know you both are known for your attachment to your wives, but visiting the Barque of Frailty was hardly unusual behavior."

"No, but it might have bothered a young woman who had not yet committed herself to marriage," Harry said. "In some ways, a woman has power as a fiancée that she doesn't have as a wife."

Beverston inclined his head. "I'll own that had occurred to me."

"Had you tried to blackmail Derenvil?" Malcolm demanded.

Beverston took another turn about the room. "I had frank conversation with him a week ago."

"Before Miss Dormer was killed."

"Yes, damn it. But if you think—"

"Miss Dormer could have damaged his marital and career prospects."

"I knew of their involvement. Any number of people could have placed Derenvil at the Barque of Frailty. Miranda's death doesn't protect Derenvil from truths coming out that could damage him in the eyes of his betrothed. Or her father."

That, Malcolm acknowledged, was a fair point. But—"If Derenvil knew you put Miss Dormer up to spying on him, he might have been quite angry."

Something sparked in Beverston's eyes that might have been fear. "Few men aren't angry in such circumstances. He told me to go to the devil. But I imagine he'll come round eventually. And I didn't tell him Miranda had been working for me."

"But he might have worked it out. It isn't easy to be betrayed by someone one was intimate with."

"As you should know."

Malcolm didn't flinch from Beverston's gaze. "My point precisely."

Beverston's face relaxed with sympathy, yet Malcolm was sure Beverston knew exactly to what use he was putting that sympathy. "You have to be one of the most tried men in history in that regard, Rannoch. And yet I doubt you came anywhere near close to killing your wife."

"But I'm not Derenvil."

A shadow of doubt flickered across Beverston's face.

"We'll talk to him," Malcolm said. "Is there anything else we should know?"

"No," Beverston said.

Which was almost certainly a lie.

~

FAITH HARKER REGARDED Malcolm and Harry across the small

bedchamber across the passage from the sitting room. "You'll do everything you can to learn who killed Miranda?"

She sat on the edge of the bed, Danny napping in her lap. Lumley hovered protectively nearby.

Malcolm nodded. "I can make no promises, but we've had success in the past, and we have some leads to follow. Meanwhile, should you and Danny have need of anything, don't hesitate to send word to me." He held out one of his cards. Odd that the Berkeley Square house was once again, for the present, the place to find him.

Faith Harker took it and nodded, but said, "Lord Beverston left me a generous sum and says he will send more. I don't pretend to agree with everything he's done, but he cares for Danny. And I think he cared for Miranda, in his way."

"And you know you may rely upon me." Lumley reached for Miss Harker's hand and lifted it to his lips.

Miss Harker gave him a quick smile that suggested this was the first time he had made such a gesture, and also that it was not unwelcome. "Thank you, Gerald."

"Do you know of anyone who would have had reason to harm Miss Dormer?" Malcolm asked.

Miss Harker frowned, as though she'd been puzzling over this herself. "She didn't talk about her life much when she was with us. Mostly she played with Danny. Her greatest fear was Mr. Smythe finding her. It was a great relief to her when we learned he was dead." Her gaze flickered from Malcolm to Harry. "I know that sounds dreadful—"

"It's understandable," Malcolm said.

"More than understandable," Harry muttered.

Miss Harker nodded. "It was a relief for me, too." She smoothed Danny's hair. "Then, a month ago, Mrs. Smythe came to see us."

"Mrs. Smythe?" Malcolm said. "Not Diana?" Diana Smythe had

been in Italy with her father and the Contessa Vincenzo when the Rannochs had left, little more than a month since.

"No, Mrs. Roger Smythe. Roger is John's younger brother," Faith added. "He married Dorinda. Miranda's cousin."

"And Miss Dormer was in touch with her?" Malcolm asked.

Miss Harker shook her head. "No one from Miranda's family had contacted her once she ran away. Not that I know, at least. Miranda was as shocked as I was when Dorinda—Mrs. Smythe—called here."

"Do you know how Mrs. Smythe found Miss Dormer?" Harry asked. "Or why she came to see her?"

"No." Miss Harker frowned down at Danny's fair hair between her fingers. "I took Danny in here, and they spoke in the sitting room. The sound of the voices carried at times. Not the words, but the tone." She hesitated. "It wasn't the tone of reconciliation."

"Did Miss Dormer say anything to you about the visit after Mrs. Smythe left?" Malcolm asked.

Miss Harker met his gaze, fingers trembling slightly on Danny's hair. She'd likely known Dorinda Smythe most of her life. "Miranda said if Dorinda ever called again, I was to forbid her the house."

CHAPTER 23

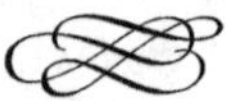

"I KNOW DORINDA SMYTHE A BIT," Cordelia said. "My stepfather has a distant connection to the Smythe family. It should be enough for us to call on her."

They were gathered in the Berkeley Square library, Mélanie and Malcolm, Cordelia and Harry, Raoul and Laura, sharing information and a cold collation Valentin had assembled. Andrew had gone to talk to Gisèle's friends who were in London, to see if any had seen or heard from her. The children were spending the day at Frances's.

"I don't think I ever met Miranda Dormer," Cordelia added. "But it's difficult to credit—"

"Anyone being so barbarous to his daughter, among other things." Harry's voice was as grim as Mélanie had ever heard it.

"It's not easy," Laura said. "Being a woman without resources." Laura had once been a woman without resources. She hadn't landed in a brothel, but she had fallen into the control of the Elsinore League.

Raoul put his arm round her. "It does shake even my supposed lack of illusions about human nature." He was frowning. Mélanie found herself wondering, as she had so often lately, what he was thinking.

"I should have realized John Smythe likely had other victims," Malcolm said.

"We were in Italy, darling." Mélanie reached for her husband's hand. "You wouldn't have known where to look for them."

Malcolm slid his fingers through her own, but his face remained grim. "Roger Smythe was elected as a Whig in the General Election. Rupert wrote to me about it. But I've never met him personally."

"Cordy and I'll talk to Dorinda Smythe," Mélanie said.

Malcolm nodded. "Harry and I should seek out Hugh Derenvil. And Matthew Trenor."

"And I'll see if I can find a trail for Thomas Ambrose," Raoul said.

"Do you know him?" Mélanie asked. She'd shared her interview with Manon, but with the news about Miranda Dormer, there'd scarcely been time to discuss it.

"A bit. I engaged his services once or twice, over a decade ago. A competent agent, though the sort with whom one always watches one's back. There can be advantages to agents who work for hire rather than belief, but with Ambrose I was always very much aware he might in fact be serving another master."

"More so than with Julien?" Mélanie asked.

"Oddly enough, yes."

"Anyone could have hired him to break into Dunmykel and search for the information about the Wanderer," Malcolm said. "But presumably not the League, since they sent Tommy, who already knew his way about the house. And presumably not Carfax, who sent Oliver. He might have hired a professional as well, but Carfax knows the house enough I wouldn't think his agent would have had to ask the locals for information, either."

"So we're back to a third person or group who are after the

Wanderer," Harry said. "Though no closer to knowing what or who the Wanderer is."

"Whoever or whatever it is," Mélanie said, "the search seems to have brought both Ambrose and Tommy to London."

"Do you think Ambrose is the one who attacked Tommy outside Dunmykel?" Cordelia asked. "Could he be behind the attack on Malcolm and Andrew? And the one on Malcolm and Harry?"

"I'd say it's likely he attacked Tommy," Malcolm said. "Or set up the attack. As to the other attacks—it could be Ambrose. Or it could be Tommy and the League trying to slow us down."

With or without Gisèle's knowledge. Malcolm didn't add that, but the shadows in his eyes said that he was full well aware of it.

"Tommy knew John Smythe growing up," Mélanie said. "He must have known Roger and Dorinda Smythe as well. And he'd likely have met Miranda Dormer."

"Yes," Malcolm said, his gaze hardening. "So he would."

DORINDA AND ROGER SMYTHE lived in a smart house on Upper Grosvenor Street. Everything from the glossy red paint on the door to the red and cream striped window curtains bespoke new and stylish. Mélanie and Cordelia had spent the brief walk from Berkeley Square strategizing what to do if Dorinda declined to receive them, but the footman who answered the door glanced at their cards and then conducted them up a mahogany-railed staircase to a sitting room filled with satinwood furniture upholstered in red and cream stripes to match the window curtains.

Dorinda Smythe rose at their entrance. Mélanie's first impression was of dark hair cut in a fashionable crop, perfectly groomed brows, and direct dark eyes. Her gown of dove gray cashmere trimmed with black braid and fastened down one side with gold clasps was almost an exact copy of a fashion plate Mélanie had seen in a copy of *La Belle Assemblée* Gisèle had at Dunmykel.

"Lady Cordelia," Dorinda said, when the footman had withdrawn to procure tea. "It's some time since we've met."

"I don't believe you've met Mrs. Rannoch." Cordelia performed introductions quite as though it were an ordinary social occasion.

"It's kind of you to receive us, Mrs. Smythe," Mélanie said, shaking hands.

"I almost didn't. But I decided on the whole it would be best to confront the inevitable questions." Dorinda Smythe gestured to the sofa and matching chairs grouped before the fireplace. "I trust we can dispense with any pretense that this is an ordinary social call. You're investigating Miranda Spencer's murder. If you're here, you must have learned that Miranda was in fact my cousin Miranda Dormer, and that I called on her and quarreled with her."

In all Mélanie's experience of interviews in the course of murder investigations, this was unusually direct.

Dorinda paused in the midst of settling her perfectly gathered skirts and raised a brow, as though to acknowledge as much. "No sense in not admitting what we all know. I don't suppose any of us wishes to prolong this interview. I've heard of the murder investigations you and your husband undertake. All Mayfair have. I know Lady Cordelia and Colonel Davenport work with you. I have no desire to confront questions in public or to remain a prisoner in my home. And whatever our quarrels, I truly would like to know what happened to Miranda."

"Faith Harker said you hadn't been in touch with your cousin since she disappeared," Mélanie said.

"That's true. Until a little over a month ago, I didn't have the least idea what had become of her." Despite her assertion that she wanted to learn what had become of her cousin, her voice was as cool and brittle as the crystal girandoles that glittered on the wall sconces.

"And so, understandably, you went to see her. Why did you

quarrel?" Mélanie plunged to the heart of the question, hoping to break Dorinda's shell of control.

Dorinda put up a manicured hand to tuck a perfect ringlet behind her ear. "Because I'd learned she was my husband's mistress."

"Your—Roger?" Cordelia had been leaving the interrogation to Mélanie but she was startled into speaking.

"I've only had one husband. You're understandably surprised, because she had run off with my husband's brother? Yes, that surprised me too. More than her being Roger's mistress, truth to tell. Not that it was a pleasant revelation. Oh, here's Edward with the tea."

Conversation ceased as the footman set a silver tray on the sofa table. Dorinda Smythe poured tea into translucent silver-rimmed cups. She was going against her own words and acting as though it were a social call, but perhaps she had recognized the advantage of a distraction.

"It was early in December," she said, when the footman had withdrawn, settling back on the sofa with a teacup carefully balanced in her steady hands. "I'd come up to London with Roger to do some last-minute shopping for Christmas while he attended to legal business. I encountered Maria Worcester in Fortnum's and she informed me—in that odious way one's supposed friends can talk about one's husband—that she'd heard Roger was seen outside a house in Mayfair with a quite lovely fair-haired woman." Dorinda took a sip of tea. Her hands were still steady but her knuckles were white round the delicate handle of the cup. "I should probably have left it there. A wise wife would have. But I wanted to know. So I made some inquiries. I learned what sort of a house it was. I couldn't go there myself, obviously. So I engaged a Bow Street runner to investigate for me in his spare time." She met Mélanie's gaze. "Not the runner you work with, I think. But it did occur to me that word of the investigation was likely to get back to your friend now, and then to you. Yet another reason it seemed best for me to speak with you. In any event, this runner—Jenkins is his name—learned the young woman in question was named Miranda Spencer. From his description, I began to have suspicions. Jenkins told me Miranda visited rooms in Fenchurch Street regularly. So I had him send word to me the next time she did so. For all my suspicions, until I actually called at those rooms, a part of me couldn't believe it really was Miranda."

"It must have been a shock," Mélanie said.

Dorinda leaned forwards to refill the teacups, back straight, mouth taut. "From what Jenkins said, Miranda obviously charmed the people at the Barque of Frailty. Miranda charmed people her whole life. It's my first memory of her. Miranda with jam and biscuit crumbs on her face charming everyone at a garden fête while I got scolded for having a stain on my frock." She set the teapot down precisely on its lace cloth. "My mother is Sir George Dormer's younger sister. My father was a soldier. He was gone most of the time. I was the third of eight children. Sir George and Lady Dormer took me in when I was eight. It was kind of them." She picked up a wedge of lemon and squeezed it into her tea. "That was what I was told growing up, again and again."

"It's not easy to be a charity case," Mélanie said. She knew such arrangements were not uncommon, wealthier relatives taking in a niece or nephew whose parents were still living, but she couldn't but think of it as barbaric.

Dorinda met her gaze. "No. The idea was that Miranda and I would play together. Which we did. But I don't think Miranda wanted another sister. One can't blame her. A lot of children don't want siblings, and I wasn't even her real sibling. She and her sister Elinor weren't that close as it was, but Elinor was three years older. Miranda and I shared a nursery, but the toys were hers. I grew up wearing her cast-off frocks." She smoothed the skirt of her gown. "I was always trying to behave myself, so I wouldn't get in trouble and be sent home, and Miranda was always up to something."

"She was restless in her life," Cordelia said.

Dorinda raised a brow. "Some of us never had the luxury of being restless. I'd have gone mad, I think, if it hadn't been for Roger."

"Your husband," Mélanie said. John Smythe's brother. Miranda Dormer's lover, according to Dorinda.

"He wasn't my husband then." Dorinda's hands curled round her cup. "He was Lord Beverston's second son. One of the crowd of children who played with the Dormer children. We both liked books better than games, so we'd sit and talk while the others were playing."

"You must have been lonely when he was away at school," Cordelia said.

"Dreadfully. I lived for the holidays when he'd come back. I never thought much of the future, never expected anything, until —" Dorinda's fingers locked together in her lap. "I overheard Lady Beverston telling my aunt that it might be advisable to make sure I didn't have any unrealistic expectations when it came to Roger." Her mouth tightened. "It actually took me a moment to understand what those expectations might be. Until then I'd thought of him as my friend. My one friend. A friend is a rare and precious thing, so I won't say 'nothing more', but I hadn't considered—"

Yet once she had realized people were thinking of her and Roger as a couple, even in a negative sense, she had realized her own attraction to him. She didn't say so, but her face betrayed as much. Her careful poise cracked to reveal both the wonder and the embarrassment of her girlhood discovery.

"I couldn't think how I was to face Roger when he returned from Oxford for the Christmas holidays. I both wanted to see him and was terrified to do so. But as it turns out, I needn't have worried. He walked into the Dormers' drawing room for their Christmas party and saw Miranda standing beneath a pine garland and had eyes for no one else. I saw the whole thing happen."

The man she had just realized she loved, realizing he loved the cousin she was constantly being measured against. No wonder Dorinda Smythe was bitter.

"He couldn't take his eyes off her all night," Dorinda said. "He and I scarcely spoke, but if I'd had any doubts, when we met the next day he confessed the whole to me. How he felt he'd never seen Miranda before. How he could scarcely imagine how he could fall in love so quickly. I listened, of course."

"That must have been painful," Mélanie said.

She shrugged, shoulders hunched. "It's what a friend does. And we were friends, after all. Before anything else. We weren't anything else at all. Save in other people's imaginations." Dorinda picked up the spoon and stirred her tea, though she had added no more lemon. "He asked me how Miranda felt. And I couldn't honestly tell. She flirted with him. But Miranda flirted with a lot of gentlemen. She liked the attention. She seemed happy with Roger, but not more so than with other gentlemen. I asked her about it once, and she said she had no thought of marriage. She was determined to enjoy herself first. I said if she didn't have a partiality for Roger, she should indicate as much. That he loved her desperately and it wasn't fair to keep him hanging. She just laughed and said at Roger's age he couldn't know the meaning of love." The fabric of Dorinda's sleeve pulled taut as her fingers curled inwards. "I asked her if she did."

"What did she say?" Mélanie asked.

"That she thought perhaps she might. But it was too early to be sure. She wouldn't say if it was Roger. But I don't think it was." Dorinda spread her fingers in her lap, as though willing them to unclench. "We went on like that all winter. Roger writing letters from Oxford, asking after Miranda. Through the Easter holidays. Watching Roger watch Miranda. Watching her dance with him. Letting him bring her a glass of champagne or fetch her fan or her shawl. Giving him just enough encouragement to keep him glued to the flounce of her gown. Not that I'm sure he'd have unglued himself even if she'd stopped talking to him. But if she knew she didn't want him herself she could at least have tried, instead of crooking her little finger whenever it amused her. It was worse that summer. Roger home. The rounds of parties. Country society—the only society I really knew at that point—where one sees the same people five nights a week at various engagements. Roger and I still went for walks or sat sketching, but he talked about Miranda the whole time."

"When you loved him yourself," Mélanie said. It was a bold move, but she sensed she could catch Dorinda off guard. Which could be vital in interrogating a suspect.

Dorinda's gaze widened and locked on Mélanie's own. The gaze of a girl in her late teens, set in the controlled, plucked, delicately rouged face of a fashionable matron. "He was my friend. I was shocked to hear Lady Beverston suggest there could be more between us."

"Yes. People are often shocked when friendship turns to love."

Dorinda glanced away. "I never hoped—I never had a chance to hope. I'd no sooner had the idea put in my head than I realized he was head over heels in love with my cousin." Her fingers curled inwards again. "But Miranda could have had a care for my feelings as well as Roger's."

"Perhaps she didn't realize," Cordelia said.

"She couldn't have failed—No, that's not true. Miranda was always self-absorbed. She'd promise me something—to help me with sums, to lend me a pair of earrings—and then not do it. Eventually I realized she didn't mean to go back on her word, she just completely forgot." Dorinda pushed a strand that had somehow escaped her carefully coiffed hair back into its pins. "I knew all that summer that Miranda was going to break Roger's heart. I just didn't know how. Two weeks after he went to London to study at one of the Inns of the Court, she disappeared."

"You didn't know where she'd gone?" Malcolm asked.

"Is that so hard to believe? We may have been raised like

sisters, but we'd never been the sort for confidences. Some sisters aren't."

"Quite. But you're obviously a perceptive woman."

Dorinda looked at her hands. "I suspected there was a man. Not Roger. I hadn't suspected for long, actually. But there was that remark about perhaps understanding love. For the month before she disappeared, there was an air of suppressed excitement about her. I caught her tucking a paper into her bodice once or twice. And once, I'm quite sure she slipped out of the house after everyone was abed. I heard a creak and peeped out my door to see her vanishing down the servants' stairs. When she disappeared, I suspected she'd run off with this man. Knowing Miranda, I kept expecting her to return with a wedding ring on her finger, saying what a lark it had been to go to Gretna Green, and charm everyone into offering felicitations and heaping wedding presents on her." Dorinda bit her finger. For the first time something that might have been guilt flashed in her eyes. "Even when Uncle George returned from London and told us we weren't to speak of Miranda again, I didn't know whom she might have run off with. Roger came home when he heard. He was beside himself. He searched for her, but he couldn't find her. Six months later, he asked me to marry him."

"That must have been—" Cordelia hesitated.

"The summit of all I wanted?" Dorinda turned her cup on its saucer. "In a way. In that I became Roger's wife. He told me he knew we'd deal well together. That I'd always been his best friend and always would be. He didn't add that I was Miranda's cousin, and by marrying me he could attempt to make it up to Miranda, even though he couldn't find her, but I knew that was part of it. Perhaps I should have taken pity on him and turned him down. But I didn't. And so I got the man I wanted, and I went from being a poor relation to being the wife of a baron's son with a comfortable fortune." She gave a tight smile, her eyes bleak. "I should be grateful. Just as I should have been grateful as a girl in the Dormer nursery. And I have far more now than I did then, in terms of creature comforts. But it's an odd thing. Having the man one wanted—or rather, being married to him—and knowing one doesn't have him at all. When we were growing up, I felt I could talk to Roger about anything. Since we've been married, it seems all we talk about is the household, or social engagements, or our little girl. At times, I'd find myself thinking Miranda had won. I know that must sound monstrous, given what's happened to her, but for the longest time I was convinced she'd somehow managed to land in an enviable situation. She always wanted to break free of Surrey. I pictured her married to a poet, or possibly some rich man's mistress. Not—" Dorinda gripped her hands together.

"What did she say when you saw her?" Mélanie asked.

"She denied she was Roger's mistress." Dorinda gave a hard laugh. "Just like childhood. Miranda could claim she hadn't broken Lady Dormer's Sèvres vase with shards of porcelain all over her hands and the most earnest look in her gaze. And nine times out of ten, people believed her. But not me. I reminded her of that. I accused her of having run off with Roger in the first place. Miranda simply said, did I know Roger so little I believed he would abandon a woman and child? Even in my anger, I realized she was right. Roger would never behave so dishonorably. That was when Miranda told me about John." She set down her teacup as though it burned her. "Diana had a bruise on her throat once. She'd hidden it with a fichu, but it slipped, and I saw. I asked about it, and she said she'd slipped getting out of the bath, though I couldn't quite imagine how that could leave a bruise in that place. Then, a few months later, she had a mark on her jaw she'd tried to cover up with powder. Diana and I have never been particularly close, though we've known each other since we were children. She was Elinor's friend, and not an easy person to get close to. Which I suppose I'm not either. But when I saw the second mark, I asked her straight out if John did it, and if she needed help. She just told me not to be silly. I wish now that I'd said something to Roger. Until I heard Miranda's story, I didn't have the least idea how bad it must have been. Miranda was afraid of John. And Miranda had never seemed afraid of anything."

"You hadn't ever suspected about her and John?" Mélanie asked.

Dorinda shook her head. "I suspected there was a man, but John, of all people—how in God's name could he have bewitched her when Roger was right there, desperately in love with her and offering her marriage—"

"Sometimes danger and risk can be the lure," Cordelia said in a quiet voice.

Dorinda met Cordelia's gaze, no doubt recalling that Cordelia was no stranger to risk and scandal. "Yes, but John never seemed—though I suppose he was dangerous, but I can't imagine Miranda knew he was violent when she left with him." Dorinda reached for her teacup. "I fear my sympathy turned to anger when I thought of how she'd ignored Roger for John, only to turn to Roger now. I accused her of trying to take my husband. I called her a lot of unfortunate names. Miranda just repeated that she wasn't Roger's mistress. I said, did she take me for a fool, and if she wasn't his mistress why on earth was he visiting her? Miranda said she couldn't explain now. In just that high-handed way she'd talked since we were in the nursery. She said that if I really appreciated Roger, I'd try to focus on salvaging my marriage. I said she was a fine one to talk about appreciating Roger—or anyone else, for that matter. I stormed out. So you could say I had an excellent motive to kill her."

Dorinda drew a harsh breath and put a fist to her mouth. "I can't believe she's gone."

CHAPTER 24

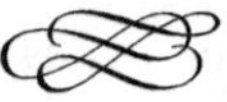

MALCOLM AND HARRY found Hugh Derenvil in Hyde Park, on the banks of the Serpentine, beneath a tangle of leafless branches, hands jammed in the pockets of his greatcoat, gaze on the gray water as it swirled in the wind. He was a tall man with regular features and fair hair. His face was usually set in serious lines, but not in the sort of frowning concentration that now suffused it.

He looked up at their approach. Recognition and surprise jumped in his blue eyes, but not fear. "Rannoch. Davenport. I didn't realize you were back in London."

"We just arrived," Malcolm said. "A rather unexpected visit."

Derenvil nodded. "I hope this means you'll be back in the House. I may not agree with your speeches, but I've missed them. They're certainly livelier and more thought-provoking than many."

"I could say the same for yours."

Derenvil met Malcolm's gaze for a moment and nodded. "Sorry, I'm a bit distracted."

Malcolm considered the other man. This was hardly the first time he'd interrogated someone he knew and liked in the course of an investigation. "It's always a shock, losing someone one's been close to."

Derenvil's gaze jerked to his face.

"We know about your relationship with Miranda Spencer," Malcolm said. "We've just spoken with Lord Beverston."

Derenvil's gaze stayed fastened on Malcolm's face as the implications sank in. "This is one of your investigations."

"It appears to be."

"But I thought Carfax—"

"Not necessarily."

He expected fear to leap in Derenvil's eyes at being a suspect, but instead his face twisted. "So, whoever killed her may still—dear God." He pulled his beaver hat from his head, pushed his dark blond hair back from his forehead, replaced his hat. "I'm not the sort—" He glanced away. "I don't spend time, as a rule, in places like the Barque of Frailty. I expect a lot of men say that, but—"

"Actually," Harry said, "some men would boast about it. Not to their credit."

A muscle flexed beside Derenvil's jaw. "I was out one evening with Hewitt and Cooperthwaite. We were going to go to White's, but Hewitt wanted to avoid his father, so we ended up in a coffeehouse and shared a bottle of claret. Well, several, actually. Then Hewitt said something about convivial company, and the next thing I knew we were in Mrs. Hartley's sitting room, and Miranda walked over to me while I was still taking in the sort of establishment we were actually in." He looked from Malcolm to Harry. "I don't suppose that sounds very believable."

"Actually," Harry said, "it sounds like a story no one would make up."

Derenvil gave a twisted smile that didn't reach his eyes. "I didn't—I knew what I was doing. And I wanted to do it. Wanted Miranda. But from the first, from that first moment she came up to me in the salon, before anything else—transpired—between us, she was someone I could talk to." He drew a breath. "I find that surprisingly rare."

"You aren't the only one," Malcolm said.

Derenvil met his gaze for a moment. "I saw you saying goodbye to Mrs. Rannoch at the Duchess of Richmond's ball. I didn't have anyone to say goodbye to. Not then. I was chiefly conscious of relief that the battle we'd been waiting for was finally here. Not that I had any illusions it would be easy. But after the Peninsula, I thought I knew what to expect."

"I think a lot of us felt that way," Harry said in a quiet voice.

Derenvil met his gaze, and for a moment what passed between them was something Malcolm knew even he couldn't fully understand, for all he'd been on the field at Waterloo. "And of course, in the end it was like nothing I'd ever experienced," Derenvil said. "I was in Edward Somerset's brigade."

Malcolm remembered carrying a message from Wellington to Somerset late in the battle, and finding Somerset beside the road with only two squadrons. When Malcolm asked where his brigade was, Somerset had said simply, "Here."

"The cavalry charge," Derenvil said. "I'd never been in anything like it. The excitement. Everyone was drunk on it. We took an eagle. But then we were surrounded. I'd never experienced sheer chaos until then. I remember running my sword through the throat of a young Frenchman who couldn't have been more than sixteen. Seeing two lads I'd gone to Harrow with fall to bayonet thrusts. I still can't remember the last part. How I was wounded myself. I spent the rest of the battle with my face in the mud, unconscious most of the time, two dead comrades and a dead horse on top of me. That's the only way I survived."

Harry put out a hand, a rare gesture for him.

"I don't mean to exaggerate my own situation," Derenvil said. "You were wounded yourself. Many of my comrades who survived lost limbs. I was comparatively fortunate. Once my wounds had healed, one could scarcely tell I'd been in battle at all."

"Hard, that," Harry said. "Sometimes it makes others forget."

Derenvil nodded. "It was easier in Paris, somehow. Surrounded by others who'd been through the same thing. I could never forget, but it was easier to live with the memories. Then I sold out and came home. I thought the distance would be good. I took rooms in London, stood for Parliament, visited my parents in the country. Went to my sister's come-out. Danced with her friends. People didn't talk about Waterloo so much. Or if they did, it was as a grand and glorious memory. Some people seemed to forget I'd ever even been in the army. It seemed to me that should make it easier. And during the day I could focus on my work. But alone at night I'd find myself dwelling on the memories. Hard to sleep when one fears what one will see in dreams."

"Odd," Harry said, "when one's survived battle, to fear sleep. But I know precisely what you mean."

Derenvil met his gaze again in understanding. "Brandy helps at times. So does staying busy. I talked a bit to other chaps who'd been at Waterloo, but we began to scatter. After a time, it starts to seem silly for the ex-military men to spend entertainments talking together in the library. I tried to get on with my life." He looked from Harry to Malcolm. "I'm betrothed. I don't know that you know that. It's since you left Britain."

"Yes. I didn't know. But Davenport did." Malcolm paused. Under the circumstances, it hardly made sense to offer his felicitations.

"Caroline is—I'm beyond fortunate to have won her. In fact, when she first agreed to my suit, I went about in a daze for several hours, sure I'd imagined it. She's beautiful. She's accomplished. She's kind. I could see a life with her from almost the moment we met. The sort of life I'd been fighting for, really." He looked from Malcolm to Harry. "Caroline also has thirty thousand pounds in the funds and her father is influential in Tory politics. I'm well aware of what people are saying about that. I imagine you won't believe me if I say I love her."

"I don't know about that," Harry said. "Love can come in many forms. What some call love others might not recognize as it."

"I thought marriage would change things," Derenvil said. "Be a way to move forwards. How could the past haunt me when I was building a new life with Caro? I'm always happy when I'm with her. But it's like sitting in my grandmother's drawing room enjoying tea and jam tarts and being terrified the whole time I'd break a cup or drop crumbs on the floor. I can't believe my happiness is real."

"I know a bit about that," Harry said. "Quite a lot, actually. Though it was before I was a soldier."

Derenvil regarded him for a moment. He must know about Harry and Cordelia's past. "I've always been sure of myself when it comes to speaking. At Harrow. At Cambridge. In the House. With Caro, I'm never sure what to say. I feel as though I'm walking on eggshells. I haven't the least idea why she chose me."

"Perhaps because she's fond of you," Malcolm said. Sympathy could be a good way to draw a suspect out, but in truth he felt more sympathy for Derenvil than he'd have anticipated when he and Harry set out to find the other man.

"She can obviously tolerate me or she wouldn't have accepted me. At one point, I think, I hoped we could share more."

"Have you thought about talking to her about your time at Waterloo?" Harry asked.

Derenvil stared at him as though he'd suggested he take Lady Caroline into White's, or to look at horses at Tattersalls, or something else equally unthinkable for a wellborn lady. "Good God, Davenport, I couldn't. Caro's had the most sheltered upbringing. She could scarcely imagine even a fistfight, let alone—" He shook his head. "I thought I'd be able to move beyond that past. Sometimes I'd feel it wash over me and come back to the present to find Caroline pouring me a cup of tea, or offering me a plate of cakes, or asking if I wanted to see the new comedy at Drury Lane. It all seemed so completely pointless—" He shook his head.

"My wife nursed soldiers at Waterloo," Harry said. "So did Mélanie Rannoch. They saw their own horrors. It made it easier, I think, afterwards, for all of us to move forwards together."

Malcolm cast a quick glance at Harry. They'd never discussed their wives' response to Waterloo. They'd never really discussed their own, save in the most oblique terms.

Derenvil nodded. "I don't think Caroline's ever been close to anything so horrible. I did hope that one day she would take an interest in my work. Would take an interest in things beyond my work. But she's never given any indication that she feels anything —anything stronger. Certainly not that she'd welcome—"

"Amorous advances?" Harry said.

Derenvil colored. "One doesn't—I would never—"

"You save that for girls like Miranda Spencer?"

"Damn it, Davenport, it's not the same."

"No." Harry's gaze had the hardness of a glass that reflects back uncompromising truth. "Lady Caroline has agreed to be your wife and your partner in life. Mrs. Spencer was paid to accept your attentions because she had no other options in life."

"I'm human. I don't deny the appeal of all Miranda could offer."

"It can be an escape," Malcolm said. "When demons keep one from sleeping." An escape he'd sought with his own wife, though he'd always balked at the idea that he was using her in that way.

He expected Derenvil to shy away, but the other man nodded. "In truth, I slept better in Miranda's bed than I had in months. Years. But not just because of—of our intimacy. I could talk to her. She never offered any judgment. She seemed genuinely interested. Talking to her—meant a great deal to me. She'd even ask me questions. I found myself telling her about the bills I'm trying to steer through Parliament. I even read her some of my speeches and she made suggestions."

"I do the same thing with my wife," Malcolm said.

Derenvil stared at him. "Your wife is a remarkable woman. Rannoch. But it's hardly the same—"

"Isn't it? It's talking through ideas, getting advice, planning strategy. Sharing one of the most important parts of one's life. Difficult for a woman to be a politician's wife without sharing that. Lady Caroline is the daughter of a politician. I don't know her well, but I would think it's in her blood."

"Caroline's father isn't the sort to share such things with his daughter. Caro has been very sheltered. It's not the upbringing I'd want—"

"For your own daughters?" Harry asked.

Surprise shot through the fog of self-disgust and regret in Derenvil's gaze. "No," he said. "It's not what I'd hope for my daughters. Should I be fortunate enough to have them."

"Did you talk to Mrs. Spencer about more than politics?" Harry asked.

"You mean did I talk to her about the war? About Waterloo?" Derenvil squeezed his eyes shut. "I'd never have thought to. But I woke one night in her bed, sweat-drenched, screaming like a frightened child—If I'd had my wits about me I'd have taken myself off at once. But before I'd even recalled where I was, she was putting a cold cloth on my head and asking me if I'd been in the war." He hesitated a moment, gaze lost in the past. "I said things to her I've never said to another living person."

"It must have been a great relief," Malcolm said.

"So often since, I've asked myself why. Why I could talk to her, when she hadn't been anywhere near Waterloo. Why she could seem to understand so instinctively."

"Did Mrs. Spencer talk to you about her past?" Malcolm asked.

Derenvil shook his head. "Very little. Save to indicate she preferred not to dwell on it. It did occur to me that she'd obviously been educated."

"She had an upbringing very much like that of your fiancée," Malcolm said.

Derenvil's eyes widened. "They're not—"

"Their lives have gone in different directions," Harry said.

"They began in much the same way. Though arguably, by the time you met her, Mrs. Spencer was less sheltered."

Derenvil frowned. "Once she said she'd come to realize that one had to accept the past. Not to be happy with it, but to understand that it didn't define the future. That one had to move on. I did wonder—what had brought her to the Barque of Frailty. But I didn't like to ask. I confess I talked about myself more than I asked questions of her." He looked at Malcolm for a moment. "Do you know—had she—"

"She ran from her family with a man who expressed himself through violence," Malcolm said. "She may not have been through battle, but she must have had more than her share of demons to face at night."

Derenvil's face twisted. "I wish—but when I learned truths about her, they were of a very different sort."

"It must have been a great shock," Malcolm said. "To realize she had been set to gather information on you."

Derenvil's gaze jerked to Malcolm's. For a moment, his gaze blazed with stark anger, an anger that took Malcolm back to the moment he had punched a street lamp, to the rage that had clouded his vision when he confronted Mélanie in a dusty theatre.

"I couldn't believe it." Derenvil's voice was low and harsh, the words seemingly torn from his throat. "I heard what Beverston was saying. I could guess where he'd got the information, but I simply couldn't credit that Miranda would have done that. Listened to my thoughts, held me through my nightmares, encouraged me to say more, and all the while—"

"It's painful," Malcolm said. "Particularly when one has a hard time making confidences in any case." He could feel Harry's gaze on him, but he didn't risk a glance at his friend.

"I'd never—" Derenvil glanced away, gaze on the roiling water. "I said things to Miranda I'd never said to anyone else. I know I was betraying Caroline, but it never felt cheap and sordid. I never doubted what was between us was real."

"It was real," Harry said. "Even if it didn't mean what you thought it did. And you don't know that Mrs. Spencer's feelings were all feigned."

Derenvil stared at him. "She was being paid by Beverston—"

"You were paying her to begin with," Harry said.

Derenvil's hands curled into fists. "I never thought to find myself the subject of blackmail. I told Beverston he could tell whom he liked whatever he liked about my past. I knew it probably meant I'd lose Caroline. Probably does mean I'll lose her. Though to own the truth, the thought of her not being upset enough to call off our betrothal was almost worse. I knew her father could end my prospects for advancement in the party. But chiefly I was aware that I'd been a fool. And that if I let Beverston make me destroy my integrity I'd never forgive myself. I could scarcely see when I walked away, I was so angry."

"Did you see Mrs. Spencer again?" Malcolm asked.

Derenvil's gaze shot to his face. "Didn't you know? I thought that was why you came to find me. I confronted Miranda the night she died."

"You were at the Barque of Frailty?" Malcolm could scarcely keep the surprise from his voice.

"Yes. The footmen let me in, and I went right upstairs. I found her alone in her bedchamber."

"What time was it?" Malcolm asked.

"Past midnight. Just. I heard the clock striking twelve-fifteen as I climbed the stairs."

"Did you see Carfax?" Harry asked.

Derenvil shook his head. "Only Miranda. I realized I might find her with a man, and to own the truth, I was so angry I didn't care, but she was quite alone. She was standing by a shelf of books holding a paper, with an odd expression on her face. Surprise, and maybe hurt as well. But as soon as she looked up and met my gaze, I think she knew I'd learned the truth. I—wasn't kind."

"Did you—" Malcolm hesitated.

"What? Strike her? No, of course not. But I called her names I thought would never cross my lips when it came to a woman. She just stood there and took everything I said. I'd never seen her face so drained of color. Finally, when I stopped my rant, she just said she could make no excuse for herself, but that she owed Lord Beverston more than I could possibly understand. I said, 'Including being completely faithless?' And she said she'd lost the luxury of being able to think about being a good person a long time ago. I said, 'Was that really a luxury?' And she said, with the life I lived, could I really know? I just stared at her. I felt as though I was looking at a stranger."

For days after he'd learned the truth about Mélanie, Malcolm would glance at his wife's familiar features and find himself thinking the same thing. "And then?" he asked.

"I turned on my heel and stormed from her room and down the backstairs. That was the last moment I saw her." He drew a sharp breath.

"You didn't see Carfax?" Harry asked.

Derenvil shook his head. "I didn't see anyone."

Which meant Carfax had left Miranda's room and returned—either to kill her or to find her dead.

"This paper she was holding when you came in," Malcolm said. "Do you have any idea what it was?"

"No. It seemed to be a sheet of notepaper. I didn't give much mind to it, but when we were quarreling—when I was calling her names—Miranda looked down at it and said people could disappoint you. That someone had just disappointed her." Beverston frowned, as though picturing the scene. "There was an open book next to her. I had the sense she'd taken the note from the book. Perhaps a letter from someone from her past that she'd kept hidden there? She was still holding it when I left."

"Can anyone vouch for your timing?" Malcolm asked.

"The footman on duty, if he remembers letting me in. No one saw me leave."

"Where did you go after you left?"

"I walked the streets for hours. Miranda's words kept repeating in my head. In particular, what her life had been as opposed to mine. I can't say I forgave her, but my perspective shifted. I wanted to—talk to her again. And now, of course, I'll never be able to do so."

Loss shone from his eyes. Malcolm had no doubt that sense of loss was real. But Derenvil wouldn't be the first killer to feel a sense of loss at the realization that he'd never see his victim again.

Derenvil met Malcolm's gaze. "You're thinking I don't have an alibi, aren't you? That there's nothing to prove I didn't kill Miranda when I confronted her. And it's true there's no proof. A week ago, I think I'd have asked how you could think such a thing of me. But learning the truth about Miranda destroyed my faith in everything."

CHAPTER 25

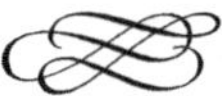

HARRY AND MALCOLM walked from Hyde Park to Brooks's, where, thanks to a communication from Rupert, they suspected they could find Matthew Trenor. They covered most of the ground in silence, gazes on the hard path through the park or the paving stones along the street. But as they turned into St. James's Street, Harry said, still with his gaze fixed ahead, "No sense pretending we'll ever forget. And I'll own to the occasional nightmare. More than occasional, at first. But recovering from my wounds to find Cordy at my bedside, reconciling with her right after the battle—that changed things. God knows what a wreck I'd be otherwise."

Malcolm nodded. "Mel has nightmares. She has as long as I've known her." She'd had the first one in the Cantabrian Mountains when they'd just met. He still remembered how stiff and awkward he'd felt holding her. "From losing her family, I thought. Which was true, though not in quite the way I thought it was. She doesn't have them as often now. But they haven't gone away."

"I don't suspect they will," Harry said. "Just get easier to put up with."

Malcolm turned, met his friend's gaze, and nodded.

The yellow brick and Portland stone of Brooks's were

suddenly before them. Once Malcolm had avoided it as a bastion of the establishment, even if it was a Whig bastion. But since he'd gone into Parliament, it had become a place he met to strategize with colleagues, to commiserate, or even occasionally celebrate. And if he preferred such meetings in Berkeley Square, where Mel could be present, he could not deny the bittersweet bite of the memories as he stepped beneath the fanlight.

"Rannoch. You back?" Henry Brougham's voice stopped them at the base of the stairs.

"Temporarily," Malcolm said.

"Pity. We need all the sanity we can get." Brougham paused to clap a hand on Malcolm's shoulder.

"A number of people, including several I used to work for, have been known to call my speeches mad."

"Precisely why we need you, old fellow." Brougham nodded to Harry. "Are you looking for someone?"

"Matthew Trenor."

Brougham's eyes narrowed. "Oh, Christ. You're here about the Carfax business."

"Do you have reason to think Trenor was connected to it?" Harry asked.

"Only that I heard rumors he was there that night. Thank God I wasn't. Never been there at all, as it happens. Think I saw him about somewhere. Try the small drawing room."

They did indeed find Matthew Trenor in the small drawing room, and alone, as luck would have it, a glass of claret at his elbow, the *Morning Chronicle* spread before him. He looked up at their entrance, his gaze narrowing with understanding but not alarm. "I was wondering when you'd seek me out."

"How did you know?"

"You're very thorough, Rannoch. I assume eventually you and Davenport will talk with everyone connected to events at the Barque of Frailty. Or your wives will, though this may be a particularly difficult investigation for them to undertake. Besides, my brother mentioned he'd seen you, though he was a bit vague about the circumstances."

Malcolm sent silent thanks to Alexander Trenor. Matthew Trenor was not very like his brother. Fair-haired where Sandy was dark, solidly built where Sandy was lanky, assured where Sandy had a boy's puppyish awkwardness. Matthew Trenor and Malcolm had overlapped briefly as attachés in Paris. Trenor had always struck Malcolm as diligent and engaged with the work he was doing. Which was more than could be said for a number of diplomats.

Malcolm dropped into a chair opposite Trenor. The sort of leather-covered, deeply cushioned chair designed to invite sporting talk over a glass of port rather than an interrogation about a murder. "You knew Miranda Spencer," Malcolm said.

"I knew her." Matthew Trenor's hand tightened round his glass. "I liked her." He picked up the glass, as though determined to keep his hand steady, and took a sip. "It's difficult to tell for a certainty with a woman in her profession, but I think she liked me too."

Harry moved to a chair beside Malcolm. "According to one of her friends at the Barque of Frailty, she had marks on her wrists after having spent time with you."

Trenor's gaze moved from Malcolm to Harry. His mouth was still a tight line, but it held faint amusement. "My dear Davenport. My dear Rannoch. Surely I don't have to explain to either of you that there could be reasons for a woman—or a man, for that matter—to have such marks after an amorous interlude without anything occurring that either participant found disagreeable."

Certain things Mélanie had told him about her encounter with Julien St. Juste shot through Malcolm's memory. Six years of marriage in which physical intimacy had come more easily to them than any other sort of intimacy, and there were still things about his wife's tastes that could surprise him. "Tell us about the night Mrs. Spencer was killed," Malcolm said.

Trenor took another drink of claret. "I didn't—spend time with Miranda that night. I had gone there hoping to do so, but I arrived to find she was already engaged. With Lord Carfax. Which I confess startled me."

"It startled me as well," Malcolm said.

Trenor settled back in his chair and crossed his legs. "I don't know Carfax anything like as well as you do. But given the general opinion about him and Lady Carfax, it did occur to me to wonder if he was there in search of information."

"Did you have any reason to think Mrs. Spencer would have information Carfax might want?" Harry asked.

"No," Trenor said, with every appearance of not having the least idea Miranda Spencer had been an agent for Lord Beverston. "But given the sort of men who frequent the Barque of Frailty, I imagine there could be any number of reasons Carfax would have found her a useful source of information. I might even have asked her." His face clouded. "Had I seen her again."

"You stayed at the Barque of Frailty that night," Malcolm said.

"Oh, yes. I spent a convivial couple of hours with another of the girls. Charity Wentworth." He raised a brow. "Shocked? You knew I frequented the Barque of Frailty. I liked Miranda, but I was hardly in an exclusive relationship with her. I'm not married. I'm a busy man. I find an establishment such as the Barque of Frailty suits my needs better than keeping a mistress."

"How you arrange your life is your own business, Trenor," Malcolm said. "Were you with Miss Wentworth until you learned of Mrs. Spencer's death?"

Remembered horror shot through Trenor's tightly controlled expression. "No, I'd gone to one of the sitting rooms for a smoke. I heard a scream. Ran into the passage. The screams were coming from Miranda's room. I ran straight down and stopped in the doorway, staring at her. I dropped to my knees. "

"What did you see?" Malcolm asked.

"Miranda lying on the bed. I couldn't take my eyes off her."

Trenor passed a hand over his eyes. "I didn't even notice Carfax at first. He was off to one side, talking to Mrs. Hartley. I think Daisy Singleton was the one who screamed. She was crying." Trenor took a drink of claret. "I confess I started to cry myself. Then Mrs. Hartley said Bow Street were on their way and asked us all to wait downstairs. The footmen poured the liquor plentifully, which I availed myself of. Eventually, a constable came in and took down our names and directions and told us we could go home. I was a bit surprised not to be questioned more fully, until the next day when I heard they'd arrested Carfax." Trenor looked from Malcolm to Harry. "You don't think he did it?"

"Do you?" Malcolm asked.

Trenor turned his glass in his hand. "If so, he's a remarkably cool customer. But then, I suppose he is in any case. He was certainly composed that night. Though also shaken, I think."

"Did Mrs. Spencer ever talk to you about her past? "Malcolm asked.

Trenor raised a brow. "Certainly not. Nor did I talk to her of mine, if it comes to that. We had more—present—matters to engage us. I assumed there was a sad story that had led to her presence at the Barque of Frailty, but it wasn't my place to ask, and Miranda wasn't the sort to dwell on the past or to ask for sympathy."

"Did anything she said lead you to think she feared anyone?" Harry asked.

"Feared?" Trenor frowned, then shook his head. "No. But there was one odd thing. I actually learned it before I learned Miranda had been killed. Charity told me a woman had been to the kitchens to visit Miranda the previous day. Apparently she claimed to be an errand girl, but from the length of her conversation with Miranda, everyone was convinced she wasn't. Miranda wouldn't talk about it, so naturally the whole house was speculating. It may have nothing to do with Miranda's murder, of course. But it is interesting it happened just the day before."

"Yes," Malcolm said. "So it is."

LAURA ACCEPTED LADY FRANCES's coachman's hand and descended from the elegant barouche in South Audley Street. Mostly her pregnancy didn't impede her, but there was no denying climbing in and out of carriages was more awkward than it had once been. When she'd collected Emily from Frances's to visit her family, she could not deny her relief that Frances had insisted she take the carriage. Far more comfortable than a hackney. It was even more of a relief now as they returned to Frances's after a comforting afternoon with her father, stepmother, and half-siblings.

Emily had already scrambled up the steps of Frances's house. South Audley Street was quiet in the middle of the afternoon, with much of the beau monde still in the country. Two ladies were descending from a carriage at the corner and a gentleman was walking down the street towards them, but no one she knew. No need to decide whether to raise a hand in greeting or make it easy for them by pretending not to see them. Laura nodded to the coachman and moved to the steps. The footman was already opening the door.

"Lady Tarrington."

Laura paused, one hand on the area railing, and turned. It was the man who had been walking down South Audley Street. Middle years, impeccably tailored coat, highly polished boots, sandy hair showing beneath his curly-brimmed beaver, level gaze. She was quite sure she had never met him.

"You're correct," he said, a trace of amusement in his voice. "We have not been introduced. But you might say I'm one of your former employers."

Laura's hand tightened on the hard metal of the railing. She could sweep away and refuse to speak with him. Satisfying, in a number of ways. But it would not give her any new information.

She turned to her daughter. "Run inside, darling. Tell Aunt Frances I'll be there presently."

Emily looked at her for a moment, then, as Laura smiled with reassurance, ran into the house. The footman met Laura's gaze, and at her nod, closed the door.

"You're a wise woman, Lady Tarrington," the man said.

"I'm not at all sure about that. But I am curious. However, you have the advantage of me. Whom do I have the pleasure of addressing?"

"My name is Brandon."

"Sir Lucius Brandon." She had heard the name from Trenchard. He hadn't mentioned names often, but she'd made careful note when he did. Even then, she'd known knowledge was power.

"The same." He regarded her for a moment. Appraising her, she thought, not as a woman but as an agent. "You may not credit this, Lady Tarrington, but we still take an interest in your welfare."

"Oh, I credit it. But not a disinterested interest."

"You did able work for us. We haven't forgot that. We could hardly fail to be concerned that you've allied yourself with a very dangerous man."

"My dear Sir Lucius. Coming from anyone associated with the League, the word 'dangerous' quite loses its sting."

"That's understandable. But I don't think you can have the least notion of what O'Roarke is involved in."

"Coming from the League, I also find that highly humorous." Though slightly less humorous than she would have done before her realization last night that Raoul was keeping something from her.

"I can see how he could seem a haven. But he won't put you before his work, you know. He's never put anyone before his work."

"I wouldn't ask him to." She wasn't going to be drawn into a debate, but she wasn't sure it was true Raoul had never put anyone before his work.

"We could protect you. And your children. It may seem impossible, but we could arrange things so you could step back into your place in society."

Laura gave an unfeigned laugh. "My dear sir. If you imagine I care a damn for my place in society, you know me even less well than I'd have thought."

Brandon's eyes narrowed, the look of one recalibrating. "If O'Roarke means so much to you, we could offer him protection as well."

"The man you've been trying to have killed?"

"You must realize we aren't above making tactical changes. You've always struck me as a pragmatist. Surely you can see the advantages of a pragmatic alliance."

"My dear Sir Lucius. Are you seriously asking me to spy for the League?"

"Call it rather an exchange of information. You can't expect me to believe you aren't curious about O'Roarke yourself. Learn what you can about what he's up to. If you still want to protect him, we'll assist you. If not, we'll protect you from him."

"You'll forgive me if I find the word 'protect' laughable in any context coming from the League."

"Say what you will, Lady Tarrington. We can protect you and your loved ones. Or make life very difficult for them."

It was the most direct threat he'd given. Laura willed her fingers to be steady "Are you so desperate to find the Wanderer?"

Brandon's eyes widened, then narrowed. "I see you aren't above gathering information."

"You see Mr. O'Roarke isn't above confiding in me." Laura drew a breath, conscious of the feel of Raoul's signet ring on a chain round her neck. He had given it to her before he left for Spain the last time. "Good day, Sir Lucius."

CHAPTER 26

"TO THINK that a member of the League dared to assault a friend on my front steps." Frances pressed a cup of tea into Laura's hand. "I cannot apologize enough, my dear."

"It was by the area railings, not the front steps, Lady Frances." Laura forced a sip of tea down her throat. She had her voice under control, but her fingers—curse them—were not quite steady. "And he hardy assaulted me. I could have walked away at any point. I was the one who wanted information. In any case, it can scarcely be considered your responsibility."

Lady Frances gave the snort of a woman used to ordering her world. "If I can't protect a friend from nuisance within feet of my door, I don't know what the world is coming to."

"Your friends these days have a number of enemies," Archie said. "Spies can be difficult to protect."

"What do you know about Sir Lucius Brandon?" Mélanie asked. She and Cordy had been sitting with Frances and Archie when Laura came in.

Archie took a meditative sip of tea as though it were port. "One of the senior League members. Not on a par with Beverston or Glenister, or Alistair or Trenchard in their lifetimes, but was a member from the beginning. I remember him at the earliest League parties I attended. The sort to be trusted with delicate errands by the senior members."

Laura tightened her grip on the delicate handle of her teacup. "I can't believe they actually thought I'd work for them or trust them. Or that I'd take their insinuations about Raoul seriously."

Mélanie leaned forwards to add milk to her tea. Her gaze seemed to linger on Laura's for a moment, but perhaps that was her own overactive imagination, Laura thought. She wasn't used to keeping secrets from her friends. "It is hard to imagine," Mélanie said. "Perhaps they're desperate enough they thought it was worth a try. Or perhaps they hoped to read something in your response."

"Or that they could frighten you and drive a wedge between us," Cordelia said. "But in that case, they don't know you very well. For that matter, if you had agreed to work with them, I can't believe they'd have trusted you weren't turning the tables and spying on them."

"Don't imagine I didn't think of it." Laura pushed a squeezed bit of lemon to the edge of her saucer. "I might well have tried it, if it weren't for Emily and the baby." She forced another sip of tea down her throat. "They controlled me for years by threatening Emily. Perhaps I shouldn't be surprised they thought threats to my family would still work."

"Then they don't know you." Mélanie's smile was quick and warm and bracing. "They don't control Emily now. And we're going to be very certain they have no chance to."

"No chance to what?" Malcolm came into the room, Harry at his side.

Laura had to tell the story again, though at least that gave her the opportunity to prove she could do so while holding her teacup steady.

"What damnable cheek," Harry said. "To dare to think they could intimidate you."

Laura found herself smiling. For someone who claimed to have no talent for human interactions, Harry had a way of knowing precisely what to say.

Malcolm was frowning. "They're very brazen. Or very frightened. Or both."

"My thoughts exactly," Mélanie said.

Malcolm met Laura's gaze. "Obviously we'll be more careful than ever with the children in particular. But we already knew we had to be."

Little more could be said about Sir Lucius Brandon. To Laura's relief, the conversation turned to the much more interesting—and less unsettling—topic of what Malcolm and Harry and Mélanie and Cordy had uncovered in their day's investigations.

"I couldn't but be sorry for Derenvil," Malcolm said. "But he certainly has motive. Matthew Trenor elicits less sympathy, though he does seem to have had some feeling for Miranda as well. But he also doesn't have an obvious motive."

"'Which doesn't mean he doesn't have one we haven't discovered yet," Harry said.

"I couldn't help but feel sympathy for Dorinda Smythe," Cordelia said. "But she certainly has a motive as well."

"As, potentially, does her husband, if Miranda was his mistress," Malcolm said. "Both of them might have had reason to take Miranda's pendant. Roger's more likely to have been in the Barque of Frailty—though he's not on Mrs. Hartley's list of those present that night—but it's possible Dorinda managed to get in."

"There's the mysterious woman Matthew Trenor heard had been to see Miranda the day before the murder," Laura said. "Could that have been Dorinda Smythe?"

"She said she hired the runner, Jenkins, because she couldn't go to the Barque of Frailty herself," Mélanie said. "But perhaps after their quarrel, she realized that was the only way she could see Miranda again. It wouldn't be the first time a suspect has admitted a great deal but also held something back."

"I wonder if the paper Hugh Derenvil saw her holding could have been a family letter," Cordelia said. "And the person who'd disappointed her was Dorinda. Or Roger."

Malcolm frowned. "Rupert wrote to me when Roger Smythe secured his seat in the election. Rupert said he had high hopes for him. So long as he didn't turn cynic because the world didn't live up to his ideals."

"He seems to have idealized Miranda Spencer—Dormer—once," Mélanie said. "One wonders what may have happened if she disillusioned him."

"Whatever happened later, when he found his lost love he didn't rescue her from the brothel," Malcolm said.

"She couldn't have gone back to her old life," Frances said. "They may both have seen that."

"That's no excuse for leaving her where she was." Malcolm's gaze swung to Frances, sharper than Laura had ever seen it when he looked at his aunt. "I hope you aren't defending the way the world is ordered."

"When have I ever done so?" Frances asked. "Even before I began consorting with Radicals. But Roger Smythe may have felt differently. Just because he's a political Radical doesn't mean he was prepared to defy society and drag his family into scandal."

"He could have set her up in rooms. With her child." Harry stirred the tea Frances had given him, clattering the spoon against the saucer.

"He'd have had to get her away from his father," Mélanie pointed out. "We don't know if Roger knew Miranda was gathering information for Beverston. For that matter, we don't know what Roger Smythe may know about the League and his father's involvement. Beverston recruited John into the League."

"And his godson, Tommy Belmont." Malcolm's mouth tightened. "Roger's politics are very different from his father's, but Beverston could think that makes good cover for him to collect information."

"For that matter, Roger's politics could actually be cover," Harry suggested.

Malcolm swung his gaze to his friend. "True enough. Though I don't like to think of Rupert being so deceived."

"Anyone can be deceived," Mélanie said in a quiet voice.

Malcolm reached for his wife's hand and gave her the sort of smile that defied the past. "True enough. We need to talk to Roger. And try to find the woman Trenor says called on Miranda at the Barque of Frailty just before her death."

"Where's Raoul?" Cordelia asked.

Where indeed? "Still combing his sources for word of Gisèle and Tommy," Laura said. "He's supposed to come here when he's done. I hope the delay means he's having some success."

"He's going to be furious when he hears about Lucius Brandon," Archie said.

Laura squeezed another wedge of lemon into her tea. "He knows I can take care of myself. I trust the rest of you do as well."

Malcolm touched her hand. "Always. It doesn't stop any of us from worrying." He set down his teacup. "I went to Rupert when I first got to London. He's been making inquiries about Gisèle. Bertrand and Gabrielle too. I'll see what Rupert can tell me about Roger Smythe before I talk to Roger. " He looked from Mélanie to Harry. "We should update Roth. Perhaps—"

"On it," Harry said, even as Mélanie said, "Of course."

"I'll put in an appearance at Brooks's," Archie said. "It's the equivalent of one of Raoul's coffeehouses for gathering information."

"I can make some more calls," Frances said.

"So can I," Cordelia said. "Laura—"

"I'd be delighted to come with you if you don't think I'd be in the way. Scandal can be a bar to talking."

"It's far more likely to be the lure that gets us in the door."

"Right." Malcolm nodded. "We'll reconvene here when we can."

"O'ROARKE." Carfax looked up from the book he had been reading as the door of his cell in Newgate swung closed. "Have you come to gloat?"

Raoul surveyed the man who had been his opponent for over half his life. Carfax's face looked perhaps sharper than usual, but he appeared every bit as much in command. "You can't believe I feel any particular satisfaction at seeing you in prison."

"No?" Carfax closed the cover of the book. Burke. "I thought your life's work was stopping mine."

"I have no illusions that your being imprisoned will stop the policies you advocate. Though, admittedly, I have a hard time imagining a spymaster taking your place who is quite your equal."

Carfax raised a brow. "Thank you."

Raoul hooked a chair with his foot to pull it out from the table and dropped down across from Carfax. "The Elsinore League are searching for the Wanderer. So are you. So, apparently, is someone else."

Something flared in Carfax's eyes that was not quite surprise. "I can't imagine the League told you."

"No. Collectively the three of you gave yourselves away."

Carfax's gaze narrowed. "How much does Malcolm know?"

"Too much for comfort, but not the truth. Not yet." Raoul regarded Carfax for a moment. "We're on the same side in this."

"Can you really claim we're on the same side in anything?"

"In that we both think the Wanderer needs to stay buried. At least, I assume you think so. I rather suspect that's responsible for your silence now."

"No comment." Carfax removed his spectacles and folded them, perhaps because he'd finished reading, perhaps because he knew the value of a commonplace gesture in maintaining command of the scene. "I'd have thought the Wanderer might prove useful to you."

"I'm too keenly aware of the dangers."

"So you say."

Raoul settled back in his chair. "You might have uses for the Wanderer yourself."

"I might." Carfax sat back in his chair as well. "You haven't thought of telling Malcolm?"

"I trust Malcolm as I trust few others. But there are choices I don't want him to have to make. And dangers I don't want to expose him to. If possible."

"Or Mélanie."

"Or Mélanie." Raoul didn't even blink at Carfax's use of her real name. They were beyond that. "Or their children. Or Lady Tarrington."

"If possible."

"As I said."

Carfax gave a short laugh. "You've always had a mad belief you could bring about the impossible, O'Roarke. In this, as in many things, I fear you will be disappointed. Though for all our sakes, I very much hope not."

"MALCOLM." Rupert Caruthers came forwards quickly round his desk. "Bertrand's been out all day making inquiries. Much of last night too. Gaby's been paying calls on émigré friends. I was just going to stop by the United Services Club and see what I could glean."

Three and a half years ago, in Paris after Waterloo, Rupert had been a man tormented by the past and secrets. Now he was one of Malcolm's closest colleagues in Parliament, the one Malcolm had entrusted with his notes and strategies when he left Britain.

Rupert was also reunited with his lover Bertrand de Laclos, who rescued endangered Bonapartists from Paris as he had once rescued Royalists, and had helped the Rannochs flee to Italy. Bertrand had an extensive network in London he was making use of to help look for Gisèle. Rupert's marriage to his wife Gabrielle had become one in name only, but they were still close friends.

"We can't thank all of you enough," Malcolm said. "I'm glad I caught you at home. It seems I need to talk to Roger Smythe."

Rupert's gaze flickered across his face. "About Gisèle? I know he's Beverston's son, but they've never been on good terms—"

"Not about Gelly. At least, I don't think so. About Miranda Spencer."

Rupert frowned. "He was one of her clients? I wouldn't have taken him as the sort for brothels, but perhaps that's naïve of me."

"He was apparently one of her clients, but he'd also known her since childhood." Malcolm explained about Miranda Spencer in fact being Miranda Dormer.

"Good God." Rupert shook his head. "I don't think I ever met Miranda Dormer, but we certainly move in the same circles. I don't know why it seems worse when it's someone one might have known, but—"

"It brings it home," Malcolm said. "She had an appalling life."

Rupert's brows drew together again. "I can't swear to Roger not visiting a brothel. But finding a woman he'd loved there, making her his mistress, not trying to get her out—that doesn't sound like him."

"People can be difficult to judge. Political ideals don't always go with personal ones."

"True enough. But Roger's always struck me as fundamentally decent. I could be wrong, of course. Perhaps it's just that I don't like to think that I am. Roger's serious. Focused. Keeps himself to himself. Doesn't talk about his family much, but I thought I detected strong affection. He has the zeal to change the world of one who hasn't come up against the realities yet. If—"

He broke off as the footman rapped at the door. "I'm sorry to interrupt, my lord. But Mr. Smythe has called."

Malcolm bit back an ironic laugh and saw Rupert do the same. "Show him in," Rupert said.

Roger Smythe went still on the threshold, taking in Malcolm's presence. "Rannoch. I came to ask Rupert for advice, but perhaps it's as well I've found you here."

Rupert looked between Roger and Malcolm and moved to the door. "I think I should leave you to talk. I'll be in the library if you need me."

Roger Smythe advanced into the room. He was dark haired like his late brother John, but taller and leaner. Malcolm would have said he had a more open countenance, but now his features were set in a contained mask. He turned to face Malcolm, the light from the windows at his back, his face in shadow, his eyes blazing with torment. "It's past time we talked. Considering we have the same goal."

Malcolm closed the study door. "Which is?"

"To learn who killed Miranda."

"My condolences." Malcolm walked to one of the two green velvet chairs in front of the desk and gestured to Roger to take the other. "I understand you and Miranda Dormer were close."

A dozen emotions shot through Roger Smythe's gaze, overlaid by loss that is still a stab wound one can't comprehend. For a moment, Malcolm was thrown back in time, to the days in Vienna when his sister Tatiana's murder still seemed scarcely real to him.

"We grew up together." Roger's voice was a hoarse rasp. He moved to the chair and sank into it, almost like one sleepwalking, unaware of his actions. "I'd been fond of her."

"You hoped to marry her."

"Wanted to." Roger's fingers curled white round the carved chair arm. "For all my mooning after her, a part of me knew I never had any real hope of success. But yes I—loved her. I couldn't bear not knowing what had happened to her. God knows I searched."

As even now they were searching for Gelly. Malcolm shut his mind for the moment to his fears for his younger sister. "Did you suspect—"

"That my own brother had seduced and abandoned her—Good God, no. If I'd had the least suspicion, I'd have called John to account. And I abhor dueling."

"So do I, but I understand the impulse in this case. When did you find Miss Dormer?"

"Last autumn." Roger drew a breath, a man trying to marshal his thoughts. "I'd just been elected to Parliament. I spent time in London, meeting with Rupert and Brougham and a few others." He hesitated a moment, met Malcolm's gaze, his own more direct. "I was sorry you were out of the country. I'm glad you're back. In any case, Dorinda and our daughter stayed in the country and I was bunking at Brooks's. One night I was walking back from a coffeehouse where I got supper, and I was sure I saw Miranda. On the other side of the street, but her way of walking was always distinctive. She was with another young woman—shorter, dark-haired—and two young men. I almost called out, but I was afraid she'd run. So I followed and saw them go into a house in Jermyn Street. I asked someone who lived there and got a sharp laugh and a comment that I'd need to move in rarified circles if I aspired to the Barque of Frailty."

"Had you heard of it?"

"No, but the tone was enough to tell me what sort of establishment it was. I don't know why I was shocked. I knew Miranda's family had cut her off. But I suppose I hoped—" He shook his head. "I wanted to storm in then and there and pull her out, but I had enough sense to realize I might not get past the footmen and Miranda might not come with me. I went back to Brooks's and talked to Gilbert Featherstone. I got some ribbing about my wife being in the country, but he wasn't as surprised as

I'd have thought he'd be. He admitted to having visited the Barque of Frailty. He also told me my father was a regular." This time both Roger's hands curled round the arms of his chair. "I can't tell you the thoughts that shot through my mind then. Worse perhaps than the truth, and God knows the truth makes our family look bad enough. I insisted Featherstone take me to the Barque of Frailty at once. I got some more ribbing, but he didn't seem to mind." Roger drew the breath of a man who's been punched in the stomach. "I'll never forget my first sight of Miranda in the drawing room. She was standing by the piano talking to two gentlemen. In many ways, not so different from the way I'd seen her in her parents' drawing room or at Beverston Court. She turned and met my gaze. I saw her shock and I saw her control it. I always knew Miranda was strong, but never how much, until that moment. She made some excuse to the men she was talking to and wandered over to me. She murmured, quite as though she were making casual conversation, that we'd better talk and it would be best if we did so upstairs. She took my arm and drew me out of the room. And upstairs to one of the bedchambers. That's how we talked, in one of the rooms where —" He looked away. "But whatever she went through at the Barque of Frailty, I don't think it could compare with what my brother put her through." He looked back at Malcolm. "John and I were never the friends brothers should be, but after that I can't call him brother anymore." Roger's hands curled into fists. "John was a brute. I hate to think what he may have put Diana through."

"Something very similar to what Miss Dormer experienced."

"Good God." Roger stared at Malcolm. "If John and I'd been on better terms, if I'd spent more time with them, perhaps I'd have noticed—"

"A number of people close to her didn't notice. But I think she'll be all right now. She's a very strong woman."

"So was Miranda." Roger glanced away, his face twisted. "I keep going over everything that happened, from the moment I saw her again. If I'd—"

"You'd loved her," Malcolm said into the silence. "It's perhaps not surprising—"

"That what?" Roger stared at him. "That I loved her still? I suppose I did, in a way."

"And in the circumstances—"

"In the circumstances what? Are you suggesting I made Miranda my mistress?"

Malcolm met Roger's intent gaze. "Your wife is under the impression you did."

"My—you've talked to Dorinda?"

"No. My wife and Lady Cordelia did. You didn't know your wife had been to see Miranda not long before she died?"

"Dorinda'd been to see Miranda?" Roger pushed himself to his feet and took a turn about the room. "How could she have thought—"

"She found out you'd seen Miranda more than once. By your own admission, Miranda is a woman you'd loved and hoped to marry. Whom you loved still."

"Yes, but—Oh, Christ." Roger spun away, drew a harsh breath. "Dorinda and I were friends from childhood. You may know that."

"Yes, that's what your wife told my wife and Cordelia."

"When we were children, I could talk to her as to almost no one else. So, of course, when I realized I loved Miranda I confided in her. She was always the one I confided in. It was only after Miranda disappeared that I began to think of Dorinda—"

"I think that may be the problem, as far as your wife sees it."

"Yes, but—It's not like that." Roger stared at Malcolm, as though pleading for understanding of a situation Malcolm was only barely beginning to grasp on the edges. "Dorinda and I may have grown closer because Miranda was gone, but that's not why I offered for her. I made a fool of myself over Miranda in more ways than one. Not the least of which was not realizing the woman I really wanted to spend the rest of my life with had been right there all along." He raked a hand through his hair. "I don't know why the devil I'm asking you to understand all this. Except that on top of everything else, not recognizing my feelings for my wife seems like sacrilege."

"Do you think your wife recognizes them?"

"I thought—" Roger's mouth worked. "I thought she did when we married. It was not long after Miranda disappeared. Hardly the time for moonlight and roses. Since then, I've wondered—Dorinda had a difficult life. One can't blame her for wanting an escape."

"For what it's worth," Malcolm said, "as I understand it, she was quite jealous of her cousin's supposed relationship with you."

Roger scanned his face. "You don't believe me."

"To own the truth, I'm not sure. But your denials have the ring of truth. And your wife told Mélanie and Cordelia that Miranda denied being your lover. But she refused to explain her relationship with you."

Roger drew a hard breath. Malcolm recognized the struggle in his face. The conflict of one sifting through how much to reveal. "When Miranda and I spoke in that room where everyone was convinced we were doing other things—I wanted her to leave with me at once, to come and live with Dorinda and me and our daughter, with her child. She said she didn't want to be a scandalous relation in our house. And she told me she couldn't, that my father would stop her. She couldn't just leave the work she was doing for him. That was when I realized what she was embroiled in." His gaze locked on Malcolm's own. "My father is part of an organization."

Malcolm pushed himself to his feet to face Roger. "Which my supposed father started along with him and some others."

"Quite." Roger released his breath. Relief, perhaps, at having made the right choice. "I wasn't sure you knew."

"I found out a year ago." Malcolm studied the other man. "Did Miranda tell you?"

"Miranda? Oh, no. I told her. That is, she was already working for my father, but she didn't really understand what she was working for, if you take my meaning. I learned not long before I found Miranda. Just after we learned of John's death." He hesitated again. "Kit Montagu sent me a message."

Kit Montagu, who would also have been Roger's neighbor in Surrey. Who must have known him since childhood. Whose sister had married John Smythe and who himself had almost married Elinor Dormer, Miranda's sister and Dorinda's cousin. Who shared Roger's politics. Who was part of an organization of young Radicals. "You're one of the Levellers," Malcolm said.

Caution shot through Roger's gaze. "I never said—"

"You didn't need to. I got to know Kit quite well in Italy. He put me in my place with his concern about my having worked for Carfax, but in the end I think he recognized we share much of the same ideals."

"Kit has a great deal of admiration for you."

"Even though I sit in the Parliament that enacted laws he's fighting against?"

"You didn't vote for those laws. Kit was a bit unsure about my decision to stand for Parliament, I think. But I think there are many ways to change our country."

"So do I." Malcolm studied Roger. "Kit saw the list of Elsinore League members. He sent word to you your father was on it?"

"He wanted to warn me. That my father might be an even more dangerous opponent than we had thought just based on politics. It was a message in code. He couldn't say much. But I did some more investigating. It was all shadowy, but I learned enough to be deeply concerned. I wasn't sure what to do. Whom I could trust." Roger hesitated. "I've never been on the most comfortable terms with either my father or my brother."

"I know the feeling." Though he and Edgar had been close,

once. Before their mother died. Before their lives took them in different directions.

"I've always taken the law seriously," Roger said. "It's why I see a road to reform through Parliament. I take my work in Parliament and the cause of reform seriously. As I know you do."

Malcolm inclined his head.

"I knew my father and I differed politically. I knew my brother and I did. But this was something I couldn't oppose across the House." He hesitated a moment. "I was sure John's death wasn't the accident Father told us it was."

Malcolm met Roger Smythe's gaze. Secrets were dangerous to share. But Roger was already in the midst of the Elsinore League tangle. He deserved to know how his brother had died. "It was an accident. But we were confronting John over his work for the Elsinore League. And for Lord Carfax."

"John was betraying the League? To Carfax? While Miranda was reporting to Father—" Roger shook his head. "It's almost beyond belief. Did he—"

"John was trying to escape. He fell and hit his head." Malcolm didn't add that John had been using his wife as a hostage and that she had pushed him. Diana Smythe had been through more than enough. "I know that may not sound believable—"

"It has the ring of truth. If you were making up a story, I expect it would be more coherent."

"I'd like to think so."

"I was still adjusting to the news of John's death when I learned about Miranda." Roger hesitated a moment, fingers taut on the marble of a pier table. "God help me, that was when I realized she could help me learn more about the League. I told her what I knew. I said it would be risky to take them on. She wanted to help. I thought it would give me time to persuade her to leave the Barque of Frailty. I knew it was dangerous if Father learned what she was doing. But it would be dangerous if she left as well. I hoped we'd uncover something that would give her the leverage to break away from my father."

"Did you?"

This time Roger didn't hesitate, though Malcolm thought he might. "Father was opposing a fishing rights bill. And there was talk about something else. Something called the Wanderer."

CHAPTER 27

"DIFFICULT TO KNOW WHERE TO START." Cordelia pulled on her gloves, smoothing the French gray kid over each knuckle. "Of course, Miranda Spencer—Dormer's—murder will be on everyone's mind, but one can scarcely ask a woman if she thinks her husband—or son or brother—was a patron of the Barque of Frailty. And it's also difficult to ask about Gisèle without giving rise to all sorts of talk."

Laura tightened the ribbons on her plum velvet bonnet. "At this point, I'd say protecting Gisèle from scandal takes second place to finding her. This family have a number of resources when it comes to combating scandal. And I use family in the more expansive sense."

"Thank you." Cordelia smiled as she smoothed her second glove, then turned to the mirror to adjust her blue and gray satin hat.

"It must have been unbearable for Miranda Dormer," Laura said, picking up her own gloves and reticule. "At any moment she could see someone she knew on the street. Or in the drawing room of the Barque of Frailty. I felt much that way myself when we first returned to Britain from France."

Cordelia turned from the glass to look at her. "I wish I'd known."

Laura met her gaze with a dry smile. "Considering I was spying on your friends, you scarcely have anything to apologize for. But—

She broke off as the door opened. Gilbert, Lady Frances's senior footman, stepped into the room. "Forgive me." He managed to address the remark to the two of them impartially. "But Lady Caroline Lewes has called. She's asking for Lady Cordelia, not Lady Frances."

The fiancée of Hugh Derenvil who had been Miranda Dormer's lover. Cordelia exchanged a quick look with Laura. "Do show her in, Gilbert."

Scarcely before Cordelia had pulled the pins from her hat and Laura had untied the ribbons on her bonnet, Gilbert announced Lady Caroline. She hesitated on the threshold. She wore a dark blue velvet pelisse over a gown of paler blue merino, just darker than her eyes. Her hat was blue velvet as well, lined in a silk that matched the gown. Her hair, a paler blonde than Cordelia's, escaped in ringlets from beneath the brim of the hat. Her brows were carefully groomed, her face set with composure.

"Caroline." Cordelia went forwards to take the younger woman's hands. "I don't believe you've met Lady Tarrington?"

Lady Caroline inclined her head with the correctness of a conventional drawing room. "I'm sorry to bother you both. It looks as though you were about to go out."

"Don't be silly." Cordelia tossed her hat onto an ormolu pier table where she had already deposited her gloves. "Nothing that can't wait."

Lady Caroline hesitated, as though the dictates of good manners warred with whatever had driven her to call. "I have something I need—your advice about."

"I'll go check on the children," Laura said.

"No, please, Lady Tarrington." Caroline put out a hand. "I know you're involved in the Rannochs' and Davenports' investigations. I'd prefer you heard this as well."

Laura cast a quick, surprised glance at Cordelia, but moved to a chair. "Of course, if you wish."

Lady Caroline sat on the sofa beside Cordelia, settling the folds of her pelisse and gown with care. "My father is close to Lord Castlereagh and Lord Liverpool." She folded her kid-gloved hands with

precision round her embroidered velvet reticule. "I heard that Colonel Davenport and Mr. Rannoch are looking into the murder for which Lord Carfax has been arrested. The girl who was killed at the Barque of Frailty, a place about which they have all deceived themselves that I am in ignorance."

"Mr. and Mrs. Rannoch have looked into more than one murder in the past," Cordelia said. "My husband has assisted them, as have I. Given Mr. Rannoch's close relationship to the Mallinson family, he has naturally taken an interest."

"And you wonder why I'm asking questions. Though you're much too polite to say so, you probably think it's some sort of fascination with the lurid." Lady Caroline tugged off one of her gloves.

"I'm not in the least polite," Cordelia said. "And I can certainly understand a crime being interesting. But I don't think you've called just because of that."

Lady Caroline gripped the fingertips of her second glove. "I was betrothed just before the holidays. You may not have heard."

"On the contrary. I confess I don't pay as much attention as I once did to the latest news from the beau monde but of course your name jumped out at me." Cordelia hesitated for just a fraction of a second. "My felicitations."

"Thank you." Lady Caroline smoothed the gloves in her lap and stared down at the stitching on the pale blue kid. "That's actually why I'm here." She drew a breath. The gaze she lifted to Cordelia held the anguish of uncertainty. Laura realized that for all her composure and impeccable grooming, she was very young. Probably more than a decade younger than Laura herself and at least five years younger than Cordy. "My betrothed, Mr. Derenvil. He knew her. The murdered girl. Miranda Spencer."

Laura could feel the shock that ran through Cordelia. It could scarcely be stronger than her own astonishment. Not at Mr. Derenvil's relationship to the dead girl, of which they already knew, but at his fiancée knowing of the relationship and speaking of it.

"I'm so sorry," Cordelia said. Words suited to cover a variety of eventualities.

"He doesn't know I knew," Lady Caroline said quickly. "Like my father, I imagine he's convinced himself I know nothing of establishments like the Barque of Frailty. But it was quite clear to me shortly after we came back to town after the New Year that he was keeping something from me." She dragged her gloves through her fingers. "One of the things that drew me to Hugh—Mr. Derenvil—from the start was that he was so easy to talk to. But after we became betrothed that seemed to change. He seemed unsure of what to say to me, and I didn't have the least idea of how to draw him out. It's an odd thing, contemplating being married."

"A huge change in one's life," Cordelia said.

"Yes, quite." Lady Caroline pressed a wrinkle from one of the gloves. "It doesn't surprise me that there had been—women in his life before his betrothal. In truth, it doesn't surprise me that there still are." She looked up and met Cordelia's and then Laura's gaze, coloring slightly. "After all, we aren't intimate yet. I understand that gentlemen have needs."

"They aren't the only ones who do," Cordelia said, "but yes."

"After we were married, I hoped—But again, I realize fidelity doesn't always go with matrimony in our world. Mr. Derenvil and

I hadn't talked about that. We hadn't talked about a great deal." She linked her fingers together. A sapphire betrothal ring showed on her left hand. "It wasn't that I was jealous so much. No, that's not true. I was. Rather painfully. More so than I'd have expected."

Laura recalled her instinctive response to Lisette Varon, Raoul's former agent. "It can take one by surprise," she said. And she had been older than Lady Caroline, with less cause for jealousy, and less of a commitment from her lover.

Lady Caroline met her gaze, almost shyly, and nodded. "But it was more than jealousy. I could tell Mr. Derenvil was troubled. I tried to draw him out, but the more I tried, the more tongue-tied he seemed to get. I had to know what was happening—because I wanted to help him, but also, I confess, to satisfy my own curiosity. One night we'd been to dine with the Castlereaghs. Mr. Derenvil was particularly distracted in the drawing room after dinner. At last he excused himself with a mumbled explanation that scarcely made sense. I couldn't bear it any longer. I told my father Lady Liverpool was escorting me home, but instead I slipped from the house and followed Mr. Derenvil."

Cordelia's eyes widened. "You're very enterprising."

"Isn't it the sort of thing you'd do?"

"Yes. Now. Perhaps also when I was younger."

"But you thought I was more spineless?"

"More cautious, perhaps."

"Caution didn't seem to be getting me very far when it came to the man I—to my betrothed." Lady Caroline opened her reticule, pushed her gloves inside, snapped it closed. "I followed him to a house in Jermyn Street. I didn't recognize it. I couldn't make sense of whom he might be calling on that I didn't know. I pulled the hood of my cloak over my head and stood by the area railings. I saw a number of gentlemen go in together and some leave, but no ladies. I started to wonder, but I didn't fully work it out until a crossing sweeper asked if I needed help finding a hackney and said this was no place for a lady like me. Then I understood what the house must be. I felt such a fool."

"It would be a shock," Cordelia said.

"I hurried home in embarrassment. But then I began to think about it. Simply visiting a house of ill repute didn't explain how troubled Mr. Derenvil had been. In fact, one would think he'd have treated it as rather commonplace. Most gentlemen seem to. I began to wonder if it was something about a particular woman at the house. If his feelings were engaged. That was when I began to truly feel jealous."

"I can understand that," Cordelia said.

Lady Caroline's gaze fastened on Cordelia's face. "Can you?"

"It's one thing to think of the man one loves sharing another's bed. Not pleasant, but it doesn't necessarily destroy one's place in his life. Or his place in one's own. But if he's formed a lasting bond—" She shook her head. In her gaze, Laura saw echoes of the time six months ago when an investigation had drawn Harry back into the life of a former mistress from the time when he and Cordelia had been apart.

"Yes." Lady Caroline gripped her elbows, arms hugged across her chest. "I actually thought about calling off the betrothal. But that wouldn't resolve whatever was troubling Hugh. I had to know."

"Did you think of asking him?" Laura asked.

"Yes." Lady Caroline's eyes widened, as though she was surprised Laura had thought of that as an option. "But I knew he wouldn't confide in me. He might even deny the whole thing. I couldn't bear to imagine him drawing back even more. So that perhaps I could never reach him."

"And so?" Cordelia asked, in the gentle voice Laura had heard her use to draw out her daughters.

"My friend Sally Arbuthnot has three brothers. I talked to her. Her youngest brother's been to the Barque of Frailty. Perhaps they all have, but Sally could get him to talk. He'd seen Hugh there. He knew the name of the girl Hugh had—been intimate with. Miranda Spencer." Her voice shook slightly as she said the name.

"It must have been hard," Cordelia said. "Having an actual name."

"It made it easier in some ways. The next evening I borrowed a gown from my maid and went to see her."

Laura saw the start of surprise in Cordelia's eyes. It was scarcely less than her own. "You went to the Barque of Frailty?" Cordelia said.

"I had to find out why Hugh was so troubled. She seemed to be the only one who could tell me. It's in Mayfair, after all. Only a few streets away from my father's house. I went to the area door and told the kitchen maid who answered that I had a message from Mr. Derenvil for Mrs. Spencer. That he'd been very specific that I give it to her personally. I wasn't sure it would work, but a few minutes later Mrs. Spencer came down to the kitchen. When she realized who I was—I couldn't think of any way of getting her to talk without admitting it—she said I should leave at once, but when I said I was desperate for information about Hugh, she took pity on me. She took me into a little sitting room near the kitchen. The maid who'd let me in brought us tea. So odd to be sitting there drinking tea with this woman whom my fiancé—" Lady Caroline bit her lip.

"It must have been terribly difficult," Cordelia said.

"Yes. Though in truth, she couldn't have been kinder. She said at once that I must realize the fact that gentlemen visited establishments like the Barque of Frailty had nothing to do with their fiancées and wives. I asked her if she'd want a man she was betrothed to to frequent such a place. That silenced her."

"Yes, I would think it would," Laura said.

Lady Caroline locked her hands together in her lap. "I sat there across the table from her, the teapot between us, and all I could think was how very much alike we were."

Surprise again flickered across Cordelia's face. "From what I've heard of her, she rather resembled you. Perhaps she even reminded Mr. Derenvil of you."

"Yes, a bit—that is, I don't know if she reminded him of me but we do—did"—her breath caught—"both have fair hair and blue eyes. But that isn't what I meant. She poured tea in the way I do, the way my governess taught me. She folded her hands in the same way. Used many of the same expressions. It was quite obvious we'd come from the same world."

"There aren't a lot of options for a wellborn young woman who is cast off by her family," Laura said.

"No, I can see that. I'd never really considered—that is, one doesn't expect—"

"I don't imagine anyone expects it," Cordelia said. "Falling in love with the wrong person isn't comfortable for anyone. But for a woman it can mean ruin. Damnable."

Lady Caroline's brows lifted. At the idea as much as the curse, Laura thought. "I wish I'd—but I was more focused on my own situation. I told Mrs. Spencer it wasn't just that Mr. Derenvil had been—patronizing her. It was that I knew he was troubled about something. She said sometimes it was hard for men to talk to someone they put on a pedestal. That she believed Mr. Derenvil cared about me very much. I said this was an odd way of proving it."

"Good for you," Cordelia murmured.

Lady Caroline colored. "She chose her words with care. But she conveyed that she didn't believe Mr. Derenvil was sure that his feelings for me were returned. I said what on earth did he expect me to do, fling myself at his head? I'd agreed to marry him. She said that in our world—funny she said that, 'our world'—marriage and love often didn't go hand in hand. I must confess she had a point. I admitted as much but said that simply went to show that Mr. Derenvil very likely didn't love me and had offered for me because it was a sensible and prudent match. He never said he loved me, not in so many words, and what words he did say could be considered pretty platitudes. Mrs. Spencer said she understood that. But that she'd rarely heard a man talk of a woman the way Mr. Derenvil talked of me. That, for what it was worth, she'd give a great deal to have a man speak that way of her. I asked her if she'd ever been in love. Odd and terribly presumptuous of me to have asked such a question of her, of all people. But somehow I found I could talk to her. Which I suppose is the same thing that happened with Hugh and her. Though under very different circumstances."

"Did she answer you?" Cordelia asked.

"Oh, yes. She didn't seem to mind the question. She said she'd had the misfortune to give her heart foolishly to a man who didn't deserve it. She said I had every right to be angry, but Mr. Derenvil was a good man, and that counted for a lot." Lady Caroline drew a breath, as though suddenly struck by something. "Mrs. Spencer must have come from a background not unlike my own. If she had met Hugh instead of this undeserving man who was responsible for her ruin, she and Hugh might have become betrothed. I wonder if he'd have found her as easy to talk to then."

"I doubt it," Cordelia said. "I imagine part of her attraction was that she was from outside his world."

"So he'd have been whispering his secrets across the pillow of some other girl at the Barque of Frailty?"

"People have a tendency to put other people in categories and to make assumptions about them," Laura said. "Mr. Derenvil seems to categorize the type of woman he might marry as the type of woman he couldn't confide in."

"I could shake him." The words burst from Lady Caroline's lips with sudden force.

"*Brava,*" Cordelia said.

"I'm sorry." Lady Caroline pressed her hand to her lips. "But it makes no sense. Isn't the person one chooses to spend one's life with precisely the person one should be able to talk to most about that life? I asked her that. Well, not that specifically, but I said if I married Mr. Derenvil would this go on? Would he still come to her for confidences and leave me to sit at the head of his table and go into ballrooms on his arm? She hesitated, as though she feared she was betraying a confidence, then said that he'd been through a great deal in the war and it was difficult for him to speak of it to someone who hadn't shared that past. That stopped me for a moment, but then I blurted out that she hadn't shared it either. She got quiet for a moment and then said, no, but she knew what it was to be haunted by one's past. Then she got very busy refilling our teacups and said Mr. Derenvil could talk to her now, but she doubted their relationship would continue that long and that she hoped mine with him would strengthen. If I went through with the marriage. It was the sort of thing I could imagine my mother saying. Except that it seemed more direct from her. Less like platitudes. I'm not sure I believed her, though. I mean, if he couldn't talk to me now, why should being married change that? And even if he didn't—seek out intimacy elsewhere—I don't know that I could be happy with a marriage where my husband couldn't share himself with me." Her brows drew together. "I rather suspect that's the sort of marriage my parents have. But I don't think it would do for me. I didn't realize that until we went through all this."

"Perhaps, for all the pain, it's a good thing you did," Laura said.

"Yes." Lady Caroline met her gaze. "Marriage is so irrevocable."

"Very true," Laura said.

"Oh, dear." Lady Caroline colored. "I'm so sorry. I didn't mean to—to allude to your situation, Lady Tarrington."

"Not in the least. It's scarcely something I can ignore. And it's common knowledge in the world now, for better or worse. I'm far happier than I ever thought to be. Far happier, I confess, than when I was married to my late husband. We were spectacularly unsuited. But at the same time, I'm keenly aware of the challenges. I would certainly counsel my daughter to think very carefully before she committed herself to marriage."

Lady Caroline nodded. Somehow her expression at once held

the trust of a schoolgirl and the worldly wisdom of a woman with much more experience. "In truth, when I left the Barque of Frailty I wasn't sure what I planned to do next. Not even what I wanted to do next. I lay in my bed staring at the canopy for the longest time. I couldn't possibly discuss it with my mother. Or even Sally. She's still inclined to view these things like something out of a lending library novel. And I needed to determine what would make me happy. And Mr. Derenvil. I couldn't be sure marriage to each other meant that for either of us anymore. At the same time, when I thought of calling off our betrothal I felt as though I were cutting myself in two. When Mr. Derenvil sent me a message the next day saying he must cry off his promise to take me driving in the park, I was conscious of a craven relief. I couldn't imagine how I was to face him until I had come to some sort of decision. I went about in a sort of daze all day, hoping something would help me arrive at some clarity. Then the next morning, my maid brought me my chocolate, all agog with the news that Lord Carfax had been arrested for murder in a Mayfair brothel."

"Did you know it was Mrs. Spencer?" Cordelia asked.

"Not at first. But it was easy enough to pretend to curiosity with my maid, and she got the information for me." Lady Caroline spread her hands in her lap, fingers taut against the blue velvet of her pelisse. "To think I'd spoken with her only twenty-four hours before—I saw Mr. Derenvil at Lady Sefton's rout that evening. I had thought I couldn't be more uncomfortable in his presence, but the look in his eyes—as though he'd retreated into some sort of hell where I couldn't reach him. And of course if I hadn't been able to speak to him before, I truly couldn't now. I knew he must know she was dead. I knew it must mean a great deal to him, but I couldn't offer him comfort. I couldn't be sure when he'd last seen her. Couldn't be sure she hadn't told him about my visit. Couldn't even be sure—" Lady Caroline broke off, as though not willing to finish the thought even in her own mind. "If you and the

Rannochs are investigating, you must not be sure Lord Carfax killed her."

"The evidence so far doesn't entirely support that," Cordelia said.

Lady Caroline gave a quick nod, gaze on her hands. "We have to know the truth. I don't think he'll have any peace otherwise. I still don't know if we can risk marriage, but I know for a certainty we can't with this hanging over us. That's why I came to you. I couldn't bear it if anything I held back might help you arrive at the truth."

"You were very brave to do so." Cordelia watched for her for a moment. "Caroline—"

"I know." Lady Caroline met her gaze, like a duelist receiving fire. "For weeks I've been questioning how well I knew Mr. Derenvil, but when I heard of Mrs. Spencer's death my first response was that he couldn't have had anything to do with it. I couldn't be so wrong in choosing him, in giving my heart—" It was the first time she'd referred to her heart, and she drew a breath as though pulling herself back from a precipice. "But truly, how can I be sure, especially after everything else I've learned these past weeks? If that proves anything, it proves how impossibly difficult it is to ever really know another person. " She looked from Cordelia to Laura. "I expect you can't even be sure about me, can you? I've admitted I went to the Barque of Frailty and got myself admitted. That I spoke to Mrs. Spencer. I could have gone back the next night. Dressed as a maid, I probably could have slipped up the service stairs more easily than any gentleman and gone into her room. I don't deny I was jealous. That must be one of the strongest motives for murder."

"Among others," Cordelia said. "But I'm not sure why you'd have come to us, in that case."

"I might have done if I'd thought you'd learn about my visit. If I wanted to put you off your guard," Lady Caroline said. She pulled her gloves from her reticule and began to pull them on, smoothing each finger. "I no longer believe anyone is what they seem, so I can quite imagine the questions you must have about me. I'll confess that I'm afraid of the truth. But it has to come out. I don't see any peace for Hugh unless it does. Even if he killed her. Because, if he did, I don't think he'll be able to live with the guilt."

CHAPTER 28

"DID you see Hugh Derenvil the night of the murder?" Malcolm asked.

"Who?" Carfax took a sip of tea from the cup on the table in his cell in Newgate.

"Don't play games, sir." Malcolm dropped into the chair opposite Carfax. "Derenvil's enough of an up-and-comer you'd be keeping an eye on him."

"Not a man one would think to find at the Barque of Frailty."

"That seems to be a pattern. He was a client of Miranda Spencer's. He found her in her room alone just after midnight. Given that you went upstairs with her and later found her body, that means you left her room and then returned to it."

"I said as much."

"But you refused to say where you went."

"Into a sitting room."

"Alone?"

Carfax shifted in his chair. "I didn't say more to Bow Street, Malcolm. What makes you think I'll talk to you?"

"Are you protecting a source in the house?" Malcolm studied

Carfax. "I assume you knew Miranda Spencer was spying for Beverston."

"I take it that's a rhetorical question."

"That's why you went to see Mrs. Spencer."

"Given Beverston's position in the League, that woud seem a sensible move, wouldn't you say?"

"Why didn't you tell me the first time I came to see you?"

Cafax took another sip of tea. "I didn't ask for your help, Malcolm."

"Was it because you know Beverston's looking for the Wanderer?"

Carfax's hand froze for just a fraction of a second on the delicate handle of his teacup. "What on earth is the Wanderer?"

"You tell me."

Carfax took a sip of tea as though to prove he could do so without sloshing the liquid. "This isn't your fight, Malcolm. Stay out of it."

"That's what Castlereagh said." Malcolm folded his arms over his chest. "Are you working with him or against him?"

"Malcolm—"

"I can't stay out of it. It's connected to Gelly's disappearance."

Carfax's brows snapped together. "What makes you think that?"

"You're not the only one who can choose to keep secrets, sir." Malcolm met his former spymaster's gaze over the delicate teacup. "You don't seem surprised that she's missing."

"I have sources of information even in here." Carfax turned his cup on its saucer. "Have you heard from her?"

Malcolm chose his words with care. Carfax, after all, was looking for the Wanderer himself. "She's unhurt. We're hoping she comes home soon."

Carfax released his breath. "If she's run off with Belmont—"

"I should have known you'd know about that. Whatever's going on between her and Tommy, I think she's going to want to return to her husband. I'm doing everything I can to make it possible for her to do so. For Gisèle's sake, I'd ask you to do the same."

"Good God, Malcolm, can you think I'd do otherwise?"

"Good God, sir, after six months ago can you think I wouldn't?"

Carfax sat back in his chair. "I thought you'd probably hate me, given the leisure to reflect in Italy."

"Don't flatter yourself, sir. I hated you when we left. But not as much as I hated myself for working for you."

"You were working for your country."

"I'm not sure I believe in countries anymore."

Carfax frowned.

"In any case, I was working for policies I abhorred in the service of a war I opposed, often using tactics I found repellent."

"And you think O'Roarke's tactics are so much better?"

"Yes, actually. Not that I find myself in entire agreement with them either. When I was at Oxford you did me the honor of thinking we were dangerous enough to set Oliver to spy on us. Then you turned me into your creature."

"You found yourself as an agent, Malcolm."

"I rather think I lost myself, sir."

"A matter of opinion. In any case, when you went into Parliament you went right back to advocating the sort of views you espoused at Oxford, so I don't think you can accuse me of doing permanent damage. More's the pity." Carfax reached for his tea. "O'Roarke came to see me earlier today. You may be pleased to know he was no more successful at getting me to talk than you've been. But I don't deny his brilliance. He's dazzled you."

"No. He's perhaps helped me remember who I am. But I take full responsibility for my decisions."

"You trust him. Blindly."

"After what I've been through, can you imagine my trusting anyone blindly?"

"Perhaps." Carfax took a sip of tea. "If I pushed you too far in the other direction."

"Don't take too much credit."

"You'll look round one day and find he's stabbed you in the back."

The moment he'd been sure Raoul had lied to him about Julien St. Juste stung Malcolm's memory. "I don't think so. But I fully acknowledge I can't be certain." Malcolm regarded Carfax. "And of course I'm quite used to being stabbed in the back."

"Information is power, Malcolm. One is a fool not to use it."

"With no thought to the cost?"

"Oh, I always calculate the cost." Carfax returned his cup to its saucer. "I was afraid of this from when you were a boy. That you'd fall under his spell."

"I think you were afraid I'd see the world his way rather than yours."

"I never had any illusions that you'd see the world my way, Malcolm. Though I did my best to point out the flaws in your logic to you. You have the brains to have seen them, though what I imagine you would call your heart interferes with your rationality. And of course O'Roarke's had his claws into you since you were a child."

"We all have our biases, sir. You included. But I'll take mine over yours any day."

THIS WAS NOT Mélanie's first visit to the Brown Bear, the tavern that adjoined the Bow Street Public Office. The Bow Street runners often used it for meetings or to interview or even detain suspects. Laura had been confined in one of the upstairs rooms before she'd been moved to Newgate when she was accused of the Duke of Trenchard's murder. Perhaps Carfax had been held here. Mélanie attracted less surprise than she once had when she stepped over the threshold. But though she'd been there, usually with Malcolm, to speak with Jeremy, she hadn't been in the habit of sitting down at one of the scarred tables, let alone drinking anything. Things had changed, however. After Italy, already being cut by the likes of Lady Langton, with Gisèle missing, the world tumbling down about them, it was hard to bring herself to worry about the dictates of polite society that had governed her life for so long.

She moved at Harry's side across the room to the corner table where Roth sat. Roth got to his feet and pulled out a chair for her. Harry raised a brow at her before he went to get himself a pint. "I'll have a stout," Mélanie said. A small act of rebellion, but it bolstered her spirits to a surprising degree. She pulled off her gloves, tucked them into her reticule, and smiled serenely at the runners and constables at the other tables, several of whom she had met in the course of investigations.

Harry returned with the pints and a fresh one for Roth. It took the better part of half an hour for Harry and her to update Roth on the discussions and revelations they had each been privy to. Roth jotted down some things in his notebook, but for the most part listened without interrupting. He let out a whistle when they had done. "No shortage of suspects."

"No." Mélanie took a sip from her tankard. Rich and bracing. Sometimes it was a relief to be unrefined. "Though so far it's difficult to see a pattern."

"I can't lay claim to as much success," Roth said. "Officially, I'm not supposed to be investigating, so all I can do is ask questions under the guise of gathering details for our case against Carfax. But I did find one of the Barque of Frailty kitchen maids unexpectedly forthcoming. She said Miranda Spencer had been very kind to her and she wanted to do anything she could to help. According to her, Beverston spent the night at the Barque of Frailty the night before Mrs. Spencer—Miss Dormer—was killed. Not necessarily surprising, but apparently he spent it not with

Miranda Spencer or another of the young women, but in Mrs. Hartley's chambers."

"We know they'd been lovers," Harry said. "Not entirely surprising that they were still."

"No," Roth agreed. "But according to Mattie—the kitchen maid—Beverston arrived in the early hours of the morning, looking quite agitated. In her words, 'He's a cold customer, never thought to see him looking as though he'd seen a ghost.' Apparently he went right to Mrs. Hartley's private sitting room and she joined him there. Mind you, Mattie didn't see any of this, she got the description from one of the footmen. But later she says she was in the passage outside Mrs. Hartley's sitting room, and she's quite sure she heard Beverston crying."

"Not so surprising if it had been after Miranda had been killed," Harry said. "I have very little use for the man, and I think it's entirely possible he killed her, but he did seem upset by her death. But if it was before she died—"

"Quite," Roth said. "Something else is apparently troubling Lord Beverston. Something that drove him to seek out Mrs. Hartley."

Mélanie pictured Lord Beverston, whom she had last seen over six months ago. "And it would take a lot for Beverston to let himself cry, I imagine. Distinctly coincidental that whatever it was happened the night before Miranda was killed."

"That's what I thought." Roth turned his pint on the dark, stained wood of the table. "I hesitate to confront Mrs. Hartley. If Carfax is guilty, and officially Bow Street's position is that he is, whatever was going on with Beverston is of no moment. But—"

"We could," Harry said. "Or perhaps Archie would be best." He took a drink from his pint. "They were rather well acquainted once. Before she was involved with Beverston."

"You lot do manage to be in the midst of an amazing number of events, don't you?" Roth said. "I'd be grateful for anything he can do to help."

Harry nodded. As much as Roth knew, there were secrets to which he still wasn't privy. Such as the fact that Archie had been a French agent.

"Do you have any more idea of who wants Carfax arrested?" Mélanie asked.

Roth shook his head. "The word from the top is to take it slowly. Make sure the case is airtight. Which gives us some time. And gives me latitude to ask further questions—so long as I don't stray too far afield."

"Sir Nathaniel and Lord Sidmouth must know we're investigating," Mélanie said.

"Oh, yes." Roth gave a dry smile as he took a drink from his pint. "I've been told to keep an eye on what you're doing. And not reveal anything sensitive. Which I don't see that I have, since if Carfax is guilty, Beverston's behavior is of no moment whatsoever."

"You have the makings of a politician, Jeremy," Mélanie said.

"Hardly that." He lifted his pint to her. "But I do learn from my friends."

"PUTTING TOGETHER THE LATEST INFORMATION," Laura said, "I wonder if Beverston could have been upset because he'd learned his son Roger was working against him and had turned Miranda."

"It's possible," Malcolm said. "Given what I've seen of Beverston, though, I'd have thought that would elicit more anger—and a quick response to contain the damage—than tears. But if he had learned, it certainly gives him motive to have killed Miranda or had her killed."

"In which case, he could have been crying at the realization that he was going to need to get rid of her," Mélanie said.

Malcolm met her gaze. "So he could."

They were gathered at one end of Frances's drawing room

while the children played at the other. Frances and Archie had not yet returned, and there was still no sign of Raoul or Andrew.

"I could imagine Beverston being shaken," Harry said, "but that would mean he places an extraordinary amount of trust in Mrs. Hartley."

Malcolm met Harry's gaze. "I liked her too. But we know she didn't tell us the truth about how Miranda came to her—that she and Beverston set up Miranda's meeting with Daisy Singleton. We don't know what else she may be hiding. Or what else she may know—about Beverston, about the League."

Harry gave an abashed smile. "Are you accusing me of giving way to sentiment?"

"Nothing wrong with that, darling. Even in a scholar." Cordelia tucked her hand through his arm.

Harry grinned at his wife and put his hand over her own. "Malcolm's right, there's a great deal we don't know about Mrs. Hartley, and we do know she lied to us. If—"

He broke off as the door opened and Lady Frances stepped into the room. "Oh, good, you're all back." She set down her reticule and began to pull off her gloves. "I can't claim to have met with a great deal of success, but I have brought someone back with me who I think may change that. Mélanie, Emily Cowper was most interested to hear you were back in London. She's in the small parlor and most desirous of speaking to you. Not, I think, about Italian fashions."

Mélanie, who had thought she was beyond surprise, stared at Frances for a moment, then exchanged a look with Malcolm and one with Cordelia and got to her feet. Scarce an hour after she had been sipping stout in the Brown Bear and thinking she didn't have a care for London society, she was going to have a tête-à-tête with one of the patronesses of Almack's.

~

EMILY COWPER PUSHED herself up from the sofa in Frances's small parlor in a stir of jade green gros de Naples and dark ringlets perfectly arranged despite the damp weather. "Suzanne, dearest. What a wretch you are for not letting me know you were back in town."

Mélanie went forwards and returned Lady Cowper's embrace. Emily's dark eyes held nothing but kindness, and Mélanie had come to think of her as a friend, but she was also keenly aware the other woman held the power of social life and death in London drawing rooms. Patroness of Almack's. Daughter of a powerful Whig family. Sister of Malcolm's friend William Lamb. Mistress of the up-and-coming Tory Lord Palmerston. "It's a flying visit. We've scarcely told anyone we're here." Mélanie drew back and smiled at Emily. Sometimes it was best to confront controversy head on. "And I didn't want to put you in an awkward situation."

"Awkward? Heavens, one of my sisters-in-law ran round after Lord Byron in public and another of them ran off to the Continent with a Radical politician. Mind you, I think someone should have told Lady Tarrington that she could amuse herself all she wanted if only she gave people the ability to ignore it in public. A bit difficult to do that when two people are actually living together."

"Not to mention having a child."

"Yes." Emily wrinkled her nose. "Sometimes having a husband can be useful. Provided he's the compliant sort. Mind you, having met Mr. O'Roarke, I can understand the temptation. And of course you're loyal to her."

"I could scarcely be otherwise."

"No, you wouldn't be."

They moved to the violet-striped sofa where Emily had been sitting. Emily settled back against the fringed cushions, the velvet-edged flounces of her gown falling effortlessly about her. "It may be awkward about Almack's. Dorothea's inclined to draw firm lines and Lady Castlereagh always worries about appearances, though I know she's fond of you. Let me see what I can do."

"You're very kind, Emily."

"Stuff. Almack's would be much less amusing without you. And though I know you don't care much about it for itself—"

"Emily—"

"Don't pretend otherwise, dearest. I know you want to be where you need to be for Malcolm's career." Emily frowned again, gaze thoughtful beneath the green velvet brim of her bonnet. "Your wifely devotion should help with Lady Castlereagh, if not with Dorothea. I doubt I can go so far as to get vouchers for Lady Tarrington, not at first, though if we could resurrect Cordelia's reputation—"

"Cordelia is living with her husband."

"Yes, there is that." Emily adjusted the brim of her bonnet. "That's not why I came to see you, though, believe it or not. Not that I wouldn't have come simply to see you, but—Is it true you and Malcolm are looking into the murder of that girl Lord Carfax has been arrested for killing?"

"News travels fast."

"Surely you haven't forgot how Mayfair works, dearest. The violent death of a girl in a brothel that half our husbands—and brothers and fathers, not to mention lovers—very likely frequent would have been talk as it is. But when one of the most powerful men in the country was arrested for killing her—Well, you can only imagine. And then when it got out that Malcolm was back in London and had been to see him—"

"People know that?"

"You don't think reporters are paying the jailers at Newgate to report on Carfax's every visitor? Though I confess I didn't realize you had joined Malcolm until Lady Frances called on me today." Emily scanned Mélanie's face. "You don't think Carfax killed her?"

"Malcolm knows more than I do, at this point. But there are certain details that don't add up."

Emily twisted her hands in her lap in an uncharacteristic display of nerves. "I'd say it was a relief. I can't claim to know Carfax well—can anyone claim to know him well, except possibly Lady Carfax? But I've known him all my life. I played with the Mallinson girls. I danced with David at my coming-out ball. Impossible to imagine a man one's sat down to dinner with—But if he may be innocent, I need to talk to you."

Mélanie scanned her friend's face, waiting.

Emily tugged at one of her rings. "Harry and I had a stupid quarrel before the holidays."

That wasn't particularly surprising, and there was no need for Emily to say she didn't mean Harry Davenport. Emily and Harry Palmerston were always quarreling and reconciling. But Mélanie couldn't immediately see what the connection might be to Carfax and to Miranda Dormer's death.

"I did what I often do when he provokes me," Emily said. "I flirted. Which made Harry jealous. Which made us quarrel again. Which made me flirt more. Yes, I know. We scarcely behaved like mature adults. But isn't part of the fun of being in love that one doesn't have to?"

"An interesting way of looking at it. Emily?" Mélanie began to have a sense of where this might be going. "Did you flirt with someone in particular?"

Emily let out an abashed sigh. "Lord Gildersly. He's rather silly, but he is amusing, and one can't deny his good looks. And I may have let it go a bit beyond flirtation. Oh, all right, I did. I knew almost at once that it was a dreadful mistake, but I couldn't simply drop him. I had to find a graceful way out. So when we came back from Panshanger after the holidays, I saw him once or twice." She smoothed one of her braided cuffs. "He came to see me on the night Miranda Spencer was killed, though of course I didn't know it at the time. But there was something odd that whole night. He arrived without our having a rendezvous. He'd obviously been drinking. Well, he generally drinks, but he was more impaired by it than usual. I very nearly showed him the door, but I was afraid he'd make a fuss in the hall—or in the street—and that would be worse. It was only later that I saw blood on his shirt cuff. I didn't think a great deal about it, but I did ask if he'd injured himself. He glanced down for a moment as though surprised it was there, and said he'd broken a glass earlier in the evening and cut his hand. He hadn't realized it was on his shirt. It seemed logical enough, and I had no reason to doubt him. Not at the time. Though he had an odd look in his eyes as he said it. As I said, there was something odd that whole night. We didn't—he wasn't able to do more than give me a clumsy kiss. I confess I was rather relieved. I put it down to drink. He took himself off soon after." Emily gripped her elbows, fighting off a shiver.

"Em," Mélanie said. "There's no reason to think—"

"And I didn't. Not then. It was only a few days later, when Miranda Spencer's death and Carfax's arrest were the talk of Mayfair, that Sally Jersey mentioned that one would be shocked at the men one knew who frequented the Barque of Frailty. She was sure the names she'd heard were only a fraction of the number—then she rattled off a list of names, including Lord Gildersly."

Mélanie stared into her friend's eyes. Emily's gaze held a glimpse of a horror she wouldn't let herself define. "That doesn't mean—"

"That he knew Mrs. Spencer?"

"I imagine he knew her, it doesn't seem to have been that large an establishment. But you don't know that he patronized her."

Emily's brows lifted and Mélanie wondered if she'd been too frank. She'd been so good at staying within the persona of Suzanne Rannoch, but months of living in Italy, among people who knew the truth of her past, had changed her. Made her careless. "And you certainly don't know that he killed her," she concluded.

"That's what I've been trying to tell myself. Believe me, it would be much easier not to feel I had to involve myself. In some ways it's gratifying that Harry can be so jealous, but I do occasionally wonder if I could push him away entirely. But Gildersly frequented the Barque of Frailty. He was very likely there the night she was killed. He was upset. Distracted. And he had blood on his shirt. Tell me as an investigator you wouldn't want to know all that."

"I would," Mélanie said. "I do. And I'm intensely grateful to you for telling me. I know it wasn't easy."

"To own the truth," Emily said, "it's rather a relief to talk to you about Gildersly. I can't bear to think that I let a man touch me who may have done—"

Images from her own past rushed into Mélanie's mind. After all, she'd slept with Julien St. Juste, and God knows what he was capable of. And Frederick Radley, who made her skin crawl. "Whatever he may have done, Gildersly can't touch you now." Mélanie surveyed her friend. "Have you seen him since?"

"He called two days later. Apologized for his behavior. I wasn't sure if he meant his being drunk or his inability to perform or both, and I wasn't interested in discussing it further. I managed to say that it had been an agreeable interlude, but I thought it should draw to a close. He appeared relieved. My pride would have been piqued, save that I was distinctly relieved myself."

"Do you think he sensed any of your suspicions?"

"I don't think so—that is, my suspicions were scarcely formulated at that point. Do you think I need to worry about him?" Emily asked with the shock of one who has stumbled into an unfamiliar world and can't quite believe it is real.

"Very likely not. But I'd avoid being alone with him until we know more."

"That won't be difficult. I haven't the least desire to be alone with him, for any number of reasons."

Mélanie touched her hand. "We'll try to keep you out of it, Emily."

"But I may have to talk." Emily inclined her head, a soldier facing possible battle. "I understand. Our family are hardly strangers to scandal, after all. And I daresay Harry and I will manage to weather it. We've weathered so much else."

"You think Emily Cowper knows something about Miranda Dormer? Or Gelly?" Malcolm asked his aunt.

"I can only assume so. She jumped at the chance to talk to Mélanie when she learned she was in London. She'd known you and Harry were, but not Mélanie and the children and Cordelia and Laura. She seemed to feel the need to confide, but I don't think she'd have done it in you as easily."

"No, I can see that." Especially if it was connected to one of her love affairs. Malcolm had known Emily Lamb—Emily Cowper now—since babyhood, had danced with her and ridden with her, but she and Mélanie had become friends. Mélanie had a way of making friends and drawing out confidences.

"Emily can be fiercely loyal to those she cares for," Cordelia said, as though she read the flicker of unease in Malcolm's gaze. "And she's very fond of Mélanie."

Malcolm nodded. He knew that was true. He also didn't trust Emily's reaction if she learned the truth about Mélanie.

The door opened again. "Tea," Frances said. "Good."

But though it was Gilbert, he was not bearing a tea tray. "We've had another caller, my lady." He sounded almost apologetic. "He's asked to wait downstairs in the library, though I assured him you'd be happy to see him upstairs. For Mr. Rannoch. It's Lord Worsley."

CHAPTER 29

MALCOLM'S THROAT tightened as he stepped into Frances's library to face David Mallinson, Viscount Worsley, Carfax's son, his own closest friend of twenty years. So many months since they had seen each other. It was by no means the longest time they'd been apart in all the years of their friendship. But it was the longest following a quarrel. For that matter, they'd never had a quarrel like the one they had parted on. Their angry words hung in the air between them, swirling like dust motes in the light. Words spoken in haste, yet that had given shape to a gulf that had always been between them. They'd exchanged letters in the intervening six months. Letters that had brought them closer than Malcolm had dared hope they could become on that night he and Mel had left Britain. But so much remained unspoken. So much that perhaps they could never put into words. So much they would have to attempt to say if they were to regain any sort of friendship. And yet they were finally meeting in circumstances in which their own quarrel couldn't be the first thing they addressed.

David held Malcolm's gaze for a long moment. For an instant in his eyes Malcolm thought he saw a twin of his own conflict and longing. Then his gaze went shuttered. He drew a breath in, shoulders going taut, and took a half step forwards. "I just arrived in London. Simon's still in Paris with the children." David and his lover Simon Tanner were raising David's late sister Louisa's children. "When I got to our old rooms in the Albany I found a letter from Bel waiting for me telling me you were here. And that you're trying to help Father."

"I'm trying to ascertain the truth of what happened."

"That's very generous of you."

"You thought I'd abandon your father to his fate?"

"I was sorely tempted to do so myself." David's mouth tightened. "I was concerned for my mother and sisters."

"So am I, if it comes to that."

"I appreciate that, Malcolm. Very much. But they'll be all right. It's always going to mean something to be a Mallinson."

"That doesn't make up for losing a father."

Something that might have been fear shot through David's eyes. "Do you think it will come to that?"

"It very well may not. I've never seen him so at risk. But he doesn't act like a man afraid."

David's gaze flickered over Malcolm's face. "You don't think he did it?"

"I think he's capable of it." Once Malcolm wouldn't have spoken so bluntly with David about his father, but they were beyond that. "But the facts don't add up. And there are a number of others with motive."

"Tell me."

They sat before the fireplace, and Malcolm recounted the investigation. Most of it. He didn't mention Sam Lucan's story about seeing Julien St. Juste with Raoul, and Mélanie's and his own conviction that Raoul was lying to them. So far they had shared those with no one but each other.

David listened intently, only interrupting when Malcolm's narrative got round to Gisèle.

"Gelly's missing? You should be looking for her, not worrying about Father."

"I am. But there are a surprising number of connections between the two. The Elsinore League are involved in Gisèle's disappearance, the Elsinore League and your father are searching for whatever the Wanderer is. Gelly takes precedence. But I can't not look into your father's case."

"Malcolm—" David half stretched out a hand across the table between them, then let it fall. "You can't trust him."

"Believe me, David, I'm well aware of that. I was before last June, but if I hadn't been, those events certainly left an impression on me."

"He won't—" David gripped the arms of his chair. "He won't hesitate to use Suzanne's— Mélanie's—past. Against her. Or you. There's no telling whom he might tell. You're clever, Malcolm. Brilliant. But you're not devious enough to be a match for him."

Something in the sincerity and intensity of David's expression tore at Malcolm's chest. "David—You're right. I'm not a match for him. But I'm on the watch for what he may try. So is Mel. I've had rather more experience of this side of him than you have."

"Malcolm." David scanned his face. "I know you've been playing this game for a decade. But it's not really a game now. You do realize that, don't you? This is the safety of your wife. And your children."

"And it means a great deal that you're concerned for them." For her, but he wasn't going to quite say it.

"You can't imagine I wouldn't be."

"There's been a lot for us all to adjust to in the past months."

David drew in his breath, a harsh rasp that sliced the air. "When I realized why Father had done what he did—I always knew he wanted me to marry. I always knew he wouldn't give up. But I hadn't properly considered what that might mean. What a risk it was to Simon. I suppose I was a fool."

"You were a son. Who couldn't quite imagine the lengths to

which his father would go. I couldn't imagine it myself, and I had far more experience of his machinations than you did."

"I knew then." David's right hand closed on his signet ring. "What I had to do to protect Simon. What we had to do together to protect the children. I understand why you did what you did to protect Suzanne and your children."

"I didn't forgive Mélanie to protect her," Malcolm said in a quiet voice. "That is, I'm not sure she needs forgiveness. I didn't come to understand her to protect her."

"No." David's gaze skimmed over his face. "I understand that, if I don't understand her. I couldn't bear the thought of any harm coming to her. I hope you know I'll do everything in my power to ensure her safety. And yours."

"That—that means a great deal, David."

"Not that you need my help."

"On the contrary. Right now, we need all the help we can get."

"And I know—Malcolm, I know you'd never betray your country."

Malcolm drew a breath. "It's odd—Lately I've been questioning that."

"Questioning what?"

"If I'd have been better off working for the other side during the war."

"For the *French*?"

"If I'd gone to work for O'Roarke instead of Carfax."

"O'Roarke's not—"

"He was a French spymaster. Your father knows."

"And you've always been close to him."

"He's my father."

Shock flared in David's gaze. "I didn't—"

"I learned just before I learned about Mel. There wasn't time to tell you. It's not the sort of thing one puts in a letter."

David shook his head. "Malcolm, I can scarcely—"

"You knew Alistair. It was a relief to be sure he wasn't my father. And to know someone I loved was."

David held his gaze for a long moment. To Malcolm's relief, he didn't see horror in it. "You've always been good at seeing situations from others' viewpoints, Malcolm. Even the worst of the bullies at Harrow."

"Well, perhaps *see* their viewpoint. Doesn't mean I thought it had any merit."

"No, but it's a knack. I get too locked into looking at things from my own perspective. As my father does, I suppose."

"Your father can appreciate other perspectives. He just discounts them."

"So now you wish you'd fought for Irish independence?"

"Or fought the British in Spain."

"I can't see you doing it." David sounded more certain than horrified.

"I'm as much French as English. And Scottish, Irish, and Spanish."

"But you grew up here. It doesn't change your being British."

"In truth, I'm not sure what I am anymore. But I'll always be a husband and a father. And a friend."

Six months ago, Malcolm would have sworn their last exchange would have shocked David. Now his friend merely regarded him and inclined his head.

MÉLANIE WENT BACK into the drawing room after seeing Emily Cowper from the house. The group she had left a half hour since were all still there, but a new arrival had joined them. Sitting bolt upright on the edge of a shield-back chair, a teacup clenched in rigid fingers, his elegant profile outlined against Lady Frances's French violet watered-silk wall hangings. David Mallinson, Viscount Worsley, her husband's childhood best friend, whom she had last seen almost seven months ago, before her world fell apart, before he'd learned the truth about her.

Frances looked to the door a split second before Malcolm. "Oh, good, Mélanie. As you see, David has just arrived in London. I think we've caught him up on nearly everything."

Malcolm's gaze locked on Mélanie's own. He was on his feet. So was David.

"Suzanne. Mélanie. It's good to see you." David walked forwards, his hand extended. Mélanie took his hand. It had been the longest time before he'd come to kiss her cheek, as Harry did. As Simon did. But when last she'd seen him, before he learned the truth, he'd been comfortable doing so. She hesitated, then leaned slightly forwards. David hesitated too, then bent his head and brushed his lips against her cheek.

"It's good to see you too, David." Mélanie's voice was not quite steady.

David smiled back, gaze grave but unwavering.

Mélanie moved into the room, aware of the gazes upon her, and sat beside her husband. "Emily Cowper had some interesting news." She recounted the story Emily had told her about Lord Gildersly.

"Interesting," Malcolm said. There was a relief in his voice that she suspected betokened more than having a new line of inquiry.

"Gildersly doesn't have a connection to the League," Harry said. "That we know of."

"But Miranda could have been gathering information about him for Lord Beverston," Laura said. "Or for Roger Smythe. Or both."

Cordelia leaned forwards, frowning. The air in the room seemed to have lightened since they had moved on to the investigation. "If—"

She broke off as Gilbert once again entered the room. This time he held a silver salver with a sealed paper on it. "Valentin just brought this round from Berkeley Square," he said. "He said Mr. Rannoch will want to see it at once."

Malcolm stared down at the handwriting on the paper and went still. "It's Gelly's," he said, even as he slit the seal.

He took in the note in one glance. "It's in code. A code Allie and I taught her."

He moved to an escritoire, reached for a sheet of writing paper and dipped a quill in ink. Mélanie watched over his shoulder as the contents emerged.

Malcolm,

If you want to find the Wanderer, go to Hyde Park. Dig beneath the third oak from the left in the grove by the Serpentine. The one with the tree Edgar fell out of. Go as quickly as you can.

Gelly

P.S. I know you'll be asking if you can trust me. Don't be stupid, Malcolm.

"She was wise to add the postscript," Harry said. "But it could still be a trap. If she's that much under Belmont's influence—"

"Quite," Malcolm said. "Or she could have come to her senses and be trying to warn us."

"There's a third possibility," Mélanie said. "We've already discussed it."

Malcolm met her gaze. "That Gelly's been playing Tommy from the first. That she was going undercover when she ran off with him."

"It's in her blood," Mélanie said. "And more important, it's the world she grew up in."

"Good God," Cordelia said. "I know we talked about it, but —The risk."

"Mélanie makes a good point," Frances said. "This family thrive on risk."

Cordelia shook her head. "I'm the last to say a woman can't dare as much as a man. But she's scarcely twenty—"

"I became an agent when I wasn't much older," Malcolm said. "Mel was one before her sixteenth birthday."

Cordelia frowned. "It's a good point. Perhaps I don't want to admit a girl with my background could be so enterprising when I was still focused on romantic intrigues and which bonnet to order."

"Gelly's obviously very good at this," Malcolm said. "If we're right that she's gone undercover."

"That's the question," Harry said. "We could be walking into a trap. But I don't see how we can not go. It won't be the first time we've had to be prepared for a trap. If it comes to it, it won't be the first time we've walked into one."

"I'm quite sure I've been followed since I got to London," Malcolm said. "We'll do our best to shake them, but it's a risk we'll have company whether or not it's a trap."

Laura glanced at the decoded paper. "Do you think the Wanderer is a thing, not a person? Something you can dig up? Unless—"

"She's directing us to a body?" Malcolm asked. "Always possible. But it's hard to see a dead body being such a source of interest twenty years later."

David, less used to these scenes, was watching in frowning silence. "So you'll keep the appointment?" he asked.

"I don't see how we can do otherwise," Malcolm said.

CHAPTER 30

MÉLANIE GLANCED at the spreading branches of the oak. "This feels oddly like the last scene in *Merry Wives of Windsor*."

Malcolm rubbed his hands together against the cold. "I have a feeling we're likely to face dangers far more serious than pretend fairies and sprites."

According to their plan, Mélanie, Harry, and Cordelia slid into the trees to keep watch while Andrew dug and Malcolm watched his back. A reluctant Laura had been persuaded to stay home because of the baby. She'd given in at last, saying she didn't want to slow them down if they had to run. Archie, whose bad leg could slow him down, had agreed for the same reason—and with the same reluctance. Malcolm had persuaded David that the rest of them could handle it and that he should go to Spendlove Manor and update his mother and sisters and Oliver, without actually coming out and saying that David was a civilian and might slow them down. Andrew was a civilian too, but Mélanie knew Malcolm had seen him in action against the Dunmykel smugglers, and with Gisèle involved there was no way he was going to stay back. Harry had asked if they should wait for Raoul, and Malcolm had said merely, "We don't know when he'll be back. We don't want to wait on this." Mélanie thought she'd caught a gleam of speculation in Harry's gaze, but he hadn't asked questions.

The wind cut with the bite of January. Worse, its rustling through the leafless branches made it harder to listen for unexpected movement. Mélanie could feel Harry's watchfulness. Cordy was admirably still. She didn't have their experience of surveillance, but she'd argued that they needed all the watchers they could get, and she promised to stay out of any fights. Harry had at last given a crisp nod. Mélanie saw him now cast a quick glance at Cordy, then turn his gaze to the distance. It was always a challenge going on a mission with one's spouse. And more so when the spouse wasn't a trained agent.

Mélanie eased her pistol from the folds of her pelisse, turned her attention from her own spouse, who had things well in hand guarding Andrew, and focused her senses on the world about them. The smell of loamy earth and cold air. The damp of the Serpentine carried on the wind. The call of an owl (a real call, unless it was a very good imitation). The rustle of a mouse or a squirrel or a hedgehog in the underbrush. All sounds that belonged in Hyde Park in the middle of the night. They'd traveled in pairs by different routes and detoured three times, but it could be difficult to shake off determined pursuit.

"Got something, I think," Andrew murmured. He dropped down and scrabbled in the ground.

And then a stir to her right that was heavier, firmer, than the animal sounds. Like the fall of a foot. She spun round and leveled her pistol just as a crash sounded on the left. Two men hurtled through the trees and tackled Andrew.

Andrew somersaulted and knocked one of the men over backwards. Malcolm jumped on the other. Harry ran from the trees. Two more men ran forwards from the right, the direction from which she'd heard the noise. One leaped on Andrew. But instead of going for Harry or Malcolm, the other hit the man Andrew had knocked over backwards, who was scrambling to his feet.

Malcolm grabbed Andrew's attacker by the shoulders, spun him round, and hit him in the jaw.

Mélanie tucked her pistol away. It wouldn't be much use in a mêlée. She picked up a large stick she'd spotted earlier instead and flashed a quick look towards Cordelia meant to remind her of her promise to stay out of a fight. Not that Mélanie would have made much of such a promise herself.

Andrew scrambled up, but one of the other set of attackers caught him by the feet. Mélanie ran forwards and hit Andrew's attacker over the head. He stumbled, but the two men who were fighting each other broke apart and both went for Andrew. Andrew tossed the box he'd recovered to Malcolm.

Cordelia let out a low whistle from the trees. Two more men ran into the clearing. One leaped on Malcolm. Malcolm tossed the box to Harry. One of the men—she could scarcely tell them apart in the dark—tackled Harry. Harry shoved the box through the leaves at Mélanie. Mélanie dived to catch it.

She dragged the box to her and pushed herself up from the leaves and dirt as her husband gave a grunt of pain. One of the men had jumped on his back and had a knife at his throat.

Another man ran from the shadows and pulled the man off Malcolm. Malcolm broke free and grabbed his attacker's knife as the man who had saved him pulled the man's hands behind him.

"Thank you, O'Roarke," Malcolm said.

Of course it was Raoul. He had a way of showing up at times like this. Though, given recent developments, his arrival raised concerns she didn't care to examine at present.

Four of the men ran off into the night. Harry had hold of the sixth. Cordelia emerged from the trees.

"Who hired you?" Malcolm demanded, looking between the man Raoul held and the man Harry held.

The man Raoul held gave a harsh laugh. "What sort of fool do you take me for?"

"I don't take you for a fool at all. I take you for a man who knows a good bargain when he hears one. Tell us whom you work for, and we'll let you go. Refuse to talk and we'll march you both to Bow Street."

Rather surprisingly, the men didn't look at each other.

"You're lying," the man Harry held said.

"Am I? Then we'd best be off to Bow Street. Assault and attempted theft carry a heavy penalty. I did mention that we have a good friend who's a runner, didn't I? And that I sit in Parliament. Colonel Davenport, who's holding you, is a hero of Waterloo."

"You may not trust us," Harry said. "But you can be quite sure the consequences will be worse if you don't comply. If you're betting men, I'd say the bet's worth taking."

The wind cut through the clearing. Another owl screeched.

"He were a gentleman," the man Raoul held said. "Leastways, he spoke like one. And dressed like one. Yellow hair. Blue eyes. 'Bout the same age as you gentlemen." He nodded from Malcolm to Harry.

"Was his hair straight or curly?" Mélanie asked. Tommy had wavy hair. Julien's was smooth.

In the shadows, she saw the man frown in an effort of memory. "Curly, ma'am. He had his hat off in the tavern. Just like a lady gets it with her curling tongs, only shorter."

"Tavern?" Malcolm asked.

"The Anchor in Wapping. A few days since. Let it be known he was looking for someone for a job. Was waiting in a room at the back. In the shadows, but his hair gleamed."

"What did he tell you to do?" Malcolm asked.

"Watch the people staying in a house in Berkeley Square. Stay back. But if they ever seemed to discover anything grab it and bring it back to him."

"Did he say what 'it' was?"

"Probably a box. Said not to open it. Asked if I could read. Seemed pleased I couldn't."

"And you hired the others?" Malcolm glanced at the man

Harry held.

"Him?" the man Raoul held gave a snort of derision. "Never seen him before. Brought one mate with me tonight. Had the devil's own work following you. My mate got away. Never seen the others."

"Were a woman hired me," the man Harry held said in a sudden rush, as though eager to reap whatever benefits the other man was getting from talking. "Word on the street someone was looking to hire for a job. Went to the back of a used clothes-seller in Rosemary Lane. Place people often meet to set up deals. Fair shocked when I saw it were a lady."

"What did she look like?" Malcolm asked.

"Black hair. The bits I saw escaping her cloak. Kept the hood up. Lovely face though. Sort to get a man in all types of trouble. Blue eyes."

"Did she also tell you to watch a house in Berkeley Square?" Malcolm said.

"That's the right of it. She said the people there might discover a box or papers we were to recover at all costs."

"How many men did she have you bring with you?"

"Just one. We lost you. Only got here because we picked up the trail of that lot." He nodded towards Raoul's captive.

Malcolm's gaze flickered between the two captives. "So the other two men who ran off—"

"Never seen them," Raoul's captive said.

"Me neither," Harry's captive said. "Would have asked twice the payment if I'd known how complicated it was."

"How were you supposed to collect your payment?" Malcolm asked. "And deliver the goods you'd recovered?"

The two men looked at each other for the first time, as though testing out who would speak first.

"I was supposed to leave word at the used-clothes seller's," Harry's captive said.

"And I was supposed to be back at the Anchor and wait for

instructions," Raoul's captive said.

Malcolm glanced at Mélanie. She knew at once what her husband was thinking. Tempting to try to trap whoever had hired both men, but even assuming those people hadn't had others watching the Hyde Park confrontation, their escaped confederates would have given the game away. If whoever had hired them had any degree of professional experience, they'd be on guard for such a trick. Mélanie inclined her head in agreement.

Malcolm reached into his coat. Both men tensed, as though anticipating a weapon. Instead, Malcolm drew out his card case. The metal gleamed in the moonlight. He flicked it open and pulled out two cards. "Should your employers contact you again, send me word at once in Berkeley Square. You can have someone read the direction on the card for you. You'll be generously rewarded."

Malcolm jerked his head at Raoul and Harry. They released the two men. The men stared at their former captors and then Malcolm for a moment, frozen by shock.

"I take my word seriously," Malcolm said. "And you can be far more useful to us on the street, where you may encounter your employers again."

Raoul's former captive gave a quick nod. "You ever need a job done, you leave word at the Anchor and ask for Charlie, guv'nor. I'd do a lot for someone whose word can be relied on."

Malcolm returned the nod.

Harry's former captive rubbed his hands where Harry had gripped them. "No hard feelings. I'll send word if I hear anything."

The men ran off into the shadows in opposite directions. Malcolm looked at Mélanie, at Harry and Cordy, at Andrew, then at last at Raoul. "No one's hurt?"

Mud adorned all of their clothes and most of their faces. But no one appeared to have been injured. Mélanie shook out her skirts and wiped a smudge from her face. The box was secured in the special pocket Blanca had sewn into her pelisse.

"So it was a trap," Andrew said in a flat voice.

"I don't think so," Malcolm said. "If Gelly wanted to trap us, why send us to the place the treasure was actually buried? And the man who hired one set of attackers definitely sounds like Tommy. Apparently he's had people watching us since we got to London, as I suspcted."

"So Gelly's turned on Belmont?" Andrew said.

"Or she's been trying to play him from the beginning, as Mélanie suggested." Malcolm's voice was grim, but Mélanie caught an edge of admiration for his little sister.

"And the other two sets of attackers?" Cordelia asked. "Who sent them?"

"The woman with the dark hair and blue eyes could be Charlotte wearing a wig or with her hair dyed," Raoul said. "Though that would mean she and Tommy were working against each other."

"Changing hair color is one of the easiest disguises for a woman," Mélanie said. "For that matter, Julien's very effective disguised a woman. And he'd certainly change his hair. Though Julien could have just dug up the papers on his own."

"We know besides the League, Carfax and at least one other person or group were after the papers Arabella took at Dunmykel," Malcolm said.

"You think Carfax hired someone from prison?" Andrew asked.

"I think Carfax is entirely capable of that," Malcolm said. He looked at Raoul. "Laura told you where to find us?"

"And Frances and Archie. They're in Berkeley Square. I could barely persuade Archie not to come with me. Not to mention Laura."

Malcolm nodded, though Mélanie caught questions in his gaze. But instead of voicing them, he glanced round their small company. "More discussion needed. But not here. Berkeley Square, I think."

CHAPTER 31

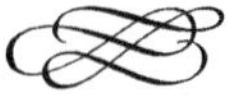

LAURA OPENED the door in Berkeley Square. "I sent Valentin to bed," she said. "Frances and Archie came with me. They're in the library." Her gaze went to Raoul. "You found them."

"Fortunately," Malcolm said, though there was a faint edge to his voice.

Frances and Archie appeared in the library doorway. "I see there were complications," Frances said, surveying the mud and leaves that adorned their clothes.

"A few," Malcolm said. "No damage done. But it's as well O'Roarke arrived."

Mélanie drew the box from beneath her pelisse.

Laura released her breath. "You have it."

"Whatever 'it' is," Malcolm said.

They all went into the library. Malcolm lit the brace of candles on the library table. Mélanie set the box on the brown-veined Carrara marble in the candles' glow. It was small, the size of a necklace box, but plain black with a brass lock. She pulled her picklocks from the pocket in her pelisse and worked at the hinge. It gave in only a few minutes. The hinges were rusty and the lid crusted with dirt. Once the lock was undone, Malcolm had to use a letter opener to pry it open. He pushed back the lid to show a folded, sealed sheet of paper with no inscription.

Malcolm picked the paper up and slit the seal while the rest of them gathered round in the circle of candlelight. A series of letters and numbers, obviously code, covered the single sheet.

"It's Julien's hand," Mélanie said.

"Burying clues seems a bit fanciful for him," Raoul said, "but I assume he had his reasons."

Julien's codes were challenging and he changed them for almost every communication with a quixoticness that was entirely in key with his personality. Malcolm, Mélanie, Harry, Raoul, and Archie clustered round the paper and began to sketch tables. Cordelia, Laura, Frances, and Andrew went to the kitchen to make coffee.

They had the basic framework by the time the party returned from the kitchen. By the time Laura was refilling the coffee cups, Mélanie had sketched out the plain text. A single sheet with two words on it lay among the jumble of code tables.

Rivendell, Kent.

"Where the Wanderer can be found?" Cordelia asked.

"Presumably," Malcolm said.

"As a fallback in case something happened to Julien himself?" Mélanie said. "For someone who knew Julien had hidden the Wanderer but not where?"

"Or as one step in a treasure hunt," Harry said. "It's not very specific. Perhaps there's another clue hidden at Rivendell."

"That sounds like the sort of elaborate way Julien might have chosen to hide information," Mélanie said. "The other papers Lady Arabella intercepted were written to whoever hired him to hide the Wanderer. Which makes it likely the ones that led to this box were too. In which case, his employers wanted him to hide the Wanderer but didn't want to know where the Wanderer was."

"But wanted the information available should they chose to dig it up?" Laura asked.

"It seems a bit odd," Mélanie admitted. "But I can't figure out another explanation."

"If that's what happened, I wonder if whoever it was ever learned where it was hidden?" Cordelia said. "The paper that led us to the box ended up with Lady Arabella. Unless—she couldn't be the one who hired M. St. Juste, could she?"

Mélanie drew a quick breath. Used as she was to contemplating different scenarios, she hadn't thought of that. She cast a quick glance at her husband and then at Raoul.

"These days it's difficult for me to be remotely sure of what my mother might have done," Malcolm said. "O'Roarke?"

"It was a shock to me that she even knew St. Juste," Raoul said. "Given that, I suppose anything's possible."

"Lady Arabella climbed in through Frances's window with the papers," Andrew said. "And was at pains to hide them."

"And we've been assuming that meant she stole them," Malcolm said. "But it's possible she was meeting with St. Juste on the Dunmykel grounds, that she wanted to keep evidence of whatever job he'd undertaken for her, but that she didn't want anyone else to find it."

"Bringing us back to the question of who or what the Wanderer is," Harry said.

"A trip to Rivendell is in order," Malcolm said. "But not tonight."

Andrew was leaning forwards in his chair, frowning at his hands. "If Belmont's the curly-haired man who hired two of the men who attacked us, and if he learns Gelly sent us that message, he'll know Gelly's deceiving. And she's still with him."

"We don't know that he knows about her message," Malcolm said. "He had us followed in any case."

"But if he learns—"

"If Gisèle has put herself undercover with Tommy Belmont, we have to assume she can take care of herself." Lady Frances's voice was level but had an undercurrent of iron.

Andrew swung towards her, gaze raw with fear. "Ma'am—"

Frances's fingers closed on his wrist. "Believe me, Andrew, I'm as worried as you are. But I think we've all been failing to remember that Gisèle's taking after Arabella may not be entirely something to fear. Arabella was a formidable woman."

Raoul turned his coffee cup in his hands. "Yes," he said, "so she was."

Frances and Archie and Harry and Cordy went home with promises to return early in the morning. Andrew went up to bed, voice contained, gaze haunted but at the same time indicating he wanted to be alone to think. With the unerring instinct that had served her so well as a governess, Laura murmured that she'd go upstairs and check on the children. Mélanie had no doubt that Raoul would have preferred to follow her, both to look in on the children and to escape further talk, but he made no move to leave the room. He, Mélanie, and Malcolm were alone in the library. It was, Mélanie realized, the first time the three of them had been alone since their talk after the visit to Sancho, the talk in which she and Malcolm were sure Raoul had lied to them.

Raoul had returned to the Queen Anne chair where he'd been sitting. Malcolm was on the sofa beside Mélanie. A fire glowed in the grate. Two lamps were lit, as was the brace of candles on the library table. The edges of the room were in shadow. Malcolm surveyed his father. Malcolm's face was neutral, but something in the set of his shoulders took Mélanie back to a time, less than a year ago, when Raoul's presence in their home and in their lives—particularly Malcolm's life—had been by no means a settled thing. "We need to talk, O'Roarke."

Raoul returned Malcolm's gaze, his own pleasant, yet more armored than it had been of late. "By all means. What about?"

"You've been lying to us."

Raoul lifted a brow. "About?"

"You said you just happened across Julien St. Juste in the Chat Gris."

Raoul picked up his cooling coffee and took a sip. "Which I did. Improbable as that may sound. If I wanted to make up a story, surely you know I could make up a better one."

Malcolm held his father's gaze. "I know you, O'Roarke. Mélanie knows you. We're both sure you were lying."

"And it was very convenient that you returned to Berkeley Square just in time for Laura and Frances and Archie to send you after us tonight," Mélanie said. "Did you hire Julien?"

"Did I what?" Raoul clunked his coffee cup down on its saucer with unexpected force. "No, of course not."

Mélanie regarded her former spymaster. "There's no 'of course' about it. You might very well not tell us if you had hired him."

Raoul blotted out a splash of coffee on the silver-rimmed saucer. "What are you accusing me of? Hiring Julien to overthrow the British government?"

Mélanie cast a quick glance at her husband. They had been thinking something of the sort, though put like that it sounded a bit mad. Which of course was precisely how Raoul would have made it sound had he truly been embroiled in such a plot.

"You tell us," Malcolm said.

Raoul took another sip of coffee. "I won't deny my quarrels with the British government, but I've never tried to actually overthrow it. I have my hands full in Spain at present. And even that is on hold, given the search for Gisèle."

"You know more about the Wanderer," Malcolm said. "Don't pretend you don't. Did you and my mother hire St. Juste to hide the Wanderer?"

"Did we—" Raoul stared at Malcolm for a moment. Mélanie would swear a shade had slipped from his eyes. "No. Whatever Arabella knew about the Wanderer, she didn't share it with me."

"But you know what the Wanderer is," Mélanie said. "You were lying to me eight years ago when you said you'd never heard of it."

Raoul returned his cup to the saucer and twisted the handle. "Did you think so then?"

"No. I thought you were telling the truth, though I knew perfectly well you didn't always do so." Once she'd been used to the idea that he kept things from her. Now it cut like a knife thrust. "But I know you were lying about Julien. And I'm quite sure you were holding something back about the Wanderer just now."

"You're very good, both of you," Raoul said. "But I thought we took it for granted that we all have secrets."

"Secrets." Malcolm said. "Not outright lies."

"My dear Malcolm, sometimes it's impossible to keep secrets without lies."

"Your work in Spain is one thing." Malcolm's voice was even and firm as iron. "But the Wanderer and St. Juste concern all of us."

"Everything seems to be damnably interconnected. One would think I'd have learned that by now." Raoul drew a hard breath that seemed to shudder through him. "Probably folly to have tried to keep any of it from either of you, but in the circumstances I felt I had to try. You're both owed an explanation, but Laura is as well. I suspect she's also aware I've been holding things back."

Malcolm crossed back to the library table and poured more coffee into his cup. Mélanie could almost hear the words he wasn't saying. *I thought things had changed. I trusted you, against all expectation. I let you into our lives. Into our family*. But instead of angry words, only the slosh of coffee and the clink of a spoon filled the library. He turned towards Mélanie, as though to reach for her cup and refill it, but she got to her feet and crossed to him, partly in solidarity, partly because she couldn't bear to simply sit.

The door opened on this silence. Laura hesitated on the threshold, taking in the scene before her.

Raoul got to his feet. "We were about to share secrets."

"I can go back upstairs," Laura said.

"On the contrary," Raoul said. "I've been holding back too much from you for too long, sweetheart."

She met his gaze for a long moment. "We never promised to share everything," she said.

"Probably as well, because it's a promise neither of us could keep. But much as I thought it wouldn't be the case, I think we've got to the point where this secret is more dangerous kept hidden than shared." He glanced from Laura to Malcolm and Mélanie. "Sit down, all of you."

He spoke quietly, but something in his tone had them all seated within moments, Mélanie and Malcolm on the sofa, Laura in one of the Queen Anne chairs. Raoul remained standing, one arm on the mantle. His gaze moved among them. "I know I can't ask you to promise to keep quiet about this, but I will ask that you think carefully about what you do with the information I'm about to reveal."

Raoul had always had a sense of the theatrical, but this was exaggerated even for him. "For God's sake, Raoul," Mélanie said. "We may keep secrets from each other, but isn't it a given at this point that, once shared, we all keep each other's secrets?"

"We've never shared a secret precisely of this sort."

"Yes, but—"

"I'm serious. Deadly serious. And I use the term advisedly."

CHAPTER 32

MÉLANIE HAD ONLY HEARD that edge in her spymaster's voice once before, when he'd rescued her from the bandits who had nearly killed her for information. From Laura's silence and fixed expression, Mélanie didn't think she'd ever heard him talk in that way.

Beside Mélanie on the sofa, Malcolm had gone completely still. "The only other time I heard you talk like that was when I was six and ran too near a stream with a swift-moving current."

Remembered fear flashed in Raoul's gaze. "I was afraid of your being swept away. As I am now."

"I've never been one to idly reveal a confidence," Malcolm said.

"Nor have I," Mélanie added.

"Nor I," Laura said.

Raoul's gaze moved among them. Had she not noticed in the old days how those cool gray eyes could warm? Mélanie wondered. Or was he the one who'd changed?

Raoul scraped a hand over his hair, much in the way Malcolm did when he was searching for the right words. There was something unexpectedly schoolboyish about it that she was used to from Malcolm, but not Raoul. It sat oddly with his intense seriousness. "This goes back to when you were all children," he said. "I met Josephine Bonaparte—Josephine de Beauharnais then—when we were both imprisoned in Les Carmes. You know that. I don't think either Josephine or I expected to live. When I wrote the letter that Hortense gave to Malcolm in d'Arenberg, I fully expected never to see him again. I wasn't at all sure Josephine would survive to get it to him, but I hoped there was a chance. There are things one says at such a time that one would never dream of saying in the light of freedom and sanity. There are bonds that form that have nothing to do with the more conventional relationships between men and women." He glanced down at the fire for a moment, his gaze more than usually hooded. "I tell you this as context for what comes after."

Mélanie stared at her former lover. She'd heard the story before, in bits and pieces. But never quite like this, in these words. "You were both released from prison," she said.

"When Robespierre fell. Josephine escaped death by a day. I went back to London as soon as I could, to see Arabella and Malcolm."

"I remember," Malcolm said. He hesitated a moment, then added, "I don't think anyone's ever hugged me so tightly."

Raoul's gaze met Malcolm's for a moment, memories echoing between them. "I went back and forth between Paris and London and Ireland for some time after that."

"I remember," Malcolm said. "You'd appear at unexpected moments."

"Much as you do with Emily now," Laura said.

Raoul gave a faint smile. "It was a heady time. The sheer relief of having escaped the Terror—I know I felt it and it seemed in the very air. We'd cheated death and we were all a little drunk on freedom. There was unbridled license in all things. It was much the same in Britain, but in Paris we could be open about it. No more hiding behind the veneer of marriage and social convention. Josephine was a widow with two children and no money. She needed a protector."

"Barras," Mélanie said.

Raoul nodded. "Paul Barras, the most powerful of the directors who ran the country."

None of this was new information, though Raoul was drawing it together with unwonted seriousness. "Julien was her lover too," Mélanie said.

"Yes, her relationship with Barras was hardly exclusive on either side. In fact, he'd later encourage her relationship with Bonaparte. But she made him an admirable hostess. And he used her to extract information."

"What a surprise," Mélanie murmured.

Raoul regarded her for a moment, his gaze like dark, still water. Memories echoed between them as well. "She wasn't a trained spy. But her salon was the ideal place to gather information. It was there that I first met Julien St. Juste. I've never been sure if St. Juste seduced Josephine for information, or she seduced him, but by the time I met him they were already lovers. My first glimpse of him was turning the pages of her music in her salon. I think he was still in his teens, with fair hair and the sort of smile that prompts young girls to scribble madly in their journals. He and I left Josephine's together that same evening and walked to the Palais Royale. That was the night I saw a man fall to the ground as we walked past and realized St. Juste had stuck a knife in his side without barely breaking his stride."

"Was it random?" Laura asked. "I mean, is he a crazed killer on top of everything else?"

Raoul turned to his lover. "He's certainly a killer, but his targets are chosen. The man was an Austrian agent. Someone had tasked St. Juste to kill him." Raoul shifted his position, one hand on the mantle, as though to anchor himself. "Louis XVI and Marie Antoinette had been executed, but the dauphin and his sister Marie-Thérèse were still imprisoned in the Temple. What to do with them was a constant tension." He was silent for a moment, as though he, to whom words came so easily, was choosing his exact words with care. "As principal director, Barras, Josephine's protector, had charge of the children."

Mélanie felt the jolt that ran through her husband, on the sofa beside her, at the same moment the possibility occurred to her. But surely—

Raoul stared down into the fire for a moment. "The dauphin was ill and failing in prison. Josephine had a soft heart. Barras knew the value of a bargaining chip. And didn't trust his fellow directors. I've sometimes thought it should have occurred to me what they might try, but it didn't. Failure of imagination, perhaps. In any case, I didn't have a suspicion until Josephine confided in me years later."

The dauphin, heir of Louis XVI and Marie Antoinette, rumored to have died in prison. Also rumored for years to have been smuggled out and hidden away. Rightful King of France, if he resurfaced.

Laura drew in her breath. Raoul's gaze moved to her, softening with concern. "Not my cleverest moment, sweetheart."

The room was gone so still Mélanie could hear the hiss of the Argand lamp. Malcolm was staring at his father. Mélanie was quite sure he had seen it, but he seemed to hesitate to put it into words. "My God. Are you saying that Josephine and Barras spirited away the dauphin—"

"There were always rumors," Mélanie said. "That Barras and Josephine smuggled the boy away."

"We even heard them in India," Laura said.

"Tsar Alexander actually told me in Vienna that Josephine had confided as much to him." Mélanie pictured the tsar's intent face as he spun the story. "But I never really believed—"

"Quite." Raoul shifted his arm along the mantle. "We know the tsar's penchant for elaboration. To put it charitably. But for once he appears to have been telling the truth. According to Josephine, she and Barras switched the dauphin for another boy with similar coloring in early spring of 1795. The substitute boy died of natural causes a few months later. The real dauphin was smuggled off to a safe location."

The implications settled over the room like the Queen of the Night's cloak. "Let me guess," Mélanie said. "Julien St. Juste was employed to make the exchange."

Raoul met her gaze. "Precisely. Josephine told me in 1809. Bonaparte was being pressured to divorce her and marry a foreign princess. By Fouché, among others. Josephine was afraid Fouché would get hold of her coded instructions to St. Juste about the boy's transfer."

Mélanie pressed a hand to her temple. "*Sacrebleu*. That was the paper you wanted me to steal from Julien."

"It was unpardonable of me to involve you. But I needed someone I could trust implicitly."

Mélanie recalled the terror on Josephine's face that night, when Mélanie had confessed she'd failed to steal the paper but that Julien St. Juste had given it to her voluntarily and said Josephine was the one person on earth he'd never betray. Hortense had been there. Mélanie had watched them burn the paper together. "I understand her desperation. If Bonaparte had learned his wife knew the dauphin was alive and had kept it from him—"

Raoul nodded. "Not to mention the uses Bonaparte's enemies could have made of the information, either finding the real dauphin or using the story to put forwards an imposter. God knows there were enough imposters at the Restoration as it was."

"You must have been terrified as well."

"I was. On multiple counts. Mostly the danger I'd put you in."

"The Wanderer," Malcolm said.

Raoul nodded. "Josephine told me that was the code name."

"Where?" Malcolm's voice came out as a hoarse rasp. "Where is the boy?"

"Josephine claimed she didn't know herself, for the boy's own safety."

"But St. Juste does."

"He'd have had to."

"In Rivendell?"

"Perhaps. Or perhaps you're right that there's another clue in the treasure hunt in Rivendell. My guess is that Josephine was telling the truth that she and Barras didn't know the boy's location, but that they told St. Juste to hide evidence of where he was somewhere they could uncover it if they ever chose to and weren't in a position to ask St. Juste himself."

"Last summer in Italy," Malcolm said. "When we found out the League were looking for St. Juste. You must have guessed it was because he knew where the dauphin was."

"Suspected," Raoul said. "Though there could be a number of other reasons they wanted him." His gaze moved from Malcolm to Mélanie to Laura. "It seemed safer for all of you not to know."

"For once, I agree with you," Mélanie said.

Laura was frowning. "If Fouché knew this ten years ago, why didn't he blackmail or torture it out of St. Juste long since?"

"I don't think Fouché knew the whole story. Only that St. Juste was in possession of a document that could be damaging to Josephine. In the end, Bonaparte did divorce her, the war worsened, and Fouché's attentions turned elsewhere."

"And you." Malcolm was studying his father. "You've known the rightful King of France could be out there somewhere for over a decade?"

"*Could* be."

"So St. Juste hid the boy in England?" Malcolm asked.

"Possibly. There could be a clue in Rivendell that leads us to Prussia or Austria or God knows where."

"Yet England has certain advantages. It would be unexpected for a French agent to hide him in the heart of the enemy. And at the time, England had a number of Royalist sympathizers who could be counted on to protect him. Not to mention the surviving members of the royal family were here. It's where I'd have chosen."

"So would I," Mélanie said.

Raoul's mouth curved slightly. "All right, yes, I might—I probably would—have done so as well."

"The boy's never been more valuable," Malcolm said. "Whoever could put him on the throne could control France. The only people who might not want him back are the current king and his adherents. And the Comte d'Artois, as the heir. Just about everyone else could use him to further their own agendas. The British, the Russians, the Austrians, a dozen different factions in France—"

"Bonapartists who might see a puppet king as preferable to the current monarch," Raoul added. "But no, I haven't been trying to find him."

"Why not?" Malcolm asked.

"France should be a republic."

"That didn't stop you from supporting Bonaparte."

"I thought I could count on Bonaparte to preserve some reforms. And I was right to a large degree. Rival monarchs lead to weak countries and infighting. You have only to look at your own country's history."

"Does Hortense know about the dauphin?" Mélanie asked.

A shadow crossed Raoul's face. "If Josephine confided in the tsar—it's possible she confided in Hortense."

"Hortense was there when her mother burned the paper from St. Juste," Mélanie said. "But I don't think she knew what it was. At least, not then. And I don't think she knew what the Wanderer meant when those men attacked us and tried to capture Julien in Switzerland."

"How long has Carfax known about the Wanderer?" Malcolm asked in a taut voice.

Raoul met his gaze. "I saw Carfax today. He admitted to knowing about the Wanderer, but not for how long. What do you think?"

"He never gave me the least indication that he knew anything of the sort. But that's just what I'd expect if Carfax had known all along."

"I don't think St. Juste would have told him," Raoul said. "On Josephine's account. But he didn't tell him about Mélanie either."

"No, he told Sylvie St. Ives," Malcolm said.

"Probably in bed," Mélanie added. "So he might have let something slip to Sylvie about the Wanderer as well. And she might have told Carfax."

Malcolm put his head in his hands.

"Carfax seems to have just started looking now," Mélanie said. "Perhaps he's only just learned."

"What do you think he'd do if he found the dauphin?" Laura asked.

"Carfax fears instability, almost above all." Malcolm looked up. "I think he'd see the return of the dauphin as dangerous, oddly for some of the same reasons Raoul fears it."

"Not entirely odd," Raoul said.

"So I think Carfax would likely be quiet but keep watch on the dauphin," Malcolm continued. "But if Carfax was upset with Louis XVIII or his successors, I could see him deciding to make use of the dauphin. On the other hand, if he thought the League or Bonapartists were going to get hold of the dauphin, I could see Carfax deciding he needed to be eliminated."

"So could I," Raoul said.

"And now we know the League are searching for the dauphin," Laura said. "And it's quite clear what they'd see. A way to control France."

Malcolm was staring at Raoul. "How the devil did my mother get mixed up in this?"

"I wish to hell I knew." Raoul took a turn about the hearthrug. "I didn't know any of it until after Arabella died. Arabella seems to have taken the papers from Wyncliffe three years after the dauphin's disappearance. As to how Wyncliffe got them— "

Malcolm studied his father. "Who else knows? About the dauphin?"

Raoul hesitated. "I can't be sure whom Josephine may have told. When I spoke with her she was terrified of the news getting out. But if she actually said something to Tsar Alexander, she may have told others. On the other hand, it's possible Alexander really was making it up. It wouldn't be the first time. As I said, I don't believe Josephine told Hortense, but she may have done, towards the end of her life. But I know of only one other person who knows for a certainty. Talleyrand."

"God in heaven. And yet, how strangely logical," Malcolm said. "Was he part of the plot?"

"Oh, no. I can't imagine Josephine and Barras trusting him," Raoul said. "I didn't find out he knew until after Mélanie met St. Juste and St. Juste burned the paper. Talleyrand came to see me a few months later and said we hadn't always agreed on everything, but he trusted I'd understand how vital it was to keep the information about the Wanderer secret."

"How did he learn about the Wanderer?" Mélanie asked.

"He didn't tell me."

"Could he have learned from Arabella?" Mélanie asked.

"It's possible, if Arabella knew the meaning of the papers she had. It's also possible Talleyrand put the idea of retrieving the papers into her head. After the first discussion, Talleyrand and I didn't discuss the Wanderer again. Until recently at Dunmykel."

"Of course," Malcolm said. "What did Talleyrand say?"

"We were both trying damnably hard not to let on how shaken we were. I promised to try to learn more. Though once Gisèle disappeared, I told him that had to come first. He said he'd had no notion Arabella knew about the Wanderer. But it wouldn't be the first time Talleyrand had lied to me."

"Damnably coincidental Talleyrand happens to be in Britain—in our house—just when all of this begins to unravel," Malcolm said. "And you know how I feel about coincidence."

"You think Talleyrand told Carfax and the League about the Wanderer?" Mélanie asked.

"It's hard to imagine that, even given Talleyrand's extreme flexibility in the alliances he'll make," Malcolm said. "But if he knew or suspected that the others were looking for the Wanderer, it could have helped bring him to Britain."

"Most definitely," Raoul said. "But I will say he looked genuinely shaken the night Aline decoded the first of the papers."

Malcolm looked at his father. "However Talleyrand felt about the dauphin ten years ago, now he could see his restoration as a way to get himself back into power."

"And his shock was fear that we were about to uncover his plan? It's possible." Raoul's brows drew together. "But it doesn't explain why Carfax and the League are searching for the Wanderer now."

"The League and Carfax and seemingly someone else," Mélanie said. "Whoever hired Thomas Ambrose and was behind the attack on Tommy before he came to Dunmykel and hired the third set of people going after the papers today."

"Unless the third player is Talleyrand," Malcolm said.

"He had Tommy attacked?" Mélanie asked.

"I wouldn't put it past Talleyrand," Malcolm said. "He has a long reach. I'm sure he still has contact with agents in Britain. The biggest argument I can see against it is that if Talleyrand is searching for the dauphin, I'd be shocked he let Carfax and the League learn of it."

"So would I," Raoul said. "But something brought it up now."

Malcolm met his father's gaze. "If the secret was still buried, I'd agree it would be best to leave it that way. But given the number of people searching for the dauphin, we need to find him. For his own sake."

"And then?" Laura asked.

"I don't believe in hereditary monarchy," Malcolm said. "God knows we've all felt the need of employment, but helping a king regain his throne isn't what I had in mind. Any more than I am going to turn Jacobite."

"Parliament put the Hanoverians on the throne," Laura said. "One could argue with the choice, but it was a choice. Whereas the dauphin lost his throne because he was spirited away."

"That assumes one even recognizes the restoration as legitimate," Mélanie said. "And not something imposed on France from the outside." She glanced at Malcolm. "Sorry."

"No apology necessary. I'm more concerned with who might try to make use of the dauphin if we do find him. What we might be unleashing. But at this point, if we stay quiet and someone else finds him and tries to use him or eliminate him, that will be on our heads."

Raoul nodded. "It's damnable. And, as so often, there are no easy answers."

"I never heard a breath about it from the League," Laura said. "But apparently Wynclife knew twenty years ago. Could this be why they want you dead? Because you know about the dauphin and they're afraid you'll stop them?"

"That seems to be putting rather a lot of faith in my ability to stop them," Raoul said. "But it's true that if they have some long-range plan involving the dauphin, they might see me as a threat. Or at least as someone who could guess the game they were playing at."

"The League in control of a country." Mélanie shivered. "That goes beyond even what we've feared."

"It's true their interests have circled round France from the beginning," Raoul said. "They were smuggling art treasures across the Channel when Alistair and Glenister founded the League."

"And Alistair and Dewhurst tried to use the queen's diamonds to ruin Cardinal de Rohan and inadvertently helped bring on the Revolution," Malcolm said.

"How much do you think Gisèle knows?" Laura asked.

Malcolm frowned. "Gelly obviously gleaned the location of the box we found tonight from more fragments hidden in Mama's jewels—probably the necklace she got from Judith. She knew it was important from our conversation before she left Dunmykel. So she might have sent me word just because of that."

"Assuming she's gone undercover with the League by running with Tommy," Mélanie said, "something made her decide the stakes were high enough to leave her family and run the risk. Which I'm not sure she would have done just based on what we all knew before she left."

Malcolm met her gaze for a moment. "I think she was looking for occupation."

Mélanie returned his look. "Even so, darling. I'm quite sure she wouldn't have run lightly."

"Could Mr. Belmont have told her?" Laura asked. "At least, some of it? In an attempt to win her over?"

"Telling her about the dauphin would be a huge risk," Raoul said. "But he has to have told her something. I think it's more likely to have been to do with her father. But if he implied the Wanderer was crucial, and connects to her father, that might have made her more determined. And then, it's possible Tommy let something slip on their journey or in London. Or Gisèle uncovered something spying on him. She's obviously far more adept than any of us suspected."

"Far more," Malcolm said.

"Beverston must know," Laura said. "He sent Mr. Belmont to Scotland. And Miranda Dormer was reporting to him as well as reporting on his activities to Roger Smythe."

"And caught the eye of Carfax, who almost certainly knew about the dauphin," Malcolm said. "It seems more and more as though Gelly's disappearance and Miranda Dormer's murder are connected."

"This could explain why Carfax isn't talking," Mélanie said. "If he thought any explanation he might give could lead to it coming out that the dauphin was alive and possibly hidden in Britain—"

"Yes, Carfax might risk his life for that," Malcolm said. "At least long enough to buy himself time."

"Do you think St. Juste would help any of these groups?" Laura asked.

Mélanie exchanged a look with Raoul. "Always difficult to predict what Julien might do," Raoul said. "While Josephine was alive, he'd have tried to protect her. Now that she's gone, that may not hold him."

"He wouldn't like to be played by anyone," Mélanie said. "Though he might enjoy playing them off against each other."

"He hired Nan and Bet Simcox's brother Robby for something," Malcolm said. "And obviously not searching for his own clues. But he seems to have been anticipating violence. Or breaking and entering." He looked at Raoul. "We've wondered if Arabella could have worked with St. Juste. Could they have been lovers?"

Raoul went still for an infinitesimal fraction of a second before saying in a level, conversational tone, "I don't see why not. In fact, realistically, if they knew each other, I'd say it's likely. They'd each have challenged the other."

"So he could be Gelly's father," Malcolm said in a level voice that was the twin of Raoul's own.

CHAPTER 33

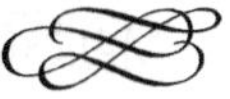

Raoul drew in and released his breath. "Hypothetically. If Bella actually knew him. If they were lovers."

"She hid the papers when Gelly was a baby."

"So she did."

"It could explain why the League want Gelly."

"To try to negotiate with St. Juste, saying they have his daughter?"

"Would that matter to him?" Malcolm asked.

Raoul exchanged a look with Mélanie. "Difficult to predict anything when it comes to Julien," Mélanie said. "But he does have a certain sense of loyalty. To Josephine. To Hortense."

"To you," Raoul said.

"Yes," Malcolm said, "we all saw that, Mel, don't deny it."

"I'm not denying it, though I think you're both exaggerating. But if Julien knew he had a daughter, I think it would mean something to him."

"You think he's trying to rescue her?" Laura asked. "That's why he wants Simcox?"

"Interesting," Raoul said. "I'd have thought Julien would just demand they return Gisèle, though. Or try to get a message to her."

"What if she's known Julien was her father for a while?" Mélanie said. "What if she and Julien are in touch? What if—"

Malcolm met her gaze as he sometimes did when their minds clicked together. "St. Juste suggested she go undercover with the League?"

"It would be like Julien," Mélanie said. "Learning he had a daughter and promptly making use of her."

"It would," Raoul said. "If we're right about any of it. And there are a lot of 'ifs.'"

Malcolm pushed himself to his feet and strode to the fireplace. "We'll have to decide how much to tell the others. Before Harry and I leave for Rivendell in the morning." He picked up the poker and pushed a log back into the fire, then turned his gaze to Raoul.

Raoul's gaze locked on Malcolm's own. It was one of the rare times Mélanie had seen genuine uncertainty in her former spymaster's gaze. "For almost a decade, I've lived with the fear of this getting out."

"Contain the information," Malcolm said in a carefully neutral voice. "It's the practical response to anything this dangerous."

"And I fell back on the training of a lifetime," Raoul said. "That's true. It's also true I didn't want any of you burdened with the choices. Or the implications."

The gaze he turned to Malcolm was somehow at once armored and more vulnerable than Mélanie had ever seen it.

Malcolm returned Raoul's gaze for a long moment, his own gaze giving little away. "I'm not sure I'd have done what you did. But I think I understand."

"That's generous."

Malcolm inclined his head. For a moment, he seemed on the verge of saying more. When at last he spoke, Mélanie wasn't sure it was what he had originally intended to say. "Which doesn't settle the question of what, if anything, we tell the others." He returned the poker to the andirons, without rattling the metal.

"The revelation of how much Gisèle apparently knows changes things," Raoul said. "God knows my instinct is still to contain the information. But I think we need to share the information, at least with the Davenports and Andrew—because of Gisèle—and Archie. Probably Frances as well. I'd rather she didn't know, given her connections to the British royal family, and the fact that she isn't trained to this life. But I'm not sure it's fair to ask Archie to keep it from her."

"You kept it from us," Laura said in a quiet voice.

Raoul turned his gaze to her. "So I did. It was damnably uncomfortable." He glanced into the fire. "Talleyrand would probably kill me for suggesting we tell anyone else. And I'm not necessarily speaking metaphorically."

"He didn't want you to tell us," Laura said.

"He accused me of going soft."

"And now you have?"

"I think I've been reminded of what's important. Which doesn't mean I'd do it differently if I could do it again."

"No, I don't suppose you would," Laura said. Her voice too was neutral.

"You're worried about telling Lady Frances, but not Cordy?" Mélanie asked.

"Cordelia has the instincts of an agent," Raoul said. "And it's clear where her loyalties lie."

"And Fanny was once loyal to Alistair?" Malcolm asked.

"Fanny's loyalties are complicated. But I don't doubt she loves her family and Archie. Above all, I don't doubt she wants to find Gisèle."

Malcolm's gaze continued steady on Raoul's own. "You don't think she'll be able to let the secret of the dauphin go."

Raoul was silent for a long moment. "I think she'll have the hardest time with it of any of us. Assuming, at the end of all this, we really are able to keep the secret."

Or have to choose sides in a potential contest over the throne of France. Mélanie's fingers locked on her elbows. And yet they had all agreed that saving a young man's life came before the risk of international instability. A choice she'd have once said she'd have been uncertain about, that she wasn't sure Raoul would have made, that she'd have thought might have divided them from Malcolm, had seemed obvious to all of them.

"I understand your qualms, but I think we need to tell Frances," Malcolm said. "It could be more dangerous for her not to know."

Raoul nodded. "A good point."

"We'll tell them in the morning," Malcolm said. "For the moment, I think we need to try to keep David out of it."

"He won't thank you," Mélanie said.

"No," Malcolm agreed. "No one likes being kept out of a secret."

"Quite," Raoul said.

LAURA STUDIED her lover in the privacy of their bedchamber. The man she'd barely known a year ago, who now knew her deepest secrets. Who had helped her find her daughter, and become her daughter's father. Who was the father of the child she'd give birth to in a few months. "You've been shouldering a lot."

Raoul gave a dry laugh. "That's one way of putting it."

Laura turned so she could see him in the light. He was standing by an armchair, his coat held in both hands, his fingers rigid on the black fabric. "My love, it's a fearful burden. The fate of a country. Potentially, the fate of the Continent. I can see why your instinct would be to hold it close. Anyone who knows it is put in a hellish situation as well. Malcolm's still a Member of Parliament, which complicates things further. As to you and me, we never promised to tell each other everything. Though I did assume—"

"Yes?" His gaze was taut on her own.

"That we'd share things that affected both of us, I suppose. And I can see how in some ways it would seem this doesn't. Or, at least, didn't. But once the papers were discovered at Dunmykel, we were all impacted. The children too."

"A good point. But keeping secrets has been the habit of a lifetime for me."

"So you fell back on old habits?"

"I behaved as I've always behaved, by the rules that have governed my life. And when I slipped out of our bed I felt I was violating something precious."

"But you did it anyway," Laura said.

"I did."

"To protect us."

"In part."

"You're not used to sharing your life with anyone."

"True enough." He studied her for a moment, head tilted to one side. The shadows cast by the Argand lamp slanted between them. "In theory, spies probably shouldn't have families. But one can rarely live one's life entirely according to theory."

"You never promised to share your life with me. And I certainly never asked you to."

"I know, beloved. It's one of the remarkable things about you."

Laura watched him in the lamplight. His face, his crisp voice, his contained movements seemed designed to hold secrets. Yet she had seen his intense gaze stripped with honesty before he'd so much as touched her hand. "We began knowing each other's secrets. We played a chess game with them. One could say we fell in love over them. Part of that was circumstance. We learned things about each other I doubt either of us would reveal to anyone willingly. But we also had the understanding to guess at more. Before that night in Maidstone, I could imagine taking a lover. I couldn't imagine—what we have."

For an instant, something flared in his hooded gaze. "You can't think I could imagine it. One moment I was telling myself to be cautious for both our sakes, the next I was pledging fidelity in the Berkeley Square garden—"

"With a warning of all the things you couldn't offer me—"

"And then I was buying you earrings, thinking about you like a boy half my age, and kissing you in an antechamber the moment we had an instant alone. I was in the midst of it before I realized—"

"What a fool you were being?"

His gaze, steady on her face, was level, yet oddly like a caress. "What I was risking. For both of us."

"It seems to me you dwelled on it entirely too much. For months I had to tell you it didn't matter, when all the while I was afraid you were looking for a way to end things."

"My darling, I'd never have—"

"You might have done. If you thought it was for my own good." He wouldn't now, because of the baby. Not for the first time, she felt the smallest twinge of guilt. She had no doubt he was as happy about their child as she was. But she also knew it wasn't something he'd ever have actively chosen. Mostly for her sake, but also for his own. She hated the thought that she'd trapped him in any way.

"But perhaps you were right, in a way," she continued. "No, I don't mean that," she added, at the shadow of concern in his gaze. "But because we started off having shared so much, we never had to worry about taking risks. We never had to worry about—"

"What we weren't sharing?"

"What lines we couldn't bear crossing." Laura drew a breath. "Gisèle may be at risk because she's St. Juste's daughter. The same could happen to Emily. Or our unborn child." She touched her stomach. The baby was a constant presence now, kicking, stirring, warm beneath her hand. "You can't keep secrets to protect us. If you do, and one of our children is hurt, I'll never forgive you."

"I wouldn't—"

"No?" She held his gaze with her own. "You're going against the instincts of a lifetime. You admitted it yourself."

"My love." He crossed to her side, but hesitated before he touched her. "I went against the instincts of a lifetime when I pledged myself to you."

She put her hands on his chest. "We're going to have to go on doing what we've always done."

"Which is?"

"Make it up as we go along."

He gave a rough laugh. His arms closed round her with unexpected force. He held her close for a long moment, as though she was anchoring him to sanity. His breath was ragged against her hair. His arms shook. She drew back and looked up at him. What she saw in the depths of his eyes shook her to the core. She'd seen him stripped with vulnerability, but she'd never seen raw fear in his controlled gaze.

She put her hand against the side of his face. "We'll get through this. We always do."

He caught her hand and pressed it to his lips. But she saw the ghosts of his fears alive in his eyes. Countries shaken. Relationships smashed.

"So often there are no easy answers," she said. "You're usually the first to say that. Surely you knew we'd all understand."

"Hoped."

"Surely you'd have understood, in the same circumstances."

"I like to think I would have."

"You know perfectly well you would have done."

"It was a reminder," he said. "Of the challenges of being what I'm trying to be. And at the same time—three decades fighting the Elsinore League, and we're now facing what we feared most. The League controlling a country."

And not just any country. France, for which he had risked so much.

Laura put her hands on his chest. "There's something else to report about the League." She kept her voice as conversational as possible. "One of their members approached me today."

She told him about Sir Lucius Brandon, as succinctly and with as little drama as possible. Raoul listened without interruption, his gaze steady on her face, but his brows drew together.

"I got you into this."

"Not this," Laura said. "I got entangled with the League on my own. I'm rather insulted they know me so little they think there's the least chance they could turn me against you. Or convince me they could or would protect you."

"They're desperate."

"Which could be an advantage."

"Or could make them more dangerous."

"We've always known the League were a potential threat."

"But they hadn't verbalized it this directly." He pulled her to him again, his chin on her hair. "I don't think I could survive anything happening to you."

"That's nonsense," Laura said, voice muffled by his cravat. "You know you could survive anything if you had to. And you'd have to, for the children."

"There are different definitions of survive. I'd find a way to go on."

Laura pulled her head back to look up at him. "I feel the same way when you're gone. I know I can't completely deny the risks. I trust you're taking every precaution. I trust you. I trust you trust me."

"You know I do, sweetheart. It doesn't make the terror go away."

"It's part of the lives we lead."

He gave a bleak smile and pressed a kiss to her forehead. "That's my Laura. Throwing my own words back at me."

Laura put her hands on his chest. "I don't want you to turn back into the man you were when I met you."

"Nor do I." Raoul pressed a kiss to her forehead. "And I don't think I could. You've changed me irrevocably."

"We've changed each other. And I wouldn't go back either. But that isn't what I meant."

His gaze shifted over her face. "What, beloved?"

"When I first met you in France. In Malcolm and Mélanie's salon. You had the most alive eyes I've ever seen. But at the same time, when you let your guard down—which was only for the briefest moment in all those first months I knew you—you looked like a man who's seen into hell and isn't sure he'll ever escape it."

"I expect a lot of people had that look after Waterloo."

"Yes, but it was more than that for you. You said it to me yourself, driving back from Maidstone. That you'd spent much of the past three years trying to mitigate the damage done at Waterloo, but now in Spain you had a chance to make a difference again. I could see the life sparking in your eyes."

Raoul's hands settled on her shoulders. "I felt alive on that drive back from Maidstone as I hadn't in years. But it had nothing to do with Spain."

Laura found herself smiling in response to the spark in his eyes, but she shook her head. "Yes, my love, and I did as well. But I know what your work in Spain means to you. I can read it between the lines of your letters—even the ones I have to decode. I see it in your eyes when you talk about your work there. I taste it in your goodbye kiss. Sometimes I see it in your eyes in unguarded moments when you're here thinking you should be there."

"My darling. If I've ever given your the sense—

"It doesn't lessen what I mean to you. Or Emily. Or the baby. At least I don't think it does. And I want you with us as much as possible. Never doubt that. But I don't want to see you lose what drives you. For your sake. And for the sake of change in Spain."

"You're what drives me. You and our children."

"Sweetheart." She put a hand against the side of his face. "You know it's never that simple. You've been fighting this fight more than half your life. I want you to be able to be true to the man I fell in love with."

"That you fell in love with me at all never ceases to amaze me."

MALCOLM PUT his head in his hands. "God in heaven."

Mélanie leaned against the closed door of their bedchamber. "It could have been worse. My imaginings were worse."

"Raoul plotting revolution?" Malcolm looked up. He had stopped in the middle of the bedchamber. He was tugging at the folds of his cravat as though he wasn't aware of what his fingers were doing. "Yes, mine too. This doesn't put us on opposite sides. But it—"

"Puts us in the middle of a thicket worse than the one round Princess Aurora's castle." She hesitated. "It's always going to be hard. Knowing what we can share and what we can't. We're all going to have to make judgment calls."

"I can see why he kept it secret," Malcolm said. "Angry as I was when I knew he had kept something secret. I probably would have kept this secret myself. Probably." His voice, as when he'd spoken to Raoul, was carefully neutral. "In any case, it's difficult for me to blame O'Roarke for wanting to protect his loved ones."

"Because you're guilty of it yourself?"

He gave a faint smile. "Guilty as charged."

"It's a very dangerous secret. You're a Member of Parliament still. You could feel obligated to do something."

Malcolm nodded. "And he might have thought we'd disagree on what to do with the information."

Mélanie stared at her husband. "You think he thought I'd want to make use of the dauphin?"

"As we discussed, it would be one way to change France. Or he might have thought I'd feel we should restore him to his rightful place. Or that that was my duty as an MP."

Images and impulses raced through her brain. "I wouldn't—"

"We weren't sure how O'Roarke would jump, sweetheart. He wondered the same about us."

"Thank God we're both sensible." She pressed her fingers against the door panels. She realized she was shaking. "Malcolm—"

He stepped forwards and drew her into his arms. "Yes. I know."

"I was terrified," Mélanie said into his cravat. "The whole time we've been trying to sort out what was happening. I didn't want to admit it, but I couldn't bear to contemplate what we'd find at the end of it."

"And we've found a thicket, as you said."

"But at least we're all on the same side."

His arms tightened round her. "We've been in a fight. We have three unseen enemies. We're looking for the lost heir to a throne whom none of us wants to see restored. Gelly's still missing. But yes, I feel relieved too."

"And we're in the midst of two investigations which seem to be getting tangled into one." Mélanie drew back to look at her husband. "Speaking of which, I don't know that Dorinda Smythe has the strongest motive. But after our interview today, I'd say she felt more strongly about Miranda than perhaps anyone we've talked to. Jealousy can be a powerful motive."

"It sounds as though Lady Caroline was jealous too."

"But Dorinda Smythe had been jealous for longer. And I can see her being horrified at the idea that Roger might bring Miranda into their household—" Mélanie broke off.

"Yes," Malcolm said, "there are certain parallels. But the thing is, I like O'Roarke, and I don't think Dorinda Smythe liked Miranda."

Mélanie looked up at her husband, torn between shock and laughter. "Darling—"

"Simple statement of fact. There's no point in pretending our situation is other than it is."

"It's odd," Mélanie said.

Her husband raised a brow in inquiry.

"Derenvil and Lady Caroline. And Roger and Dorinda Smythe. They're very different. But neither can seem to talk to each other."

"It can be the most challenging thing for a couple to do. Talking." Malcolm smoothed a strand of hair off her temple. "I remember being terrified to speak to you. At least, about anything that touched on emotions. And there were so many things you couldn't say to me."

She looked steadily into his eyes. "I still managed to say a lot."

"But it's better now."

She pressed her cheek against his shoulder. "Infinitely."

Odd. Only ten months ago she'd been keenly aware things would never be the same between them. And she'd given a bleak smile at the suggestion that they might be better.

"We'll tell the others in the morning, before Harry and I leave for Rivendell," Malcolm said. "One step at a time. Much as I want to cut a path straight to Gelly, we have to pick our way through the thicket."

Mélanie nodded. "Meanwhile, we have another night in our bed."

He bent his head and kissed her. "So we do."

CHAPTER 34

HARRY REACHED FOR HIS COFFEE. "Well, this certainly explains why everyone is so interested in the Wanderer."

"Damnable that he can't simply be left safely where he's been for twenty-some years." Frances met Raoul's gaze across the table and must have caught a flash of surprise in his eyes. "You thought I'd argue we should risk war and disruption to restore the rightful king to his throne? That doesn't really sound like me. Or did you think I'd feel differently because I knew Louis and Marie Antoinette and met the boy as a child?"

"I have a healthy respect for the role personal feelings can play," Raoul said.

Frances turned her coffee cup in her hands. "I'm delighted the dauphin survived, but I suspect he'd be far happier staying wherever he is than becoming a pawn in this game you all play."

"Do you think he feels that way?" Cordelia asked. "He was old enough when he was taken away that he must know his rightful heritage."

"He certainly hasn't made any effort to claim it," Malcolm said.

Raoul took a swallow of coffee. His posture gave little away, as usual, but Mélanie thought he sat more easily now the truth was out among their friends. At the same time, the weight of the secret still seemed to sit on his shoulders. "The dauphin wasn't treated well in prison. It's one of the reasons Josephine wanted to get him away. By the time he was smuggled out of the Temple, it's difficult to tell what state he'd have been in, physically or mentally. He may not wish to be king. He may not be equipped for the role."

"But he may be just the sort who could be manipulated by those who want a figurehead," Archie said.

Raoul met his friend's gaze. "Quite."

"Once we find him, the question is, can we keep his existence a secret, even if he wishes to remain anonymous," Malcolm said.

Or would they be embroiled in somehow vouching for the rightful King of France, the last thing Mélanie had ever thought to find herself doing.

"How much do you think Castlereagh knows?" Harry asked.

"I've been wondering." Malcolm took a sip of coffee. "This could be why Castlereagh warned me off the investigation so strongly. If the dauphin turned up and his identity could be proved conclusively, our government would have no choice but to back him. But I doubt Castlereagh wants France disrupted any more than Carfax does. And the thought of the League or anyone else controlling the dauphin would terrify him."

"So you think he and Carfax are working together?" Cordelia asked.

"Possibly." Malcolm frowned into his cup for a moment. "It's difficult to see what advantage they both gain from Carfax remaining in prison."

"Stopping the investigation?" Laura suggested.

"Because one or both of them is behind Miranda Dormer's death?" Malcolm shifted his cup on its saucer. "It's a possibility we have to consider. But if Carfax is, I keep coming back to why he didn't have an escape route. I could see him keeping quiet if he thought more investigation would uncover the dauphin's whereabouts, though. Which gets to whether there is a connection between Miranda Dormer and the dauphin."

"We'll have to see what we find in Rivendell," Harry said.

Andrew had been frowning into his scarcely touched coffee cup, saying little. Now he lifted his head and looked at Malcolm. "You really think Julien St. Juste is Gelly's father?"

"We have no proof," Malcolm said. "But it fits some of the facts."

"A number of them," Raoul said. He glanced at Frances.

"I never heard of the man until last September, in Italy," Frances said. "But from what you say, it could explain why Bella said I was much better off not knowing. And I could certainly see a man such as you describe appealing to Bella."

"And you think Gelly may have been working for him—for how long? Weeks? Months? A year?" The strain of the past weeks tore at Andrew's voice.

"We don't know that she's working with him at all," Malcolm said. "And if she is, we don't know how long it's been going on. But it might explain Gelly's apparently going undercover with Tommy."

Andrew looked from Malcolm to Mélanie to Raoul. "From what you've said, St. Juste is extremely dangerous."

Mélanie met Malcolm's gaze, then saw Malcolm glance at Raoul. "Julien's dangerous," Mélanie said. "But if Gisèle is his daughter, I think he'll protect her."

"Think," Andrew said.

"Difficult to be sure of anything with St. Juste," Raoul said. "But as dangerous an opponent as he can be, he can be an even more powerful ally."

"You don't think any of these groups could have bought him?" Andrew asked. "The League or Carfax or this third person or people?"

"If so, they wouldn't need to search for the Wanderer," Harry pointed out.

Andrew nodded and scraped a hand across his face. "You're right. I'm not thinking. Your lives are dangerous enough. St. Juste's sounds beyond imagining. But perhaps if Gelly is his daughter, that accounts for a lot."

"Biology doesn't create people," Raoul said. "We're the sum of our own pasts and our own choices. If St. Juste is Gisèle's father, that hasn't made her who she is any more than being Louis XVI and Marie Antoinette's son has made the dauphin whoever he is now. Blood doesn't define us. My whole life is built on that."

"I won't argue with that," Frances said. "But you can't deny one can inherit traits. I can see that looking round this table. If Gisèle inherited St. Juste's brilliance and ruthlessness, combined with Bella's, it explains a lot."

Andrew met her gaze across the table. "My point precisely, ma'am." *Because neither of them was capable of loving.* The unspoken subtext hung in the air.

"What on earth are you going to do in Rivendell?" Cordelia asked, looking from Harry to Malcolm. "Dig up the ground looking for more boxes? Question every young man in his mid-thirties?"

"We can't know until we're there." Malcolm said.

"The people who hired the attackers last night know you have the box," Laura said. "They were following you already. They're bound to follow you to Rivendell. "

"Right. But they won't know which of us is going after the box." Harry glanced at Malcolm. "They're likely to assume you are, though. Perhaps we should rethink who goes to Rivendell."

Malcolm met his friend's gaze. "You're almost certain to be followed even if I don't go with you."

"And there's no one I'd rather have at my back in a fight. But if there's one thing I learned as an agent, it's to use deception to avoid a fight whenever possible. I wonder if we can't disguise the visit to Rivendell as something different."

"I could go with you," Andrew said. He glanced round the

table. "All these people must know we're looking for Gelly by now. If I go, they may think we're off after a clue to her whereabouts."

"Mary Dartford lives not far from Rivendell," Frances said. "One of Gisèle's girlhood friends. You could call on her. Mention at a post house that that's where you're bound."

Andrew nodded. At the possibility of action, his face was more animated than it had been all day.

Malcolm frowned. Mélanie saw the competing pulls of logic and the need to shoulder the burden—not to mention take action—in his face. "If—"

He broke off as Valentin entered the breakfast parlor. "Forgive me, but there's a Mr. Montagu who's just called asking for Mr. Rannoch. He says it's urgent."

VALENTIN HAD SHOWN Kit into the library. In the circumstances, Malcolm thought it was better to speak with him alone. He found Kit standing by the library table, hat and gloves in hand, blue eyes blazing with an intensity that bordered on desperation.

"Is it true?" Kit spun towards Malcolm and slammed his hat and gloves down on the table. "Is the girl Lord Carfax murdered Miranda Dormer?"

Malcolm closed the door. "Yes, unfortunately. We've only just learned. I'm so sorry. You must have grown up with her. I know her sister Elinor—"

"Is the girl I was unofficially promised to." Kit scraped a hand over his hair. The last time Malcolm had seen him in Italy, he had been headed home to escort his younger sister and spend Christmas with their mother, but also to tell Elinor Dormer, the girl he had been on the verge of marrying, that he had fallen in love with Sofia Vincenzo, the daughter of the woman his father had run off to Italy with fifteen years before.

"Yes, we were all in and out of each other's houses when we were small," Kit said. "But how on earth did Miranda—"

"She ran off with John Smythe."

John Smythe had been married to Kit's sister Diana, and it was only a few months ago that Kit had learned how badly Smythe had treated her. Now he stared at Malcolm for a moment in disbelief, then gave a gasp of outrage. "By God—"

It was perhaps as well that Smythe was beyond Kit's reach when it came to challenging the other man to a duel. Malcolm quickly told Kit the rest. Kit went very white. "Smythe was a monster. I knew that. After Diana, perhaps this shouldn't shock me. But—and Beverston had her spying for him?"

"Does that shock you?"

Kit drew a breath. "No. On reflection. Which doesn't speak well for my opinion of Beverston. But I've always thought he was the sort to cut ethical corners. And now we know he's one of the Elsinore League's founders." Kit took a turn about the room, as though trying to make sense of this tumult of new information. "I came to town because I had a message from Roger saying the dead girl was Miranda. I had another waiting for me when I got here saying I should talk to you. Why the devil did Carfax kill her? It seems a strange way to attack the League."

"Carfax may not have killed her."

Kit's gaze clashed with Malcolm's. He was angry and wanted justice for his friend, but not so angry he'd lost the ability to analyze. "That's why you're investigating. I should have realized."

When they first met, Kit had mistrusted Malcolm because Malcolm had worked for Carfax, a man who stood for everything Kit opposed politically and who would dearly love to shut down Kit and his Radical friends. For that matter, Carfax stood for everything Malcolm opposed, and had the whole time Malcolm worked for him. Despite or because of that, Kit's mistrust had been like a shock of cold water. "I have no doubt Carfax is capable of murder," Malcolm said. "I'm just not sure he's responsible for this one. The facts don't add up."

Kit gave a slow nod. "He didn't know who Miranda was?"

"He says not. With Carfax one can never be sure how much that means." Malcolm surveyed Kit. "You must have seen the Dormers since you returned to Britain."

Kit nodded. "Elinor took it well when I told her about Sofia. She couldn't have been kinder. She said she wanted me to be happy, and she was delighted I'd found someone I cared for so deeply. She'd never want to build a life on denying that. But to own the truth, I sensed she was relieved herself. Which, of course, I found a great relief. While at the same time—"

"Wondering how you could have misread her?"

Kit met his gaze. "Yes. To think that, if I hadn't met Sofia, we might have stumbled into a marriage neither of us wanted." He shook his head. "I spoke with Sir George as well, to make sure he understood things would not progress as he'd expected between Elinor and me. He was less sympathetic."

"Likely because he was less relieved."

"Yes, very likely. He wanted the alliance between our families. But he said if Elinor and I were agreed, of course he could make no objection. He did add that he hoped I'd think it through carefully before I allied myself with a foreigner." Kit's jaw tightened. "After that, it didn't seem appropriate to spend much time at Dormer Manor. But I did call to wish Elinor a happy Christmas on Boxing Day. She seemed happy. She wished me well. The odd thing is—" He drew an uneven breath. "She said she always thought about Miranda at Christmas. That she'd wonder where she was, and remember holidays with her. Only she couldn't discuss it with the family, because no one spoke of Miranda." He shook his head. "It's hard to believe. Growing up, we were so much a part of each other's lives—Diana, Selena, and I, and Miranda, Elinor, and Dorinda. Sir George tried to help out after my father left. And perhaps because he didn't have a son of his own. He'd take me fishing while the girls played. Elinor and Diana were friends. Selena would trail round after them. Dorinda was always a bit sharp tongued. But then, I don't think Miranda made it easy for her. She tended to get her own way. I can't remember a time she couldn't wrap everyone round her finger." He drew a sharp breath. "Sorry, with her gone, I shouldn't—But it's true."

"It's very helpful, actually. The other two girls resented her?"

"Elinor mostly ignored her. It was harder for Dorinda because they were of an age."

"And now she's married to your comrade, Roger."

Kit met Malcolm's gaze. "Roger said he told you about the Levellers. I know I hadn't told you—"

"There was no particular reason for you to share the membership, and you could be pardoned for keeping it close. Roger Smythe impressed me."

"But he's a suspect."

"To the extent that everyone who was close to Miranda is."

"And Roger was besotted with her. He was the only one who really talked about her when she disappeared. You could see how desperate he was." Kit took another turn round the hearthrug. "Miranda wasn't the easiest girl. But I couldn't understand it when she disappeared. How quiet they all were. How they could pretend she'd never existed."

"Do you think she could have been in communication with any of them?"

"Not that I know of. Elinor certainly seemed to have no idea of her whereabouts." Kit shook his head. "I asked Sir George about it once. He bit my head off. Said when I had a family I'd understand. But I rather think when I have children of my own I'll find it even more inexplicable."

"Yes," Malcolm said, "I imagine you will."

"Roger said Miranda has a child."

"He appears to be well looked after."

"Thanks to Beverston." Kit's mouth twisted. "But Beverston's been using her all this time."

"Beverston's a spymaster to all intents and purposes. Which may explain his actions, but doesn't excuse them. Did you know Roger had found her?"

"Good God, no. Why—"

"She was spying on Beverston for him."

"And on the League." Comprehension flashed in Kit's gaze. "Because I told Roger his father was a League member."

"You had to do so, Kit. And apparently Miranda wanted to help Roger against Beverston and the League."

"But if Beverston had learned the truth—Do you think he killed her?"

"It's possible, if he learned she was reporting to Roger, or if he thought she was going to talk to Carfax."

"And you're also wondering about Roger. And Dorinda."

"They're not easy questions to ask about people one has known since childhood," Malcolm said. "But as I said, one has to ask them about the people close to the victim."

Kit frowned. "Roger adored Miranda. Leaving aside that he's my friend, it's difficult for me to imagine a reason why he'd kill her."

"And Dorinda?"

The instinctive protest against accusing a woman died on Kit's lips. The investigation last September had taught him to suspect everyone. "I said Miranda wasn't the easiest person. And perhaps, in particular, not for Dorinda."

"And Dorinda's husband was in love with her."

"*Was*." Kit continued to frown. "I remember when Roger told me he was marrying Dorinda. He said he'd been far too slow to see what was in front of him. I'd swear he genuinely cares for her."

"That doesn't necessarily make the other feelings go away," Malcolm said.

Kit regarded him with the gaze of one just coming to understand love's complexities. "No," he said, "it doesn't."

CHAPTER 35

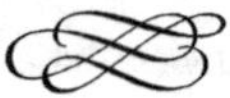

HENRIETTE VARON SMILED AT RAOUL. "It's good to see you. Lisette told me you were happy. Looking at you, I can see she spoke the truth."

Raoul smiled at the mother of one of his best agents. "Lisette has always been a very discerning young woman. Though perhaps she sees things with the optimism of the young."

"She wouldn't thank you for saying so. She sees herself as a determined realist. But I can tell you're happy with forty-some years' knowledge of the world. You're going to be a father. Or perhaps I should say a father again."

"Yes." Odd, Raoul thought, as he settled back in a petit-point-covered chair in Henriette's sitting room, to be able to admit it so simply. "In truth, I'm happier than I ever thought to be. Certainly than I ever deserved to be. None of which lessens the gravity of the situation we're in."

Henriette poured coffee. A whiff and they could have been in the gardens at Malmaison where Henriette had been seamstress to both Josephine and Hortense. Or in a salon in Hortense's chateau in d'Arrenberg. In times that had been at once simpler and more fraught.

"I'm not a spy," Henriette said. "This isn't my world."

"No, but you're a good observer of people. And you've lived on the edge of this world for decades. You've put up with your daughter being drawn into it."

"I very nearly didn't forgive you for that."

"Recalling my reaction to my own son's becoming an agent, I can only thank you for your forbearance. But this is a question of what Josephine knew."

Henriette handed him a cup of coffee. "We were close through the years. As a woman is with her dressmaker. But she hardly confided in me as she did in you."

"I was in Ireland for most of '98. I scarcely saw her. Do you remember anything particular that year? "

Henriette frowned. "Madame had been married to Bonaparte for two years. Hortense turned fifteen in April, Alexandre turned seventeen in September. My own Lisette turned four in August. Minette wasn't born yet, though I was expecting her by the end of the year. Bonaparte went to Egypt. Josephine was concerned about him, desperate for news. Anxious about what the separation might mean. The news from Ireland was concerning as well. Madame was worried about you. And—" Her gaze froze on her coffee cup for a moment. "Yes it must have been that year. Lisette was chattering away, but I hadn't begun to think about another child yet. In the summer, Bonaparte had left on the campaign. I was taking in a gown for a dinner that evening when I heard Josephine give a cry from the next room. Normally I wouldn't have disturbed her privacy, but there was something about the note in her voice—her maid had gone downstairs, so it was just the two of us. She was paler than bleached muslin. I poured her a glass of wine and persuaded her to sit down. I'd seen her in almost every conceivable mood, but never quite like this. She took a swallow of wine—though I had to hold the glass to keep it from spilling—and said she'd lost something that could destroy her. At last she went to her escritoire and scribbled a note and asked me to see it delivered." Henriette turned her cup on its saucer and met Raoul's gaze. "It was to M. St. Juste."

"Do you know if he responded?"

"Oh, yes. Josephine asked me to slip down to the salon and let him in through one of the French windows that night, then bring him up to the sitting room that was kept for my use. If anyone saw, they would just think I was smuggling in a lover. I didn't care for my reputation, and I knew I could explain to my husband. I brought M. St. Juste upstairs. He was as imperturbable as usual, though rather more serious than in general. I still remember the way Josephine turned to St. Juste when I let him in, hands locked together. She came towards him and he took her hands. I left at once. I have no idea what they said. But Josephine was calmer when she summoned me back to the room. I saw St. Juste press her hand and assure her all would be well. I don't think I've ever heard such sincerity in his voice. When I saw him out of the chateau he said, 'Try not to let her worry. It will do little good.' When I went back upstairs, Josephine said, 'Julien has the strangest ability to instill confidence in me.' She was calmer in the days after, though I could tell it was still weighing on her. Then she received another message from him. I saw her read it, and it was as though a weight lifted from her shoulders. I asked if all was well. And she said, 'Julien says it will be, and I've learned to trust him.' After that—I'd still see fear at the back of her eyes at moments, but with time it lessened." Her gaze flickered over Raoul's face. "Does that help?"

"Very much." Raoul sat back in his chair. "Do you remember who had visited just before Josephine first told you these papers had disappeared?"

Henriette took a sip of coffee, brows drawn together. "I don't recall particular guests who'd been to stay, though of course people were in and out of the house. But Josephine had given a ball two days before. She brought in extra footmen for it. Not unusual, and in general I wouldn't remember them particularly.

But there was one man. I saw him upstairs the night of the ball when I went up to fetch a fresh pair of gloves for madame. Not entirely unusual—he said he'd gone up to collect empty glasses. He did have a tray of them, and guests did leave glasses upstairs. It was a bit odd he was so near the family's rooms, but he was new, he might have got lost. Then fifteen years later I was at the theatre with Lisette and Minette and saw the same man. It took me a bit to remember why he was familiar, but I was sure it was the footman from that ball. I could tell Lisette recognized him for different reasons. She told me she didn't know his name, but he was an agent for hire."

"What did he look like?"

"Tall. A thin face. Dark hair, the first time. Gray fifteen years later—either because he'd aged or because it was dyed. Deepset eyes. Do you recognize the description?"

"I think so. I strongly suspect it's Thomas Ambrose, who broke into Dunmykel a month since, looking for the same thing Josephine was so afraid to have lost—and shot Mélanie Rannoch."

Malcolm found Aldous Morningtree, Viscount Gildersly, playing tennis at an indoor academy. Malcolm stood by the half-rail and peered through a curtain of netting at the blue-painted court. Gildersly played well. Some five years older than Malcolm, he had the physique of a man who hunted, sparred, and otherwise indulged in the sporting life, but he was beginning to run to fat. Malcolm remained at the net, aware with every volley of the tennis ball that Harry and Andrew were getting closer to Rivendell.

It had been the sensible decision to let them go without him. He was quite sure he'd been followed to the tennis academy, but no one had attempted to interfere with him, and there was no harm in leading pursuers to Gildersly. It might be a good bit of misdirection. And hopefully it was giving Harry and Andrew protection. None of which lessened the tang of guilt at the back of his mouth, because his friends were running risks in his place. The bite of frustration, because they were probably closer to answers he was desperate for than he was himself.

"Rannoch." Gildersly drawled Malcolm's surname so that it was almost more than two syllables as he strolled from the court, towel draped round his neck, racket still in one hand. "Didn't know you were one for tennis."

"I am on occasion, but generally in the country. I can't claim to your expertise."

Gildersly laughed, though Malcolm thought he caught a gleam of calculation in the other man's blue gaze. "Practice, that's what it takes. Good match, Pomfret," he called to his erstwhile opponent.

"I actually came hoping for a word with you." Malcolm positioned himself in front of the gate that led from the court.

Gildersly raised a brow. "I can't remember the last time I set foot in Parliament."

"I haven't for some time either. This is about Miranda Spencer."

Gildersly's skin turned green against the blue-painted walls of the tennis court.

"There's a coffeehouse across the street," Malcolm said. "Unless you want to discuss it further here."

In the coffeehouse, Gildersly tossed down a third of his pint, with far less finesse than he had shown on the tennis court, before he clunked down the tankard and met Malcolm's gaze across the table. "I know you're looking into her murder. I don't deny I went to the Barque of Frailty on occasion. But I never frequented Miranda Spencer."

Something about the wording made the coffee Malcolm had ordered rise up in his throat. "You had a cut on your hand the night Mrs. Spencer was killed."

"Who the devil says so?"

"A lady who was brave enough to share the story."

"Oh, Christ." Gildersly took another swig from his pint. "I forgot Emily was a friend of your wife's."

"And of mine."

"She may not care what her husband hears, but she won't want Palmerston to know."

"I don't expect she does. And she'd prefer to have her name kept out of it. But she's prepared to talk if necessary."

Gildersly stared at him for a moment. "Damn. Always knew Emily's brother was capable of romantic gestures, but didn't think she was too."

"Emily is not a woman to underestimate."

Gildersly took another swig from his pint. "Well, in this case she's wrong. I was with another girl that night."

"What was her name?"

Gildersly frowned for a moment. "Janie. I think. Maybe Julie."

"And your hand?"

Gildersly reached for his pint again. "If you must know, when we heard that ghastly scream, I dropped the glass I was holding and cut my hand. Made a damned mess of my coat. Hurried out of there and went to Emily's. Thought it would steady my nerves."

And provide him with an alibi? Gildersly might not be brilliant, but he had a certain cunning. He might have thought that far ahead.

"Did anyone see you leave?"

Gildersly shifted his pint on the tabletop. "Don't think so. House was in chaos. No, wait a bit. I brushed past Beverston on the stairs. And Matthew Trenor."

"Together?"

"They were both running to see what had happened." Gildersly frowned. "But yes, I had the sense they'd been talking."

~

ROSAMUND HARTLEY SMILED at Archie across her sitting room. She wore a high-necked day dress of corded lavender silk and her hair was elegantly coiled, but the smile was the same one that had captivated him from the stage when her filmy gown showed her shapely ankles and her hair escaped about her face in tendrils.

"I was wondering when you'd come," she said.

Archie settled back in his chair, stretching out his bad leg. "I thought it was best to let Malcolm and Harry form their own impression first."

Rosamund poured two glasses of sherry and put one in his hand. "You place a great deal of trust in them."

"I do. I also knew they wouldn't be biased."

Rosamund raised a brow in that way she had. "You suspected me."

"I knew I should suspect you if I could be unbiased. Which I fully realize I'm not where you're concerned."

"I'm flattered."

Archie took a drink of sherry. "I have quite agreeable memories of our time together. Which I wouldn't trade for the world. None of which diminishes my love for my wife."

Rosamund lifted her glass to him. "I confess I wouldn't trade my memories either. Which doesn't diminish my satisfaction with my current state." She took a sip. "You should be quite proud of Harry. He's remarkably like you."

Archie found himself smiling, though he said, "I'm not sure he'd take that as a compliment."

"Oh, I'm quite sure he would."

Archie sat forwards in his chair. "Beverston arranged with you for Miranda Spencer—Dormer—to come here."

Rosamund shrugged. "I should have realized they'd discover that. But I was so accustomed to keeping Miranda's history secret."

"And you were protecting Beverston."

She took a sip of sherry. "Yes, I suppose I was. You aren't the only one I share happy memories with."

Archie kept his gaze steady on her face. "He was heard crying in your room the night before Miranda Dormer was murdered."

Rosamund went still for a moment. Her indrawn breath was like the snick of a knife. Then she lifted a brow in acknowledgment of a hit. "Yes, I confess we spent that night together." She folded her hands in her lap, composed despite her wording. "No, we haven't been involved in that way for some time. Except on occasion. And this was one of those occasions. He'd had an uncomfortable break with his current mistress."

"Sylvie St. Ives?" Archie asked.

Her eyes narrowed. "You do have good sources of information. Yes. Apparently he'd learned Lady St. Ives was spying on him. One might quarrel with his taking exception to something he was fully capable of doing himself, but Beverston has always hated to be used." She regarded Archie for a moment. "Did you know?"

"I wasn't sure if they were allies or enemies. This resolves at least part of that."

"You know Lady St. Ives." Rosamund made it not quite a question.

"Not in the intimate sense, but yes, we've crossed paths. One might say she's a formidable woman."

"I think Beverston's feelings were unusually engaged. Until that night I'd never seen him cry. Though I saw him cry the next night over Miranda." Her brows drew together.

"I'll at least credit Beverston with the wit to appreciate formidable women," Archie said. "Sylvie St. Ives. You. Miranda Dormer, it seems."

Rosamund set down her glass and smoothed her hands over the delicate fabric of her skirt. "He wasn't Miranda's lover."

"I know. That is, I believe what I've heard of his denials. Knowing what I do of Beverston, I'm not sure why, save that I've learned people tend to draw certain lines, whatever compromises they're capable of. Perhaps the more so the more they're capable of compromise."

Rosamund inclined her head. "He was oddly protective of her, for all he exposed her to great risk. With Lady St. Ives, I think he'd let his guard down. His feelings seemed genuinely engaged, but I think he was also horrified at what he might have revealed to her."

"Yes, I imagine he was. Beverston was engaged in some very dangerous games. But then, you know that."

Rosamund held his gaze. "I've never been anything but a minor player in Beverston's games. That hasn't changed."

His instinct was to believe her. But with Rosamund, he wasn't entirely sure he could count on his instinct. "Do you think Beverston would have been capable of killing Miranda?" he asked.

Rosamund hesitated, fingering a fold of her gown. "I don't think he did," she said. "Perhaps I don't want to think he did. But yes, I think he'd have been capable of it."

"Thank you." Archie set down his glass.

Rosamund clasped her hands together. "I trust you're being careful. You're scarcely in a comfortable position with the League."

"I think the League are convinced I'm not to be trusted. They find it useful to maintain a connection to me. But you know me enough to know I'm watching my back."

Rosamund regarded him for a moment. "You're in love with her."

Archie found himself smiling. "It's not a word I use easily. But yes. I am."

She nodded. "I'm glad. Go carefully, Archie."

"You too, Rosie."

He started to push himself up from his chair. Rosamund moved as though to rise as well, then said suddenly. "Archie."

Archie sat back in his chair. "Yes?"

"The night Miranda was killed. Lord Carfax wasn't with her the entire time after they went upstairs."

"Yes, we know that. Do you know where he was?"

Rosamund fingered a fold of her gown, as though even now not sure about speaking. "I went upstairs just after midnight. I usually do, during the evening, to make sure there's no disturbance. I didn't see Miranda. Her door was closed. But when I glanced down one of the passages, I saw Carfax in an alcove."

"Alone?"

Rosamund's fingers twisted in the folds of her skirt. "No. He was talking to Beverston."

"Interesting. Do you know what they were talking about?"

"No. I didn't get close enough to hear. I assumed they wished to be private. But as I turned away I caught a glimpse of Carfax's face." Her fingers stilled. "He looked like a man who's been dealt a mortal blow."

CHAPTER 36

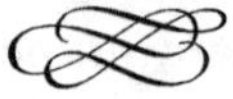

"RAOUL!"

A woman's voice called Raoul's name as he left the house where Henriette and her daughters lodged. A familiar voice, save so out of context that he started and looked round in surprise. A veiled woman waved to him from the window of a barouche drawn up across the street.

He started across the street only to hear another cry from the woman in the carriage, this one a warning. He sprang back, just as a dark, closed carriage thundered down the street. He fell back against the wall of a tobacconist's, inches from being trampled under wheels and horse hooves.

He dusted his coat off and made his way to the carriage the woman had called to him from, wary but more determined than ever.

"Are you all right?" The carriage door opened and the woman leaned out, her veil pushed back. As he'd suspected, Raoul found himself looking at Margaret, the woman to whom he was married, the woman he had last seen in Italy. Where he had learned she'd been working for the Elsinore League for two decades.

"This is unexpected, Meg." He swung up into the carriage and pulled the door to.

Margaret leaned forwards on the carriage seat, veil falling back from her hat. "That carriage nearly ran you down."

"So it did. My thanks for the warning."

"Was it a deliberate attack?"

"I'm not sure. Are your friends in the League still trying to kill me?"

Margaret's gaze darted across his face. "You think I'm part of it? That I called out to you to get you to cross the street?"

"You did get me to cross the street. But then you gave me a timely warning. But the last time I saw you, you were still allied with the League."

"A lot's changed since then."

Raoul leaned back against the soft leather squabs. "What are you doing here, Meg?"

"I'm in London on my way back to Ireland." She hesitated a moment. "Desmond and I thought it best to return separately." It was like Margaret to be careful when speaking of her long-time lover, even when the only one present was Raoul, who was well aware of the relationship.

"And why do you happen to be in the street outside where I was paying a call?"

Margaret clasped her gloved hands in her lap. "I followed you when you left Berkeley Square. I need to talk to you, but it seemed best not to call openly."

"Because of the League?"

"Partly. I could explain away why I needed to talk to you—we are still married. But you can't deny it would be awkward if I called at the Rannochs' house."

"It's not as though Malcolm and Mélanie aren't well aware of you. Are you worried about meeting Laura? I think we're rather beyond awkwardness, don't you?"

"Speak for yourself." Margaret spread her hands over her lap.

"I've told the League I won't work for them anymore. They haven't pressured me. So far. Lord Beverston asked me to call on him. But it was because he wanted to know more about his son John. I don't have a great deal of sympathy for Beverston, but it was impossible not to feel some."

"What did he ask you about John?"

"Mostly about his mood those last days. And if he'd approached me. I told him he had but hadn't said much."

"Did you tell him Vincenzo warned you not to trust John Smythe?"

Margaret held his gaze across the carriage. "I don't think it would be much comfort for Beverston to know his son was working against him, do you?"

"Not much comfort at all. But for the sake of the League I imagine he'd like to know."

"For the sake of the League, I imagine he would. But I told you I'm not working for them anymore." Margaret hesitated a moment. "Beverston also warned me against you. Reading between the lines, I think you're still a target. That's why I came to see you."

"Thank you."

"I don't want any harm to befall you, Raoul. In fact, just now I realized—" She shook her head, stirring the folds of her veil. "You were nearly run down crossing the street because I called to you. I'd never forgive myself if I was responsible for your death."

"Whyever the League are after me, it's nothing to do with you, Meg."

"That wouldn't stop me from feeling guilty if they used me to get to you." She adjusted the folds of her veil. "It occurred to me of course that Beverston might want me to warn you. But I didn't think they might use me to set up an attack."

"We don't know that's what happened. The League don't need you to find me."

She nodded. "I didn't expect to see you back in London."

"It's a short visit."

"You're looking into Carfax's arrest with the Rannochs."

"Among other things. Did Beverston say anything about Carfax?"

Margaret frowned. "When Beverston warned me about you, I said he must be relieved to at least see one of his enemies behind bars. Beverston said he placed no very great reliance upon that lasting. But that there were ways to control everyone. Even Carfax. Do you know what he meant?"

"No. But the implications are interesting." Raoul studied Margaret in the light slanting through the carriage window. Her veil fell back over her shoulders. It was a long time since he'd seen that brilliance in her eyes and complexion. "Meg," he said. "How long have you known?"

"Known what?"

He reached across the carriage and caught her wrist. "Don't forget I've seen you like this before. Does Desmond know?"

"For God's sake, Raoul." She pulled away from his grasp. "It's no concern of yours."

"Of course it's a concern of mine. I'm what's standing between you and a stable future for yourself, your child, and the man you love. But we can fix that."

"Madly idealistic, as usual."

"Meg, you can't tell me you're still opposed to divorce under these circumstances. What are you planning to do? Have the child in secret? Smuggle it away?"

"'Don't be ridiculous. But we scarcely have time—"

"Not before Laura's and my child perhaps. But we should for you."

"You're being very kind."

"What did you think I'd be?"

Margaret sniffed into her handkerchief. "You can't deny it's ironic. Considering how—"

"How opposed you've been to divorce? Yes, but children

change things." He watched her for a moment. "I hope it's also a cause for joy."

"Is that what it is for you?"

"Yes, though I'm fully aware of what I'm putting Laura through." He leaned across the carriage and tucked a strand of hair behind her ear. "I want you to be happy, Meg."

She regarded him for a moment. "As I said in Italy, you always wanted children more than I did. I'd long since given up even thinking about it. And there's no denying it's a fearful complication. But yes, I am happy."

"I'm glad." He squeezed her shoulder. "We'll make this work, Meg."

Margaret shook her head, but her smile was the affectionate sort he'd never thought to see from her again. "Still an incurable optimist."

"I'm not in the least optimistic."

"My dear. What do you call your blind conviction that you can change the world? Or that the masses you want to liberate will behave as rationally as you hope?"

"My dear girl. I long since gave up thinking I could do more than make a difference round the edges."

"Ha. If that were true, the League wouldn't be so determined to get rid of you."

"I THINK we know the woman who hired one of the sets of people who attacked us in the park last night." Mélanie took a sip of tea in the Berkeley Square library where they were sharing news. "I took a sketch when I visited the used the clothes-seller in Rosemary Lane. When I darkened the hair, the people at the shop recognize her as Sylvie St. Ives."

"And based on Rosamund's story about Beverston, she wasn't working for the League," Archie said.

Malcolm poked up the fire for the third time. He seemed too restless to sit. "It's just possible she's working for Carfax again despite their break six months ago. But I think it's more likely she's working for the third actor."

"Lady St. Ives's cousin is an agent for Fouché," Raoul said. "And they've worked together before."

Malcolm met his father's gaze. "You think Fouché is the third actor?"

"I begin to suspect so."

"Fouché's always wanted power and hasn't cared much—if at all—if he served Royalists or Republicans," Malcolm said. "He'd certainly have reason to want to control the dauphin."

"A puppet to give him control of France," Raoul said. "It's an open question whether that or the League's controlling France is a more frightening prospect."

"So he hired Thomas Ambrose?" Cordelia asked. "But it sounds as though Ambrose is the man who took the papers from Josephine twenty years ago."

"Yes, I'm quite sure he was," Raoul said. "I suspect Wyncliffe hired Ambrose to steal the papers from Josephine for the League. St. Juste reassured Josephine about the papers, but we know he didn't get the papers back. I suspect when he realized Wyncliffe was behind the theft and had gone to Dunmykel, he contacted Arabella and asked her to recover them."

"So they already knew each other," Malcolm said.

"They must have done if this scenario is right," Raoul said. "And it's the only one I can think of to explain Arabella's knowing to take the papers from Wyncliffe and Julien's being assured the papers wouldn't be used against Josephine."

Malcolm set down the poker and dropped down on the sofa beside Mélanie. "But Arabella kept the papers."

"Whatever was between Bella and St. Juste, I doubt she showed him blind loyalty," Raoul said. "She'd have known the papers were vitally important even if she didn't know precisely what they were.

She may have promised St. Juste she wouldn't use them so long as he did something for her or complied with her wishes in some other way. In any case, St. Juste seems to have believed they were safe."

"Eleven years later, Josephine was afraid Julien would use a letter against her," Mélanie said.

Raoul nodded. "A lot had shifted by then. St. Juste had worked for a number of other masters. He remained loyal to Josephine, but I don't think she recognized it. At least not until before he gave you the paper. After that she trusted him enough that she sent him along with you to escort Hortense into Switzerland."

"So Thomas Ambrose stole the papers for Lord Wyncliffe twenty years ago," Frances said. "The papers Bella took from Wyncliffe and gave to me briefly. And then Ambrose is also the man who broke into Dunmykel just before Christmas and shot Mélanie?"

"I think so."

"And shot Tommy?" Mélanie asked. "I've always thought the man who broke in and shot me is likely the one who shot Tommy as well."

"So have I," Raoul said. "And I do think it's Ambrose. In which case, he's likely working for Fouché now. Through Sylvie St. Ives. We know that on his deathbed Wyncliffe told Beverston about the papers concerning the Wanderer that he stole and Arabella in turn stole from him. That probably started Beverston and the League searching for the papers. I suspect Lady St. Ives learned from Beverston and informed Fouché in exile."

"And Carfax got wind of it through his sources," Malcolm said. "That's probably the news he got at Carfax Court that Bel said sent him to London. So we have the League, Cafax, and Fouché all seeking the lost dauphin. And we can only hope Harry and Andrew get to Rivendell before any of them."

Mélanie could feel her husband's coiled tension on the sofa beside her. She knew how much it had cost him to remain in

London. "Gildersly's story is interesting," she said, reminding him of the work for them in London. "Matthew Trenor seems to know Beverston. Not necessarily surprising, but they were talking together just after Miranda was murdered."

"Yes, and it doesn't entirely agree with Trenor's account of his actions. We should follow up on it," Malcolm said. "Though I'm more intrigued by Mrs. Hartley's account of seeing Beverston and Carfax together just before Miranda was killed, and by her description of the look on Carfax's face. It would take a lot for Carfax to look as though he'd been dealt a mortal blow."

"I had an unexpected meeting with Margaret when I left Henriette's," Raoul said. "She spoke with Beverston, but his questions seem to have been about his son. Margaret didn't tell him John was working for Carfax. But she did comment to him on Carfax's being in prison. Beverston said he placed no reliance upon it lasting, but that there were ways to control everyone, including Carfax."

Malcolm's eyes narrowed. "Which together with Mrs. Hartley's story makes it seem Beverston tried to blackmail Carfax the night of the murder. Which could be why Carfax is keeping quiet in prison."

"But surely—" Cordelia stared at him. "Surely Beverston wasn't blackmailing him into accepting the blame for the murder. Miranda wasn't even dead at that point."

"We don't know precisely when she was killed," Malcolm said. "It's possible Beverton had already killed her or knew someone else had done so and blackmailed Carfax into taking the blame. Though I still have a hard time seeing Carfax simply going along with that, whatever Beverston had on him. But it's also possible Beverston tried to blackmail Carfax over something else, and then once Carfax was accused of the murder, he was afraid Beverston would use whatever he had if Carfax revealed too much. At the very least it explains why Carfax wouldn't tell me where he was when he left Miranda's room. He didn't want to risk my asking Beverston about it."

"Do you think the League really did manage to get evidence of David and Simon's relationship?" Cordelia asked.

Malcolm's brows drew together. "I'm not sure where they'd have found it. But it's a possibility we have to consider."

"Did Margaret say anything else?" Laura asked Raoul.

"Nothing that can't wait." Raoul reached for her hand. "If—"

He broke off as Valentin opened the door. "A Miss Simcox and Mr. Trenor are asking to see Mr. and Mrs. Rannoch."

"Show them in," Mélanie said without hesitation.

Bet Simcox and Sandy Trenor came into the room quickly but hesitated on the threshold. "It's all right." Mélanie walked forwards to draw them into the room. "Mr. Trenor, I believe you're acquainted with everyone here." She turned to Frances, Archie, Raoul, Laura, and Cordy. "May I present Miss Elizabeth Simcox?"

Bet was pale and wide-eyed but she curtsied and inclined her head. If the others had any idea of Bet's origins and profession they gave no sign of it. "We're sorry to barge in," Trenor said, when he'd handed Bet into a chair. "But we thought this was important."

"I've had word from Robby." Bet sat bold upright in her chair, hands folded in her lap. "That is had word *of* him. My scapegrace brother hasn't been in touch with Nan or me. But Gwen at the Dolphin says he was there last night. Had a quick pint and said he had to be back out on the street. That it might be a matter of life or death." Bet shook her head. "Robby always could exaggerate. But Gwen says he only drank half the pint, said he wanted to be sure to keep a clear head. That doesn't sound like Robby. I can't but think—"

She broke off as Valentin entered the room again. He'd learned not to stand on ceremony in the midst of an investigation. "There's a Mr. Lumley in the hall

CHAPTER 37

GERALD LUMLEY PUSHED the library door to behind him. "Someone's following me."

"You're sure?" Malcolm got to his feet and walked towards the new arrival. Lumley's face was pale and his hair disordered, as though he had tugged his hat off with no concern for it, but his gaze was level and alert.

"I caught a reflection in the window when the street turned," Lumley said.

"Clever," Malcolm said.

Lumley drew a breath, then went still, taking in the number of people gathered in the room.

"It's all right," Malcolm said. "They're all part of this." Which was probably true—all the mysteries seemed to be intertwined. He quickly introduced Lumley to the others.

Lumley nodded with punctilious courtesy, then looked back at Malcolm. "I feel quite out of my depth. Why on earth would anyone be after me?"

"I don't know, but let's try a test. Give me five minutes and walk back outside with O'Roarke."

Malcolm went out into the garden, round through the mews,

and back into the square. The sky had turned inky purple and twilight shadows slanted across the square. Lumley and Raoul emerged from the house shortly after, chatting with a good appearance of ease. Lumley was handling this well. Moments later, Malcolm saw a dark form detach itself from the area railings of the next house over and fall into step behind them. Malcolm leaped from the shadows and landed on the follower's back. The man he tackled kicked but Malcolm tightened his grip on the man's shoulders. He twisted with the instincts of a street fighter. Raoul ran up and grabbed the man's arms. Malcolm got to his feet. Raoul pulled the man up, an iron grip on his arms.

"What the devil do you want with Lumley?" Malcolm asked the man. He was young, probably not much more than twenty, with disordered fair hair and blue eyes that were somehow familiar as he stared at Malcolm with a mixture of alarm and belligerence.

"Who?" the young man asked.

"Me." Lumley ran up.

The young man's jaw tightened. "Haven't been—"

"Spare us." Malcolm said. "I saw you."

"What do you have against me?" Lumley asked.

"I'm not—"

The door of the Berkeley Square house thudded open. "Robby!" Bet Simcox ran into the street. "What are you in the midst of?"

Malcolm stared into Bet Simcox's blue eyes, the twin of those of the young man Raoul held. "This is your brother?"

"My idiot brother." Bet stared at him, arms folded across her chest.

Mélanie ran out of the house after Bet, Cordelia and Laura behind her. "Inside, I think. Mr. Simcox, we promise no violence if we aren't met with any in return."

"I'm not going to be violent," Robby said. His face was still set with determination but he was making no attempt to break Raoul's hold.

"Julien St. Juste hired you to follow Mr. Lumley?" Mélanie said when they were all gathered in the library. Raoul had patted Robby Simcox down for weapons, retrieved a knife, and then steered the young man to a chair and released him, though he continued to stand watch.

"No, he—that is"—Robby sucked in his breath. "Never heard of anyone called St. Juste."

"Robby." Bet fixed her brother with a firm stare. "We know he hired you. Sam told us. We didn't know why, but it's clear now."

"Though not why St. Juste would be after Lumley," Raoul said. He was standing where he could block the path to the door.

"He's not after him," Robby insisted. "That is, St. Juste isn't after Lumley. All right, yes, he did hire me to follow Lumley, but I was supposed to protect him."

"Protect me?" Lumley said on a note of amazement. "From what?"

"He didn't say. Just that I was to follow you and report on where you went, and be prepared to protect you if you were attacked."

Lumley scrapped a hand through his hair. "It's daft."

"Maybe so, but it's the truth." Robby Simcox's lower lip jutted forwards. "Are you calling me a liar?"

"Not necessarily, " Malcolm said. "But with everything we're involved in, it's hard to imagine a man like St. Juste's main interest is in Lumley. At least on the surface. " He looked at Lumley. "Could Miranda have told you something?"

"You mean something that got her killed?"

"Miranda was murdered. And Julien St. Juste, who, whatever else he is, is no fool, thinks you're in danger."

"But St. Juste didn't know Miranda," Cordelia said. "Did he?"

"Not that we know of," Raoul said. "Which especially with St. Juste is no guarantee of anything."

"Miranda didn't tell me anything," Lumley insisted. "Even if she knew this St. Juste, she never mentioned him to me."

"It's likely something you don't realize is important." Archie sat forwards in his chair, gaze on Lumley. Assessing, as Mélanie knew all the spies in the room were doing. Was he an innocent caught up in something over his head or a very good agent playing them?

"Do have a cup of tea, Mr. Lumley." Lady Frances lifted the teapot from a silver tray on the sofa table. "In fact, I think we could all do with one. Perhaps—"

A crack cut through the library. Mélanie felt something sharp hit her neck. Malcolm slammed her to the floor and fell on top of her. Only then did she realize the sound had been the report of a gun.

CHAPTER 38

Mélanie pushed herself to her knees. Archie had flung himself over Frances. Sandy Trenor had his arms round Bet Simcox. Raoul had somehow crossed the length of carpet to Laura's chair. Laura looked at him and shook her head. Cordelia had a hand to her head. Lumley was staring at the broken glass that littered the carpet beneath the shattered window.

"Is anyone hurt?" Malcolm asked as wind whistled into the room through the hole in the glass.

As the others shook their heads, Mélanie put a hand to the back of her neck and felt blood.

"Are you hit?" Malcolm's voice was sharp.

"Just a scratch. A piece of broken glass hit me." She plucked the glass from the carpet and set it on a rosewood table where no one could step on it.

Malcolm was on his feet and drew the curtains in an instant. Raoul touched his fingers to Laura's cheek and then was across the room again, running his fingers over the paneling.

"Laura, Cordy," Malcolm said in a conversational voice, "let's get the children out of the parlor and gather them up at the back of the hall. Behind the stairs. Make a game out of it. Tell Valentin to stay with you."

Laura and Cordelia were on their feet and out of the room without questions.

Raoul pulled the knife he'd taken off Robby Simcox from beneath his coat and pressed it into the golden oak of one of the bookcases. "A rifle," he said, holding the bullet out. "Downward angle."

"The Hollingsworth house across the square is being painted." Malcolm glanced behind one of the curtains. "The painters will be gone at this hour and the family are away with no staff left on duty. I suspect he shot from the first floor."

"For God's sake, darling, come away from the window," Mélanie said.

"I doubt he'll try again now we're alerted." Malcolm moved back to help her to her feet. "Not this way."

"Someone shot a rifle across Berkeley Square?" Trenor asked, his arm still round Bet.

"Yes, that's something we've never encountered before," Malcolm said.

"This proves it," Robby Simcox said. "Someone's after Lumley."

"Probably," Malcolm said.

"Probably?" Lumley demanded. "What else—"

"They could have been shooting at Raoul." Frances blotted the tea that had spilled in her lap.

Robby swung round to look at Raoul. "Someone's trying to kill you too?"

"Possibly."

"Probably," Laura said.

"A carriage came close to running me down earlier today," Raoul said. "It could have been an accident, but I doubt it."

Malcolm glanced at the wall where Raoul had dug out the bullet, at Raoul, at Lumley. "Lumley was sitting in front of where you were standing. Difficult to be sure which of you the sniper was aiming at. Let's all go in the hall with the children. No access from the windows if we stay behind the stairs."

Laura, Cordy, and Valentin had dragged chairs in from the breakfast parlor and wedged them beneath all the doors that opened onto the hall. The children were sitting on the floor. "Is someone trying to break into the house?" Colin asked when his parents appeared.

"Something like that." Malcolm touched his fingers to Colin's hair, then went to stand with Mélanie, Raoul, and Archie, who had drawn together by the stairwell.

"That was the work of a professional," Archie said. "And also a desperate shot. Trenor's right, people, thank God, don't go about shooting off rifles in London, even agents. Perhaps especially agents. Much too risky."

"Quite." Raoul studied the bullet he still held in his hand. "So something's happened to escalate things and he'll try again quickly." He looked from Archie to Malcolm to Mélanie. "How would you do it?"

"I wouldn't wait for the target to leave the house," Mélanie said. "He has to know we're professionals as well and that we're on our guard now. And he'll know we'll have the wit to stay away from windows."

"So he has to get inside the house," Malcolm said. "The area door or the kitchen windows are most likely. If he's done any research he'll know we're understaffed."

"You're mad." Trenor had drawn close and was staring at them. "All of you."

"Quite mad," Malcolm agreed. "But we're in the midst of a mad world. " He glanced round the protected portion of the hall. Bet was holding her brother's arm, as though to anchor him to the spot. Frances, pressed into a chair by Archie, was stroking Chloe's hair. Chloe looked a bit surprised but was putting up with it. Laura was kneeling with her arms round Emily and Jessica, and Berowne in her lap. Valentin was on the floor between Colin and Livia. Cordelia, Drusilla in her arms, had been talking to Lumley, the sort of seeming nonsense designed to soothe, but now she broke off and looked at Malcolm.

"You should all be quite all right here," Malcolm said, in the same level voice he'd been using ever since the rifle bullet ripped into their house. "Mel, Raoul, and I need to reconnoiter. Uncle Archie's going to stay here."

Archie nodded. His bad leg, which could slow him down, wouldn't be much of an issue should—God forbid—anyone get into the confined portion of the hall.

Mélanie smiled quickly at the children. Best not to stop and think too much. She followed Malcolm and Raoul through the baize-covered door at the back of the hall that led below stairs. Midway down the pine stairs they all caught it. The smell of smoke.

"Damnation," Malcolm said. "Why didn't I think—"

He and Raoul already had their coats off. Mélanie yanked at the tapes on her petticoat and ripped it off. They caught the glow of flames as they rounded the last bend in the stairs, fabric pressed over their faces.

The door to the kitchen was ajar, probably to allow the smoke to escape upstairs. They raced through and met a blast of heat. The flames were in the center of the room, on the deal kitchen table. They threw coats and petticoat over the fire. Mélanie and Raoul flung themselves on top. Malcolm jerked open the area door. Draped across the table, smoke in her nose and eyes, Mélanie heard a thud and a crash and a muffled cry. Raoul helped her to her feet. Malcolm came through the area door, dragging a compact, sandy-haired man. Even in the gray, smoky light, Mélanie recognized the hunch of his shoulders and the set of his face.

"Billy," she said. Billy Hopkins might serve other masters, but in all Mélanie's encounters with him he'd been working for Lord

Carfax. Save once, when Carfaxs daughter Louisa had engaged his services with tragic results.

"Don't look at me like that, Mrs. Rannoch," Billy said. "I know I've been a damn fool."

"Quite." Malcolm tightened his grip. "Though in fairness, if you hadn't got your feet tangled in the area railings, I wouldn't have caught you. At least we know who is behind this. Out with it, Billy —whom does Carfax want killed, Lumley or O'Roarke?"

"O'Roarke?" Billy said on a note of disbelief. "Granted he gets in the way, but why would Carfax want to get rid of him now?"

"Why indeed?" Raoul grabbed a kitchen knife and pressed it to Billy's throat. "Why does Carfax want Gerald Lumley dead?"

Billy went very still but didn't appear particularly perturbed. "You won't use that."

"Not usually, perhaps," Raoul said, the blade steady against Billy's throat. "But you just shot a rifle into a room where my entire family were assembled, including the woman I love who is carrying our child, and then set fire to the house they're all in. Such moral scruples as I have have been severely strained. Talk."

"I can talk," Billy said. "But you won't know if I'm telling the truth. In fact, I probably won't be."

"Try this," Malcolm said. "Don't talk, and I'm taking you with me to see Carfax. You can sit there while I tell him how you failed."

Billy snorted. "It was mad anyway. I told him so, but he insisted. Usually he's more practical."

"Why?" Malcolm folded his arms across his chest. "Why does he want Lumley dead?"

"When does Carfax ever say why he wants anything done? If he explains at all, he explains more to you than me."

That was a good point.

"When did he hire you?" Malcolm asked.

"This morning. That's what I mean about mad. Summoned me to Newgate—don't ask how, there are ways—told me if Lumley got anywhere near you, he had to be eliminated. By whatever means necessary. That isn't the way Carfax normally talks."

"No," Malcolm said, "it isn't. Is anyone working with you?"

"When have you ever known me to work with someone else?"

Malcolm watched Billy for a moment, then nodded. The smell of charred cloth and burnt wood drifted through the smoky air. "Mel, can you get me a rope?"

Mélanie found a length of kitchen twine. Malcolm lashed Billy's wrists, loosely bound his ankles, so he could walk but not run, took the knife from Raoul, and pressed it against Billy's side. "Upstairs, Billy, march. And though I might not use this to get you to talk—mostly because I don't think we could trust anything you might say—I won't hesitate to use it to keep you from escaping."

Billy gave a grunt of acknowledgment and the four of them trooped up the stairs. Malcolm and Raoul took Billy into the library. Mélanie went to the back of the hall, and said it was quite safe for the children to return to their game of hide and seek in the parlor. Laura and Cordy went with them with looks that implored Mélanie to tell them the whole later.

"I'm afraid there's a bit of a mess in the kitchen," Mélanie said to Valentin.

"Nothing I can't handle, madam. I'm very grateful the threat is over."

The others went into the library, where Malcolm and Raoul had Billy seated in a chair in the center of the room, away from any exits or anything that could be turned into a weapon.

Lumley stared at Billy. "Was he—"

"You were his target," Malcolm said. "We still aren't sure why."

"Not so mad now," Robby said. He frowned. "Didn't do a very good job of protecting him."

"You may have kept him safe on his way here," Malcolm said. "And you put us on our guard. Without you we wouldn't have known whom he was shooting at."

Lumley continued to stare at Billy, as though he were a creature from an alien realm. "I've never seen you before. I don't have anything against you."

"I don't have anything against you." Billy's tone was matter-of-fact for all he was tied to the chair. "It was a job."

Lumley shook his head. "God, if I was back in Rivendell—"

Malcolm swung round to look at Lumley as Mélanie drew in her breath. "But you grew up in Surrey," Malcolm said, voice taut with the effort to maintain control.

"We moved there when I was eleven," Lumley said. "When my father got the living. Before that, he was the curate in Rivendell. That's where they lived when I came to them."

"Came to them?" Mélanie asked.

"Yes." The gaze Lumley turned to her was wide and open. "They took me in when I was ten. I'd been living in an orphanage."

"Where?" Malcolm asked in the same taut voice.

"Where?" Lumley looked confused by the questions as though he couldn't see the point. "In Brittany. I know I don't have much of an accent—Miranda used to tease me about how I'd lost it. But I'm actually French."

CHAPTER 39

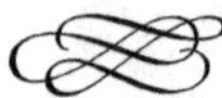

MALCOLM SLAMMED his hands down on the scarred table. "You tried to have the dauphin killed."

Carfax cast a quick glance round his cell.

"Damn it, sir. We have Billy Hopkins. He shot a rifle into my house. Into the room my wife was in. And Aunt Frances and Laura, who are both pregnant. My children were across the hall."

Carfax's face seemed to go pale, though it might have been a trick of the shadows. "Billy's too good a shot to miss."

Malcolm dropped into the chair across from Carfax. "Billy did miss. O'Roarke dug the bullet out of one of our bookcases. And then Billy set fire to our house."

"I presume the house is still standing."

"No thanks to Billy."

"Don't exaggerate, Malcolm." Carfax unhooked his spectacles from behind his ears. "Using smoke to get people out of a building is an old trick. I've used it myself as a field agent."

"And we've had it used on us before. It doesn't change the risk. Or the fact that you tried to have the rightful King of France killed. Do you deny it?"

Carfax folded his spectacles. "I don't know whether to say your shock shows naïveté or a sort of touching faith in my scruples. You know perfectly well I've never caviled at what's necessary to protect Britain."

"And this was necessary?"

"France in control of the Elsinore League? Or Fouché? Could you seriously support that?"

"Of course not. But he could be got away from them."

"You'd prefer that I backed him and controlled France?"

"I think the question is what you'd prefer."

Carfax set down his spectacles and spread his hands on the table. "Instability is dangerous. France has a government. Not ideal, perhaps, but it's working."

"So you decided murder was preferable?"

"You're surprised I'd cavil at murder?"

"Not of a crossing sweeper or a dockyard worker. Or of a woman employed in a brothel. But of the legitimate claimant to a throne? Yes."

Carfax tugged a handkerchief from his coat. "I'd say this to few people, but you of all people should know that it's not the actual bloodlines that matter. It's what they represent. There's a perfectly adequate representative of the monarchy on the throne of France now."

"That's quite an admission."

Carfax unfolded his spectacles and polished them with the handkerchief. "As I said, it's one I'd make to few people."

"Billy says you only gave him his orders this morning. That you insisted Lumley had to be eliminated before he got to us."

Carfax set spectacles and the handkerchief down on the table. "I was concerned about what you'd do if you found the dauphin. I think this conversation proves my fears right."

"I haven't told you what I'm going to do."

"Or what O'Roarke's going to do?"

"O'Roarke doesn't want him on the throne of France any more than you do."

"Or so he tells you."

"Don't. I've had enough of people trying to sow discord between us." Malcolm got to his feet. "The only thing I'm not sure of is if you killed Miranda Dormer to bury the secret of the dauphin. Whether or not you did it, I'm quite sure you're capable of having done so."

"Malcolm." Carfax's voice stopped him. Unusually sharp. "What are you going to do?"

"Protect Gerald Lumley. Who was perfectly ready to admit he comes from France but didn't give a hint of his true origins. He doesn't seem like a man who wants to reclaim his heritage. I'm not sure how much he even remembers. It's no secret his jailers tried to render him unfit to ever be king."

"That won't stop others from trying to use him." Carfax watched him for a moment. "It will be on your head, you know. If this brings about a war."

"And I don't relish that. But if you taught me nothing else, sir, you taught me that one has to live with the consequences of the decisions one makes."

"We can lock him up," Jeremy Roth said as two constables marched Billy down the steps of the Berkeley Square house and into a waiting carriage. "I can't vouch for how long it will last. It didn't very long last time."

"Carfax will have more difficulty pulling strings from prison," Raoul said, "though I have no doubt he'll be able to pull some. But at least it gives us a bit of time."

Mélanie glanced towards the back of the hall. The door to the breakfast parlor was slightly ajar and she could just hear the high-pitched voices of the children. The company were gathered there sharing a makeshift collation. It was a long time since any of them had eaten and feeding everyone had seemed a good solution to fill the time until Malcolm returned from his visit to Carfax. "Thank you, Jeremy," she said.

Roth nodded. "Billy Hopkins is clearly guilty of a number of crimes only today, let alone in the past." He looked from Mélanie to Raoul. "Do you have any idea why he attacked Lumley?"

"It's a bit of a mystery," Raoul said in an easy voice.

"We think Lumley may know something about Miranda Dormer that Carfax is concerned about," Mélanie added. Most of the people currently sitting in her breakfast parlor knew about the dauphin, but not all. And Lumley was either carefully avoiding talking (ingrained instinct, perhaps) or genuinely didn't remember his heritage. "Something about which he doesn't realize the significance."

Roth's brows drew together. "So you're inclined now to think Carfax killed her?"

"Malcolm never ruled that out," Mélanie said. And indeed, Lumley's being the dauphin and Carfax's trying to kill Lumley made it more likely that Carfax had killed Miranda Dormer. "But whether or not he killed her, Carfax plainly had an interest in what Miranda Dormer knew."

Roth nodded again, with the gaze of one piecing together the evidence. He had a quick mind. If they weren't careful, he'd piece together the truth about the dauphin, just as Mélanie had always been afraid he'd piece together the truth about her. And they really couldn't afford for Jeremy, in his position, to know the rightful King of France was hidden in Britain.

Assuming Lumley managed to stay hidden.

Roth pressed Mélanie's hand, nodded at Raoul, and followed his constables from the house. Mélanie closed the door—Valentin was in the breakfast parlor taking a well-deserved break—and looked at Raoul.

"So far, so good," he sad.

Mélanie nodded and glanced down the hall again. The rightful Louis XVII was sitting at her breakfast parlor table having supper.

For all they'd been through, she'd never envisioned a situation like this. And close as they'd been to major events, she wasn't sure they'd ever been involved in something that could so irrevocably shake their world.

"We're not going to be able to keep this quiet," she said.

"One step at a time," Raoul said. "We don't know what he wants. We don't know what he remembers."

"Whatever he remembers, I'm not sure he's going to be allowed to have what he wants."

The front door swung open and Sylvie St. Ives stepped into the hall.

"Forgive me, the door was open," said the woman who had been Beverston's mistress, Carfax's agent, and was now presumably working for Fouché. "I know you're understaffed. Since we're old friends I know you won't expect me to stand on ceremony."

Curse it, Mélanie thought, she'd been about to bolt the door. Though she wouldn't have put it past Sylvie to come in through a window. Mélanie faced Lady St. Ives, whom she had last seen in an antechamber in Apsley House the night Mélanie accused Sylvie of murdering Ben Coventry. The night before they'd had to flee London. "I'm sorry, Lady St. Ives. As you say we're understaffed. I fear we aren't even officially at home."

Sylvie pulled off her gloves, exquisitely stitched pale blue kid to match her pelisse and bonnet. "Seeking refuge in formalities. It's what I'd do myself. But we can stop the pretending. I know he's here. And I can take him off your hands."

"A very obliging offer, Lady St. Ives," Raoul said. He was positioned between her and the hall to the breakfast parlor. Not that there was a great deal she could do on her own against all of them, and theoretically she didn't want Lumley dead. But she had killed before. "But surely there's no point in detailing the reasons we wouldn't accept it."

Sylvie raised a well-groomed brow. "Would it really be so much worse than the situation in France now?"

"Fouché in charge of the country? Probably. And we'd have a lot of bloodshed getting there."

"So you'd rather he fall into the League's hands? Because that's what will happen you know. Unless Carfax kills him first. You're a master of control, Mr. O'Roarke, but you won't be able to control this."

"My dear Lady St. Ives, as I'm sure Fouché could tell you, I've never been one to listen when anyone tells me I can't do something."

"You can't keep him in this house forever. We can at least protect him."

"Call us arrogant," Mélanie said, "but I'm quite sure we can do that ourselves."

"The secret's out," Sylvie said.

"Yes, but you won't spread it about," Raoul said. "You don't want even more people after him. And the League's resources are greater than Fouché's."

"It's kind of you to call, Lady St. Ives," Mélanie said, "but we really aren't equipped for guests, and as you see there is nothing more to discuss, so—"

She broke off as the sound of the bell cut through the hall. She was, she realized, so used to having servants to answer it, that it was a moment before she quite realized what had happened. A glance through one of the windows that flanked the door showed a footman on the steps in a red-and-buff livery that she thought belonged to Lord Beverston. She exchanged a quick look with Raoul, then opened the door while Raoul kept an eye on Lady St. Ives.

The footman blinked at seeing her open the door rather than one of his peers. "Yes?" Mélanie said, and had the absurd thought that the story that she had opened her own door might prove to be the greatest scandal of their time in London.

"From Lord Beverston." The footman held out a sealed paper.

"It's for Mr. Gerald Lumley. I've been instructed to put it into his hands personally."

Mélanie hesitated. She could deny the footman the house, but they needed to know what Beverston wanted. The footman looked conventional enough but he could be an agent. She wouldn't put it past Beverston. Still, she and Raoul were both there, and Beverson, like Sylvie, didn't want Lumley dead. Quite the reverse, in fact. "Come inside," she said. "I'm afraid I must ask you to let us search you for weapons."

The footman's eyes widened. Either proof that he was who he said he was or that he was a very good actor—or agent—indeed. But he stepped into the hall and stood as still as if he were on duty at a ball as Raoul patted him down for weapons, while Mélanie kept an eye on Sylvie.

"He's clean," Raoul said.

Mélanie nodded. Nothing to be done about Sylvie. Save watch her. She met Raoul's gaze for a moment, then walked to the breakfast parlor.

Lumley was staring into a cup of tea. He frowned at the news that Beverston had a message for him, but did not appear anything like as alarmed as he should. At a look from Mélanie, Archie also accompanied them into the hall, as did Robby Simcox, who evidently took his commission to protect Lumley seriously.

"Lady St. Ives is also there," Mélanie said to Lumley. "She'll ask you to trust her. Don't."

Lumley turned a confused gaze to her. "I don't even know her."

"And you don't need to," Mélanie said. "She'll want you to leave with her. On no account are you to do so."

"Mr. Lumley," Sylvie said, right on cue, when Lumley appeared. "I don't believe we've met."

"No, madam, we have not," Lumley returned with surprising firmness.

Mélanie and Archie beside him, Lumley took the letter from the footman. "Lord Beverston said to wait while you read it," the footman said. "He said you might want to leave with me afterwards."

"You can wait outside," Mélanie said, as Archie opened the door. The footman hesitated. Mélanie gripped his arm, Archie propelled him outside, pushed the door to, and set his shoulders to it.

Frowning, Lumley slit the seal. Mélanie had no compunction about reading over his shoulder.

Lumley,

Miss Harker and Danny are with me and asking for you. I trust you will join us at my villa in Richmond. I know how important they both are to you.

Beverston

Lumley read it through twice, then looked up at Mélanie, his face pale. "I should go."

"Mr. Lumley." Mélanie put a hand on his arm. "You can't trust Lord Beverston."

"For God's sake, Mrs. Rannoch, I've known him half my life—"

"He knows who you are."

Something flickered in Lumley's gaze. Perhaps recognition. The dawning of a memory?

"And he may have killed Miranda." At least it was a possibility.

Lumley's jaw tightened. "All the more reason I need to go. He has Faith and Danny."

"Mr. Lumley, we'll make sure—"

"Can you deny he's threatening them?" Lumley waved the note.

Mélanie, whose mind had been working rapidly on how to protect Faith Harker and Danny from the moment she saw the note, met Lumley's gaze. "I'm quite sure Beverston won't hurt his grandson from everything I've heard."

"But he won't have such qualms with Faith. He's not a man who's careful with servants."

"Mr. Lumley—"

"I have to protect her."

"And we will, but—"

The bell rang again.

"Your husband appears to be at the door," Sylvie St. Ives said.

Mélanie unbolted the door and let Malcolm into the hall. "I assume there's a reason one of Beverston's footmen is on our doorstep?" He paused and took in the company.

Lumley held out Beverston's note. "I have to go. I need to rescue Faith and Danny. If I understand nothing else that's going on, I understand they're in danger."

"We certainly need to rescue them. But not by risking you."

"You can't keep him shut in here forever," Sylvie said.

"Good day, Sylvie." Malcolm met her gaze. "Kind of you to call."

Sylvie regarded him with a shrewd gaze and faintly mocking smile. "You don't want this, Malcolm."

"No, but I seem to be stuck with it."

"Rannoch," Lumley said. "I can't just stay here—"

"My point precisely," Sylvie interjected.

The door from the study swung open. A slender figure strolled into the hall, fair hair gleaming in the candlelight. "Well, well. Glad to find you all here," said Julien St. Juste.

CHAPTER 40

"DO YOU EVER RING, ST. JUSTE?" Malcolm asked.

"We came through a window. It seemed more prudent overall."

A woman followed St. Juste from the study. It was Gisèle.

Malcolm stared at his sister.

"You found him," she said.

"We rather stumbled across him." Malcolm's voice was not quite steady.

"Sylvie," Julien said. "I should have known I'd find you here. You really should learn to keep information to yourself, you know."

"You really should learn not to share it," Sylvie said, though Mélanie thought her skin was paler than it had been a few moments before.

"I tried, Mr. St. Juste," Robby Simcox said. "I've done everything I could to keep him safe."

"Thank you, Simcox," Julien said, his gaze still on Sylvie.

Lumley was studying Julien. "You're—"

"You recognize me? I fancy you've changed more than I have."

"I have to get Faith and Danny."

"Beverston's Richmond villa is secluded," Malcolm said. "He'll try to keep you there, Lumley."

"That's not—"

"And he won't let Miss Harker and Danny go." Malcolm glanced round the hall. "Out through the breakfast parlor, I think."

"What—?"

"Across the garden to the mews. Beverston's footman will figure out we're gone before long, but he won't be able to follow us. Archie, you're in charge of Sylvie. Aunt Frances!" Malcolm called.

Lady Frances emerged from the breakfast parlor with a celerity that indicated she might have been listening at the door. She went still as her gaze fell on Gisèle.

"I'm sorry to have caused you trouble, Aunt Frances," Gisèle said.

Frances squeezed her eyes shut and reached out to grip the edge of a console table. "Dear God."

Malcolm moved to his aunt's side. "We have a great deal to discuss. But first, if I ever needed you to call in a favor with the regent, I do now."

Frances met his gaze, her own now clear and alert. "Gladly, but you've always told me to keep him out of it."

"Not this time. Only he can get us what we need. O'Roarke and Mel will go with you." He turned to Gisèle. "For God's sake, at least stay here with Archie until we're back, Gelly.

Gisèle inclined her head. She was standing very still, her hands at her sides. "I promise."

Malcolm held her gaze for a long moment, then nodded and turned to Julien. "You're coming with us, St. Juste."

Julien raised his brows. "I have every intention of doing so. But I thought I'd have to follow."

"On the contrary. We need you to convince Beverston of who Lumley is."

BEVERSTON SURVEYED the trio his footman (a different footman from the one who might still be in Berkeley Square) had shown into the library of his villa in Richmond. Malcolm, Lumley, St. Juste. His gaze settled on St. Juste and lingered.

"St. Juste. What are you doing here?"

"Observing, for the moment."

Beverston gave a grunt that might have been acknowledgment. Or an indication of suspicions. "I wasn't prepared for such an entourage. Or if this many of you descended on us, I thought some might sneak in the back. Or try to." He raised a brow.

"No," Malcolm said. "We didn't bring others."

"I don't believe you, of course. But I think I have the house well guarded."

"We've come for Miss Harker and Danny. Send them out and we'll trouble you no further."

Beverston stared at him for a moment, then gave a guffaw of laughter. "You've got guts, Rannoch, I'll give you that. In your shoes, perhaps I'd have tried the same. You have few other options. My grandson isn't going anywhere, and Miss Harker, as his nurse, is naturally staying with him. Mr. Lumley is welcome to join them. In fact we would be quite desolate should he not do so."

Lumley cleared his throat. "Lord Beverston."

Carriage wheels and horse hooves sounded on the gravel drive outside. Malcolm glanced out the window. "Oh, good. My wife and O'Roarke. And our other guests."

Mélanie and Raoul came into the room a few minutes later, accompanied by Jeremy Roth and Lord Carfax.

"Good," Malcolm said. "I knew Aunt Frances could pull it off."

"Carfax," Beverston said. "I must say this is a surprise."

"To me as well," Carfax said. He was pale but managed, as usual, to look in command of the situation, despite the fact that he was wearing handcuffs. He met St. Juste's gaze for a moment. St.

Juste, leaning against the oak-paneled wall, his ankles crossed, raised a brow but said nothing.

"It helps to have an aunt who can ask for favors from the prince regent," Malcolm said.

"I should have considered that," Beverston said. "Though I fail to see why you want Carfax present."

"So do I," Carfax said.

"Lumley," Malcolm said, "tell Beverston who you are."

Lumley stared at him. But behind the confused gaze was a hint of what might have been recognition. Or fear. "Who I am?"

"Just so." Malcolm kept his voice gentle. "Are you the son of Louis XVI and Marie Antoinette of Austria?"

The air in the room turned still and thick, as though he had uttered an incantation or breathed the true name of a magical creature. Shock reverberated against the Chinese wallpaper and oak paneling. Shock at Malcolm's voicing the words, but not at the words at themselves, except from Roth. And Lumley.

"Am I *who*?" Lumley said. "Of course not."

"Good try," Beverston said. "But there's no need to pretend. I assure you, Your Majesty, you have a friend in me. And I have many other friends who will help you regain what you've lost."

Lumley looked like a man who's stumbled into Bedlam in the last of Hogarth's engravings of the rake's progress. "Lord Beverston, you've known me since I was eleven years old. You know who I am."

"I knew who I thought you were." Beverston's voice was surprisingly gentle, the voice he'd used with Danny. "And I'll never forgive myself for not knowing the truth sooner and helping return you to what is rightfully yours."

"My father is a vicar—"

"Your adoptive father. I may not have known the truth, but I always knew the Lumleys adopted you from France."

"Yes, I was adopted. From an orphanage in Brittany. My mother was a ladies' maid who someone got with child. My actual birth is far less exalted than my adoptive birth. Ask him." He spun to face St. Juste. "He brought me here."

"Quite true," St. Juste said. "And if I thought there was the least chance Lord Beverston would believe me, I'd have tried to tell him the truth long since, and saved us all a lot of bother."

"Spare us, St. Juste," Beverston said.

"Point taken, I think," St. Juste said.

"Carfax," Malcolm said, "tell Beverston the truth. Unless you want him to start a war trying to put the wrong person on the throne of France."

Carfax had gone paler, but he returned Malcolm's gaze like a general returning fire. "I confess, if Lumley is not the dauphin it would be quite a relief. But I can't imagine what you think I know about it. Or that Beverston would believe whatever story you evidently wish me to make up."

"You tried to have Lumley killed only a few hours ago."

"I deny doing anything of the sort. But surely if I had that would make it even less likely that he's an imposter."

Malcolm regarded his former spymaster, holding Carfax's gaze with his own. "Whatever you recently told me, I'm not sure you'd have tried to kill the rightful King of France. Not at this point, not given what you knew."

"But you think I'd try to have an imposter killed?"

"Yes. If it could cover up the fact that the rightful dauphin remained in the Temple prison and died there because of you."

Comprehension flashed in Raoul's gaze and in Mélanie's in almost the same instant.

Beverston was behind them. "A good try, Rannoch. But why would Carfax—"

"Because he didn't want a child ruler who could easily become hostage to God knows whom. Just as he doesn't want a restoration now."

"Precisely. So he'd say anything to discredit the rightful heir." Beverston swung towards St. Juste. "St. Juste hid the boy. He buried evidence of his whereabouts, for God's sake. Made a damned treasure hunt out of it. Why would he have done that with an imposter?"

"Why indeed?" St. Juste examined his nails. "Barras and Josephine didn't want to know where the boy was. For their own sakes and the boy's. But they insisted—well, Barras did—that I leave clues to the boy's whereabouts where they could find them should they ever wish to bring him to light—and should I not be reachable for whatever reason. I'd have been a fool to think Barras wasn't having me watched. To avoid arousing his suspicions, I needed to behave precisely as I would have done had I really extracted the dauphin from the Temple."

"But why?" Beverston said. "Why not extract him when you'd gone this far? You can't claim you, of all people, were distracted by political motives on either side. Any side."

"Hardly." St. Juste uncrossed and recrossed his ankles, his polished boots gleaming in the candlelight. "In truth, I'd have been curious to see how you'd all have played the true situation. But Carfax got wind of it and told me not to."

"Carfax?" Beverston said in disbelief. He glanced at Carfax.

"Yes, I know," St. Juste said. "But he was my first employer. And he had rather more of a hold on me then than he does now.

"You're just taking his side now," Beverston said. "For whatever reason. Your Majesty"—he turned to Lumley—"I assure you this does not affect my belief in you."

"My God," Lumley said. "What will?"

"Of course, with the story, and the hidden papers, and the rumors that are out there already, you could make a good case that he's the dauphin," St. Juste said. "Even a good enough one to put him on the throne if you had the right backing. God knows there've been enough pretenders already, with less creditable stories to prove their identity. There's a certain romance to the story of a lost heir returning to claim his heritage. Don't you agree, sir?" He glanced at Carfax.

"I've always been singularly deaf to the power of that type of story," Carfax said.

"No, but you know the power it can have on the public imagination. Probably why you decided it was safer to kill Lumley."

"But you didn't." Lumley regarded St. Juste. "You hired Simcox to protect me. At least, that's what he said."

"Yes, he was telling the truth. Simcox has his talents, but I don't think dissimulation is one of them."

"Why?" Lumley said. "Why protect me?"

St. Juste inspected his nails again. "I did bring you here. I confess I felt a certain responsibility."

"Julien," Mélanie said. "Did you just admit to a conscience?"

St. Juste looked up and met her gaze with a crooked smile that might almost have been called sheepish. "I don't like being used. Or being the means of others being used."

"Or you might have wanted to protect the real dauphin because you know just how valuable he is," Beverston said. "That seems far more likely."

"I had a feeling you'd say that." St. Juste settled his shoulders against the paneling. "As I said, it's a conundrum."

"Josephine never knew?" Raoul said.

"No. And she never asked me where he was." A shadow crossed St. Juste's face. "She'd have been furious I didn't follow her instructions, for all she later feared her rescue of the dauphin coming to light. But I rather think she'd want to protect Lumley."

"I need hardly point out that St. Juste's word is the last we should be taking for anything," Carfax said.

"No, but you might take mine." The door from the hall creaked. A walking stick thudded on the Axminster rug. A tall figure entered the room, powdered wig not a hair askew, diamond shoe buckles gleaming. Prince Talleyrand paused on the threshold, gaze sweeping the company. "I told your footman I'd show myself in, Beverston. In truth, I didn't give him time to argue. It seems I arrived in London just in time."

"Well, well," St. Juste said. "I confess this is a surprise. Don't tell me *you've* had an attack of conscience, sir."

"What an overwrought way of putting it." Talleyrand turned back to Beverston. "I know it's difficult to believe St. Juste. And generally unwise. But in this case he really does happen to be telling the truth."

Malcolm studied the prince. Another of those who had helped shape his childhood. "You were in on it with Carfax."

"I don't believe I said anything of the sort."

"You didn't have to." Malcolm kept his gaze locked on Talleyrand's. "You were afraid of the threat the dauphin could be."

"Or he's afraid of it now," Beverston said. "Like the rest of you."

"An exiled boy king would have been a receipt for disaster," Carfax said. "Every faction in Europe would have wanted to use him for their own ends. And if someone had managed to put him on the throne, we know what a *débâcle* can come from a child monarch."

"I should have guessed." Raoul was looking at Talleyrand. "It wasn't the first or last time you worked with Carfax."

Carfax's face was white, but he didn't move a muscle.

"Did you know about the dauphin's aborted rescue?" Malcolm asked Talleyrand. "Did you agree with Carfax that he should stay in prison? Or did Carfax tell you later?"

"My dear Malcolm. I really don't think you can expect me to answer."

"But you're convinced the boys weren't switched."

"I'm convinced," Lumley said. "Someone might listen to me."

"A struggle over who belongs on the throne of France could do incalculable damage now," Talleyrand said. "But there was a time —for instance, just after Bonaparte abdicated the first time— when I would have found a plausible alternative heir distinctly useful. You don't think I'd have made use of him if he really were the rightful King of France?"

Beverston stared at Talleyrand, as though he were a toad that had appeared in his perfectly manicured garden.

"Try to use him," Talleyrand said, "and you'll have my word to contend with. It still counts for rather a lot in France."

Beverston held the prince's gaze for a long moment. At last he drew a rough breath. "You make a good case. But what both you and Carfax seem to fail to consider is that if I do take this improbable story for the truth, you've given me a very useful weapon to use against the pair of you."

"But you won't use it," Carfax said.

"No?" Beverston swung towards him. "You underestimate me, Carfax. Which is a mistake I'd not have thought you'd make."

"Not in the least. I give you credit for being prudent enough not to use the information because then I will reveal that you've been stealing state secrets for personal gain."

Beverston held Carfaxs gaze, but Malcolm thought he'd gone a shade paler. "You can't possibly prove that."

"I can't prove how you did it. But I know the result. So does Castlereagh. And believe me we will uncover the truth."

"That's why you were talking to Miranda Dormer," Malcolm said to Carfax. "Because you knew she worked for Beverston."

"In part." Carfax was still looking at Beverston. "Also Hugh Derenvil went to Castlereagh today and signed a letter accusing you of trying to blackmail him for his vote."

"Oh, my God," Beverston said. "The man's a fool."

"Or a very brave man," Malcolm said.

"Quite possibly both," Carfax said. "But he's willing to speak out against your tactics."

Lumley was looking at Carfax. "You didn't seek out Miranda because of me? When I heard all this, I was afraid..."

"What?" Mélanie asked gently as he trailed off.

Lumley looked at her with the gaze of one desperately searching for answers. "Miranda didn't know who you all think—thought—I was. *I* didn't know. But I knew there was some mystery about my being brought from France. And that I wasn't supposed to talk about it. It was impressed on me so strongly that I really didn't talk about it. Except to Miranda, much later, after I found her in London. I suppose because we both had secrets at that point. I told her there were secrets about my coming to the Lumleys that even I didn't understand. And that on the journey here, I'd heard people refer to me as 'the Wanderer.'"

"Did she tell you?" Malcolm asked Beverston

"No," Beverston said.

"He's telling the truth," Lumley said. "Miranda promised she wouldn't tell anyone anything. She used to sometimes call me the Wanderer just as a joke, but she promised she wouldn't tell anyone else. But then, only a fortnight or so ago—the last time I saw her—she was worried. She'd had a dream and she was afraid she mumbled something about 'the Wanderer' in her sleep. She wasn't sleeping alone."

"I never—" Beverston said.

"No," Lumley said, "it wasn't you. It was another gentleman who visited her. Mr. Matthew Trenor."

"Oh, my God," Malcolm said.

Because suddenly he knew who had killed Miranda Dormer. And why.

CHAPTER 41

Bet Simcox undid the ties on her cloak and draped it over the back of the sofa in the sitting room of Sandy's rooms in Piccadilly.

Sandy turned up the lamp. "As it happens, Robby was doing something rather splendid."

"Yes, he was behaving far more sensibly than usual." Bet smoothed the worn blue velvet of the cloak. "Though it wasn't without risk."

"But he'll be all right now. No need to worry."

"I'll tell Nannie and Sam." Bet twitched a fold of the cloak straight. "I can go back to St. Giles. No more need for you to worry."

"Don't be silly, Bet." Sandy took a quick step towards her. "That is, yes, there's no need to worry, but you can't go back to St Giles. Much more comfortable here, isn't it?"

Bet glanced round the sitting room. You could fit two of her rooms in St. Giles in here alone. A log fire burned in the grate, banked by Sandy's manservant, but easy for them to poke up. The clean light and soft scent of real wax tapers filled the air instead of greasy tallow. "Of course it is," she said, swallowing a desperate laugh. "But I don't belong here."

"Don't know where else you belong. Much more agreeable to meet here than for me to come to your rooms. And I thought—" Sandy shifted his weight from one foot to the other. "I'd like it to be just the two of us."

A lump rose up in her throat. There hadn't been anyone but him for some time. In truth, it was difficult to contemplate anyone else now, though of course one day she'd have to. These past days living with him, for all her worries about her brother, had been a taste of something she'd never thought to have. "Sandy, I can't thank you enough for what you've done. But I can't stay here."

"Why not?" Hurt shot across his face, so that for a moment she wanted nothing more than to take him in her arms. "Don't you—"

"You can visit me. I'd like nothing more. And it can be just the two of us for as long as we can make that work." For as long as she could make ends meet, for as long as he didn't tire of her. "But men like you don't—"

"My father makes me a very good allowance. And he's always telling me to take more initiative."

"I don't think he meant setting up a mistress." Besides, gentlemen didn't take their mistresses to live in their homes, they set them up in rooms somewhere. And though they might visit St. Giles for a lark now and then and bed a girl, they didn't find their mistresses there. They chose opera dancers or actresses or shop girls or pretty governesses. There was hierarchy in all things.

"Bother that. I want you with me, Bet. You shouldn't have to worry about anything else. Unless you don't want to be with me." Sandy crossed to her, or started to when the skirts of his greatcoat caught on the sofa table. He shrugged out of it in impatience and tossed it on the sofa. Something shiny tumbled from one of the pockets. Sandy picked it up and stared at it. "That's odd."

"What?" It was a necklace with a green stone, she noted with a pang. Not hers.

"I don't know where this came from." Sandy picked up the coat and examined it. "Oh, poison. The footman must have given me Matt's coat when I left Mother and Father's, and Matt must have mine. It's happened before. We both ordered them from Weston at the same time. I'd best—"

He broke off as the door burst open and his brother came into the room with purposeful force. "Sandy. Glad you're home. Cursed nuisance, we seem to have left Grosvenor Square in each other's coats again. Really must sew something in the linings or something so the footmen can tell the difference."

He came quickly into the room. Despite his wording, Bet thought he looked more than mildly perturbed. There was something in the set of his shoulders and the way he lunged forwards that made her take a step back.

Sandy picked up his brother's coat and handed it to Matthew. "I just found this in the pocket." He started to hold the pendant out, then drew his hand back. "Who were you giving this to? It's odd, seems like someone was just talking about a jade pendant."

"Mr. Lumley." Bet sucked in her breath. Gerald Lumley had mentioned Miranda Dormer's necklace when they were all sitting round the Rannochs' breakfast parlor table.

"That's it." Sandy stared at his brother. He didn't quite seem to have seen the implications she had. "Matt, why do you have this?"

"I knew her, you know that." Matthew jerked his head at Bet. "You should understand visiting a girl like that."

"But why do you have her necklace? Why—"

Matthew lunged across the room to seize the pendant from Sandy. Sandy jumped out of the way. Matthew lurched into the drinks trolley. Two decanters and a set of glasses clattered to the Turkey rug. The smells of brandy and sherry filled the room. The door burst open. Mr. and Mrs. Rannoch ran into the room.

"It's over, Trenor," Mr. Rannoch said, as Matthew pushed himself up from the wreckage of broken glass. "We know Miranda Dormer had discovered you were selling secrets to Beverston. And we know you killed her for it."

"I found this." Sandy thrust the pendant into Mr. Rannoch's hand.

"You were passing information to Beverston by hiding it in a book in Miranda's room, weren't you?" Mr. Rannoch said. "Clever, you and Beverston didn't have to actually meet. But she found one of your communications. She told Hugh Derenvil she was disappointed in you."

Matthew Trenor hurled himself across the room. Almost before she realized he'd moved, Bet felt his arm round her and the press of a knife at her throat.

MALCOLM STARED at Matthew Trenor's knife against Bet Simcox's throat and cursed himself for a fool. "Don't be stupid, Trenor. There's nowhere for you to go."

"Of course there is. A whole world beyond Britain. Sandy's little friend and I are going out that door. Then you need no longer concern yourself with me."

Malcolm cast a sidelong glance at Mélanie. The knife was too close to Bet's throat to risk a jump.

"Don't you dare go one step with Bet." Sandy Trenor ranged himself in front of his brother.

"You care for her." Matthew's gaze fastened on his brother. "I cared for Miranda, you know. Don’t think I didn't. Which made it all the harder to realize—" Matthew drew a rough breath. "If you love her you won't stop me. And Rannoch's the chivalrous sort." Matthew, dragging a white-faced Bet, edged to the side, round his brother. "Don't worry, once I'm away you'll have her back."

Sandy stared at his brother as though he'd never seen him before. "You won't. You won't let her go. She's one more loose end to you. You'll kill her like that other girl."

"Don't be stupid, Sandy—"

Sandy hurled himself at his brother. The knife went flying.

Sandy caught Bet in his arms and pushed her behind him. Mélanie snatched up the knife. Sandy flung himself on top of his brother, one hand closed round Matthew's wrist. Malcolm grabbed Matthew's other arm.

"They'll never prosecute me for it," Matthew said. "Not the death of a girl like that."

"Sadly, perhaps not," Malcolm said. "But they will for treason. Which is why Miranda died in the first place."'

GISÈLE WAS in the Berkeley Square library when Malcolm and Mélanie returned. Malcolm felt himself breathe a sigh of relief, stronger than his response to any of the myriad crises of the day. In addition to Frances, Archie, Laura, and Cordelia, Raoul had returned from Richmond. Lumley had come with him. Another man had accompanied him as well, to Malcolm's surprise. Julien St. Juste was sitting in one of the Queen Anne chairs. Malcolm had rather expected St. Juste to melt into the shadows as Talleyrand had evidently done. St. Juste raised a brow of acknowledgment at Malcolm but said nothing while Malcolm and Mélanie recounted the events of the night for those who had missed various parts of them.

"So Trenor didn't kill Miranda because she mentioned the Wanderer?" Lumley asked.

"No," Malcolm said. "I think he passed that along to Beverston, but I don't think he had the least idea what it meant."

"Her death wasn't even so much to do with the Elsinore League," Cordelia said.

"Only tangentially, in that Beverston was paying Trenor for information," Malcolm. "I don't think Trenor even knows about the League."

"Carfax didn't know Trenor was the leak?" Frances asked.

"Apparently not. He seems to have sought out Miranda

because she was close to Beverston. Which probably panicked Trenor. And Carfax's questions may have prompted Miranda to search her room. She found the communication Trenor had hidden for Beverston. Trenor probably went to Miranda that night to learn if she'd revealed anything to Carfax. And Miranda must have confronted him. She told Derenvil she was disappointed in Trenor. She seems to have had some genuine feeling for him. As he did for her. But when she confronted him, Trenor realized she wouldn't keep quiet. In point of fact, I suspect she'd have told Roger Smythe if she'd lived."

"And he took the pendant because it was a reminder of her?" Cordelia asked.

"It may have got tangled up in his clothes as Harry suggested," Malcolm said. "The chain's broken. He may have just stuffed it in a pocket to get it out of the way. But guilt's an odd thing. Perhaps keeping it was a way of keeping her alive. Perhaps he couldn't bear to look at it and acknowledge what he'd done. Perhaps he simply wasn't sure how or where to get rid of it."

"And Carfax thought his staying in prison would reveal Beverston's source?" Laura said.

"He and Castlereagh were hoping Beverston would betray himself if he thought Carfax was out of the way," Malcolm said. "At least that's my theory. I doubt either would admit it. But I think Carfax also knew Beverston was looking for the dauphin, so he was treading very carefully. And then there's whatever else Beverston was threatening Carfax over at the Barque of Frailty the night of the murder."

"I didn't know, you know," Lumley said. "That I was supposed to be he." Even now, Lumley couldn't quite seem to say the dauphin's name. "I knew there was secrecy about my being taken from France. I knew I wasn't supposed to talk about it, or about my past. I suppose my hesitation to talk about it must have made it seem as though I were he." Lumley drew a breath. "The dauphin."

"A bit," Malcolm said. "Or rather it made it harder to see that you weren't. Mostly we were all making assumptions based on erroneous evidence."

"Evidence laid by you." Lumley looked at St. Juste.

"Barras and Josephine weren't fools," St. Juste said. "I had to make it convincing."

"But it's gone now, isn't it?" Lumley said. "The evidence? No one will suspect in the future."

"It's always a possibility," Malcolm said. "There've been pretenders in the past, and no doubt there will be in the future. But I think the story has been sufficiently discounted. Especially as you have no desire to promote it yourself."

"Good God, no." Lumley drew a breath, the breath of a man looking to the future after a crisis. "I'm going back to my law practice. And I'm going to marry Faith, if she'll have me." He looked at Raoul. "I still don't know quite how you got her and Danny out of Beverston's villa."

"Perseverance," Raoul said. "Not the first time I've extracted people." He glanced at Laura. "Not the first time I've extracted a child. It helped that Beverston was in shock."

"It was masterful." Lumley got to his feet. "I told Faith I'd call once she had Danny settled. I know it's late, but in the circumstances—"

"I don't think anyone's watching to cavil at the proprieties," Malcolm said.

Lumley nodded, and took himself off soon after.

"All this," Malcolm said, returning to the library after he had seen Lumley out, "because of a name people could put to him."

"Names can have a lot of power." Raoul leaned back on the sofa, his arm round Laura. "And sometimes it doesn't matter if it's the name one was born to or not. Which sounds as if it should be a good thing."

"But not if someone is pretending to bloodlines," Laura said. "Thank goodness Mr. Lumley isn't the sort to want a throne."

"You don't think he could still be used?" Cordelia asked.

"There's always the risk," Raoul said. "There'd be a risk of a pretender even if there'd never been an actual plot to switch another boy for the dauphin. But I don't think the League or Fouché will try again. They'll turn their sights elsewhere."

"Will Mr. Lumley be all right?" Gisèle spoke for the first time.

"All the pertinent actors know he's not the dauphin now," St. Juste said. "And seem to believe it. Even Sylvie, whom I had a long talk with when I returned to Berkeley Square."

"That's why you came back?" Malcolm turned from poking up the fire. Not that he'd trust anything St. Juste might say.

"Partly. I felt impelled to get her off your hands. And I wanted to thank your sister for her invaluable assistance." He smiled at Gisèle.

Malcolm felt his fingers clench round the poker. But they were going to have to discuss this, and perhaps it was as well to do it in front of everyone. They'd all have to know, one way and another. He returned the poker to the andirons. "How long were you working for St. Juste, Gelly?" Malcolm asked.

"I'm not sure I'd call it working for him," Gisèle said in a level voice. "I first met him when I was fourteen in the Elsinore League caves at Dunmykel."

"In the—" Malcolm forced his fingers to unclench from the gilded iron. "You knew about the caves?"

"I found them the summer before while Allie was working on her equations and Judith was playing with her dolls. You have to admit they're educational."

"They could give you a distinctly warped sense of all kinds of things," Frances said. She looked rather as though she swallowed hot coals.

"Yes, well, fortunately you made sure we all had plenty of accurate information about such matters. It's all right, Aunt Frances. It's not as though I actually saw any of the things that must have one on in the rooms. I never saw anyone in them at all until I encountered Julien. He told me he'd been a friend of Mama's. He was looking for something she'd told him was hidden there. He didn't say anything about the Elsinore League, but I assumed it was something of Alistair's, so I helped him sort of on general principles. We found the papers hidden in one of the finials on the bed post in the *Midsummer* room. After that Julien would appear occasionally, in the caves, or on the Dunmykel grounds, when I least expected it. I liked that I could talk to him about Mama." Gisèle's fingers tightened on the folds of her skirt for a moment. "And he taught me things—codes, how to pick a lock, how to wield a knife."

Things Malcolm might have taught her if he had been there instead of trying to outrun his ghosts on the Continent.

"You were a quick student," St. Juste said.

Gisèle flashed a smile at him, then looked back at Malcolm. "Julien came to Dunmykel in November and told me about the Wanderer and the papers Mama had hidden. I could tell they were important. I tried to find them for weeks, but I never thought of looking in Mama's jewels."

"And he suggested you go undercover with Tommy." Malcolm subdued the impulse to reach for the poker again.

"No, he wasn't there. When Tommy was recovering from his wound he tried to enlist me to look for some papers my mother might have hidden. I knew it must be the same papers. It seemed a good idea to pretend to be working with him and try to learn more. When Mélanie found the papers in Mama's jewels and Allie decoded them, I realized there might be more clues hidden in jewels that Aunt Frances or Judith now had. Tommy realized it as well." She looked straight into Malcolm's gaze, her own compelling. "He overheard it. I didn't tell him. But once Tommy knew, the best solution seemed to be for me to go with him and track what he was doing and try to learn the truth before he did."

Malcolm looked into the green gaze of his little sister, which was now also the gaze of a seasoned agent. "You could have told me."

"You'd have stopped me. Don't deny it, Malcolm. And once Tommy had the least clue I was working with you, I'd have lost any chance to go undercover with him."

Malcolm didn't for a moment believe it was as simple as that, but he also knew he wouldn't get Gisèle to say more in front of everyone. Maybe not even when they were alone. "When did you come back into it?" Malcolm swung his gaze to St. Juste.

"In London," St. Juste said in an easy voice. "I'd given Mrs. Thirle a way to contact me. Given that the secrets of the Wanderer seemed to be unraveling and that I'd started the whole thing, it seemed a good time to return to London. Your sister is a formidable agent, Rannoch. But I didn't want to leave her to handle this alone."

Frances's indrawn breath cut the air, like a diamond scraping glass. She had been sitting very still, her gaze trained on Gisèle. Now she said, "There's really no need for either of you to pretend in front of this group."

Gisèle looked at her aunt with a smile that was half defense, half apology. "I should think pretense comes as easily to this family as breathing, Aunt Frances."

"Perhaps. But whatever reasons your mother had for keeping the secret, there's really no point in making a mystery of it now. I think everyone in the room already guesses the relationship between you and Mr. St. Juste."

Confusion flickered across Gisèle's face.

St. Juste flung back his head and laughed. "You think she's my daughter?" He looked genuinely surprised. "No, I assure you, Lady Frances. Though I'd be proud to call her that." He paused for a moment. "What an odd thought. Though not entirely unwelcome. In any case, she's not mine, though she's quite brilliant. She takes after both her parents. Your mother was a formidable woman, Rannoch."

"We know that," Malcolm said. "And also that Gisèle's been asking questions about her father. I can't believe that isn't connected to all of this."

Gisèle sat up very straight. Her fingers were white against the dark green fabric of her skirt. "You think I'd only respond to a crisis and try to do something important with my life because of who my father is?"

"No," Malcolm said, "but I suspect it has something to do with it. It did for me."

Gisèle frowned down at her hands. She still wore her wedding band, Malcolm realized. It was her only jewelry at present. "For years I scarcely thought about it. But you can't imagine it wasn't on my mind with everything that's happened in the past six months and all the secrets, known and unknown. Learning who Malcolm's father is." Her gaze flickered to Raoul. "In many ways, I wish you were my father."

"I'd have been proud to be," Raoul said.

"But you aren't. And neither is Julien. Though Julien did tell me the truth. And Tommy reinforced it. I confess it was something of a shock. I can see why Mama kept it secret. Though I don't suppose now—"

She broke off as Valentin opened the door and ushered Lord Carfax into the room.

"Forgive me." Carfax hesitated a few paces into the room after Valentin withdrew and closed the door. "With Trenor in custody, Roth spoke with Conant, and I've been released. I wanted to offer my thanks."

Malcolm bit back a curse. For all he was relieved Carfax was out of prison, his former spymaster had damnable timing. And for all his thanks sounded genuine, they could have been delivered in the morning. Why had Carfax taken the time to come to Berkeley Square before going to see his wife and children? Was it worry over what Malcolm might do with the information—only a theory really—that he had been behind the dauphin's not being spirited out of France? Carfax's sharp features were shadowed with concern, but somehow it didn't seem like worry about political secrets. Malcolm was used to seeing that on his former spymaster's face. Instead, in the light from the brace of candles on the library table, Carfax looked uncharacteristically uncertain.

"I'm glad we discovered the truth, sir," Malcolm said. "I'm sure you must wish to reassure Lady Carfax and the rest of your family."

"Quite."

"But that's part of why you're here, isn't it?" St. Juste said. "You arrived at a timely moment, as it happens. All things considered, I really don't think it can remain secret any longer. Not from anyone in this room."

Carfax went pale as new-fallen snow, gaze locked on Julien's.

"He's right." Gisèle's voice cut across the room. "I was hoping to talk to you first, but really much better that everyone knows and stops speculating. Will you tell them, my lord, or shall I?"

"Tell them?" Carfax seemed to have trouble finding the breath to speak.

"That you're my father," Gisèle said.

CHAPTER 42

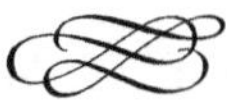

Good God. It's not possible. Of course. The thoughts raced across Malcolm's mind while his sister and former spymaster stared at each other in the warm light of the library.

Frances broke the silence that gripped the room. "This certainly explains Arabella's silence. The two of you will want to talk alone. The rest of us will remove upstairs to the drawing room. Gisèle, my dear, you have only to send word if you need us."

Mélanie slid her hand into Malcolm's as they climbed the stairs with the others. Malcolm squeezed his wife's fingers. The group was remarkably—especially for this group—silent.

"My God." Raoul shook his head as Archie pushed the drawing room door to behind everyone.

"You didn't know?" Malcolm asked.

"Good God, no."

"Or suspect?"

"Do you seriously think I could have?"

"Could? Yes. Did? I'm not sure. But I don't think you'd have told me."

"Probably not, until Gelly disappeared. Then all bets would have been off." Raoul scraped a hand over his hair. "I don't know why it shocks me so much. I knew she had lovers. I knew she had lovers in pursuit of her work."

"Of course Bella did." Frances sank down into an armchair, one hand supporting her stomach. "But this is the first I've heard so much as a rumor of Carfax's having a lover."

Archie put a hand on her shoulder. "I don't think this had much—if anything—to do with dalliance."

Raoul frowned as though puzzling over Arabella. "Whyever it started, I can imagine—they'd have each found the other a challenge. That can be very attractive." He shook his head. "Thinking back—the times Arabella and I talked about Carfax. Strategized about him." He looked at Malcolm. "Mentioned your spending time with David. I can't claim I ever picked up on any clue. Which speaks very well for Bella's talents and not at all well for mine."

"She protected it," Malcolm said. "As she protected few secrets. Perhaps because of your reaction. Though I wonder if some of it wasn't for the sake of Carfax. Or at least for the sake of his marriage."

Raoul met his gaze for a moment. "Yes. It may well have been. Arabella wasn't without sensitivity."

"St. Juste knew." Frances looked round. "Where is Mr. St. Juste?"

Where indeed? Malcolm had seen him leave the library but there was no sign of him in the drawing room.

"Julien has a habit of melting away," Mélanie said. "But I do think part of the reason he came back to the house, besides dealing with Sylvie, was to make sure Gisèle was all right. And perhaps to help her tell us about Carfax."

"Do you think he learned the truth from Lady Arabella?" Cordelia asked. "Or from Carfax?"

"At a guess, from Arabella," Raoul said. "We don't exactly understand St. Juste's relationship with Carfax, but I doubt it's a confidence Carfax would share with anyone, let alone an agent."

Laura, who had been watching Raoul with concern, went up

and slid an arm round him. "Tommy Belmont knows," she said. "So the League know, or some within the League."

Raoul nodded and drew her against him. "Probably Beverston. I suspect that's what Beverston threatened Carfax with at the Barque of Frailty the night of the murder."

"Watching Gisèle today—" Frances shook her head, her hand still on the babies she carried within her. "Part of me felt I was looking at a stranger. And part of me has never been more proud."

"She has a remarkable aptitude as an agent," Raoul said. "And she's noticed more than any of us realized."

"I should have seen more," Mélanie said. She was still holding Malcolm's hand.

Malcolm looked at her

"I know how women can be overlooked," she said.

"Undoubtedly. But there has to be more to it," he said. "I understand she was drawn to adventure. I understand she thought I'd keep her out of things. But for her to walk away from her family—"

"One doesn't always understand consequences when one's twenty," Cordelia said.

Laura met her gaze. "No, one doesn't."

Frances frowned. "God knows I didn't put my children first at twenty. And as for my marriage—well, I fear I'd given up on it. Which certainly can't be said for Gisèle."

"But I don't think one always sees the damage one's doing," Cordelia said.

"Or the people who may be hurt." Mélanie leaned her head against Malcolm's shoulder.

Malcolm pressed a kiss to her forehead. "David and I've only just begun to mend matters. And now I'm going to have to keep this from him. Unless Carfax decides to tell him."

Without speaking, Archie moved to the drinks trolley and began to pour out drinks for everyone. Cordelia helped him pass them round. A quarter hour later, Gisèle slipped into the room.

Her face was pale and she kept her hands carefully clasped together, but her voice was level. "Lord Carfax has left. He's going to Spendlove Manor tonight to see his family, but he says he'll come see you tomorrow, Malcolm."

She glanced round the room. Archie lifted his glass, jerked his head towards the drinks trolley, and raised a brow. Gisèle smiled and shook her head. "You've all been very forbearing. I'm sure you have questions. But right now, I need to speak to Malcolm."

Malcolm got up from the sofa where he'd been sitting beside Mélanie. It was the conversation he'd been wanting to have since Gisèle had disappeared on New Year's Day, and now he was gripped by unexpected dread.

"Of course," he said, "let's go into the small salon."

Malcolm lit the Argand lamp in the small salon and studied his sister in its glow. So much to say, so difficult to know where to start. "I imagine it was both a relief and a challenge to finally be able to talk to him."

Gisèle nodded, arms folded across her chest. "I'm his daughter. In a number of ways."

"You're yourself, Gelly. As we all are. Not the sum of our parents."

"Are we? Can you really claim you don't take after Raoul?"

"If I do, it's because he raised me. More than Arabella did. Certainly more than Alistair did."

"Aunt Frances raised me. But I don't think I'm very like her."

"No? Take it from an outside observer, Gelly. You have her tenacity. And her often uncomfortable insight. Her ruthlessness. And her loyalty to those she loves."

Gisèle glanced towards the door to the drawing room. "She must be disappointed in me."

"She just said she'd never been more proud." Malcolm studied his sister. "This is a shock, Gelly. I suspect one day you'll be glad you know the truth. But don't let it define you."

"I'd never do that. I knew what I needed to do long before I learned Carfax was my father. I wouldn't let a little thing like biological parentage affect me. Perhaps the strongest example of how very much I in fact take after my biological father." She hesitated. "I wonder if he knew."

"Who?"

"Alistair."

"I'm not sure." For a moment Malcolm saw Alistair Rannoch putting a sovereign into the hand of a four-year-old Gisèle. "I'm fairly sure he knew he wasn't your father."

"Oh, yes. He never made much pretense about that. I doubt he and Mama were sleeping together at all by the time I was conceived."

"He was always fond of you, though," Malcolm said.

"Don't say that to—"

"I'm not. I think he liked you best of the three of us. I'm not sure why he was so hard on Edgar."

Gisèle tilted her head to one side. "Perhaps Edgar disappointed him by not living up to you."

"That's absurd."

"Is it? I think Alistair knew just how keen your understanding was. I think a part of him wished you were his."

Tommy's words, uttered from a sickbed in December, echoed in Malcolm's head. They had been remarkably similar to Gisèle's just now. "I'll never really fathom Alistair. At this point we'll never have the chance to learn more. I suppose it's folly to refine too much upon his motives."

Gisèle hugged her arms tighter over her chest. "Yes. Hard not to do so, though. But you're right, it's a silly exercise. I don't suppose we'll ever really understand Mama either."

The urge to offer comfort welled up on his tongue. But though Gisèle would always be his baby sister in some ways, she was too old for that sort of simple comfort. If he hadn't already known it, tonight had proved it. "No," he agreed. "We won't. But we have more windows into her thoughts. Aunt Frances for one."

"And Raoul."

"Yes. Though I think he wonders if he'll ever understand her either."

"Julien says she may be the most formidable agent he ever worked with. She kept the secret of the dauphin—or what she thought was the secret—all those years. She had to have known how dangerous it was."

"I don't think Mama worried very much about danger."

"No. But she must have been afraid sometimes." Gisèle's fingers pressed into the fabric of her sleeves. "I know I was, these past weeks."

This time Malcolm did move forwards and put his arms round his sister. "It's over, Gelly. You can come home."

Gisèle clung to him for a moment, fingers clenched on his coat, face buried in his shoulder. Then she drew a breath and stepped back. "I love you, Malcolm." She set her hands on his shoulders. "We solved this crisis. But it's not over. I'm not sure it's even begun."

Malcolm's gaze skimmed over her face. "It's true there's a lot left to be done. And we'll do it together."

Gisèle looked up at him, her gaze steady. "We have different ways of fighting, Malcolm. And I'm not sure you'd agree with mine."

"I won't shut you out, Gelly. I promise."

"You're very good at what you do, Malcolm. But I can do things you can't—"

"Gelly—"

Gisèle squeezed his hands and took a step back. "I love you, Malcolm. But I can't come back. Not yet."

"For God's sake, Gelly—"

"I knew you'd object. But you understand about duty. Mama left work unfinished."

"That can't define us."

"Why do you think I agreed to stay here when you went to confront Beverston? Tommy and the League don't know I came to see you. Julien and I made very sure of that. Even if they find out, I can spin a story."

Malcolm had thought he was beyond shock where Gisèle was concerned. Apparently he'd been wrong. "You're going back."

"You have a job to do, Malcolm. And so do I."

"Away from your family."

She swallowed. For an instant, uncertainty flickered in her gaze. "For a while. Tell me duty's never taken you away from your family."

"All too often. And I've regretted it."

"Would you do it differently?"

"I'm not sure. But I wouldn't go under deep cover for an uncertain amount of time."

"I think that rather depends on the stakes."

"Gelly, you can't. Tommy may suspect you after you sent me the message that took us to Hyde Park."

She shook her head. "He was having you followed from the time you got to London. I was afraid of that when I sent you to Hyde Park, which is why I warned you."

"Charlotte Leblanc suspects you."

"But Tommy doesn't believe her. Charlotte doesn't think I'll come back. I think my going back will convince even her."

Malcolm took a half step towards her. "Gelly. What aren't you telling me?"

"We're fighting the Elsinore League, Malcolm. You know how important that is. There are things only I can do."

"At least wait until Andrew gets back from Rivendell."

Something like panic shot across Gisèle's face. "Oh, no, Malcolm. I can't see Andrew. Even I have a breaking point."

"So does Andrew, I imagine."

Gisèle swallowed. "Then I have to hope we don't reach it. Don't you think a large part of why I'm doing this is to make sure Andrew and Ian are safe? Don't you run risks for Mélanie and Colin and Jessica?"

"Yes. But if I'm honest, I also at times do it because I'm drawn to risk myself."

"All the more reason for you to understand me."

"I think I do understand, Gelly. And I understand just how great are the risks that you're running."

She lifted her chin in a way that reminded him of the girl she'd been at thirteen. "Are you going to try to stop me?"

Every instinct screamed to do just that, but he shook his head. "I don't think I could, for one thing. For another, you've proved you can make your own decisions. I'd be going against everything I believe in if I tried to control you."

Relief shot across her face. "Thank you."

"But I'll never forgive you if you don't come back safely."

"Oh, Malcolm." Gisèle gave a twisted smile. "Surely you know that's something none of us can promise."

CHAPTER 43

MÉLANIE OPENED the door of the study where Gisèle had gone to write a letter to Andrew. "I thought you might like some tea."

Gisèle looked up, the pen clenched in one hand. "You must hate me, Mélanie."

"Not in the least." Mélanie set the cup of down on a corner of Malcolm's desk. "I'm not sure I'd do what you're doing, but I think I understand."

Gisèle looked down at the letter on the blotter. "Try to explain to Andrew. I don't know that he'll ever forgive me."

"Andrew loves you." Mélanie perched on the edge of the desk. "That won't change."

"I hope not." Gisèle's voice caught. "Look after Ian." Her voice caught. "He probably doesn't remember me."

"He remembers. And don't make the mistake of thinking it doesn't make a difference because he's so little."

Gisèle turned her head away, then seemed to force herself to meet Mélanie's gaze. "You can't expect your children to live with you if you can't live with yourself. You said that to me once."

Mélanie swallowed, her throat dry. "So I did. I said it to Raoul recently as well."

"Raoul was away from Malcolm at times. He's away from Emily for long periods of time now. He's bound to be away from his and Laura's baby."

"So he is. But for myself, I'm not sure I could live with myself if I stayed away from Colin and Jessica."

"Perhaps you're a better parent than Raoul is, or than I am."

"I don't think so. I think it's something that every parent has to work out, and there's no one right answer. I just hope you've weighed the consequences. Raoul would be the first to tell you there are consequences. You're—"

"Don't say I'm very young. I'm older than you were when you married my brother to spy for the French. I know the truth," she added. "Tommy told me."

"I'm glad you know the truth. But I'd hardly hold my own actions up as a model for anyone to follow. Or claim I properly weighed the consequences."

"But you also aren't sure you'd do it differently, are you?"

"No."

"And for all he knows the consequences, Raoul's still a field agent." Gisèle picked up the tea and took a careful sip. "Ian will understand when he's older. At least, I pray to God he will."

"And Tommy?"

"Tommy can take care of himself."

"That's not what I meant."

Gisèle set the cup down, carefully aligning the silver handle. "I need Tommy. That is, I need his help and the information he can give me. I have no illusions about him."

"Illusions aren't the same as feelings."

"I love Andrew."

"Loving someone else doesn't necessarily make those feelings go away. But I don't think you're the type for an affair without strings."

Gisèle lifted her chin. "I never said—"

"No. But I am somewhat observant."

Gisèle drew a breath as though gathering a cloak about her. "I won't let myself get burnt. You and Malcolm are very good at what you do, but you have to allow that I have talents of my own."

"Obviously very formidable talents."

"Well, then. You need to let me make my own choices. My own mistakes. Fight my own battles. Face my own consequences." She picked up the pen again with white-knuckled fingers. "And believe me, I know there will be consequences."

MÉLANIE WATCHED her husband in the shadowy privacy of their bedchamber. Jessica's even breathing in her cradle cut the air. Malcolm's back was to her, his shoulders a taut line. Gisèle had left an hour since, as quietly as she had arrived. "You did the only thing you could have done, darling," Mélanie said. "You had to let her make her own decision."

"Yes, I know." Malcolm's voice was rough but steady. "And God knows she's shown she can take care of herself."

"Julien said she was a quick study. Coming from Julien that's speaks volumes." Mélanie shook her head. "I still can't quite believe—"

"I know. " Malcolm moved to the cradle and smoothed the covers over Jessica, then turned to face her. "There's been a lot to adjust to today."

"Darling, I can't imagine—"

"I know. Though given the way my family's history is intertwined with spies, I suppose it's no wonder Gisèle and I both have spymasters for our fathers."

Mélanie gripped her elbows, subduing certain thoughts about Arabella Rannoch. As a woman, she knew, none better, that one couldn't always plan these things. "To think Carfax watched her grow up—"

"I think she means something to him. Not, I think, what I mean to O'Roarke. What I think I mean—"

"You know perfectly well what you mean to Raoul, darling. But I do think Gisèle means something to Carfax. And I rather think some of that carried over to how he feels about you."

"I hope to God not. Unless you're saying Carfax would toss Gisèle aside as collateral damage."

"I don't think Carfax tossed you aside in the least, darling. I think he made a carefully calculated choice that he regrets. Though he'd probably do the same again. In that sense, he's very like Raoul. Though Raoul's motives and goals are quite different."

"And his definition of collateral damage."

"That too. I'm the last person to excuse anything Carfax has done. But he does care about you."

"You're more generous than I am, Mel." He crossed to her side and slid his arms round her. "It fits with your being the romantic in the family."

"I'm not in the least romantic."

"So you say, beloved." He kissed her nose. "Andrew and Harry should be back tomorrow or the next day. I have to speak to Andrew." A shadow crossed his face. "But there's no reason we can't begin making preparations to return to Italy. I'll talk to Bertrand."

Her gaze fell on one of the framed theatrical prints on the wall. Romeo saying farewell to Juliet because it was the nightingale and not the lark. "We should take time to make sure everything's attended to here. I don't think we have to worry about Carfax right now. And the League are going to have to regroup."

"They may be dangerous while they do so. I won't be easy until we set sail. We've been home a matter of days, and someone shot into our house tonight. This is a new low."

"Billy wasn't shooting at any of us."

"Hardly comforting."

"It could have happened in Italy, darling. Our lives are a risk.

We know that. Though I confess rifle fire through the library window was somewhat extreme."

"Quite." He drew her to him.

"At least we don't have to worry about starting a war," she said into his shoulder.

"There is that." He stroked her hair. "And Miranda Dormer's killer is at least for the present in custody. It remains to be seen if justice will be done."

"And you saved Carfax."

"Not my chief aim, but I'm relieved he's not imprisoned for a crime he didn't commit."

"You'll need to see David again before we go." Mélanie lifted her head from Malcolm's shoulder. David's gaze, the brush of his lip on her cheek, in Frances's drawing room—was it only yesterday?—lingered in her memory and brought something like hope.

"Yes." A shadow flitted through Malcolm's eyes, and she knew he was thinking that the truth of Gisèle's parentage was now between him and David. "Though I imagine he'll return to the Continent himself shortly. Perhaps we can see Simon and the children on our way to Italy."

"Perhaps they can all come stay with us." She set her mind to more positive things.

"I hope so." Malcolm set his hands on her shoulders. "I also need to write to grandfather in the morning. To try to explain about Gisèle. And to tell him his gambit failed."

CHAPTER 44

CARFAX DROPPED into a wingback chair opposite the desk in Malcolm's study.

"You're here early," Malcolm said.

"Amelia understood I had a great deal of business to see to in London. She'll be moving back to Carfax House tomorrow."

"You saw David?"

For an instant, relief, pain, and fear did battle in Carfax's eyes. "We spoke briefly. He plans to return to the Continent shortly. He's agreed to write."

Malcolm nodded. When it came to a fragile relationship with David, he could certainly empathize. "Roth was here first thing this morning. He believes Sir Nathaniel plans to bring Trenor up on charges. Unless Castlereagh quashes it."

Carfax crossed his legs. "I need to see Castlereagh. A great deal is still unclear."

"I don't think Trenor has the least notion of who the Wanderer is," Malcolm said. "I think he told Beverston that Miranda had said something about the Wanderer, though probably not until after Miranda was dead, as Beverston doesn't seem to have questioned her. Perhaps Beverston was even afraid someone else in the League had let something slip to her. But when Harry and Andrew went to Rivendell, Beverston put together that Miranda was close to Lumley and Lumley had come from France to Rivendell. Sylvie, I suspect, worked it out because she learned St. Juste had Robby Simcox protecting Lumley." Malcolm surveyed Carfax. "How did know Lumley was the supposed dauphin?"

Carfax hesitated a moment, as though he wasn't sure he'd respond. "When I spoke with Miranda Spencer—Miranda Dormer—I mentioned the Wanderer. I wanted to see how she'd react. If Beverston had her searching for information about the Wanderer. She denied the name meant anything to her, but I could tell it did. Something personal, which made me question if it was part of her work for Beverston. Obviosuly I didn't get a chance to ask her more, but I set inquiries about her in motion after her death."

"From Newgate."

"One can accomplish a great deal from a cell. And people tend to underestimate one's reach, which can be an advantage. I didn't know she was really Miranda Dormer until then. Once I learned that and learned she was still in communication with a young man in his mid-thirties who had been adopted from France as a child, I began to have my suspicions. When I had Lumley followed, I realized someone else was shadowing him as well. I didn't know Simcox was working for St. Juste, but just the fact that he was of interest to someone else was enough to confirm my suspicions."

"No wonder you didn't want me investigating. You had everything under control on your own."

"I didn't want you investigating because I didn't want you and your insights and your conscience anywhere near the Wanderer."

"And because Beverston knew the truth about Gisèle's parentage."

Carfax's mouth tightened. "He told me just after I spoke with

Miranda Dormer. Otherwise I'd probably have been gone before her body was discovered."

"What did he want you to do?"

"He didn't say. I think at that point he simply wanted me to know the power the League could hold over me. I confess I was in shock."

"Not surprising even for you."

"I went back to see Miss Dormer, in the hopes of learning more about Beverston's plans." Carfax hesitated. "I found her dead. If I hadn't been in such shock, I might have got myself out of the house before anyone else came in. As it was, once I was discovered with her, I decided I might be able to discover more from prison, with Beverston off guard."

"Castlereagh knew."

"I got a message to him that night. He already knew about the Wanderer."

"But not that Wanderer himself was an imposter."

Carfax's gaze settled hard on Malcolm's own. "Obviously." He settled back in his chair. "There was also the matter of the foreign office intelligence the League were getting. We never could work out the source. We started with everyone within the League we knew of with foreign office connections, but that got us nowhere. Finally we decided it must be someone Beverston was paying outside the League. He was known to spend a great deal of time at the Barque of Frailty. I wondered if Derenvil could be the leak. Castlereagh didn't want to think it of him, but Castlereagh was also surprised he was visiting a brothel. Part of my aim in showing up at the Barque of Frailty was to let Beverston know we were on to him, though I genuinely thought Miss Dormer might be able to give us intelligence. I certainly never intended—"

"Trenor didn't kill her because of you, sir. He may have been more on edge because you were there, but his motivation was her confronting him about passing information to Beverston. At which point he probably realized she was working for someone other than Beverston."

"She was obviously a very capable agent." Carfax gripped the arms of his chair. For a few minutes he and Malcolm had fallen back into speaking as spymaster and agent. Now something shifted in his face. His fingers curved round the chair arms as they though were made of porcelain rather than carved wood. "Gisèle—"

"She left last night." Four simple words that covered strained goodbyes, second guesses, Aunt Frances's white face, tears (his own, hidden from everyone including his wife).

Carfax fixed Malcolm with a hard gaze. "She's gone back undercover."

"No comment."

"You have a way to reach her?"

"Can you imagine I'd have let her leave if I didn't?"

Carfax relaxed back into his chair. "For all your insights, I imagine last night's revelations came as a surprise to you."

"Perhaps none more so than my sister's parentage."

"Surely at this point your mother's love affairs don't surprise you."

"It's not Arabella's actions that surprise me."

Carfax held Malcolm's gaze, though Malcolm saw a spot of color on the other man's face. "With all the other sins you've laid at my door, surely this isn't the worst."

"Not the worst. But perhaps the most surprising."

Carfax glanced away, then looked back at Malcolm. "I don't believe I owe anyone an explanation, save Amelia should she ever find out. But for what it's worth, it was an aberration."

Malcolm drew a breath. Part of him wanted to know as little as possible. And yet he had to learn more. For Gisèle's sake. Perhaps for his own. "Which of you—"

"Seduced the other?"

"I was going to say was seeking information from the other, but it's much the same thing."

"I'm not entirely sure. And I'm not sure either of us could have said at the time. Arabella wanted to discover what I knew about your father's activities in Ireland." Carfax adjusted his spectacles. "I trust we can dispense with the farce that I don't know who your father is."

"Of all the secrets in our family, that's hardly the one I'd most jealously protect. In fact, it's become a fairly open secret."

"She risked a lot for him. But then, I'm not entirely without understanding of the pull of love."

Of all the shocking things Malcolm had heard from his spymaster through the years, this was perhaps the most surprising. "You think it was love?"

"Why else would she have done what she did to protect him?"

"To further her cause. Or his own. Or both of theirs."

Carfax gave a short laugh. "All of you and your talk of causes. I swear you're more romantic fools than those acting out of romantic love. In any case, Arabella wanted information that would help O'Roarke."

"And you?"

"Need you ask? It was '97. I wanted information about Ireland. Arabella was O'Roarke's mistress and O'Roarke was at the heart of the brewing rebellion. And I knew Arabella was investigating the Elsinore League." Carfax settled his hands on the chair arms again, as though laying claim to a throne. "I know it's a gambit you've probably never employed yourself, but you must know seduction is as much a tool of espionage as codebooks. If you didn't know it before, surely your wife taught you that."

"My wife has taught me a number of things," Malcolm said in an even voice.

"Remember when I was in military intelligence, I was a field agent. Suffice it to say Arabella may have been an aberration, but not my first such."

All these years and Carfax could still surprise him.

The surprise must have shown on his face, for Carfax gave a short laugh. "I'll own I'm not the best suited for such a role, but I managed. Rather better than you might expect as it happens."

"It's not that." Well, not entirely that.

Carfax regarded him over his spectacles. "It's admittedly a difficult thing to hear about the parental generation. You're handling the discussion better than David in similar circumstances. But then, you've always been more flexible in your thinking in a number of ways."

Odd, in this world in which infidelity was so commonplace, that the truth of Gisèle's parentage to some degree explained the secrecy. It could potentially do real damage to a marriage Malcolm had always seen as amazingly strong for the beau monde.

Carfax coughed and adjusted his spectacles. "It's not easy to be married to anyone in intelligence, as you know. Amelia's given up a lot as my wife. I have no desire to cause her additional pain."

"Oddly, I don't think Arabella did either. She was at particularly great pains to keep Gisèle's father's identity secret. Even from Frances and O'Roarke."

"Probably embarrassed to be associated with me."

"I think there was more to it."

"That's the way your mind works, Malcolm."

"Perhaps. But she was quite frank with both of them about her love affairs. She never objected to my friendship with your family. Reading between the lines, I'd say she had a certain respect for you."

Carfax snorted. But something about the look in his eyes suggested the idea was not entirely lost on him. Or unwelcome. He removed his spectacles and polished them with his handkerchief. "I liked your mother. I was—sorry—when she died."

"So was I." Malcolm sat back and regarded his former spymaster. "Did you know? About Gisèle?"

"Suspected." Carfax tucked his handkerchief back into his coat pocket. "There was very little to be gained from confronting your mother, and obviously it was better that both Gisèle and the world remain in ignorance." Carfax turned his spectacles in his hands. "I was glad she seemed happy with Thirle. I certainly never wanted her to be drawn into Arabella's work."

"You never thought of recruiting her yourself?"

"Are you mad, Malcolm?"

"You recruited me. You recruited Sylvie St. Ives."

"You're a man."

"Don't let Mélanie hear you say that. Or Gisèle. And Sylvie's a lot of things, but she's definitely a woman."

"And you needed employment. And Sylvie had already put herself in play."

"You and Arabella shared a common enemy."

"True enough. As do you and I now."

"But it didn't occur to you to make an alliance with her. Like the one you offered me."

"Arabella and I both wanted to know about the League. I'm not sure we'd have put the knowledge to the same use. I imagine you've resisted forming an alliance with me for the same reason."

"Fair enough."

"And when it came to Ireland I knew we'd never be allies."

Had he even seen Carfax and Arabella together? Malcolm wondered. He must have done, at least in passing. He'd thought he was fairly sensitive to the feelings of adults, but he'd noticed nothing.

"You were a child," Carfax said, reading him well as he so often did. "An observant child. But one doesn't think of one's parents—"

"That's just the thing. I knew perfectly well how Arabella conducted her life. I had no illusions about her relationship with Alistair. Did she learn anything from you?"

Carfax shifted in his chair. "A bit. Probably enough to help her get O'Roarke out of Ireland."

"Did you learn anything from her?"

"Can you doubt it?"

"Yes, actually. You're formidable, but so was Arabella."

Carfax gave a faint smile. "I learned a bit. Not as much as I hoped."

"Gisèle's taken on Arabella's quest. And yours." Malcolm folded his arms across his chest. "You and Arabella were remarkably alike in your determination to bring down the League."

"I've interested myself in a lot more than the League for the past two decades."

"But you've been willing to sacrifice an incalculable amount in pursuit of them."

"They're an incalculably dangerous enemy."

"They still know the truth about Gisèle's parentage."

"I know. I may have to tell Amelia the truth. You of all people should know a marriage can survive that." Carfax leaned his head back against the claret velvet of the chair. "Are you going back to Italy?"

"As soon as we can tidy up loose ends here and pack our things. Nothing's changed in that regard."

"A pity. You're needed here more than ever."

"Then perhaps you should have thought of that before you moved against us, sir."

Carfax gave a wry smile. "Fair enough." He pushed himself to his feet. "Is O'Roarke here? I'd like to have a word with him before I go."

CHAPTER 45

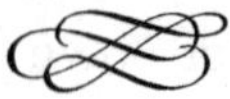

RAOUL WAS on the drawing room carpet playing with the children when Carfax found him and asked for a word. He followed Carfax into the small salon, not quite sure what he was letting himself in for.

"That's a sight I never thought to see," Carfax said.

"What?" Raoul asked, closing the door.

"You on the floor building pillow forts instead of directing snipers behind real fortifications."

"One adapts to the needs of the moment."

Carfax studied him for a moment, as though piecing together a code key. "Arabella would be pleased, I think. To see you happy."

"I hope so. I'm quite sure she'd be pleased to see you out of prison."

"Perhaps." Carfax moved across the room, where the light from the windows was at his back. "I rather think there's a great deal Arabella would blame me for."

"Gisèle's tough," Raoul said. "She's more like Arabella than I credited. But without the illness. In fact, she's also more than a bit like Malcolm."

Carfax's gaze jerked to his face. "She's scarcely more—"

"She's not a child. That's a mistake we all made, I think. At her age, Arabella was trying to bring down the League. You and I were agents. So was Malcolm."

"She's—"

"I don't know your wife well, Carfax. But I've glimpsed your eldest daughter's mettle. And I've seen a bit of Isobel and Lucinda. I would think they'd have taught you not to underestimate women. Even if Arabella didn't."

Carfax gave a nod of acknowledgment. "One doesn't stop worrying."

"We're all worried. None of my confidence means I wouldn't do almost anything to bring her back. But forcing her to give up what she feels she must do would be a disaster."

Carfax nodded again. "Malcolm will be all right, I think. Despite the strains."

"Yes, so do I."

"But it doesn't stop you from worrying."

"I don't think one ever stops worrying about one's children."

"No. One wants to give one's children the best start possible. Ideally one wants to be able to acknowledge them." Carfax held Raoul's gaze for a moment. "Even when that's not possible, it doesn't change the way one feels."

"No," Raoul said. "It doesn't."

"But easier for everyone if one can acknowledge the child to the world." Carfax pushed his spectacles back up on his nose. "It's a long time since Amelia and I've gone through it, but I'd hazard a guess Lady Tarrington's baby is due in the spring."

"May." Raoul leaned against the wall. Odd to be discussing the forthcoming birth of his child with Carfax. But perhaps no odder than other things in the past year.

"I imagine you and Lady Tarrington would like to be married before your child arrives," Carfax said.

"We don't have a great deal of time, but of course that's what we want for the child's sake. For a long time it did seem to be a possibility, but things have changed for Margaret. My—the woman I'm married to."

"Mrs. O'Roarke is willing to go along with a divorce?" Carfax said.

"She's in the same predicament herself. That's produced an unexpected unanimity of thinking."

"Convenient, perhaps." Carfax rubbed at an ash smudge on his shirt cuff. "I'm not quite sure what my position will be when all this settles, but I should still command influence in Parliament. It shouldn't be a problem to get the divorce through before May."

Raoul stared at the man who had been one of his greatest enemies for the past thirty years. A number of responses sprang to mind. Then he simply said, "Thank you. We'd be most grateful."

Carfax met his gaze for a long moment and inclined his head.

"Not that that gratitude will change my future actions," Raoul said.

Carfax gave a faint smile. "I'd be disappointed in you if it did, O'Roarke."

MALCOLM LOOKED up from writing a summary of the case against Matthew Trenor that he had promised Jeremy Roth as Valentin showed Roger Smythe into the study.

"I wanted to thank you," Roger said, when Malcolm waved him to a chair. "I understand Miranda's true killer is in custody."

"Where I profoundly hope he stays. It can difficult, bringing the son a peer to justice."

"I know." Roger's fingers curled round the chair arms. "I've met Matthew Trenor. I can't say I know him well. But—"

Malcolm leaned forwards across the desk, the moment he'd try to choke the life out of Tatiana's killer sharp in his memory. "It's intolerable," he said. "But nothing you can do will bring her back.

Leave this to the law. For your family's sake. For your own sake. For the sake of justice."

Roger gave a contained nod. "I can't answer for what I'd do if I was face to face with Trenor now, but my whole life is built on respect for justice. The law is my profession, after all. As it is Gerald Lumley's." Roger shifted his position in the chair. "Lumley came to see me this morning. I know he was a good friend to Miranda. And I know my father tried to use him though I don't quite understand how. But Lumley seems to think that's over."

"It is," Malcolm said.

Roger nodded again, his expression a trifle easier. "Lumley also told me he's going to marry Faith Harker. She's been raising Miranda's son."

"From what I've seen the boy regards her as his mother."

"That's what Lumley says as well. Dorinda and I would gladly raise the boy, but I have no wish to take him away from the only mother he's known. I've told Lumley we're happy for Danny to stay with him and Faith. And that I'll make sure my father doesn't interfere."

"I'm glad."

"We can at least snatch what good we can from this tragedy." Roger scraped the toe of his boot over the carpet. "Dorinda and I had a long talk last night. We said things to each other we both should have said years ago. I can't say we've resolved everything, but—" He gave a sudden smile. "It's amazing what the truth can do."

"The truth, and admitting one's feelings."

"That too." Roger studied him for a moment. "My father and the League still have to be stopped. Miranda's death convinces me of that more than ever. Though I think Father's worked out that Miranda was reporting to me."

"Matthew Trenor probably told him Miranda was working for someone else."

Roger nodded. "It won't be easy for me to uncover more information."

"You'd be wise to lie low for a while. But this is a long game, and we'd welcome your assistance."

"You have it without asking. I'm not going to stay on the sidelines. You'll be returning to Parliament?" Roger asked.

"No, we'll be going back to Italy within the week. But I'll stay in close touch with Rupert. I shall enjoy following your parliamentary career."

"I hope there's a career for you to follow. But I'm sorry. I'd have been honored to work with you."

"You still will be when it comes to the fight against the Elsinore League. I'll make sure you have the codes to communicate with us before we leave."

Roger leaned forwards and extended his hand across the desk. "Thank you for your trust, Rannoch."

Malcolm clasped Roger's hand. "We need people like you. Both in Parliament and against the League."

He saw Roger from the house himself. They met Raoul in the hall. He had just finished seeing Carfax out.

"Carfax talked to you?" Malcolm asked as he and his father returned to the study.

"Yes." Raoul's expression was oddly bemused. "I hadn't told you yet—I haven't even told Laura because of everything that happened yesterday and because I didn't want to get her hopes up —but when I saw Margaret yesterday I learned that she's with child as well. Which has changed her views on divorce."

"That's wonderful." Malcolm returned to his chair at the desk.

"Yes." Raoul advanced into the room and dropped into the wingback chair Carfax had occupied an hour before. "Though I wasn't at all sure it would be possible before May. Which is partly why I haven't told Laura yet. But Carfax has just offered to push the divorce through Parliament."

"Carfax offered—Good God."

"Yes, that was my reaction. Then I thanked him. Most sincerely. I think it's a very sincere offer." Raoul settled back in the chair and crossed his legs, gaze on the toes of his boots. "Partly, I think, to thank you for your role in getting him out of prison. But I also had a sense learning the truth about Gisèle has been making him think about what it means to be a parent."

Malcolm studied his own father. It was one of those moments when he felt they had switched places and he had become the parent. Or at least the one to offer comfort. "It has to have been a shock. Learning about Carfax and Arabella."

Raoul looked up, as though aware of his gaze, and gave a crooked smile. At once vulnerable and defensive. Funny how hard it had once been to read him. Not that Malcolm would precisely call it easy now, but he knew the cues to look for. "I don't know why I'm surprised," Raoul said. "I knew she had lovers she—disagreed with. To put it mildly. Not that shared beliefs or even liking each other necessarily have anything to do with attraction."

"I don't know that this was about attraction." Malcolm swallowed. He was, after all, talking about his mother. "That is, I don't think that's what started it, on either side."

"No." Raoul dug a hand through his hair. "If she did it because of Ireland—"

"You can't say you wouldn't have done the same to save her."

"No," Raoul said again, after a pause that more or less confirmed Malcolm's suspicions that he had in fact done so. "But one doesn't like—"

Malcolm shut his mind to speculation on what Mélanie might or might not do under what circumstances. "It's part of being a spy. Isn't that what you'd say?"

"Possibly. In case you haven't realized it yet, I often say things that don't quite agree with what I feel."

"I have begun to suspect as much." Malcolm smiled despite the topic.

Raoul echoed the smile with a twisted one of his own. "I think perhaps as much as anything it's a shock that I didn't suspect anything, at the time or in the two decades since."

Malcolm watched Raoul for a long moment. However matter-of-fact he might be about Arabella, Malcolm was coming to realize just what she had meant to him. "You can't tell me you'd be so sanguine—"

"If it was Laura?" As often happened Raoul read his thoughts. "God help me, no. But then, Laura and I've made promises to each other that your mother and I never did. I wouldn't do things myself now that I once wouldn't have thought twice about. I never expected that sort of a relationship with Arabella. At least not after the early months, when I was more a love-struck schoolboy than anything. I won't say I was free of illusions where Arabella was concerned, but at least I was reasonably free of those sorts of illusions. I already knew I wasn't Gisèle's father, after all." He drew a breath. "I didn't get to see much of her before she left. How has she taken learning about Carfax?"

"Difficult to tell. Defenses rather run in the family. I think there are things driving her that she isn't telling us about, but I don't think it's to do with Carfax."

It was Raoul's turn to watch him. "You had to let her go. To do anything else would have been dishonest and disastrous for your relationship with your sister. Not to mention that given what we saw of Gisèle yesterday I don't think it would be humanly possible."

"Quite, on all counts. Perhaps especially the last." Malcolm shifted his pen on the ink blotter. "I'm worried about Andrew. And I'm afraid she's ruined her marriage, though I don't think she wants to do so."

"It's a decision you have to let her make."

Malcolm looked up at his father. "Says the man who's gone to great lengths to manipulate the people he loves."

"I'm trying to learn from my past actions."

"If you'd left Mel and me to our own devices, I doubt we'd be as happy as we are today."

"If I'd tried to manipulate Laura into doing what I thought was right for her six months ago, she might be less happy."

"You know damn well she would be. So would you. But Gelly's doing what I was afraid you'd do six months ago. Pushing away the person she loves for the sake of what she sees as duty."

"Not quite the same. I thought I was denying Laura the life she could have. In point of fact, I was. Am. I don't think Gisèle thinks that about Thirle."

"No. She thinks, with the optimism of twenty, that emotional damage can be repaired later." Malcolm adjusted the pen again. "Reading between the lines, I think she's going to the Continent with Tommy. It's as well we're going back to Italy."

Raoul nodded, "Most of the divorce can be done quietly, but I'll need to come back here for some of it. No need for Laura to be present, though. In fact, much better if she's not. It will be a relief to know she's in Italy."

Now that the immediate crises were resolved, Malcolm felt the insistent tug to be out of the country "Nowhere is really safe, I suppose, but it does feel more of a haven than most places we could be."

"Carfax is even less likely to move against Mélanie now."

"Carfax is grateful to us for the moment, but he's also determined to bring down the League. And we're in the middle of it."

"We're going to be in the middle of it regardless," Raoul said.

"Quite. But we'll have more freedom to act if we don't have to worry about Mel being arrested. Or you."

ANDREW STARED down at Gisèle's letter. He seemed to have read it through twice, but Malcolm wasn't sure he had fully made sense of it.

"How much danger is she in?" he said at last.

"The League can be ruthless." Malcolm wasn't going to sugar-coat it. "Though I don't think they'd lightly move against someone with Gelly's connections. That's assuming they realize what she's doing. They're likely to underestimate a woman, particularly a very young woman. And Gelly's shown herself well able to take care of herself. She's agreed to a system where she checks in with us regularly. We'll be able to pull her out if we need to."

Andrew stared at Malcolm across the paper-strewn desk as though he were looking at a stranger. "You're talking about her as though she's one of your agents."

"I wouldn't call her one of my agents, but she is an agent, Andrew. She's made herself one. With training from St. Juste, who's a formidable agent himself."

Andrew shook his head. "It's always had a pull on all of you."

"Adventure?"

"That too. But I was going to say duty." Andrew looked down at the letter again. "What can I do to help her?"

"Act the bewildered husband for any League members watching."

"That scarcely requires acting." Andrew's fingers tightened on the letter. "I want to do more. Tell me what I can do without adding to the risks. Train me if you have to."

"Andrew—"

"This is my fight now too. If it matters this much to Gelly, it matters to me. And the sooner it's resolved, the sooner I get my wife back."

STILL MULLING what role he could find for Andrew, Malcolm went into the drawing room. Laura, Cordelia, and Harry were on the floor playing with the children. Harry looked up from rolling a ball to meet Malcolm's gaze. Malcolm gave his friend a brief smile. Given the circumstances, his talk with Andrew had gone about as well as it could.

He met Mélanie's gaze across the room. She and Raoul were standing by the windows. For a horrible instant he was reminded of the moment he had told the two of them and Laura that they had to leave London. He crossed to join them. "It could have been worse," he said, meeting Mélanie's gaze. "Andrew understands. As well as it's possible to understand. He wants to help. We're going to have to figure out something he can do."

"I'm so glad." Mélanie's gaze showed relief, but also a question. Malcolm realized she was holding a sheet of hot-pressed notepaper. "This just came from Frances," she said. "She wants the three of us in South Audley Street this evening at nine. You and me and Raoul."

"Just the three of us?" Malcolm asked.

"Yes, she's most specific." Mélanie held out the note. "She says it's not a social visit, she'll have someone there we need to speak with."

Malcolm studied the note. "Unusually secretive for Frances. Given the events of the past twenty-four hours—not to mention the past few weeks—I don't know whether to say I'm prepared for anything or that I can't imagine what she can have in mind that will surprise us. We'll go, of course. But all in all, it will be a distinct relief to get back to Italy."

FRANCES'S FOOTMAN CONDUCTED MÉLANIE, Malcolm, and Raoul to a sitting room at the back of the house on the ground floor. It had a door that opened onto the garden. Mélanie and Malcolm had made use of it for slipping in and out of the house unobserved on more than one occasion. The footman opened the door, withdrew, and closed the door without announcing them.

The lamps were turned low. A brace of candles burned on the

mantel. Frances came forwards to greet them with a rustle of silk and a waft of her lilac scent. Her hair was carefully dressed and sapphires glittered at her throat and ears. Though unsure of the reason for the visit, Mélanie had dressed in an evening gown of midnight blue silk trimmed with gold braid, pinned her hair up in loose curls, and added a pair of cameo earrings Malcolm had given her in Italy. Apparently she had chosen correctly.

Four men were by the fireplace, three standing—Archie, Carfax, and Lord Castlereagh. A third man was sitting in a carved walnut armchair drawn close to the fire. A heavy man whose girth overflowed the chair and whose diamond cravat pin and watch fob and numerous rings glinted in the firelight.

For a moment, shock held Mélanie motionless. Then instinct took over and she sank into a curtsey, even as Malcolm and Raoul bowed.

CHAPTER 46

THE PRINCE REGENT stretched out his hand, indicating they should rise. "Mrs. Rannoch. Rannoch. O'Roarke. Lady Frances tells us that, thanks to you, we have a averted a crisis that could have threatened the security of the realm."

"My aunt is a brilliant woman, but in this I think she exaggerates." Malcolm scarcely moved a muscle, but Mélanie felt him draw closer to her. "However, I can assure Your Royal Highness that you need have no further fears about the threat in question."

"Never known Fanny to exaggerate," the regent said. "And Carfax and Castlereagh confirm what she says."

Malcolm's gaze shifted to the two men who had played such key roles in his life, who could so easily destroy them and all they held dear. "That's very good of them."

"Believe me," Castlereagh said, his voice taut and precise, "we know precisely what was at stake. There's no question that the situation could have been dire indeed. And that you averted it."

The regent stretched out a hand. Castlereagh put a box into it. Gilt glinted on the red tooled leather of the cover as the regent flipped open the lid of the box. Two aquamarine cravat pins glittered on either side of an aquamarine pendant. "I pray you will accept these small tokens of our gratitude," the regent said. "Not the finest stones, but the color struck me as very close to the color of Mrs. Rannoch's eyes."

"You are too kind, Your Highness." Mélanie stepped forwards and took the box, because it seemed one of them was required to do so. "We will treasure them as a memory of your kindness."

She hesitated a moment, then took the pendant from the box. Malcolm moved behind her and clasped it round her throat. For a moment, the smile the regent gave her was frankly appreciative. Then he held out another hand without looking at Castlereagh. Castlereagh put two sealed papers into the prince's hand. The prince held the papers out. "I understand from Fanny that certain past incidents could cause trouble for Mrs Rannoch and O'Roarke should they come to light. Of course, I know something of O'Roarke's history in Ireland. I don't need to know further details about his activities or Mrs. Rannoch's. But I have no wish for either of you to live in fear. These documents give you each a pardon for all past actions involving the British crown, should questions ever be raised. Which I profoundly hope they will not be. Again, I don't understand the details, but Castlereagh assures me the documents are sufficient to protect you."

The silence in the room echoed in Mélanie's ears, as though she were underwater. Malcolm touched her arm. She realized she needed to take one of the papers. She felt as though she were moving in a dream world.

Raoul took the other paper from the hand of the man whose government he had spent much of his life fighting. "This is extraordinarily generous, Your Highness."

"We have no wish to see any of you leave Britain again. Particularly Mrs. Rannoch. Or the pretty Lady Tarrington. Or Fanny. She's been threatening to decamp herself."

Raoul's gaze shifted to Castlereagh, and then to Carfax

"Those papers," Castlereagh said, "can spare all of us a great deal of unpleasantness."

"And we need Malcolm in Britain." Carfax spoke up for the first time. "And Mrs. Rannoch. And possibly even you, O'Roarke."

MALCOLM LOOKED at his aunt across her sitting room. The rattle of the carriage wheels carrying the regent, Castlereagh, and Carfax had faded away, but the sound, the words spoken, still hung in the air. "Aunt Frances—"

"I didn't tell him anything, my dear. Save that you had done a great service and that he was better off not knowing the details. And though Prinny may not have a great deal of wit, he did have the wit to know I was right about that."

Raoul was turning the paper the regent had given him over in his hands, a bemused expression on his face. "You're a wonder, Fanny."

"I don't think it would have worked if Castlereagh and Carfax hadn't backed me up. Carfax knows he over played his hand six months ago. He knows he needs Malcolm. And he may realize this is the only way he's going to get his son back."

"And Castlereagh?" Mélanie asked. "He knows about Raoul and me?"

"He knows something," Malcolm said. "I'm not sure the whole truth. But he knows enough to know he doesn't want to know more, I think."

"He's quite fond of both of you," Archie said. "And it would hardly redound well on him if it came out that his former favorite aide had been married to a French agent."

Raoul looked at his friend. "Archie—"

"I know," Frances said. "But I don't think any of them suspects anything about Archie. So I couldn't ask for a pardon for him without rousing their suspicions. If anyone has to go back to Italy permanently, it will be Archie and I. But I don't think we will."

Archie took her hand and carried it to his lips.

"You can go get our other guest now," Frances said to him.

Malcolm raised a brow at his aunt.

"Someone else who helped us," Frances said.

A few moments later, Archie returned to the room with Prince Talleyrand.

"I must say I'm surprised, sir," Malcolm said. "When you vanished from Beverston's villa I made sure you'd gone straight to a boat for France."

"I would have done did I not see a need to see this other business to the close. Officially I'm not here. But then now that I'm a private citizen, it's really no one's business where I go. Dorothée is waiting for me on a yacht off the coast. We sailed down from Scotland. After all, ensuring you could safely return to your old life is what brought us to Britain in the first place."

"Don't tell me this was your plan to checkmate Carfax," Malcolm said. "You're a master strategist, but I don't see how you could have foreseen all the turns that got us to this point."

"No." Talleyrand moved to an armchair and lowered himself into it. "My original plan was to use Carfax's actions surrounding the Wanderer to force him to assist you in returning safely to Britain."

"That would have entailed considerable risk to yourself."

Talleyrand shrugged. "I'm out of power, and Carfax was the one giving orders to St. Juste, so he was more at risk. But I was bargaining on his determination to keep the story of the Wanderer secret at all costs. Thank you." Talleyrand accepted a glass of calvados from Archie, who then went to pour whisky for the others. "You'd still have been at risk from the League, though," Talleyrand continued, "as you rightly pointed out in Scotland. Getting Mélanie and O'Roarke pardons was a much neater solution, and entirely Fanny's idea. I merely encouraged her when I called this afternoon and she told me her plan."

Mélanie looked at Malcolm. "Darling. We can go home."

"The League are still a threat," Malcolm said.

"But they can't use the truth of Mélanie's past against her." Raoul took a drink of the whisky Archie had given him. "Even should the truth come out, she's protected."

"So are you," Frances said. "For your past actions. Not for anything you may do going forwards. Though I don't expect that will deter you."

"I'm not working against Britain at present," Raoul said. "Contrary to what some think, it's never been my aim to foment a revolution here. Britain actually offers more intriguing ways to work for change."

Talleyrand settled back in his chair and sipped his calvados. "Carfax can't blackmail you over Mélanie's past or O'Roarke's. The League can't."

"And now that you've been issued the pardons, Carfax and Castlereagh have their own incentive to keep the secret," Archie said.

Malcolm nodded slowly, as though it still wasn't quite real.

"Darling." Mélanie seized his hands. "You've had this hanging over you for over a year. It's at least one thing you don't have to worry about anymore."

"Nor do you." Malcolm twined his fingers round her own and lifted her hands to his lips one at a time. "No more ridiculous delusions that you've done anything but make my life far better than I ever dreamed it could be."

"You can return to your seat in Parliament," Raoul said.

"Mélanie can go back to Almack's," Frances said. "Assuming Emily Cowper can get her vouchers, which I imagine she can, and assuming Mélanie wants to, which is considerably more questionable. But you have options. Especially now that Raoul can make an honest woman of Laura. Carfax told me about the divorce," she added. "It's splendid news."

Archie lifted his whisky in a toast. "We have few enough victories. We can savor this one. And it will make it easier to fight the League."

"Yes." Malcolm lifted his own glass, as did Mélanie. "But we're not sharing the list with Carfax."

"And we'll probably have to be on our guard against his trying to steal it," Raoul said. "But there's no denying it will be easier here."

~

"THEY REALLY CAN'T EVER ARREST you for anything you've done in the past?" Laura looked at Raoul in the privacy of their bedchamber. He, Mélanie, and Malcolm had shared the news with everyone when they returned to Berkeley Square, but she still found it difficult to take in how dramatically their world had shifted in the short time the three of them had spent at Fanny's house in South Audley Street.

"I'm no lawyer, but I believe a pardon from the monarch—or the monarch's authorized representative in the regent's case—is ironclad for past actions. Not for future ones. They may be bargaining on that weighing with both Mélanie and me."

"It won't stop you," she said. It wasn't a question.

"No, but for the moment we have breathing room. And other things have shifted as well." Raoul turned to her, his face inscrutable. "Would you marry me if I were free?"

Laura drew a sharp breath. For all that had changed in the last few hours, his marriage wasn't part of it. "Is that a hypothetical?"

"No." An odd smile played about his mouth. "Margaret is expecting a child as well."

Laughter bubbled up in Laura's throat. "Good God."

"Yes, the irony wasn't lost on me. Or on Margaret. Carfax has offered to help speed the divorce."

"Carfax—" She shook her head.

"Possibly because he's adjusting to learning he has another child himself. I wouldn't say prison's mellowed him, but something has shifted." Raoul watched her a moment longer, then went down on one knee. "Will you do me the honor of becoming my wife, Laura?"

"Oh, my dear." She bent down, as she had once before, and took his face between her hands. "Surely you don't need to ask it."

He got to his feet and settled her in his arms without breaking the kiss. "I think we'll be able to manage it before the baby's born."

Laura nodded. It mattered, of course, for their child. There were many practical challenges to being born a bastard. And yet —"I'm glad. I don't care what people think of me, but there's no denying it will be easier for our child. Otherwise—If it weren't for the baby—"

Raoul kissed her hair. "My darling, if I'd been free, I'd have asked you in Maidstone, and damn my scruples."

COLIN LOOKED up at Mélanie as she smoothed the covers over him. "When are we going back to Italy?"

"Not for a while, darling." Mélanie kissed him. "Perhaps we'll go this summer. But we're going to stay in Berkeley Square for a bit."

Colin's eyes had been half closed with sleep, but now they widened. "You mean we get to stay home?"

A lump rose in Mélanie's throat. "Just so, darling."

Colin smiled. "What about Addison and Blanca and the baby?"

"We'll send for them, lad. First thing tomorrow." Malcolm bent to kiss their son as well.

Colin reached up to hug both his parents, then rolled to face the bed where Emily was already asleep. "Em will be glad. She's missed London. I don't think she wanted Laura to know how much. Or any of you." He looked back at Mélanie and Malcolm. "So we're safe now?"

Malcolm touched his fingers to Colin's hair. "We're safe."

"Do you believe it?" Mélanie asked her husband, when they were back in their bedchamber.

"That we're safe?" Malcolm smoothed the blanket over Jessica, asleep in her cradle. "Safe enough that I'm willing to risk staying here, at least for the present. I'm not sure we'd be any safer in Italy."

Mélanie stroked Berowne, who was curled up on the bed. "The children still see it as home."

"We haven't been gone that long. I'll own I'm not unhappy to be back myself."

"Darling—"

He gave a twisted grin. "Yes, all right, I'm happy." He looked at her for a moment, with one of his carefully neutral looks. "What about you?"

"Can you ask? I've wanted nothing more—"

Malcolm crossed to her side. "Not how do you feel for me and the children. How do you feel about being back yourself?"

She met his searching gaze. Something in it stopped the easy answer that sprang to her lips. "I'm—"

He set his hands on her shoulders. "What do you want, Mel?"

It was the question she asked him in Italy. She drew a breath, then went still. "I want you to have back what you lost."

"I have it. What do you want for yourself?"

"My life with you and the children."

"You wouldn't let me stop at that when you asked me the same question. What do you want for yourself?"

"Don't you rather think I gave up the right to want anything for myself?"

"That's nonsense."

"I put my own agenda first at the start of our marriage."

"And then you followed mine. To Paris, to Britain. To the beau monde and the life of a politician's wife. At which you were brilliant. I think you could be brilliant at anything you chose to do. The question now is what do you choose?"

"You're going back to Parliament—"

"And I can't imagine how I'd do it without your help with stategy and my speeches. But I don't necessarily need a hostess. Not that you aren't an invaluable asset, but being an asset is a waste of your talents. I can host my own damn parties if necessary. I'm never going to be prime minster, in any case. Whatever change we can bring about, I'll always be arguing on the fringe."

"I'd miss it," she said. "The political whirl. I have missed it. It will be good to be back. But—" She hesitated, searching through layers of demands, impulses, loyalties. "I'd also miss the freedom we've had in Italy."

"So would I. We're damn well not going to go out six nights a week. At least I'm not. We need time with the children. And time to explore. After the last six years, you're entitled to all the time you want."

"Malcolm." She put her hands on his chest. "We're still fighting the League."

A shadow crossed his face. "So we are. But I refuse to let that fight define us."

Mélanie looked at her husband, who always claimed, under some strange delusion, that she was the romantic between them. "You're sounding distinctly optimistic, darling."

He kissed her nose. "Perhaps that's because for the first time in a long time, I actually am. We have a future, sweetheart. It's ours to make of it what we will."

HISTORICAL NOTES

Louis-Charles, younger son of Louis XVI and Marie Antoinette, was the dauphin from his brother's death in 1789 until the new constitution in 1791 made him instead prince royal. Following his father's execution in January 1793, he was Louis XVII to Royalists though never officially king. When he died in 1795, he was buried in a common grave, but one of the doctors performing the post-mortem removed his heart. The doctor took the heart home and preserved it in alcohol though the alcohol subsequently evaporated.

From the time of Louis-Charles's death there were rumors that he had in fact been smuggled off to safety. The Restoration brought even more rumors and a parade of impostors claiming to be the lost dauphin. In 1999, DNA from the dead boy's heart, by then in Saint-Denis, was compared with DNA from a descendant of Marie Antoinette. A mitochondrial DNA sequence proved the child who died in the Temple was indeed Marie Antoinette's son.

Tsar Alexander really did claim Josephine had confided in him, shortly before her death, that she and Barras had had the boy spirited away. There is no evidence that Josephine and Barras actually attempted to do so, and it is quite likely that she never told him anything of the sort (Tsar Alexander was no stranger to elaboration, as Raoul says). But novelists often build on "what if?" and this "what if?" offered tantalizing possibilities that create all sorts of complications and moral dilemmas for Rannochs and their friends and opponents.

Deborah Cadbury's *The Lost King of France* (London: Fourth Estate, 2002) offers a fascinating account of Louis-Charles's imprisonment and death, the imposters who came after, and the way DNA solved the mystery. There is also a wonderful review of the book by Hilary Mantel in the *London Review of Books*, Vol. 25, No. 18, 17 August 2003.

A READING GROUP GUIDE

About This Guide

The suggested questions are included to enhance your group's reading of Tracy Grant's *The Duke's Gambit.*

1. How are the characters shaped by their birth, or what they believe their birth to be? What do you think shapes them more, their actual birth or how their birth is perceived by others?
2. Compare and contrast the different fathers and daughters in the book.
3. How do you think the revelation of who Gisèle's father is will impact the series going forwards?
4. Several of the characters are balancing being parents of young children with living dangerous lives. What do

you think of the various choices made by Raoul, Gisèle, Mélanie, and Malcolm?

5. At the end of the book Malcolm asks Mélanie what she wants. What do you think she wants?
6. Who do you think has the upper hand now, the Elsinore League, Carfax, or the Rannochs?
7. What do you think lies ahead for Bet Simcox and Sandy Trenor?
8. Do you think Malcolm will ever work with Carfax again?
9. What do you think David and Simon will do now the Rannochs are able to return to Britain?
10. Do you think Carfax will still try to compel David to marry? If so, what do you think he will try next?
11. What do you think lies ahead for Hugh Derenvil and Caroline Lewes?
12. Do you think being married will change Raoul and Laura's relationship?
13. The Rannochs are back in Britain. How will their lives compare to their lives in Britain before they left?

DISCOVER MORE BY TRACY GRANT

Traditional Regencies

WIDOW'S GAMBIT

FRIVOLOUS PRETENCE

THE COURTING OF PHILIPPA

Lescaut Quartet

DARK ANGEL

SHORES OF DESIRE

SHADOWS OF THE HEART

RIGHTFULLY HIS

The Rannoch Fraser Mysteries

HIS SPANISH BRIDE

LONDON INTERLUDE

VIENNA WALTZ

IMPERIAL SCANDAL

THE PARIS AFFAIR

THE PARIS PLOT

BENEATH A SILENT MOON

THE BERKELEY SQUARE AFFAIR
THE MAYFAIR AFFAIR
INCIDENT IN BERKELEY SQUARE
LONDON GAMBIT
MISSION FOR A QUEEN
GILDED DECEIT
MIDWINTER INTRIGUE
THE DUKE'S GAMBIT
SECRETS OF A LADY
THE MASK OF NIGHT

ABOUT THE AUTHOR

Tracy Grant studied British history at Stanford University and received the Firestone Award for Excellence in Research for her honors thesis on shifting conceptions of honor in late-fifteenth-century England. She lives in the San Francisco Bay Area with her young daughter and three cats. In addition to writing, Tracy works for the Merola Opera Program, a professional training program for opera singers, pianists, and stage directors. Her real life heroine is her daughter Mélanie, who is very cooperative about Mummy's writing time. She is currently at work on her next book chronicling the adventures of Malcolm and Mélanie Rannoch. Visit her on the Web at www.tracygrant.org

CPSIA information can be obtained
at www.ICGtesting.com
Printed in the USA
FSHW01n1147240518
48641FS